DEBBIE JOHNSON

A GIFT FROM THE COMFORT FOOD CAFÉ

Complete and Unabridged

CHARNWOOD
Leicester

First published in Great Britain in 2018 by
HarperCollins*Publishers*
London

First Charnwood Edition
published 2019
by arrangement with
HarperCollins*Publishers* Ltd
London

*A catalogue record for this book is available
from the British Library.*

ISBN 978–1–4448–4253–1

Published by
F. A. Thorpe (Publishing)
Anstey, Leicestershire

Set by Words & Graphics Ltd.
Anstey, Leicestershire
Printed and bound in Great Britain by
T. J. International Ltd., Padstow, Cornwall

This book is printed on acid-free paper

For Barbara Tomkinson (and Tinkerbell!)

PART 1: ON YOUR MARKS . . .

1

My name is Katie Seddon. I am seven years old, and I am preparing to run away.

This is the first time, but it won't be the last.

It is Christmas Day, and I have gathered together all of the essentials, which include the following: a selection of gifts, including my mermaid Barbie, a colouring book and felt tip pens, a musical jewellery box with a wind-up dancing ballerina inside it, fluffy pink ear muffs, elf bed socks and a four-pack of custard creams wrapped in cellophane. The biscuits weren't under the tree that morning; I pinched them from the kitchen.

I look at my stash, and decide that I am ready for all that life can throw at me.

I pack my haul into my *Toy Story* backpack, and decide I will take a trip to infinity and beyond. Or at least to my grandma's house. She only lives two streets away, so it isn't exactly an intergalactic space quest.

I sit on my bed, and pause after I've zipped everything up. I wonder if my mum and dad will hear me as I sneak downstairs, get my raincoat, and leave — but a few seconds sitting with my head cocked to one side, listening to them scream at each other, reassures me that they won't.

I can only make out the odd word, and I've learned already not to try too hard. I won't hear

3

anything good. It's a cacophony of shrieks and yells and thuds as they chase each other around the living room. The bangs of ashtrays being thrown and high-pitched swearing and the crash of plates are all perfectly normal to me. They're part of the soundtrack of my childhood; a reverse lullaby that keeps me awake and scared instead of sleepy and secure.

Looking back, with more complex thought processes than I possessed at seven, I know they are one of those couples who base their whole relationship on mutual contempt. On a good day, they tolerate each other. On a bad one, the only emotion in their eyes is hatred and bitterness. The overwhelming disappointment of what their lives have become.

I know now it's not uncommon — and that their conflicts were the glue that held them together. Maybe when they first met it was exciting. Maybe they thought the arguments were passionate. Maybe the first few serious rows were put down to fire and spice. Maybe they were different when they were young, and thought they were in love — but now, with my dad in a dead-end job and Mum stuck at home, it's not passion. It's fury.

At the age of seven, I don't understand any of this. I don't know what's going on in the big, nasty grown-up world — but I do know that I've had enough. That this is the worst Christmas ever. That they're both really, really mean when they fight. Dad is bigger and physically stronger, but Mum is like a wasp, constantly zooming in to sting him. It's horrible, and I'm leaving. Forever.

I tiptoe down the stairs and creep out of the house really quietly, although I needn't have bothered — they've reached critical mass by this stage and wouldn't pause if I did a conga through the living room wearing my flashing neon Rudolph deely-boppers. Which I am wearing, by the way — I've decided they will help me stay safe outside in the dark.

The walk to my grandma's is a bit scary. I've done it before, loads of times, but only with grown-ups. This time I am doing it alone, at night, and with nobody to hold my hand when I'm crossing the road. I'm a good girl, and do as I've been taught, waiting for the green man to come on at the traffic lights even though there are no cars at all. Mum sometimes goes when the red man is on, but she says that's all right for adults.

I knock on my grandma's door, and she opens it wearing her quilted dressing gown and tartan slippers. She lets me in without any questions at all. I realise now it's because she didn't have to ask — she knew exactly what was going on in my house, and exactly why I needed a refuge. A place to shelter from the storm of my parents' toxic relationship.

My nan was a very kind woman, and she always smelled of Parma Violets. To this day I still find it comforting whenever they turn up in a big bag of Swizzels. Halloween can be a bittersweet experience.

She settles me down with a bowl of custard-soaked jam roly-poly that she warms up in the microwave, and makes me a mug of instant hot chocolate. She even lets me sit in the big armchair that has the button that makes the footrest go up, tucked under a blanket. I hear her on the phone, but I'm so comfy and cosy and happy I'm not remotely interested in who she's talking to. The room is lit by the twinkles of her small plastic Christmas tree, and all is well with the world.

When she comes back into the room, she's all wrinkled smiles and loveliness, and we watch an episode of *ER* together. It's an exciting one, with a big fire and lots of drama. It may even have been that early brush with Nurse Carol Hathaway that planted the seeds of my later career.

By the time my mum drags herself away from her fight, Nan has put me to bed at her house. I'm in the spare room, which used to be Mum's when she was little and still has a giant cuddly lion in it that's big enough to sit on.

I lie scrunched up beneath the duvet, warm and full, and hear them talking down below. It's one of those little terraced houses with the staircase right off the living room, so the noise carries. Mum sounds tearful and her voice is wobbling and going up and down, like your voice does when you're trying to keep a cry in and can't breathe properly. Nan is telling her to leave me here for the night, and to stay herself as well. Telling her to consider staying for good — to finally leave him.

'There's never going to be a happy ending here, Sandra. You've both given it your best, but enough's enough, love,' she says, and I hear how sad she sounds. Sometimes I forget that my mum is my nan's little girl as well as my mum. Weird.

I wake up the next morning with my mum in bed with me, curled around me like a soft, protective spoon. She's already awake, watching me as I sleep, gently moving my blonde hair from my face. For a moment, all is well in the world.

Then I see that her eyes are all crusted together where she'd been crying, and her face is all puffed up, and she has finger-shaped bruises on the tops of her arms like small purple paw-marks. I burrow into her, and give her a cuddle — she looks like she needs one.

2

The second time I run away, with any serious intent, I am fourteen. I've been staying with my nan most weekends, to the point where it is my second home. Mum and Dad are still at it, the years giving them more frown lines but no extra restraint.

The fights don't get physical quite as often, but I still sometimes find the remnants of shattered crockery in the kitchen in the morning, or a mysteriously put-in window pane in the living room door, glass scattered on the floor in glistening zig-zags as I come downstairs for school.

I always creep down quietly, hoping they're still sleeping it off, praying for a peaceful bowl of cornflakes before I leave. I've learned to tread carefully in our house, in all kinds of ways.

The year I turn fourteen, though, things change. They change because my nan dies, and my escape hatch is gone. It's sudden and unexpected — a complication of diabetes. All those Parma Violets, I suppose. I am grieving and in pain and swamped with guilt — because as well as missing her, I am worried about myself as well. About how I'll cope without her, and her kind smiles, and our cosy nights in watching *ER* and *Casualty* and *Holby City*, talking about nothing but saying such a lot.

Mum and Dad had gone out for a meal

8

together, a pre-Christmas 'date night'. As usually happens on those rare occasions, what started off well was ending with a row. Something to do with him drinking four pints of cider even though he was supposed to be the one driving, I don't know.

The verbal missiles start as soon as they walk in, and had obviously been fired first on the journey home from their *romantic* night out. I make a sharp exit, stage left, not really knowing where I'm going or what I'm going to do when I get there.

They don't even see me, and I stand outside the house on the driveway for a few moments, looking in at their drama unfolding. It's dark, and it's almost Christmas, and their row takes a festive turn when Dad gives Mum a mighty push as she screams at him. It's not a push with intent — more of a push to get an irritating insect out of his face.

She loses her balance and topples backwards, staggering for a few steps before she finally lands sprawling in the middle of the Christmas tree, taking it down with her.

I stay rooted to the spot for a few seconds, just to make sure she isn't, you know, dead or anything — but am strangely reassured to see her climb back up from the fake-pine branches, strewn in red and green tinsel. She's grabbed the nearest weapon to hand — the star off the top of the tree — and is brandishing it like a shiv in a jailhouse movie, threatening to poke his eye out.

Okay, I think. *God bless you merry gentlemen*, and away I go. It's very cold, and the streets are giddy with pitching snow and slow-moving cars inching through slush. I'm wearing a hoody and leggings, which isn't really enough. I haven't packed as well as I did last time, not even a spare pair of bed socks.

I wander the streets a little, wondering if I could hitch-hike to London without getting murdered or locked in someone's cellar, before my feet finally take me where I probably knew I was going all along.

I sit on the kerb outside my nan's old house, ice-cold snow immediately soaking through the seat of my leggings, and rest my chin in my hands as I stare across the street.

Someone else lives there now, of course. The house was sold within a couple of months of her dying, which will always, always piss me off. I'm a teenager now, so I swear a lot more than I did when I was seven. And this? Imposters in her home? That pisses me off. It should have been kept as some kind of museum. At least had a blue plaque outside it. Instead, it's like she was never even there.

I pull the cord of my hoody to make it tighter around my face, and look in through the front window. I see their brightly lit Christmas tree, and the cosy room, and occasionally even see a woman walking around, carrying a baby. I have no idea who they are, but I resent them. It might not be their fault that she died, but that doesn't make me feel any better. The people who live there are pissing me off as well.

I'm so sick of my parents' dramas. Sick of the tension, of not knowing when it's all going to kick off again. There was a temporary lull after Nan died, and both of them were on their best behaviour, but it didn't last.

Sometimes it comes after a flash point; sometimes it comes after days of simmering anger and snide comments and 'your dinner's in the dog' sniping. He'll go straight to the pub after work; she'll sit at home planning her revenge.

And I know now — because my mother has said it to me — that I am apparently the cause of their determined grip on marital misery.

'We didn't want you to come from a broken home,' she said — as though this was better. As though me bearing witness to a state of warfare throughout my childhood is beneficial, rather than filling me with dread.

I wade through a state of constant nervous energy every time I come home from school, standing in the hallway with my coat still on, weighing up the mood of the house, deciding whether I can risk venturing into the living room or if it would be better to run straight upstairs to my room, put on my headphones, and pretend none of it is happening.

So that's how I live. Hiding in my room with my music; hiding at friends' houses for way too many sleepovers, and running. Sometimes here, to my nan's. Sometimes to town. Sometimes just buying a day pass for the bus and riding around all day.

It's not an easy balance, and as soon as I am old enough, I go away to college to study nursing. I choose a college far enough away that

I have to live in the halls, and think I have found paradise. Other teenagers are homesick — I'm just relieved. Relieved to have my own space, my own place, my own peace and quiet. Relieved to be alone.

3

By the time I am in my twenties, I'm sharing my own space and my own place and I don't have much peace and quiet any more. I'm definitely, 100 per cent not alone, either.

In fact, the third time I run away, I'm a grown woman, with a six-month-old baby, a job, a rented flat, and a boyfriend who never really wanted to be a dad.

That time, I run away for good. That time, I run away because of yet another screaming row — with Jason, my boyfriend.

It isn't pretty. These things never are. When we met, he was working as a hospital porter, and I was a nurse. At the time, I suppose I thought we fell in love — but now I see it for what it was. A lot of lust, some laughs, and a strange sense that this was what I was supposed to be doing. That women of my age should be looking to find 'the one' and building a relationship.

It was never, ever right between us, but when I got pregnant, we both pretended it was. Because everyone knows that having a newborn baby is really easy, and completely papers over the cracks in any relationship, don't they?

Of course, it didn't make anything better. It made everything worse. The flat was too small. We didn't have enough money. We were too young, and didn't have a clue what we were doing. Mainly, I think, we just didn't like each other very much.

While I was pregnant, we were able to pretend much better. We went to Ikea and laughed as we built cots from Swedish instructions and cooed over tiny little baby-grows. He said he'd give up drinking while I was pregnant, and even managed it for a couple of weeks.

After our son, Saul, arrived, the tensions started to build. I never slept. Jason was working extra shifts. When we did see each other, we were both filled with seething resentments — me because I was stuck at home, him because when he did get home, all I did was moan and nag.

The only good thing about any of it was the baby. He was perfect — caught between us, this chubby-faced, blond-haired angel who I always secretly thought we didn't deserve.

The night of the screaming row, I am especially tired. I've been on my own for so long, I've started talking to the kettle. It isn't answering yet, but in my delirious state of fatigue, it's only a matter of time.

Saul is teething and crying and irritable. Jason has been doing extra shifts to cover for other people's Christmas leave, and I am watching the big hand crawl around the clock in the kitchen, counting the minutes until I can hand Saul over and collapse onto my bed and cry silently into my pillow for a few moments, wondering what happened to my life.

We're out of nappies, and Jason is supposed to be getting some on the way home. Except he doesn't come home — not for another two

14

hours. And when he does, he smells of lager and cigarettes and Calvin Klein's Obsession, which is a perfume I definitely don't wear. In fact the only perfume I wear these days is baby sick and desperation.

I could overlook all of that if he'd even remembered the nappies — but of course he hasn't. He has, though, remembered to pick up six cans of Fosters and a bad attitude.

I yell. He yells. We both say things we will regret, but also probably mean. It gets louder, and hotter, and angrier. We're both like subterranean geysers, all of our frustrations rising to the surface in one big, scalding explosion.

I pick up the nearest thing I can find — a dirty nappy — and lob it at Jason's head. He retaliates by slapping me so hard across the face I feel the red sting marks shine immediately.

We're both stunned into silence by this; me standing still, holding my stinging cheek, him staring at me, shaking his head, stammering apologies.

I'm so sorry, he says. I don't know what came over me, he says. It'll never happen again, he promises. He is full of remorse, full of regret, full of instant self-loathing. In a strange way, I almost feel sorry for him — our situation has revealed a side of himself he probably never knew existed.

I am hurt, and shaken, and weirdly relieved. It's like we've finally pushed ourselves over an abyss that we can't climb out of. I don't feel scared, oddly — I can tell he won't do it again. Not this time, anyway.

I'm trying to make words come out of my mouth when I notice Saul. Saul, my beautiful son, who has been sitting in his baby chair, in a dirty nappy and a Baby's First Christmas vest, watching all of this unfold.

His blue eyes are wide and wet, his pudgy fists held to his ears trying to block out the noise, so scared and confused he is screaming as well. He's probably been screaming for a while — but neither of us noticed, because we were too lost in our own drama.

I rush to the baby to comfort him, and know that I will be running away again sometime soon — not for my sake, but for Saul's. Maybe even for Jason's.

Now, when I look back using the magical power of hindsight, it feels like so many of the important moments in my life — like that one — involve running away. I could draw a time-map of when things started to go wrong, and add in a cartoon figure of myself zooming off in the opposite direction, vapour trails behind me.

The problem with all of these memories — all of these actions and reactions and inactions and overreactions — isn't really the running away. The problem is, I never had any clue what I was running towards, and usually found myself blown around by the breeze, like the fluff from one of those wispy dandelion heads, without any sense of direction and no control over my own movements.

Now, a few years have passed. Saul will be four on his next birthday, and life is very different.

I'm less of a dandelion-head, and am trying very hard to take root.

It's different because the last time I ran away, I ran here — to a little place called Budbury, on the picture-postcard perfect coast of Dorset. I have a job. I have a tiny house. I have friends, who I've reluctantly allowed into my life. I have a community, in the Comfort Food Café that is the heart of the village. I have peace, and quiet, and most importantly, I have a gorgeously healthy little boy. Who definitely disrupts the quiet, but in a good way.

I have more than I could ever have imagined — and this time, I won't be running anywhere. This time, I am breaking all the cycles.

This time, I'm staying put — no matter how complicated it gets.

4

This year, Christmas Eve night

I've had enough. My head is pounding, and my eyes are sore, and every inch of my body from my scalp to my toes feels like it's clenched up in tension.

All I can hear is the screaming, rising in shrieks and peaks above the sound of festive music, a playlist of carols I have on my phone to try and drown it all out. The mix is horrendous: the sublime choruses of 'Hark the Herald Angels Sing' alternating with yells of abuse.

Saul is sleeping, but restlessly, in that way that children will — I can see his eyes moving around under his lids, and his little fists are clenched, and every now and then his legs jerk, like a dreaming dog. It's the night before Christmas — maybe he's thinking about Santa, flying over the rooftops in his sleigh. I hope so, anyway. I hope he's not about to wake up, and hear all the rowing, and the banging, and voices. I worked hard to protect him from this, but it's chased me down, rooted me out.

I'm in my own little house, but I don't feel safe here any more. I'm in my own little house, and there are too many voices. Too much conflict. I'm in my own little house, and I'm hiding upstairs, cowering beneath the bed sheets, paralysed by it all.

I'm in my own little house, and I have to get out. I have to get away. I have to run.

PART 2: GET SET . . .

5

Six weeks earlier

It's the weekend. Saturday, in fact. But as anyone with young children knows, kids have absolutely zero respect for the sacred concept of 'the lie-in'.

Saul has always been high-energy. I mean, I don't have a lot to compare it to, but even the other little boys at the playgroups we've attended, and at his pre-school in the next village over, seem like they're on sedatives next to him.

He's a force of nature. A bundle of energy. A whirling dervish in *Paw Patrol* pyjamas — and he never stops talking. I know this is good — he has a crazy vocabulary for his age — but sometimes I remember the days when he couldn't speak or move oh so fondly. I am such a bad mother.

Right now, I'm lying in bed, in what my friend Lynnie calls the 'corpse pose'. Lynnie is in her sixties and has Alzheimer's — but no matter how much she declines, she always seems to remember her past life as a yoga instructor. Saul adores her, and she's even managed to get him into downward dog on a few occasions — sometimes for literally whole seconds.

It hasn't turned him into a zen master though — and he seems to think that 5.45 a.m. is the perfect time to come and climb into bed with me.

We live together in a teeny-tiny terraced house in the centre of Budbury village. There's only one road, which runs through the village like a ribbon, lined with a few shops and a pub, a community centre and a pet cemetery and a couple of dozen little houses. They're quite old, and face straight onto the pavement, and were probably built for fishermen in ye olde days of yore.

Several of my friends — regulars at the Comfort Food Café, a few minutes' walk away on the clifftops — live on the same road. I used to feel a bit claustrophobic, living so close to people who were keen to be friends. I used to feel like the only way I could be independent and safe was to be alone. Sometimes, I still feel like that — but I try to beat it down with a big stick, because it's really not healthy, is it?

So, I know from my horribly early visit to the bathroom, in the grey pre-dawn November light, roughly what else they're all up to. Edie May, who is 92 and has almost as much energy as Saul, is still tucked up in bed, bless her.

Zoe and Cal, along with Cal's daughter Martha, also still seem to be a-slumber. Martha's 17, and from what I recall from that state of being, mornings are not to be touched at weekends. Lucky swines.

In fact, I can see lights on in only one other house — the one where Becca and Sam live. They have a baby girl — Little Edie — who has just turned one. She's utterly adorable and they both dote on her — but she's not one of life's sleepers.

Seeing them awake, and imagining Sam bleary-eyed and zombified as he tries to entertain Little Edie, makes me feel slightly better. There's no snooze button on a baby — he'll be up, and surrounded by plastic objects in primary colours, and elbow-deep in nappies. Ha ha.

Saul doesn't have a snooze button either — but he is easier to distract. This morning, by 6 a.m., I am not only in corpse pose — I am playing Beauty Parlour.

This is one of Saul's favourite games, and I have no idea where he picked it up. None of the women in Budbury are exactly dedicated followers of fashion.

Willow, one of Lynnie's daughters, has a pretty unique style that involves a lot of home-made clothes and a nose ring and bright pink hair. The teenagers — Martha and her pal Lizzie — definitely wear a lot of eyeliner. But there isn't a beauty parlour in the village — or possibly even in the twenty-first century. Even the words sound like something from the 1950s, and bring to mind those big space-alien dryers women sit beneath in old movies, before they go on a hot date with Cary Grant.

Anyway — I don't know where he got it from, but I'm glad he did. It's a game that can be played with me entirely immobile. The very best kind of game.

He's gathered my make-up bag and a collection of hair-brushes and slides and bobbles; even some hairspray and perfume. In all honesty, I rarely even use any of it, but like most women I've somehow managed to amass a gigantic pile of half-used cosmetics and hair products to clutter up the house for no good reason.

He's sitting cross-legged next to me, blond hair scrunched up on one side and perfectly flat on the other, working away with the foundation. I didn't know I even owned foundation, and I suspect it's some deep tan-coloured gunk I used after a sunny holiday in Majorca when I was twenty-one. He's blending it in with all the gentleness of Mike Tyson, but I don't care.

It's allowing me to stay in bed, so I just make the odd encouraging noise, and keep my eyes closed really tight when he starts on the eyeshadow. I ban him from mascara though, as I'd actually like to keep my vision.

'You're looking so beautiful, Mummy,' he says, when he pauses to inspect his work so far. 'But I think you need to highlight your cheekbones a bit more. I'll use some blusher.'

'Okay,' I mutter, half asleep. Where *is* he getting this stuff?

I hear the lids getting screwed off various pots, and know from his sharp inhalation of breath that he's probably just spilled something. In fact, the whole duvet cover will likely be covered in powders and lotions — but hey, that's what washing machines were made for, right?

He pokes at me with his fingers, rubbing in what I know will be two great big clown-like spots on the side of my face, before sighing in satisfaction. Lipstick is next, after he's instructed me to make a 'kissy mouth' first. I bet I'm looking really sexy.

I glance through slitted eyes at the clock, and see that it is now 6.20 a.m. Wow. A massive lie-in.

'How's it going?' I ask, stifling a yawn.

'Really good. Really pretty. I think I might be finished. Shall we get up so we can watch cartoons before we go to the café for breakfast?'

Ugggh. Cartoons. I shrivel and die a little inside, and make a new suggestion: 'Hey — why don't you go and get my nail varnishes and you can do my fingers and toes?'

That fills in the next half an hour, and completely finishes off the duvet cover. I must admit he does a quite good job though, and am still admiring my brand-new multi-coloured fingers a little while later, when he is safely installed on the sofa watching shows on CBBC, shoving chunks of sliced-up banana into his mouth and laughing at the antics of a cartoon mouse who goes to school.

I put the duvet cover in the washer, and change it out for a new one — it's getting colder now anyway, and I'm already looking forward to snuggling up beneath the clean brushed cotton later. I live a wild and crazy life, what can I say?

I catch up on a bit of coursework for college — I'm trying to keep my nursing skills up to date, and since I met Lynnie, I've become a lot more interested in community mental health — and organise some files. I do some ironing, in a vain attempt to get prepared for the week ahead, and I check my emails. Apart from being contacted by a Nigerian prince offering me an unbeatable investment opportunity, there's nothing.

My phone shows three missed calls from my mum, but I can't quite face that conversation just yet. It's never fun, getting Mum's weekly updates on what terrible crime Dad has committed recently. I love them both, but it's like being trapped between two angry pit bulls. Except with more spite and slobber.

I intermittently check in with Saul, making sure he's not eating the coffee table or swinging from the light fittings, and eventually take him upstairs to get ready for the day ahead. He's excited to go to the café, and I can't say that I blame him — it's become like a second home to us. A home that always has cake.

It's his favourite place in the whole world. I think it might just be mine too.

6

The Comfort Food Café is like no place else on earth. It's set on the top of a cliff on the gorgeous coastline, surrounded by the sea on one side and rolling green hills on the other.

You reach it by climbing up a long and winding path, and enter through a wrought-iron archway that spells out its name in an embroidery made of metal roses. Even the archway is pretty and welcoming.

The building itself is low and sprawling, and set in its own higgledy-piggledy garden. There are tables and benches that get packed in summer, as well as a barbecue area, a terrace, and as of this year, the adjoining Comfort Reads bookshop.

The bookshop is open by the time we get there, and Zoe — short, ginger, slim — waves at us through the window. She's sitting on her stool behind the till, a paperback propped up on her knees. Saul squeaks when he sees her, as the last time we were here she produced a Gruffalo mug for him.

Zoe moved here last year with her god-daughter Martha, who is seventeen now, after her mother died. It's not been an easy ride for them, but they're settled now — along with Cal, Martha's biological dad, who she'd never even met before last Christmas as he lived in Australia. Yeah, I know — if Budbury had a

Facebook page, it would need to set its relationship status to 'It's Complicated'.

I don't think anyone here is simple, or straightforward, or has had an especially traditional life. It's one of the reasons it's sucked me in, to be honest — these are people who lived through a lot, survived to tell the tale, and now seem to see it as their life's mission to make other people happy while feeding them carrot cake.

There's even some kind of weird vibe where they match people up with their favourite comfort foods — like me and jam roly-poly, which always reminds me of my nan. I must have mentioned it at some point, but I don't remember when — all I know is when I'm especially down or tired, that's what will be waiting for me there, even if it's not on the menu.

I still vividly remember the first time I came here. It was a couple of weeks after we'd made the move to Dorset — after leaving Jason, I lived with my parents for a while, but I soon realised that was a mistake. I knew I needed to get away properly, and started looking for a place with enough distance for a fresh start, but close enough to Bristol for me to get back and see my parents, and potentially for Saul to see his dad, if that's how things played out. It's not, but such is life.

Mum, amazingly, helped me find the money to move here — something to do with a 'nest egg' that my nan had left — but it took some sorting. Jason resisted initially, made some half-hearted attempts to persuade me to come back, but it felt hollow and fake — we were better off without each other, and we both knew it. Eventually he moved himself as well, all the way to Glasgow — fresh starts all round.

It was harder than I thought, though, leaving. Setting up on my own in a new place where I knew nobody, with a baby. I'd thought it was what I needed — but I didn't factor in how lonely I'd feel in those first few weeks. I had to stop myself from giving in, from calling my parents or Jason, from back-sliding.

Saul was almost eighteen months by that stage, and bloody hard work. I can say it now, because I'm his mum and it's in the past — but he was actually a bit of a demon child. Endless energy, constant battles, the terrible twos way before his birthday. I was exhausted, running on empty, and secretly convinced that my own child hated me. I had no idea how I was going to cope.

Then, one morning, I came here. To the café. Out of sheer desperation, really — the need to get out of the house and at least be in some proximity to the rest of the world. I was sitting there, Saul busily throwing bread soldiers at my head and mashing his egg up like it was his mortal enemy, feeling washed out and fatigued to the edge of insanity.

A woman I now know as Becca came up to me, and brought me toast. Not Saul — me. Then another lady, who I'd thought was a customer but turned out to be the owner of the café, Cherie Moon, came and took Saul away. She's a big woman, Cherie, tall and robust, in her seventies with a weather-beaten face and wrinkles she wears with pride. She has a lot of long hair that she often has bundled up into a grey-streaked plait, and she has so much confidence that it practically oozes out of her.

Anyone else, I'd have worried about handing the baby over — more for their sake than his — but I just instinctively knew that Cherie could handle it. She'd walked him around the room, while I ate my toast and actually drank a hot beverage before it was lukewarm, and the sense of relief I felt was astonishing. In fact I had to disappear off to the toilets for a minute to compose myself — by which I mean sob relentlessly into wadded-up tissue paper.

These random acts of kindness — aimed at me, a complete stranger — were my introduction to the café. To the village. To the community that now, almost two years on, I am starting to dare to call my own.

It's taken a long time, because I am wary and stubborn and always cautious about random acts of kindness, but I understand it all better now. This place is like the island of misfit toys, and someone is always on hand with a sticking plaster and a spoonful of medicine for the soul.

These days, our lives are tied up with theirs in ways I could never have anticipated. The café gang help me out with childcare. I help them out with other things. We all look out for each other. It's like a big, tangled, misshapen ball of string, all directions leading to each other.

I'm still not the life and soul of any of the parties the café hosts or organises — I still dodge the big social events — but I'm getting there. Edging towards a security and comfort that I've never known since my nan died.

Saul thinks this place is home. He's little — he doesn't remember a life before it. He thinks Lynnie is his wacky granny, and Willow is a cartoon character because of her pink hair, and Cherie is the queen of the world.

He thinks Laura, who manages the café, is the cuddliest woman ever, and that Edie May is a magical tiny-faced elf who lives in a teapot.

He thinks all the men of Budbury — and there are several — are there purely to play football with him, or take him for walks on the beach, or help him hunt for fossils. He thinks the dogs of Budbury — Midgebo, Laura's black Lab, and Bella Swan, Willow's border terrier, and her boyfriend Tom's Rottie cross, Rick Grimes — are his own personal pooches.

I may have left behind my parents, and Jason, but what I gained was so much bigger — a whole village of the biggest-hearted people I've ever met.

He's tugging at my hand as we approach the doors, his little legs pumping as fast as they can, like a puppy straining on the lead, desperate to get inside.

Inside, where a world of fun awaits. Where the café starts to get weird. Weird in a good way. There are lots of things you'd expect to find in a café — tables covered with red gingham cloths; a big fridge full of soft drinks; a chiller cabinet crammed with sandwich platters and salads and whopping great slices of cake; a serving counter and a till. So far, so normal.

Then there are the extras. The things that immediately let you know that you're not in Kansas any more, Toto. The multiple mobiles hanging from the ceiling, dangling home-made oddities like old vinyl singles and papier-mâché fish. Half a red kayak. The oars from a rowing boat. Fishing net tangled up with fairy lights. The shelves lined with random objects — an antique sewing machine; a giant fossil in a cabinet; rows of books and board games and puzzles.

It's like the anti-Ikea — as though the Old Curiosity Shop got together with a tea room and had a baby. Despite the clutter, though, it all still feels fresh and clean, and is washed over with the light flooding in through the windows on all sides.

On one side, you can see into the garden. On the other, it's the sea and the beach and the endless red-and-gold cliff tops stretching off along the horizon. It's the kind of place you can lose hours, just watching the maritime world go by.

Saul bursts through the doors and strikes a dramatic pose, his little arms raised in the air, fists clenched, as though he's Superman about to take off.

'Everybody, I'm here!' he shouts, just in case they hadn't noticed. Laura is behind the counter, round and pretty and fighting a constant losing battle with her curly hair. She pauses in her work — slicing up lemon meringue cake — and her face breaks out into a huge smile.

'Thank goodness! I was wondering when you were going to turn up!' she says, wiping her hands down on her apron and walking out to see us. She crouches down in front of Saul and gives him a cuddle which he returns so enthusiastically she ends up sitting on her backside, his face buried in her hair.

I start to apologise, but she looks up at me and raises an eyebrow. That's a stern telling off from Laura, so I clamp my mouth shut.

Laura has two kids of her own — Nate and Lizzie, teenagers now — and understands children. She's told me approximately seven thousand times that I need to stop saying I'm sorry about Saul, when he's only doing what kids of that age do. She continues to stare at me, over the tufts of Saul's hair, but I can't figure out what I'm doing wrong this time, so I pretend not to notice.

I look around, and see Cherie sitting at a corner table, her feet in red and green striped socks, propped up on the chair next to her. Her husband Frank, who is an 82-year-old silver fox, is sitting opposite, drinking his thick tea and reading the paper. They both look up at me, and grin widely. They must be in an extra good mood this morning.

There is an actual paying customer here, still wrapped up in walking gear, perusing a guide book as he eats his toast. The café is on the Jurassic Coast and is often populated by people in padded anoraks and woolly hats, taking a break from their treks. He glances at the commotion, briefly widens his eyes when he nods good morning to me, and goes hastily back to his maps.

I glance around. There's nobody else here. Or at least I don't think there is, until he walks out of the gents.

He's tall by my standards — about six foot — but short by the standards of his own family, who are all giants. He's bulky, with brawn he earned travelling the world digging wells and building schools in the kind of places you see on the news during droughts. His chestnut hair is cropped brutally short, and he's wearing his usual uniform of careworn denims and a long-sleeved jersey top.

He looks up, and our eyes meet across an un-crowded room. He has great eyes. Bright blue, on the Paul Newman spectrum. He smiles when he sees me, and I smile back, even though I feel the usual tug of anxiety I get whenever I'm around him. He's looking half-amused, as though he's remembering a joke someone told him on a bus some time, his gaze moving from me to Saul.

This is Van, and he's Lynnie's son, and Willow's brother. He came back from his life in Africa when Lynnie took a turn for the worse in the spring, and has been working for Frank as a labourer ever since. I wait, knowing that Saul will spot him as soon as he's emerged from Laura's hair.

Right on cue, I see my son look up and around, his eyes widening in excitement when he sees him walking towards us.

'Van! Van! Mummy, Van is here, look!' he

squeals, leaving Laura lying on the floor, abandoned and forgotten, and me in a cloud of dust as he runs towards him. Van braces — this has happened many times before — catches him in his arms, scoops him up, and swings him around and around in a dizzying circle.

All I can hear is the ecstatic chuckling of my little boy as he whirls and flies through the air, shrieking for it to stop in a way that suggests he really doesn't want it to. Laura looks on and grins. Cherie and Frank look on and laugh. Even the random walker stifles a smile.

It's the kind of thing that makes everyone who sees it happy — an innocent expression of pure, unadulterated joy.

Everyone apart from me, I suspect. It doesn't make me happy. It makes me nervous. It makes me want to grab Saul back from him, and run away all over again. I vowed I wouldn't, no matter how complicated it all gets — but this is a whole new level of complicated.

Because in the same way that Saul seems to think that Cherie is the queen, and Edie is a magical elf, and Willow is a cartoon character, and all the dogs belong to him, he has views about Van as well. In his world, Van seems to have become the nearest thing he has to a real-life dad.

7

This, I am starting to think, could be a problem. Van is a nice man. Okay, he's a nice man who happens to be tremendously hot as well — and maybe that's the real problem. I like him, a lot.

In a fairytale world, that would be wonderful, wouldn't it? I'd complete my new move and my new life with a new relationship. We'd all live happily ever after, in a pink castle on a hill, surrounded by unicorns and rainbows. Everything wrapped up in a sparkly bow.

But this is the real world — my world. And in my world, all I've ever seen is relationships that start off good and go very, very bad. I'm determined not to let that happen to me again — or to Saul — and the best way to do that seems to be never to have a relationship at all.

That sounds very sensible when I say it in my head. I really, genuinely mean it. In my head. It doesn't seem to be my head that's the problem though — it's the rest of my body. Even here, now, in a café on a Saturday morning surrounded by other people, I feel that twitch when I look at him. The twitch that screams 'take me, take me', even when no words come out of my mouth beyond 'hi'. That's a blessing at least.

Van has done nothing to provoke this inner sluttiness, apart from exist, and I can't blame him for that. There are lots of good-looking men in Budbury, but they're all attached. There's Matt, the local vet and Laura's boyfriend. There's Sam, Becca's partner, who looks like a surfer and has the cutest Irish accent. There's Tom, Willow's fella, who has a superhero geek thing going on. There's Cal, Martha's dad and Zoe's man, an Aussie who manages Frank's farm and is pretty much the dictionary definition of 'rugged'.

But none of them have ever given me the twitch. Maybe because they're taken, and I just don't do that kind of thing. Maybe because I simply never felt that kind of chemistry with them even before I knew who they were and exactly how taken they are. It's weird, isn't it, the way you fancy some people and not others?

Weird, and in this case, inconvenient. I'm way too busy to even be wasting time thinking about such things, never mind doing them. I'm a single mum, I have my college course, and I work part-time in the village pharmacy, which is run by Auburn, Van and Willow's sister. Not an hour of my day is unaccounted for, ever. No, I definitely don't have time for a man in my life.

Even if I did, Van's never given any overt hint that he's even interested. He's probably not. In fact he definitely isn't. I'm nothing special — I'm perfectly average in every way. I'm petite — I get that from my mum — and I'm almost-blonde. Which, if you look at it from the other direction, means I'm almost mousy. I'm not the kind of woman men look at and have sexy thoughts about.

'You look stunning today,' says Van, just as I'm

39

thinking about how plain I am. He's stopped spinning Saul, and now has him on his shoulders, where he's using the extra height to fiddle with a mobile made of sea shells.

'Yes, you really do,' chimes in Laura, now busily getting my coffee ready. 'It's good to see somebody making an effort around here.'

I'm quite confused by this stage, especially as Frank and Cherie are visibly shaking with compressed laughter as they look at me over their newspaper pages.

'Erm . . . okay? Thank you,' I say, touching my hair self-consciously, noticing that it feels a bit stiff. Probably the salty sea air.

Saul realises what's being said, and grins at me before saying: 'I did that. I made her so pretty. I did Mummy's make-up in my beauty parlour this morning. She was being a lazy bones and staying in bed.'

I feel a horrifying blush sweep over my cheeks as the realisation sinks in. Luckily, my face is probably already so red that nobody will even notice.

My hands fly up to hide myself, and everybody bursts out laughing at my reaction. Even the walker, who I've never met in my life.

Oh God. I did it, didn't I? I played beauty parlour all morning just to get an extra few minutes in bed, and then was so busy and tired I didn't even look in a mirror before I left the house. Saul is perfectly dressed, perfectly groomed, with his teeth brushed and his hair neat and tidy. Me? I probably look like an escaped circus clown.

It does, at least, explain all the strange stares when I walked in. Maybe they thought I'd deliberately done it — me, a woman who rarely even wears make-up at all, and sees not being noticed as a tick in the win column.

Laura comes over and pats me on the shoulder in consolation. She's trying to look sympathetic, but the tears of amusement rolling down her cheeks don't match her tone.

'We've all been there, love,' she says, casting her eyes over my new look. 'I once went to Tesco with my hair sprayed into a mohawk, when Lizzie was going through a creative stage. Completely forgot until I was in the checkout paying for my sweet potatoes and toilet roll. What time did he get you up?'

'Umm . . . before six,' I reply quietly. I feel embarrassed and awkward and want the floor to open up, like in one of those films about earthquakes, and swallow me whole. I want to say more — to see how funny this is and shrug it off. Play it like Auburn would, and do a spontaneous mock-fashion catwalk around the room, showing off my new look.

But I'm not Auburn. I don't have her energy or confidence or 'I'm-all-out-of-shits-to-give' attitude. I'm me. I'm almost mousy, and my default setting is to stay as quiet as possible so the predators don't notice me.

I try on a small smile for size, as Van looks at me in concern. Maybe he can see the slight trembling in my hands, or the ever-so-annoying sheen in my eyes. He nods at me once, sharply, and says: 'Come on, Saul — we're going on an

41

adventure in the garden. Buried treasure. Let's give your mum a chance to look less beautiful and have a coffee, and see what we can find. What do you say, pirate lad?'

Saul grabs hold of his ears as though they're handles, and shrieks: 'Aye aye, Captain!' as they walk towards the doors. I watch them go, feeling both relieved and worried.

I don't have time to ponder the worried part, because Laura takes me by the arm and leads me away to the ladies. She's produced a packet of baby wipes — she's one of those mumsy women who always have a fresh pack of hankies about her person — and perches on the fake zebra-skin stool that's in there while I start to clean myself up. She looks a bit tired herself, now I come to notice.

The mirror in front of me reveals that my stylish look is even worse than I'd anticipated. I have purple eyes, the colour swirling all around the socket and across my eyebrows, and my skin is the deep tan of a terracotta warrior — up to my chin, where it suddenly goes milky white again. Two giant, circular blobs of bright red adorn my cheeks like apples, and the remnants of scarlet lipstick are lining my mouth. My hair is sprayed into a kind of cone on my head, like a strange hat — he must have covered it in lacquer, and massaged it upwards like the Eiffel Tower.

I stare at my reflection for a couple of seconds, then start to attack the whole mess with the vigour of a woman vowing never to let such a thing happen again.

'I remember those days,' says Laura, watching me and smiling. 'The early mornings. The constant demands for attention. I know it doesn't feel like it now, but you'll miss it when it's gone.'

'Really?' I say, unable to keep the disbelief from my voice as my fingertips get caught in my beehive.

'Oh yes,' she replies, nodding. 'Definitely. These days, budging Lizzie and Nate from their bedrooms is a challenge. Getting their attention is even harder. They still need me — but mainly for money and food and lifts to their friends' houses. I'm not the centre of their worlds any more, and even though that means I get more sleep, I do miss them being little. Of course, it was different for me — I had David around, then.'

Laura married her childhood sweetheart when they were barely out of school, and had her kids young. From what I can gather, theirs was a perfect life — until David tragically died after an accident at home.

A couple of years after that, she packed the children up and moved here for the summer. A summer that turned into forever, after Nate and Lizzie settled so well, and she met Matt. She's another one of the Budbury survivors who has fitted into the routine of life here in this far-off corner of the world.

'Well, it's not too late, is it?' I ask, as I wipe my eyes within an inch of their lives. 'You could have another baby, if that's what you and Matt wanted.'

She snorts out a quick laugh, and slaps her own thighs.

'I don't think so!' she answers, looking part amused, part wistful. 'I'm knocking forty, you know. I think those days are behind me. Matt . . . well, he'd be a great dad. But I think he's happy with being a kind-of step-dad . . . I don't know. We've never even discussed it, to be honest. Anyway, I'm exhausted enough dealing with the kids and Midgebo.'

She gazes off at something I can't see, and I wonder if I've said the wrong thing. If I've touched a sore spot without even trying. She snaps out of it and smiles at me again, as though to reassure me.

'Anyway. You know what this place is like,' she says. 'We share our problems and we share our joys — and that means we all get to enjoy having Saul in our lives. We're glad you're here.'

I feel a sudden wash of gratitude towards her — for the baby wipes, for the conversation, for the reassurance. For the way she makes me feel so welcome.

'Thank you,' I reply, as I tackle the blusher spots. 'It's . . . well, it's taken me a while to settle in, but now I have, I'm glad I'm here as well. I'm not . . . not the sort of person who opens up too easily.'

She nods, and I can practically see her making an effort not to dive right in with a load of questions. The crowd here doesn't know much about my background, or why I left Bristol. They don't know about the way I grew up, or about Saul's dad, other than he lives in Scotland now. I have my privacy settings on high, and always have had.

Even as a kid, I was guarded. There are only so many times you can bring friends home from school just to have them walk into a parental war zone before you decide not to bother any more. It was embarrassing, at an age when you're mortally embarrassed about having a spot, never mind your mates seeing your mum whack your dad around the head with a frying pan.

'I know,' she says, when I don't add anything. 'And that's fine. We're all different, aren't we? I hope you know, though, that we're always here for you if ever you need a listening ear. Or some cake.'

'Or some baby wipes.'

'Yes! I always have baby wipes . . . even if I don't have the baby. Anyway, come on out and have a coffee and some toast. Or do you want some jam roly-poly? I know you like that.'

'Isn't it a bit early for jam roly-poly?' I ask, smiling.

She feigns shocked horror and says: 'Hush your mouth, child — it's never too early for jam roly-poly! I didn't get a figure like this by watching the clock, you know!'

She gestures down at her own body, which to be fair is a little on the round side. She's not fat, not by any means. Just . . . comfortable. And curvy. And perfect.

'Thank you. Toast would be great,' I reply, as we emerge back into the café. There's another couple of customers now, a fresh-faced teenager and what looks like his granddad, and I feel

45

momentarily bad that I took Laura away from her work. She glances at my face, and seems to know that immediately.

'Don't worry,' she says, patting my hand. 'Cherie's sorted them, look. About time she got off her lazy backside anyway.'

She says the last part extra-loud, and Cherie laughs from behind the counter, waving a spatula at her threateningly.

'Watch your cheek, lady,' she answers, grinning. 'You're never too old for a good spanking!'

Frank looks up from his newspaper, blue eyes twinkling, and adds: 'You're right there, love!'

This is something of a conversation stopper, and Laura and I exchange wide-eyed glances as we both try very hard not to imagine Frank getting his 82-year-old bottom smacked. Crikey. Grey panthers rule — and they've definitely got a better love life than me.

Laura does a mock shiver and settles me down at one of the tables. She knows I won't want company, and doesn't push it. The ladies here, in particular, tend to gather at the café for mammoth sessions of gossip and world-righting. I often see them, clustered around a couple of tables shoved together — Cherie and Laura and Becca and Zoe, Edie and Willow and Auburn. They always look so comfortable with each other; sitting there guzzling endless rounds of freshly baked scones and hot chocolates.

Sometimes, I want to join them. I want to take that simple step of walking in, sitting down and chatting with the tribe. But I never have, so far

46

— in fact I've sometimes turned away from the café once I've seen them there, not quite ready to break my solitude.

Maybe one day I'll take the daring step of joining them for one of their sessions.

Not quite yet, though, I decide, looking on as the new customers stare around the room in wonder. They'll always remember this place — the weird café on the cliff they found when they were out walking. They'll probably tell their friends about it, go home and try to describe it. I see the teenager whip out his phone and start taking photos — because, of course, teenagers don't settle for just describing something when they can post it on social media instead.

Cherie comes over with a mocha — my favourite — and a plate heaped with granary toast. The butter is laid on so thick it's melting and oozing over bread that I know Laura will have baked herself. I have died and gone to heaven.

'There you go, love,' says Cherie, laying one gentle hand on my shoulder. 'Fill your boots, as they say. That little dynamo of yours will be back in soon, so enjoy the peace. Oh, by the way, did Laura tell you there was a phone call for you?'

I already have a mouthful of toast when she asks this, and all I can do is shake my head, butter dripping down my chin, looking up at her inquiringly.

'Laura!' she bellows, so loud that small mountain ranges in Nepal probably shake and quiver. 'When did you take that message for Katie?'

Laura stops what she's doing — slicing tomatoes for the day's salads — and stares up, looking horrified.

'Oh no!' she says, biting her lip. 'I'm so sorry — I completely forgot about it; I don't know where my head is today! Katie, your mum called — she said can you call her back, please? She also said, 'Don't worry, nobody's dead.' Which is nice.'

8

Van walks back into the café at that stage, Saul trailing behind him, cheeks rosy from the autumnal chill and his hair ruffled.

'Mummy!' he shouts, dashing over full of excitement. 'We found treasure!'

He grabs hold of my knee with one muddy hand, and in the other brandishes his booty — a one pound coin. I'm guessing that Van managed to distract him while he buried it in the garden, then helped him re-discover it. He winks at me over Saul's head, and I blink rapidly in response.

'It's a Spanish doon!' Saul says, spinning it around on the table top. He looks so thrilled, it momentarily distracts me from Van, my mother, and wondering what the hell is going on back at home.

'A Spanish doon? Wow!' I say, widening my eyes in suitable awe. 'That's amazing!'

'Shop?' he asks, hopefully, his tone slightly wheedling. He might think it's a Spanish doubloon — or doon, I should say — but clearly still expects to be able to exchange it for a carton of juice and a chocolate bar.

'Later, sweetie,' I respond. 'I'll take you to the shop later. Right now it's time for me to take you to see Lynnie and Willow while I go to work. How does that sound? You can show them your Spanish doon.'

He ponders this, and I see him weigh up the

pros and cons with his little boy brain. On the one hand, no shop. But on the other — fun times! Luckily, he lands on the side of Lynnie and Willow, which is exactly where I want him. Life is much easier if you don't have to argue with a toddler. I mean, I usually win the arguments — I am technically the grown-up — but it's tiring.

'Lynnie will love my doon,' he pronounces, pulling up the hood of his coat in the way he does when he wants me to know he's ready to go somewhere. It's like his signal — *I'm ready for action, Mummy!*

I nod, and cram as much toast in my mouth as I can without choking. I swill it down with my mocha, feeling disrespectful — it deserved better than that. Life with a small child often leads to indigestion, I've discovered.

I glance at Cherie apologetically, feeling bad for my lack of appreciation, but she just nods and gives me a 'don't-worry-about-it' wave as I put my coat on. I'm wondering already how I'll manage to call my mum, and plan to try and fit it in on the walk to Lynnie's cottage. I have a few hours to do at the pharmacy, while he's on his weirdly formed playdate.

'I'm heading back,' says Van, now wrapped up in a navy fleece jacket and wearing a beanie hat that makes him look a bit like he should be in some mountainous ski resort in the Alps. 'I'll walk with you, if that's okay?'

I see Laura watching us, pretending not to, and know that she'll be thinking what a nice couple we make. Laura is a great believer in happy endings, despite all her own trials and tribulations. I catch her eye and raise one eyebrow, and she at least has the grace to blush and start bustling around with a cheese grater.

'Okay,' I say simply, as Van waits for a reply. I mean, I could hardly say no, could I? Even if I wanted to.

We say our farewells and start the short walk to the cottage. It's a beautiful day, cold but sunny, with that fresh, crisp light you sometimes get in autumn. Dazzling blue skies hover over the sea, the colour so bold and solid it looks like you could reach out and touch it.

The coastal pathways are slightly muddy from the melted morning frost, and the sound of birdsong is melodically present in the background, along with the gentle hiss and hum of calm waves lapping the sand.

We leave the cliffs behind us, and emerge onto footpaths that criss-cross Frank's farm. Tucked between glorious green hills, the fields are literally covered in seagulls and other birds, hovering and flapping over the ground like a living carpet made of fluttering wings.

'Why all the birdies?' Saul asks, tugging at Van's sleeve and looking up at him inquiringly. He correctly assumes that I wouldn't have a clue.

'Ah,' replies Van, pointing across at them. 'That's because it's after harvest, and we've been getting the fields ready for their new seeds. We spread muck on it — cow poo! — and then we plough it and all the soil gets squished and turned over. When we do that, lots of worms come out to play, and the birds come along for an extra big dinner time. It's like the Comfort Food Café for seagulls, but instead of cake, they eat long, wriggly worms!'

Saul immediately giggles at the mention of cow poo, obviously. I know from my dealings with men that this will be the case even when he's thirty. He watches the birds and makes wriggling gestures with his fingers, making them into worms and laughing.

He's trotting along, feet squelching, one hand in mine and one in Van's, occasionally asking us to 'give him a swing'. We usually oblige, and his squeals of delight as he flies up into the air are joyous to hear. Anyone looking on would assume we were a young couple out for a stroll with our son, and the thought chokes me a little.

Maybe it's that, or maybe it's an underlying worry about my mum, but I'm quiet as we walk. Smiling, so I don't look like a complete misery-guts, but not exactly chatty either.

'Are you all right?' asks Van, giving me a sideways glance. 'You seem a bit . . . off, today.'

I snap myself out of my fugue state and reply as breezily as I can: 'Yes, I'm fine. Sorry. Just a bit tired, you know?'

'I can imagine. Maybe you need a night off. Maybe . . . we could go for a pint. Together. Like grown-ups do, or so I'm told. I don't know many of those.'

'Oh . . . well, I don't think I could. I wouldn't have a babysitter.'

He sighs, and when I look up at him, his blue eyes are crinkled at the corners. He looks partly amused, partly exasperated. Wholly gorgeous.

'Katie, you have a whole village full of babysitters. Saul could stay over at the cottage. Becca and Sam would have him for a few hours. Edie would sit in with him. Cherie and Frank would love to have him. Laura would probably see it as a treat and bake a whole oven full of cupcakes for him. There are several teenagers who would be desperate to earn a tenner for the privilege of sitting on your sofa using their phones. Babysitting isn't a problem.'

'Right,' I say, trudging on, half wishing that Saul would fall face first into a cowpat or something so I could use the excuse to end this particular conversation. He remains annoyingly upright, singing a song to himself about a worm that lives at the bottom of his garden. I recognise it immediately, and find myself singing along: 'And his name is Wiggly-Woo . . . '

Saul giggles again, and carries on singing. Van is quiet, but not in an annoyed way — coming from his family, I'm guessing he's used to eccentric women who randomly burst into song. I know Willow does it all the time, often serenading us with her highly individual versions of Disney classics.

'Right,' I say again, brushing my hair away from my face and feeling annoyed with myself. I don't know quite why, but I feel silly, for a whole variety of reasons.

'Well then,' I continue, trying to stride ahead but not managing it, as Van is so much taller than me. 'Maybe I will come out for a drink some time. Maybe I won't. I suppose what I'm saying is that I'll do it when and if I want to. Is that all right?'

He grins, and then laughs. I'm not sure I expected him to laugh, but it's better than him being offended.

'I love that thing you do,' he answers, looking on as Saul trudges off to investigate a pile of Wiggly-Woos.

'What thing?'

'That thing where you say stuff in a quiet voice that makes you sound apologetic and shy, but when you actually look at what the stuff you said was, it's the opposite of apologetic and shy. You sound all weedy, but you're actually kind of channelling a Chaka Khan 'I'm Every Woman' vibe.'

I glance at him from beneath my fringe, and can't help but smile. He's totally right, of course. The new me is striving to be a strong and independent woman — but my attitude hasn't quite caught up with it. I'm like a mouse trying to roar.

'I'm a work in progress,' I reply, smiling at him. 'And by the way, I think your mother is on her way to meet us . . . '

He looks up and squints into the sunlight to make her out. Lynnie is cutting a path in our direction, wearing her pyjamas, a faux fur stole, and a pair of ancient Hunter wellies. Now, Lynnie does have Alzheimer's, but in all honesty, dressing like that probably isn't part of her symptoms — the whole family has what you might call a relaxed approach to social conventions.

The rolled-up yoga mat under her arm, though? That's usually a sign that she's decided to set off somewhere to give a class. At a guess, the café.

Sure enough, Willow isn't far behind her, eating up the distance with her stupidly long legs to catch her up, pink hair streaming in the breeze. Bella Swan, her Border terrier, is next in line.

We all meet up in the middle, Willow puffing slightly, Lynnie looking confused at all the fuss. It's hard to know how she'll react in situations like this — sometimes a gentle reminder of the here and now sets her back on track. Other times, she understandably lashes out at the fact that a group of strange people are trying to kidnap her.

Luckily, Saul is usually the salve in all of these scenarios. He runs straight up to her, and wraps his arms around her legs, making delighted sounds muffled by his scarf.

'Well, hello!' says Lynnie, squatting down to get on eye level with him. 'Where are you off to, little man?'

'Your cottage, silly billy!' he replies joyously, reaching out to stroke the faux fur around her shoulders. 'Mummy's going to work at the chemist shop and I'm coming to look after you.'

I meet Willow's gaze, and see the frown lines and anxiety on her face. She tries to hide it, and often manages, but it's all there — the worry and the fatigue. She's one of life's optimists, Willow, always seeing the best in the world and the people she meets — but having a sunny disposition doesn't always count when your mum has dementia.

We all wait to see what Lynnie's reaction is going to be, and there is almost a communal sigh of relief when she stands up straight and offers her hand to Saul.

'Come on then,' she says, heading back to the house, him ambling at her side. 'If you're going to look after me, we'd better make some toast to keep our strength up.'

She nods at me and Van politely as she goes, as though we are strangers deserving of a pleasantry as she passes. It's more than Willow gets.

'I'm the bad guy today,' she says sadly, as we follow on. 'She didn't want to take her tablets, or eat her breakfast, or get dressed. Then she waited until I was in the bathroom and made a break for it. Crazy like a fox, that one.'

Van nods and stays silent. I know he struggles more than his sisters with his mother's condition. Maybe it's because he's not been back as long; maybe it's a gender thing — he's the kind of guy who's used to being able to fix things. Build things. Make things work properly. Now he's facing something that isn't fixable, and I know it eats away at him.

'If it's too much to have Saul around, I can take him with me,' I say, touching Willow's arm as we walk.

'No, honestly, it's fine,' Willow replies, pasting a smile onto her drawn face. 'It's actually easier when he's here. It's like having a kid around somehow overrides the other impulses; some instinct kicks in and she just enjoys being with him and playing with him. Besides, can you imagine Saul in a pharmacy?'

I grin as I picture this, and bite back a giggle.

'I know. It'd be dangerous, wouldn't it? He'd be snorting athlete's foot powder and painting his face with antibacterial cream . . . '

'Not to mention swigging the Gaviscon, getting high on caffeine pills, and possibly treating the antibiotics like Skittles.'

We all pause as we let these images sink in.

'You're right,' I say, finally. 'He's banned from the pharmacy for life. Anyway . . . if you're sure?'

'Of course I'm sure,' she says, gently but firmly. 'I'd speak out if I needed to, don't worry. No, off you go — might as well make a break for it while he's distracted. I'll see you this afternoon, all right? He'll be fine. I'll be fine. We'll all be fine. Tom's coming round anyway, so he can ride Rick Grimes around the garden like he's that dog-dragon in *The Neverending Story*.'

Rick Grimes is part Rottweiler, part golden retriever, part mystery. He can be unpredictable with other dogs, but adores children. As we don't have any pets of our own, it's a good set-up — Saul gets all the fun, and I get none of the responsibility.

I nod and say goodbye to her and Van, and head off towards the village. I seem to spend my life traipsing across various fields and footpaths, juggling time and childcare and favours. Life might be easier if I had a car — but as I can't drive, maybe not. Perhaps, I think, as I leave them behind and follow a different path, I should invest in one of those motorbikes that has a sidecar I can put Saul into. He'd love that.

I'm still smiling about that particular image when I arrive at the pharmacy. It's in the centre of the village, and is imaginatively called The Budbury Chemist. It's quite quaint and old-fashioned looking on the outside, with mullioned windows and a wooden sign that hangs like the ones you find outside old pubs. On it is a painted version of an old apothecary symbol, a pestle and mortar, with a border made of green ivy. The place used to be owned by a lady called Ivy Wellkettle, who left to live with her daughter last year, and the sign has stayed as a reminder of her.

I push the door open and hear the familiar jingle-jangle of the bell as I make my way inside. The warmth of the room envelops me, and makes me realise how cold it's been getting recently. This will be my third winter here in Budbury, and last year's was a humdinger. At least Saul is walking much more now, so I won't be wrestling his push-chair through the snow as often.

I look around at the well-stocked shelves and the pristine counter and the various posters about flu jabs and controlling asthma and giving up smoking, and spot Auburn sitting on the sprawling sofa at the back of the main room, next to Edie May.

You don't often get sofas in chemists' shops, but this is Budbury. Everyone likes a place to sit wherever they go — otherwise, they might have to stay upright while chatting. This sofa was a gift from Cherie, and it shows — it's in the shape of a giant pair of bright red lips. Like an enormous lipstick-on-tissue kiss that's been stuffed and covered in velvet and given little legs. Personally, I find it quite scary, and always feel like I'm about to be eaten by a cartoon alien whenever I sit on it.

Auburn is, as her name suggests, a red-head. All of Lynnie's children were named after characteristics they had when they were born — Van had a wonky ear (it looks fine now); Willow was long and lean, and their other brother, who lives in Aberdeen, is called Angel because he was so cherubic. He's the black sheep of the family — he changed his name to Andrew.

Today, Auburn's hair is pulled back into a glossy pony-tail, cascading down the side of her white-coated shoulder. She looks professional and competent, and every inch the pharmacist, until you notice the bulge in her chest pocket. That'd be her Zippo and pack of cigarettes, which she regularly sneaks out into the courtyard at the back to puff away on. She's always saying she's going to give up, and even put one of the especially graphic anti-smoking posters in a back window so she can look at it as she wheezes. The photos of black lungs don't seem to have deterred her.

Next to Auburn is Edie, the village's 92-year-old elder stateswoman. She's tiny, with a face made entirely of wrinkles and creases, and twinkling blue eyes that belie her true age. Her white hair is recently permed, and forms a pouffy helmet around her head.

The other quirk about Edie is the fact she apparently believes her long-dead fiancé is still alive. He was killed during the Second World War, but there was never any body. Over the years, I'm told, she settled into a delusion that he was still around — and always takes home extra food for him from the café.

It's the way Budbury works that everybody simply accepts this, and doesn't allow it to get in the way of the fact that Edie, despite her age, is still one of the most active and popular people in the village. Nobody asks too many questions, nobody thinks she's any weirder than anybody else, and nobody even blinks when she mentions him.

The two of them — Edie and Auburn, not Edie and her ghost fiancé — are currently sharing a catalogue of some kind, pointing at pictures and giggling.

They look up as I walk towards them, and Edie pipes up: 'Katie! Just the girl! We were just considering a new range of novelty condoms and over-the-counter sex aids . . . what do you think? Is Budbury ready for that?'

I find myself blushing, and try to shake it away.

'I don't know . . . do you think there'd be much demand?' I ask, trying and failing to not look at the glossy photos of soft-focus boudoirs.

'Who knows?' replies Auburn, closing the catalogue, standing up and stretching. 'I think there are hidden depths of perversion in this town. It's all sweet and sugar-coated on the surface, but there's got to be some heavy-duty swinging and dominatrix action going on behind the lace curtains . . . '

My mind flickers back to Frank's comment about spanking, and I blush even more.

Auburn, being Auburn, carries on regardless: 'And you know what? That catalogue came in the same post for a brochure about Harry Potter merchandise we might want for Christmas! Imagine if they'd mixed up the two, and we'd got a Harry Potter-themed sex selection? That would be fun . . . Voldemort's Length, for *your* Chamber of Secrets!'

I shudder, and try not to show it.

'Well,' I say, hiding my discomfort as well as I can, 'you could always open an X-rated store in the back room, couldn't you? Adults only. Ann Summers kind of vibe. Laura would probably make you some cakes in the shape of penises.'

Edie bursts out laughing and claps her tiny hands together in delight.

'Oh yes! Buttercream willy cake! How funny — they'd flock here from as far away as Devon! We'd all become famous for our willy cake! Can you imagine?'

Sadly, I can — and it prompts me to offer a round of hot beverages instead of working further on our masterplan of filth. One minute it's a joke; the next I'll be selling fluffy handcuffs to the postman's wife.

'Been busy?' I ask, as Auburn follows me behind the dispensing area. This is pristine and clean, with a big fridge and well-organised shelves and various containers and pieces of equipment; reference books with exciting names

61

like *Stockley's Drug Interactions*, a computer and printer for the labels, and a big locked cupboard that contains the heavy-duty controlled pharmaceuticals. The 'Party Cupboard', as Auburn very irreverently calls it.

It leads into a tiny kitchen area, which is slightly less pristine, and beyond that a stock room. We stop in the kitchen, and Auburn leans back against the counter-tops, pulling her cigarettes from her pocket in preparation for a trip outside.

'A bit, this morning. Some repeat prescriptions for that lady who has a lot of problems with her arthritis, lives a few miles off? Plus some blue pill action for a bloke who actually lives much further towards Dorchester, but is obviously too embarrassed to get his fix locally. Few people came in for cough and cold stuff. Sold some of those hand-warmers you put in the microwave. But not exactly a tsunami of custom, no. How are things with you? Did you drop Saul off today?'

I nod and bustle around getting the cups ready. She sounds slightly edgy as she asks, and I know that's not because of Saul — it's because she's worried about her mum.

'Yep, everything is fine,' I reply, smiling at her. Okay, that's stretching the truth a bit — but it won't do her any good to know Lynnie was having one of her wandering star moments. Auburn in particular gets stressed out about those, as the first time she looked after her mum overnight, she made a run for it and ended up in hospital with a broken ankle. Not her fault

62

— but like most women, she lives to blame herself for everything that ever goes wrong in the entire universe.

'Good . . . well, while it's quiet, I'm going to nip out for a breath of unfresh air. Oh! By the way — I completely forgot. You got a phone call earlier — from your mum. Said there was no answer on your landline, and she'd been trying you on your mobile, and could you please call her back? If you're not too busy. But don't worry, nobody's died.'

9

Before I make the tea, I get out my phone and check it. Missed calls from Mum, yes, but annoyingly no messages that might shed some light on what's going on. And as for the landline, that'll be because I unplugged it and forgot — Saul called 999 a few days ago to tell the police that two seagulls were having a fight outside the house. They saw the funny side, but in that stern *warnings about wasting emergency services' time* kind of voice.

I quickly look into the shop, to make sure there's not a giant queue of customers waiting to buy hand sanitiser and Strepsils, and call my mum's number. It goes straight to voicemail, and I leave a quick message saying I'm sorry I haven't called back, I'm glad nobody's dead, and she can get me on my mobile later.

I give it a few moments' thought, then try my dad as well. Also voicemail. The landline just rings out and out, and I can picture it, chiming away in the hall at home, on the little table that has a seat attached to it — an antique relic of a bygone era when people had to sit at home and talk to each other.

It's weird that neither of them is answering. It's Saturday, so Dad might be out at the pub with his mates. Mum's usually at home, though, watching the clock and getting annoyed with him.

I chew my lip a bit, and decide there's nothing else I can do for the time being. And, as I've been told, nobody's dead.

I distract myself by making the tea, and walk back through to give Edie a mug. She's chortling away at the sex aid catalogue, and peers at me over her glasses.

'Oh my! The things these people come up with!' she says, wrapping her papery-skinned fingers around the mug. 'Where do they get their ideas from?'

'I really don't know,' I reply, smiling at her infectious amusement. 'It's probably best not to think about it too deeply.'

She nods sagely, and stands up to her spectacular height of five foot nothing. She's dressed in her usual beige cardigan and matching tights, with sensible shoes and a fluorescent orange Vans backpack draped from her slender shoulders. It's like Edie's uniform. She downs her tea in one — decades of experience.

'You're probably right, dear . . . say goodbye to Smokey McChuff Face for me, will you? Thanks for this lovely tea, but I must make a move. Busy day today — I'm judging in a sausage-making contest in the big city! I wonder what the sex catalogue people would make of that, eh?'

I grimace, and wave her off. The 'big city' actually means the next village over, Apple-church, which is a regular metropolis compared to Budbury. They have three pubs, and a school, and their very own GP surgery. Dizzying stuff.

I try my mum again and get no reply. To try and stop myself from worrying, I do some stocktaking, and by the time Auburn comes back in with her own mug of coffee and a plate of café-made cookies, I've discovered that we need more cold sore cream. Heaven forbid the lips of Budbury should go untreated. I make a note on my little pad, and take one of the chocolate chip sin-balls that Auburn offers. I have no idea why everyone in Budbury isn't obese — must be all the walking we do to offset the sugar.

I tell her goodbye from Edie, and carry on stalking the shelves, counting up boxes of Kleenex and wondering why chemist shops always seem to sell those lollipops that are made in the shape of whistles.

Auburn follows behind me like a shadow. She's hovering so close at one point that when I back up to get a wider look at our frankly stunning range of scented candles, I crash right into her.

'Sorry!' she yelps, jumping out of the way, the word muffled by her mouthful of cookie crumbs.

'Can I help you with something, Auburn?' I ask, smiling at her to take any potential sting out of my words. Full of confidence and brazen flash on the surface, she's actually pretty easily offended — like she's waiting for the world to notice she's not all that.

'No . . . I'm just bored, I suppose. I've got all the prescription requests done for Monday; I've checked my stocks in the dispensary, and I've eaten seven thousand chocolate chip cookies. So

66

now I have a massive sugar rush and nowhere to go. I talked to Van while I was outside, by the way, just to see how things were going.'

'Right — everything okay?' I ask, perching myself on the stool behind the counter. Just in case we get a mad flood of customers — and also to stop Auburn from invading my personal space. I'm very protective of my personal space.

'Yep. Mum's teaching Saul how to knit. He says he's going to make you a scarf for Christmas. And Van says he asked you out for a drink and you said no.'

'I didn't say no. I said maybe I would, maybe I wouldn't. Was he upset? I didn't mean to upset him. I just . . . didn't want to agree to something I wasn't sure about.'

She grins, full wattage, and seems delighted with it all. Van is her big brother, but not by much, and there's a definite sibling rivalry that age and maturity hasn't managed to erase.

I'm an only child, and being involved with big families is always a magical mystery tour for me — no matter how old they get, there always seems to be part of them that stays feral, and wants to hold the other one down on the floor while they dribble spit on their faces.

'No, he's not upset. In fact I think you've accidentally mastered the art of treat 'em mean and keep 'em keen without even trying. Most people would just lie to get out of something.'

'I don't think I have the imagination to lie,' I reply, quietly. 'And I spent too much of my life tiptoeing around other people's feelings to feel comfortable with it. Not so long ago, I'd have just said yes to please him.'

'But not now?' she asks, one eyebrow arched up in question.

'No. Not now. Anyway, what lie would you have told?'

She narrows her eyes slightly, as though she's letting me know that she knows that I'm changing the conversation, steering it away from any personal revelations. I nod, to show that I know that she knows, and that I'm not about to start spilling my guts like I'm on *The Jeremy Kyle Show*. Budbury, for all its many charms, is not a great respecter of privacy. So, we both know what we know — and leave it at that.

'Well,' she replies, staring off into space as she thinks about it, 'there are a variety of lies that would suit that scenario. If you'd met him in a club, you could give him a fake phone number. And a fake name. I used to pretend I was a nurse called Lorraine when I met men for the first time. This is different, though . . . you'd have to go for either something halfway believable, or a complete whopper.'

'Examples, please. I live to learn at the knees of Lorraine.'

'Okay — well, halfway believable. Tell him you're a lesbian.'

'What?? Do I look like I might be a lesbian?'

She bursts out laughing, and I have to join in.

'Not that there's anything wrong with that,' I add. 'And it has its appeal — I could be the only gay in the village.'

'That we *know* of,' replies Auburn, nodding like she's stumbled across the world's greatest

68

conspiracy theory. 'Statistically, there must be some. I should probably organise an official survey. And lesbians, I believe, can look like absolutely anybody — so that's a daft comment. Admittedly, you have a child — but you could say that was a one-off, and you've since had a personal epiphany of a Sapphic persuasion.'

'I could, if I knew what that meant. All right. That's one — how about the complete whopper?'

'Those are more fun,' she says, unwrapping a whistle-shaped lollipop and pausing to blow through it. 'You could say you're a nun on sabbatical. Or that you have a terrible sexually transmitted disease that's made your lady parts fall off. Or that your dog ate your foot. Or wait until the night you were supposed to go out, and say a giant pterodactyl shat on your head.'

'Or,' I reply, taking the lollipop out of her hand and throwing it into the bin — the last thing she needs is more sugar — 'I could just be honest. I'm really not at a point in my life where I want to be dating. Not that it was a date. Not that he implied that. Not that I'm being up myself, and assuming he's interested in me that way. Because I'm sure he's not — he's a very attractive man, and there's no way he'd fancy me. And even if he did, I'm not saying that I fancy him. Even though he is very attractive. And . . . '

I run out of steam at that point, which is a good thing, as Auburn is already practically wetting herself laughing at me.

'Aye aye, Captain Careful,' she says, giving me

a mock salute. 'Message received, over and out — you're not interested. Even if he was interested. Which is all very interesting. And as he's my big bro, and I still think of him in terms of sweaty socks and acne, I can understand you saying no. But if not him, then what about someone else? I mean, you've been here for ages, and presumably single for ages, and . . . well, don't you need a shag by now?'

She looks genuinely bewildered by the concept of someone being celibate for this long. Auburn, for all her bluster, is actually almost as guarded as me when it comes to her emotions — she covers them up under layers of sarcasm and nonsense.

She's the same with her personal history — I know she lived away from home for over a decade, travelling and working, in South America and Asia and Europe. There must have been significant others, but she's never talked about them. Now, she seems to have a selection of blokes she refers to as her 'he-man harem', who she occasionally pays visits to. Presumably not to discuss the meaning of life.

I shrug and try to look nonchalant.

'I'm the mother of a very active small child. That changes everything. For a start, I'm too tired to even think about sex, never mind actually do it. And . . . well, maybe I'm just not built like you, Auburn. You can separate sex and feelings. That's never been my strong point, and life is already complicated enough without throwing that into the mix. For now, I'm content with things the way they are.'

70

She ponders that, and nods.

'You're right. Separating emotions from pretty much everything else is one of my strong suits. And I get what you're saying — but Saul won't be around as a human shield forever, will he?'

I'm not keen on that phrase, but let it pass. She doesn't mean any harm by it, I know.

'Nope. And maybe when he's left home, I'll turn into a nymphomaniac to make up for lost time. At the moment . . . well, I'm too busy washing pterodactyl poo from my hair, aren't I?'

'That's the spirit!' she says, patting my hand. 'By George, I think she's got it!'

She gazes outside, at the quiet main street that flows through Budbury, which is sleepy even on a Saturday. I know she's thinking about her mum, and what's going on at home. She usually stays until just after lunchtime, to be available for pharmacist duties, and it's now almost twelve. Crikey, I think — I've managed to go to the in-bed Beauty Parlour, show off my new image at the café, say no to a not-really-a-date with a hot man, drop off Saul, and look at sex aids with a nonagenarian already this morning.

'Why don't you go home?' I suggest, following her gaze. 'I think we've had our rush. If anyone comes in with a prescription, I can tell them to collect it on Monday. Or if it's urgent, I'll call you and you can come back. I can lock up at three and meet you back at the cottage.'

She bites her lip, and I can see her weighing it up in her mind.

'If that's okay with you, I think I might,' she replies. 'Van said Willow had headed off to

71

the café to help out — Laura wasn't feeling too good, apparently — so that might not be a bad idea.'

She sees the concerned look sprout on my face — I can't help it — and quickly adds: 'They're fine, honest! Mum and Saul are knitting, and Van's watching football on the telly. Everything's good. But . . . if it's all right with you, I might head off, yeah. Need to walk off those cookies, apart from anything else!'

'Yep. Walk away from the whistle pops, and make a move. I'll see you later.'

She nods, and bustles about getting her white coat off and her leather jacket on, and eventually leaves — giving me a wink as she grabs one more whistle pop 'for the road'.

I sigh a little as she goes, unfairly looking forward to an hour or so on my own. Barring customers, of course.

I never get time on my own, and when I do, it's precious. Not that I don't love Saul, or enjoy the pleasant, predictable bustle of my life, but every now and then, being in a room alone, without anybody needing me to do anything for them, is balm for an aching soul. I spent a lot of time alone growing up, and sometimes I miss it.

I won't be lazy — I'll do some cleaning, or unpack a new delivery of supplies, or order some cold sore cream online — but I'll be alone while I do it. Blissful.

Unfortunately, the universe has other ideas, and literally two minutes after the bell dinged to mark Auburn's exit, it dings again. I look up

72

from my perch, and see Laura walk in. Her eyes have a slightly deranged look to them, and her pretty face is drawn and pale and . . . scared?

10

Laura glances around furtively, checking for interlopers, before heading in my direction. She's bundled up in a thick, hot pink puffa jacket, hands wrapped in black gloves that have skeleton bones painted on the fingers. I suspect she stole those from Lizzie, and I also suspect that they might glow in the dark. It's started raining outside, and her hair is bursting out from her hood in frizzy strands. She tugs the hood down, revealing a severe case of hat head.

'Hi!' she says, her voice shrill and way too perky. 'Is there anyone else here?'

'No,' I reply, coming out to her side of the counter. 'Auburn just left.'

'I know . . . I was hiding around the corner and saw her go.'

'Okay,' I say, calmly. Of course, I'm wondering why she was hiding, and why she sounds so weird, but I don't push. I've worked in healthcare the whole of my adult life, and sometimes people just need a little space. If they want to talk, they'll expand to fill the silence.

'Would you like a cup of tea?' I ask instead, in that ultra-British way that actually means 'I'm worried about you and don't know what else to do.'

She stares at me for a minute, slowly peeling off her skeleton gloves, and shakes her head.

'No, thank you. I'm just . . . well, I just thought

74

I'd pop in and see how things are going?'

She doesn't even sound convinced by this herself, and I see her automatically reach out and pick up a cookie from the plate. She takes a bite and pulls a face.

'Not as good as they could have been,' she says, frowning. 'I made these at home to take to the café, and Midgebo ran into the cottage being chased by a cat. Poor thing was terrified.'

'The cat?' I ask, not unreasonably, as Midgebo is a very large, very lively black Labrador.

'Oh no — Midgebo! The cat was a monster! Seriously, the biggest ginger tom I've ever seen. It chased him around the kitchen, trapped him in a corner, then as soon as his job was done, gave me a look, like 'yeah, puny human, your kingdom is mine' and strutted back out again. I've never seen him before, but I suppose people must have cats . . . I mean, a lot of us have dogs, don't we? And Becca has those goldfish. But perhaps other people have cats . . . '

She's wittering now, and doesn't seem able to stop. I recognise the wittering for what it is: self-distraction.

'Laura, are you all right? Auburn said you'd left the café because you didn't feel well. Is there anything I can do for you?'

I'm thinking it might be bowels. The great British public seems, as a race, constitutionally unable to say the word 'bowel' in public without at least attempting to whisper it.

She bites her lips viciously, and I'm horrified to see tears springing up in her eyes. Laura is one of the most cheerful people I know, and seeing her crying simply does not compute. I know she's had her share of hardships and tragedy, but since I've known her, she's been such a happy soul. Kind of like Mary Poppins in café cook form, always upbeat and positive, and carrying a big bag full of everything you could ever need in life.

'Yes. No. Maybe . . . is the chemist like a doctor? Or a priest? Or Vegas?' she asks, in a tumble of words, all falling over each other.

'You mean, are there rules about confidentiality?'

She nods, her curls bobbing up and down with the motion, and the tears finally spilling down her cheeks.

'Well, I have rules about confidentiality, and they're probably stricter than any laws, so don't worry. Now, come on, what's the matter? Don't be upset. It can't be that bad — and don't be embarrassed, whatever it is. I'm a medical professional, you know, even though I didn't look like one when I walked into the café this morning!'

I intend that last line as something of a joke, and she looks pathetically grateful for it, swiping her hands across her face to remove the tears as though she's angry with herself.

'Yes,' she says firmly. 'You are. And thank you. It's kind of related to what we were talking about then, anyway. I've been really tired recently, and was just putting it down to getting older and being busy and the fact that I eat way too much cake and not enough quinoa or whatever. But then me and you had that conversation, about how exhausting it is to have a baby around, but how quickly it goes, and how it completely and utterly changes your life, and how it's both the best and the worst time you ever have?'

We'd barely touched on any of that, but clearly, in her head, we had, so I just nod encouragingly.

'Well, after that, I was in the kitchen, making a toffee caramel sauce for the puddings, and I suddenly hated toffee caramel pudding. I mean, look at me, Katie — I'm not the sort of woman who hates toffee caramel pudding!'

The last few words come out in a kind of desperate wail, and I suddenly start to get an inkling of what might be bothering her.

'Ah . . . so you're wondering why you hate toffee caramel pudding? And why you're tired?'

'Yes, and . . . well, having looked at the calendar on my phone, I suppose I'm also wondering why I'm ten days late with my period as well . . . I mean, it probably means nothing. I'm probably going through early menopause. And I'm probably going to love the pudding again tomorrow. But . . . '

'You thought maybe you should check? Just to put your mind at rest?'

She nods, looking forlorn and deflated now she's finally admitted what's bothering her, and I walk over to our high shelf full of slightly adult items — by which I mean condoms and pregnancy tests and other things that would make a teenaged boy blush. I grab one of the packages, then turn the sign hanging on the door to 'closed'. I hope we don't get a sudden rush

— but even if we do, Auburn would understand.

'Come on,' I say, leading her through to the back rooms. 'Are you ready to go? Or do you need that tea?'

'No, I'm bursting,' she says, managing a smile. 'I drank a whole bottle of water on my way here, just in case. If you hadn't been in, or you'd been busy with a customer, I'd have probably just weed myself quietly in the corner and hoped nobody noticed.'

We approach the loo — a common or garden loo, with a small wooden sign showing a gnome urinating on the door — and I feel her slowing up. Like a dog who recognises the entrance to the vet's, and tries to drag its heels as you take him in.

'No point waiting,' I say, firmly but, I hope, kindly. 'If you're not pregnant, then you can start eating some quinoa and maybe take some vitamin D, which I can find for you here. If you are pregnant, then ignoring it won't make the problem go away. And it's not even necessarily a problem — just an adjustment.'

She snorts out a quick laugh, and finally takes off her puffa jacket.

'It would be less of an adjustment, and more of a 'holy fuck what am I going to do next?' kind of thing, really. I don't even know what I want it to be . . . negative would be easier, and, you know, I do like my life as it is. But positive would be . . . well, it would be a baby, wouldn't it? A new life. A bloody miracle . . . '

Laura rarely swears — at least out loud — and it's a sign of what a tizzy she's built herself up

78

into. She hands me her jacket, gives me a brave smile, and says: 'Right! I'm going in . . . if I'm not back in ten minutes, call the fire brigade!'

I nod, and tell her I'll be waiting back in the shop. I mean, nobody can pee properly while they know someone's outside listening, can they?

I feel jittery and nervous on her behalf, and calm myself down by checking up on our stocks of pre-natal vitamins and nappies. You know, just in case? By the time I've decided we're fine for both, and dusted the already dust-free shelves they're sitting on, Laura emerges from the back.

Her skin is still pale, and her lips are quivering, and she's crying again. I don't know whether it's from relief at not being pregnant, shock at being pregnant, or a combination of all of the above. I fight the urge to run across the room and shake her shoulders, screaming 'what was it???', and instead just smile. Whatever the news, she doesn't need some hysterical shop assistant getting in on the action.

'Well?' I ask, then hastily add: 'If you want to tell me, that is. It's completely fine if you don't, I respect your privacy.'

She holds out her hands, inviting me to take them.

'Don't worry, I did wash first . . . ' she says, grinning, as our fingers interlink. 'And it was positive, Katie. I might need to do another seven, just to be sure, but . . . well, I think I might be just a little bit pregnant!'

'And how do you feel about that?' I ask, keeping my tone even — she's smiling, but I still can't 100 per cent figure out what's going on in her head. Probably she can't either.

'Well, I feel terrified. And shocked. And worried. Concerned about how Matt will react, and how Lizzie and Nate will react, and how I'll manage at my age. How I'll fit in work, and how that might affect Cherie. And I'm cursing that night away we had for Matt's birthday, and all the cheap prosecco we drank that might have made us a bit careless, and that Princess Leia outfit Becca bought me for a laugh that made us definitely a bit careless . . .

'And I'm even a little tiny bit sad about David, my husband who died? Which is extra stupid — but this seems such a big deal, and I really want to talk to him about it. And . . . well, there are a lot of problems. The house is too small. I have a job that involves toffee caramel puddings. I have teenagers. I have a crazy dog. I'm overweight and middle-aged and . . . oh lord, Katie, mainly, I'm just absolutely delighted! The minute that second line appeared on the pee stick, I was just filled with joy . . . I can't believe it, still, but I'm over the moon. Thank you! Thank you so much!'

She pulls me into her arms, and we do a crazy, unbalanced jig all over the room, bumping into shelves, knocking over cardboard display stands, and generally wobbling and whooping and waving our hands around. Anyone passing by outside who happens to glance in will wonder if we've been getting high on our own supply after breaking into the Party Cupboard.

Eventually, we come to a standstill, both wearing matching grins on our faces — her hysterical level of happiness is completely infectious.

'What will you do now?' I ask. 'Apart from seven more tests. And maybe you should make an appointment with the GP. And . . . well, I'd suggest having a drink to calm yourself down, but that's not really appropriate, is it?'

Her expression momentarily clouds over — understandable, as I've just pointed out she'll be teetotal for the next few months — but soon bounces back into happy mode. Then confused mode. Then frowning mode.

'I need to tell Matt, obviously. I think he'll be okay about it, but . . . gosh, this is a really big thing, isn't it? I think I might need an hour to myself.'

'Go to my place. There's a spare key in the soil of the hanging basket. Excuse the mess, but make yourself at home — have a cuppa. Have a think. Take your time. I'll be here for a bit, then I'm off to Willow's to collect Saul, so there's no rush.'

She bites her lip, looks through the window at the rain, and nods.

'Thank you. That's a good plan. Nobody will look for me there . . . I'll just sit for a minute, and try and get my head a tiny bit straighter before I go and see Matt. Oh my . . . how do you think he'll react?'

That's a tricky one. The truth is that even though I've technically known Matt for a long time, I don't actually *know* him. Matt is the local vet, and he definitely seems to communicate better with animals than people. Like myself,

81

he's a private kind of person. Always polite, always the type of guy you know you could count on in a crisis, but also always slightly guarded. Like he doesn't quite trust you if you only have two legs and no tail.

'I couldn't possibly say, Laura. You know him better than anyone. Trust your instincts. And try not to worry — I'm sure it'll all be fine.'

'Yes, you're right . . . I'm sure it'll all be . . . shit!'

'What?' I ask, as she tries to hide behind me — a foolish decision, as she's at least two inches taller, significantly more round, and has huge hair. 'You think it'll be shit?'

'No! I meant — oh, hi, Matt! How are you?'

He walks into the room, accompanied by the sound of the doorbell tinkling, having clearly decided to ignore the closed sign. It's starting to feel a tiny bit like a French farce in here now, with all the comings and goings.

Matt — tall, brawny, looks a bit like I imagine a blacksmith would look if I'd ever met one — nods politely at me. That takes approximately one nanosecond, before he turns all his attention to Laura. His face visibly softens as their eyes meet, and for a second I see a glimpse of what Laura's Matt is like. Not the public Matt — but hers.

They share a smile, one of those smiles that makes you feel like you might just be invisible, and he reaches out to touch her amusingly large hair.

'Cherie texted me,' he says, simply. 'Said you'd gone home sick? And that you felt repulsed at the idea of caramel toffee pudding?'

Laura laughs out loud, and replies: 'Yes, well. I'm amazed she didn't call 999 at that stage. I'm all right . . . I'm . . . erm . . . '

I feel so awkward, so much of a spare part, that I begin to edge backwards out of the room. This is private. It's personal. It's special. It's nothing at all to do with me. I try and think up a quick and believable excuse for leaving the two of them alone that doesn't involve a pterodactyl with the runs, but soon realise I don't need to.

I am still invisible, and they don't even see me as I skulk off to the back of the building, through the dispensary, and into the relative sanctuary of the stock room and the tiny kitchen.

I close the door behind me, leaving them alone, which technically I'm not supposed to do in case they raid our drug supply — but I'm convinced they have other things on their minds than selling asthma inhalers on the Budbury black market.

I stand still and listen — relieved when all I can hear is the low-key hum of their voices and not any actual words. I look around, and see that I am surrounded by unopened boxes, shelving stacked with trays of plastic bottles and random objects like a pricing gun and shampoo samples and an as-yet-unassembled Christmas tree, lurking in one corner like a festive ambush.

I lean back against the counter, absentmind-edly wiping up some spilled tea with the dishcloth, not even noticing for a few moments that I'm actually crying as I wipe.

It's not sad crying — nothing sad has

happened — it's just . . . girl crying. You know the kind — when you're just feeling overemotional and a bit off balance and you don't really understand why.

I let myself have a small weep — nobody can see, it'll be my little secret — and then swill my face with cold water so I don't look too blotchy.

I'm being daft, I know — I have nothing to cry about. Sometimes, though, you just don't need a reason, do you?

I distract myself for a few moments by washing and drying the mugs and spoons that are in the sink, and then tiptoe to the door to see how things are getting on. I can still hear voices, and some laughter, and then a silence. I'm kind of hoping they don't get into some huge debate, or a mammoth life-planning session, and forget I'm here.

Just as that thought crosses my mind, I hear Laura shouting: 'Katie! Katie, where have you gone?'

I emerge back onto the shop floor, and am immediately wrapped up in a big Laura hug. I glance from beneath her hair at Matt, who looks stunned, dazed, and utterly soppy.

'He was pleased, then?' I whisper.

'Ecstatic. Honestly, if I'd known he'd be that happy, maybe I'd have done it on purpose . . . '

She smiles as she walks back over to Matt, who places a protective arm across her shoulders, and nods at me. This time, it's a nod with a lot of warmth.

'Thank you,' he says simply. 'For looking after her.'

'Not a problem,' I reply. 'Any time at all. And obviously, I won't mention this to anyone, until . . . well, until you make it official.'

After a few more moments of faffing, and Laura insisting on paying me for the pregnancy test she used and the spare she takes home 'just in case', they finally leave.

I flip the shop sign back to 'open', and watch them amble down the main street together, laughing and giggling, wrapped in each other's arms. They're a funny sight — her in the hot pink puffa, Matt in his far more sensible navy blue Berghaus — and completely lost in each other and in their own secret world. They don't even seem to notice the rain, as neither of them has bothered pulling up their hoods.

I settle back behind the counter, looking on as they pass the pub and head for Matt's surgery. I'm smiling, but I still feel a bit unsettled. A bit melancholy. A bit . . . just not quite right.

I can't put my finger on what the exact emotion is, until I realise that I can no longer see Matt and Laura and their little bubble of intimacy and happiness. They've disappeared off from view, and now I'm just staring at my own reflection in one of the pharmacy's tiny window panes. Rain is streaking down the glass, creating a weird optical illusion where it looks like my face has been chopped in two.

I look away from the double me, and let out a breath I didn't know I'd been holding. I'm one woman. Alone, on a stool. Still breathing. Still holding on.

I'm so happy for them. And I'm so sad for me.

Because all of a sudden, it hits me like a cartoon anvil dropping from the sky — I'm very, very lonely.

11

Luckily, I don't have too much time to ponder that realisation and feel even more sorry for myself, as we have a veritable rush in the Budbury Chemist.

A small group of walkers comes in, one of them looking for blister plasters, one looking for Imodium, and one looking for sore eye drops. They seem remarkably cheerful considering their shopping list, and set off again in a flurry of chatter and clattering boots and those weird walking poles that are probably helpful on hills, but out of place on pavements.

After that, Scrumpy Joe Jones, who runs the local cider cave, arrives to pick up a prescription Auburn's made up for his wife Joanne, who has 'one of her headaches'. He rolls his eyes at me as he says this, as though I completely understand what hell that implies for him.

As Joe leaves, I get a visit from the Teenagers, who roam Budbury in a relatively benign pack — less likely to vandalise the bus-stop than to walk your dog for you.

There's Martha, Zoe's kind-of-daughter, who is seventeen, and Lizzie, Laura's daughter, who is in the year below at college.

The girls look very different — Lizzie blonde, Martha dyed black; one on the short side and one getting that tall, willowy look that young girls take for granted. They both, though, feature heavy black eyeliner use, Dr. Martens boots, and various shades of black, purple and green clothes. They look like they could form a band, and be the star attraction at Wednesday Addams' birthday party.

With them is Josh, Lizzie's boyfriend, and the son of the just-gone Scrumpy Joe. Like his dad, he's tall and skinny and dark, with big brown eyes and an ever-present beanie hat. Nate, Laura's son, is a couple of years younger than them but has learned to fight for his place in the pack.

Like my Saul, I suppose, he's been without a dad since David died — but the menfolk of Budbury stepped in and he now never goes short of a footballing friend or someone to act macho with.

Last week, Laura caught him having a wee in the grid outside their cottage, and his response to her outrage was to tell her that Cal 'says it's manly'. I think it's fair to say both Nate and Cal were feeling a bit less manly by the time Laura had finished with them, and there will be no repeat performances.

Tailing along is a new face — Ollie, Martha's relatively new boyfriend. He's eighteen, and looks an unlikely boyfriend candidate for a Goth princess, with his surfer-dude blond hair and the kind of clothes and build I associate with adverts for Abercrombie & Fitch. For some reason, even though he's called Ollie, he's always known as Bill. I daren't ask why, in case they tell me.

They all mooch around for a while, sniffing

the candles and briefly perusing the abandoned sex aids catalogue until I manage to wrestle it from Martha's amused grip. Eventually they all buy a whistle pop each and disappear off down the street, trying to perform the theme tune from *In The Night Garden* entirely with sugar whistles. I watch them go, a flurry of pushing and shoving and giggling, and think how weird it will be when Saul is that age. And how my life will look by the time he really starts his.

He's already at nursery, with his little friends and miniature social life that consists of parties at soft play centres, and he'll actually be starting in reception at primary school next September. It's so weird with babies and little kids — every day of amusing them seems to last forever, but in the blink of an eye a whole year has gone. It must still seem like yesterday to Laura that her two were tiny, and now they're part of the Budbury Massive.

At the moment I'm measuring Saul's progress in small things — like when he'll be able to reach the light switch, or write his own name with the 'S' facing the right way — but before long, it'll be much bigger things. Like his first day at little school, then big school, then maybe Uni or work. One day he's stretching on his tippy toes to try and put the lights on, next he's walking down the aisle and becoming a father.

As all parents probably know — and I've just this second realised — that way madness lies. It's not worth thinking about, apart from as a reminder to perhaps tend to my own life a tiny bit more.

Once you have kids you lean towards not noticing your own birthdays, or time passing — you're so focused on theirs. This is natural, and right, and good — but it doesn't mean I should forget about myself entirely.

All of these thoughts are hurting my brain a bit, and by the time I lock up the shop and finish for the day, I'm trying really hard to think less and do more. I've had a message from Auburn saying that Lynnie has gone for a nap, and Saul is helping her make jam tarts, and there's no rush to get back for him.

Usually, I'd still rush — reluctant to believe that everything was actually fine, that Saul was behaving, that I didn't need to go and relieve them as soon as humanly possible. That relying on people was a necessary evil to be reduced to the absolute minimum.

But I've been here for a while now. These people are my friends. I've just helped one of them find out that she's having a baby. I help Auburn and Willow with Lynnie when I can. I sometimes clean Edie's windows for her, after I saw her climbing on a stepladder as I went past one day, cloth in her 92-year-old hand. I helped Cherie talk sense into her hubby when Frank sprained his ankle and was insisting on carrying on working on the farm. I babysit for Little Edie so Sam and Becca can have the occasional night out.

I do things for them, because I want to — because I like them and because I enjoy helping. Being part of their world. But so far I've been so selective with how much a part of their

90

world I allow myself to be; always backing off when things have felt too intense.

Like Edie's ninety-second birthday party earlier in the year — it had a *Strictly Come Dancing* theme, as it's Edie's favourite show. Cherie organised ballroom lessons for us at the café, and I attended all of them. I love dancing. But when it came to the big night, and everyone else was dressing up and heading to the party, I cried off. Made an excuse and stayed at home. It felt too big, too overwhelming, too public.

I think I have to start making more of an effort to change that. To believe that I am welcome, that these people like me, and that every favour doesn't make me a burden or leave me with a debt they'll demand to be repaid.

So, instead of doing my normal mad dash over to the cottage to act apologetically about ever having gone to work at all, I head to the café. I check my phone as I go, and see a text from my mum: 'Sorry not answering, love. Bit busy. Don't worry about me. See you soon.'

I tap out a quick reply, asking her if she's sure she's all right, and try not to worry too much. I remind myself that my mother is not exactly averse to creating a little drama around herself, and that maybe it's just because I haven't paid her enough attention recently.

And I haven't, really, I know that — I've been busy and haven't spoken to her as much as I should. I haven't been back to visit in a couple of months either. I feel bad about that, now. I mean, she can be a bit of a nightmare, but can't we all, in our own way? She's still my mum, and

91

I still love her. I'm sure she's always done her best.

I try not to hold onto anger about the way I grew up, because it does me no good at all. Wishing it had been different won't make it different. Fantasising about a childhood where my family was happy doesn't create an alternative reality. It all happened, it all had an effect, and none of it can be changed — all I can change is the way I build my own life, not the way my parents built theirs.

I shake my head as I climb the path up the side of the hill that leads to the café, and put my phone away. Thoughts for another time. Or not. Mum says not to worry — so I need to try not to worry.

After I make my way under the wrought-iron archway and into the garden, I pause for a moment and look out at the bay. It's still drizzling, and the sky is fifty shades of grey, but the sun is trying desperately to break through the clouds. It's a strange and beautiful effect: dark clouds, dark sky, with one or two dazzling fingers of gold poking through to cast yellow streams down onto the waves, where they shimmer and shine as the water rolls inland.

There are dog walkers down there on the beach, and a couple of mums with toddlers wrapped up so well they look like fat eggs you could roll down a hill, and someone who appears to be fossil-hunting. Out of season, quiet, but still stunningly beautiful. In summer, it's completely different — the café is bustling, the beach is full, the sounds are a blend of squealing kids and the ice cream van's tune and the chatter and buzz of holiday fun.

I reluctantly turn away from the view and walk towards the café. It's after three now, and as I'd suspected, the only people left there are the regulars. I pause and look through the windows. The light outside is dim and grey, so the contrast is stark: the café is vivid and warm and bright, its fairy lights shining, the glass panes slightly steamed up.

I can see a few tables pulled together to form one big, haphazardly assembled mega-table, and the ladies arranged around it. Cherie has her head thrown back in laughter; Becca has Little Edie on her lap; Zoe has a paperback in her hands, and Willow is doing some kind of mime to entertain them.

They look perfectly relaxed. Perfectly comfortable. Perfectly terrifying.

I take a deep breath, and push open the door. They all turn and look at me, and I see Cherie's eyes widen in surprise. I get that feeling, the one I'm way too familiar with: the feeling that I've walked into a room where I'm not welcome. Where I'm interrupting something.

'Come on in then!' bellows Cherie, waving at me. 'And don't let the weather come with you!'

I nod and shut the door — I hadn't even noticed I'd been holding it open, as though clinging to the option of running away, back down the hill.

By the time I've crossed the room, Willow has pulled an extra chair over for me, and headed to the kitchen to get me a coffee from the ancient machine. I hear it hiss and spit as I sit down, smiling politely, wondering what on earth I'm going to talk about now I'm here.

'We were just discussing the relative feminist merits of Disney princesses,' says Zoe, her ginger curls pulled up into a cascade of fire on top of her head.

'Oh . . . well. Maybe Mulan?'

'She definitely kicks ass,' replies Becca, bouncing Edie up and down on one knee. The baby responds with a series of gurgles that implies it's the most fun she's had in her entire life. 'As does Pocahontas.'

'Yes, that's true,' says Zoe, 'but for me it's got to be Merida from *Brave*. Because she's a warrior, she doesn't want to be forced to be married and, most importantly of all, she's a ginger. And as we all know, gingers rock.'

Willow places the coffee — a lovely mocha — in front of me, and pushes a big slice of chocolate fudge cake in my direction.

'Eat that,' she says, firmly. 'And then agree with me that it's *Frozen*. The film, not the cake.'

Cherie starts to hum 'Do You Want to Build a Snowman?', and within seconds, everyone has joined in. The debate is paused for a few seconds, until we run out of lyrics — apart from Willow, that is, who knows all the words to pretty much every big Disney song ever.

'I think,' Becca says, once the discordant chanting has stopped, 'that I'd also cast a vote for Moana. I know it's recent, and some of you old fuddy-duddies won't have seen it yet, but it's very cool. No princes. No magical kisses. Just a feisty chick and her friend the demi-god, saving the world one song at a time. Plus, The Rock. You're welcome.'

She sings the last two words in the tune of the song from the movie, but only me and Willow get that part — Zoe and Cherie just look confused.

Becca takes in their lack of understanding, and shakes her head.

'Clearly, we need a movie night. Maybe we can do it here. Get rid of the blokes for the evening, and ideally the kids too, and have a Disney film marathon. Wouldn't want kids at that, would we? Or . . . maybe not here, just realised there's no telly. Duh.'

'We could do it upstairs, in the flat,' replies Cherie, pointing above her head. 'Bit of a squeeze, but that would add to the ambiance. You supply the movie, I'll supply the Baileys. We'll let Laura do the cake, as soon as she's feeling better.'

Everyone nods in agreement, even me. Laura, of course, may not be feeling 'better' for a while, but it's definitely not my place to point that one out.

I'm interested in seeing Cherie's flat. I've never been upstairs, to her near-legendary bolthole. She lived there for years, after the death of her first husband, until she finally moved in with Frank at his farmhouse.

Since then, it's been used as a kind of emergency pit-stop for the Budbury ladies' brigade. Becca lived in it until she and Sam properly got together, and Zoe used it as an escape hatch when she first moved here.

I've never been up there, but I've heard the stories — Cherie was a bit of a rock-chick in her day, hanging around with a hippy crowd and going to festivals before glamping was invented, and she's still partial to the occasional herbal cigarette and cranking up the volume on her record collection. The flat, I'm told, is a perfect reflection of all of that.

'So,' says Cherie, giving me a gentle kick beneath the table, 'what brings you to our door, lady? Not that we're anything but delighted to see you. We were beginning to think that you didn't like us.'

She's smiling, so I know she's not really serious.

'What makes you think I like you now?' I ask, licking oozing fudge off my spoon. 'I'm here for the cake.'

'Cheeky! You're very welcome, anyway, my love. Much as we adore our menfolk, we do need our little get-togethers. Stops us getting lonely.'

It's interesting that she uses that word. Lonely. I mean, I can't imagine any of these women feeling lonely — not now, anyway. But when I think about it, I can see that they all have been. That they all know how lonely feels.

Looking at them now, they all have solid, robust relationships, full lives, and this circle of friendship — but it wasn't always that way. They've all been through the grinder, and somehow all emerged whole. They've pulled each other out of holes, like a human chain of emotional support — and I'm starting to think that maybe I need a bit of a tug in the right direction myself.

'That's why I came,' I say quietly, as I glance at them all. 'I was feeling a bit lonely. Took me a while to notice, because I'm basically really happy with my life. Like our Disney heroines, it's not a needing-a-man thing . . . maybe it's a single mum thing. Or a still-feeling-new-in-town thing. Or just a me thing. I don't know — but I thought I'd come along and see what you all get up to when the café's closed.'

There is a slight pause after I speak; not long, but long enough to make me wonder if I've somehow misjudged this terribly. If I'm not eligible to join their club after all. If I should just crawl under the table and pretend I don't exist.

'Well, mainly we eat cake,' says Cherie, reaching out to squeeze my hand. 'And drink coffee. Occasionally, when we're feeling really wild, we crack open a bottle of Amaretto and have a little toot . . . '

'And sometimes we dance,' adds Willow, grinning at me. 'Or even sing. We do both of those things really badly, but we don't let that stop us.'

'Willow speaks only for herself,' chimes in Becca, lowering a now-sleeping baby into her pushchair, 'I have the voice of an angel and moves that would make Beyonce weep. When we're not dancing, singing, or eating cake, by the way, we're talking about Daniel Craig.'

Zoe pipes up: 'And sometimes, looking at pictures of Daniel Craig, on the iPad. But that's only if Big Edie's here — she's a total pervert. I mainly sit here half-listening, half-reading a book, until I spot a chance to say something snarky or sarcastic. If I'm not here, Auburn takes over on the sarcasm front; we're a bit like a tag-team. Laura's job is to ask us questions about our love lives, talk way too much about *Bake Off*, and supply the cake. It's like a badly oiled machine — we all have our roles to play.'

I look from one to the other as they take turns talking, wondering what I could possibly contribute. Whistle pops?

'Mainly, my love,' says Cherie, obviously realising I may be struggling here, 'we make sure that none of us get lonely. We've all been there, and know how it feels. It's hard, sometimes, to reach out to other people — especially when you're trying to be all Little Miss Independent. But reaching out for help isn't a bad thing — it's a good thing. Come here whenever you like, and listen to us witter on. You'll soon get the hang of it. It's a bit like a club . . . a cake club.'

'Are there any rules?' I ask, looking around at their intent faces. 'Will you abduct me at midnight and put a sack over my head and I'll wake up in Frank's turnip field?'

'Not unless you want us to,' she replies, shaking her head slowly. 'Although, now I seem to have named it Cake Club . . . we probably should have some rules. And the first rule of Cake Club is: you don't talk about Cake Club.'

'Unless you want to, obvs,' adds Willow, 'then it's totally fine.'

'Yeah. Then it's fine,' says Cherie, somehow keeping her face straight.

I nod, and feel stupidly grateful for their humour, and the way they've made me feel welcome without making too big a deal of it. The way I do feel, quite suddenly, a bit less alone in the world.

'Well,' I say, eventually, eating some more cake. 'I do like Daniel Craig.'

12

The next major development in my life comes two days later, and is covered in fur.

Matt knocks on my door in the morning, just after I've got back from taking Saul to nursery. He's shuffling, looking sheepish, and not quite making full eye contact, as is his tendency when dealing with humans.

'Hi,' I say, trying not to look annoyed. I think this is possibly the first time anybody has ever knocked on my front door, and it feels strangely intrusive. 'Is everything okay? Is Laura all right?'

I gesture for him to come into the hallway, as yet again it's pelting with rain. November is turning out to be nothing but rain.

His face creases into a huge smile as he steps inside, even the mention of Laura's name transforming him into something completely different.

'Yeah, she's great — sorry, didn't mean to worry you. I was . . . well, I was wondering if you could help me out with something. Laura was all for turning up with him in tow, but . . . I wanted to ask first. It's a big responsibility. And you might be allergic.'

I am completely befuddled by this whole exchange, and it obviously shows on my face. Matt shakes his head, and apologises again.

'Let me start over,' he says, grinning at his

own ineptitude. 'Did Laura mention the rogue cat at all — the one that's been hanging around the Rockery?'

The Rockery is the holiday cottage complex where both Laura and Matt live, in separate houses — although for how long, who knows? Zoe and Martha lived there for a while too, before they moved into the house next to the pharmacy with Cal. It's owned by Cherie, who seems to have a habit of turning her holiday lets into permanent homes for the Budbury strays — now including a cat, from the sounds of it.

'She did, briefly — she said he'd had a showdown with Midegbo and won. Sounds like quite a cat.'

'He is — pretty much the biggest I've ever seen. A ginger tom, probably about three or four, but looks like he's been in the wars. He was starting to make a bit of a nuisance of himself at the Rockery, finding his way into the cottages, chasing the dogs, probably worrying the sheep, planning world domination . . . usual cat stuff. The kids all tried to catch him, but he was too clever for them.'

'Cats usually are,' I reply, smiling at the image of the teenagers chasing a ginger phantom all over the gardens.

'Yes. They are. Anyway, I did manage to catch him . . . '

'Being a professional animal whisperer and all?'

'Being someone with a lot of experience of cornering unwilling felines. I brought him into the surgery, and gave him a good look over. He's

101

a bit of a softy once you get close up — loves a fuss and a treat.

'Anyhow — he's not microchipped. No collar or ID of any kind. From the state of him, he's not been living in a home for a while, and he's been out and about getting feisty with the locals. The tip of one ear is gone, and he has a line of fur missing where it's not grown back over some scar tissue on his face. I've called around all the local shelters and the police station and checked the pet registry, and nobody's reported him as lost. I think he's been stray for a while, and sadly nobody's looking for him. I'm keeping him in for a day or two, giving him a course of vaccinations, and . . . well, performing the necessary operation to prevent a ginger tom epidemic.'

'Ouch . . . that'll make you popular!'

'It's only a small op — I'll keep him with me for a few days, make sure he's not a stitch-remover. But as I'm sure you've guessed, I'm here about what happens to him next . . . I need to find him a good home, and Laura suggested you, because Saul loves animals.'

I pause, and ponder this idea. It's not terrible — but it's not brilliant either.

'Well, Saul also loves dinosaurs, but we're not adopting one of those,' I point out.

'They're extinct.'

'I realise that — but . . . well, what do you think? What's your professional opinion? I'm out a lot, and I'm busy. I'm sure Saul would love it — he loves Midgebo and Bella and Rick, and pretty much every other animal he comes across — but Saul is three. He's not in a position to make mature decisions.'

Matt nods and looks thoughtful. This is easily the longest conversation we've ever had, and I'm finding it easier than I thought to be blunt. Matt is a straightforward man, which makes life so much simpler.

'It's better to think it through,' he agrees. 'I see too many cases of people taking on pets they're not equipped to deal with, and it ending badly. But I would say this — cats are a lot less high-maintenance than dogs, on the whole. This one in particular seems pretty independent, very robust physically, and has a nice nature. Even when the kids were chasing him around, and Midgebo was barking at him, he never once scratched or lashed out, which is usually a sign of a good, stable personality. Maybe you could come and meet him, and bring Saul?'

'If I bring Saul, it's a done deal — I won't be able to resist the pleading! If it's okay with you, why don't I pop in now, while Saul's out? I must admit, I do kind of like cats . . . '

He gives me a small and understanding smile — like I've just made a life-changing admission — and waits while I grab a coat and an umbrella. I feel like I have the umbrella permanently glued to my side these days. It should be made part of my arm, like a cyborg limb. Robo-Brolly.

Together, in what I have to describe as a companionable silence, we make our way down the slight hill to his surgery, which is closed until the afternoon. Neither of us seems to feel the need to fill the time with small talk, which is refreshing — and leaves me free to save all my spare oxygen to use in the outrageous coo-ing sounds I make the minute I lay eyes on the cat.

He's in a big kennel in the back of the building, next to a sorry-looking Dalmatian who I'm told is recovering from knee surgery. Opposite, there's a far more feisty French bulldog, who is turning round and round in circles, so happy to see Matt he's almost climbing the walls. Matt makes a few comforting noises, lets the bulldog lick his finger through the cage door, and gives me a few minutes to make the acquaintance of the ginger tom.

He is ginger — but with gorgeous stripes of so many different shades that he almost looks multi-coloured. He's absolutely enormous — especially for a stray — but a lot of that looks to be made up of a very thick, very fluffy coat. His tail is fanned, a bit like a golden retriever's, and he has bright green eyes set in a very wide face. His feet are all white, like he's wearing little boots, and I can see the ear with the tip missing and the scar Matt mentioned.

He gazes at me that way that cats can — the way that says they can see into your soul, that they know all your secrets, and that they'd quite like a can of tuna now, please.

Matt has opened the cage door, and after a few moments of getting to know each other, he finally trots to the edge, and gracefully leaps to the floor. Once there, he winds in and out of my legs, purring and snuffling, rubbing his fur against my jeans and basically totally flirting with me. I lean down and stroke his head, and he leans into my hand, giving me a quick lick with a sandpaper tongue.

Matt's right. He is a big softy. Also, I suspect, a big softy who knows a thing or two about human manipulation, and is putting on a good show of adorableness.

'So,' says Matt, after a few minutes of this dance, 'what do you think? Take some time if you like. It's a big decision, I don't want to rush you . . . '

'I'll take him,' I say quickly, tearing myself away from my new friend and standing straight. Because suddenly, I can't imagine our little home without this cat in it. He is clearly some kind of cat Jedi, and has totally mind-controlled me.

Matt lets out a quiet laugh at my undoubtedly soppy expression, and leans down to scoop the cat into his arms. Said cat looks at me pleadingly as he is reinstalled in his prison, and lets out a few plaintive meows to let me know he expected better of me as I stand by and allow him to be jailed again.

'It's okay, sweetie, I'll be back . . . ' I murmur, poking my finger through the door to touch his fur. He gives me one sad look before curling up in a giant fluffy ball, as if to say 'yeah, right . . . I've heard that one before.' I suspect he's a cat who's had a lot of humans disappoint him in his time. Or — just possibly — I'm reading too much into it.

'Okay,' says Matt, walking me back into the reception area. 'Good decision. I think he'll settle just fine, and I'm always around if you need me. What are you going to call him? Not that it makes much difference with cats.'

'I don't know,' I say, putting my coat back on, and smiling. Smiling because I'm genuinely happy — almost excited in fact — at the prospect of getting a cat. I really should get out more.

'I'll leave that up to Saul,' I decide, looking around at the posters about worming tablets and neutering programmes and the importance of vaccinations.

I stay for a few more minutes, chatting to Matt about Laura and the impending life-changing arrival, and find out that she's started back at work, that she's feeling so excited it seems to be helping override the less pleasant physical symptoms, and that they have an ultrasound booked in a few weeks' time. After that, assuming all goes well, they'll start telling people their news. Until then, it's their little secret.

Or, I suppose, mine too. Mine and the cat's — because he undoubtedly read my mind and knows all about it by now.

13

I leave the surgery and stand beneath the porch roof for a few moments, sheltering from the rain while I decide what to do next.

I have another couple of hours before I have to go and get Saul, and am fighting the urge to rush out and buy luxury cat beds and a box full of toy mice. Cats, I know, rarely care for such things — they're far happier on the luxury bed that they find in your bedroom, and Budbury is definitely full of real mice that will be a lot more fun.

Instead, I decide to go to the café. Of course. It seems to exert some kind of magnetic force on everyone who lives in the village, and there's little point resisting. Besides, I'm already halfway there, and I can get warm and dry, and eat home-baked bread slathered in fresh dairy butter. What's not to like? Especially as the only bread left in my own house is half a packet of wholemeal pittas that are destined for the bin.

Anyway, I'm overdue a visit. I've not made it there for a few days, after my initiation into the Budbury Cake Club, and feel like I need to make the effort. Like if I leave it too long, it'll be harder to join in again — like when you don't use your earrings for ages and the holes are a bit healed over and you end up having to semi-pierce the skin. Or maybe that's just me. I could, of course, start my Christmas shopping instead, but I don't quite have the energy to tackle that one — plus I have to wait for payday at the end of the month. I already know what Saul wants — I trick him into writing a very early letter to Santa so I can be prepared — and none of it is going to be difficult to get. I've already half decided that I'll probably combine the shopping with a trip back to Bristol anyway, as I really do need to see my parents.

Dad has stayed radio silent for the last couple of days, but that's not actually unusual. He's not a fan of mobile phones, and thinks social media is the work of the devil. He may of course be right on that one.

Mum has sent a few more texts, which are a strange combination of attempts at reassurance blended with a subtle sense of mystery — like 'I'm fine, love, or at least I will be . . . '; or 'Don't worry about me — what doesn't kill you makes you stronger!' Like that.

She is a drama queen, and I tell myself not to overreact. I always reply, tell her to call when she can, and make the appropriate concerned noises. But after a few days of this kind of exchange, I'm starting to think there's nothing actually wrong at all. That she's just short of attention and needing a moment in the spotlight.

My nan always used to call her Judy Garland, because of her tendencies towards melodrama and tears. Looking back, her combative relation-ship with my dad was definitely not helped by this personality trait. Maybe the fact that he always engaged with the script was part of the attraction.

It also made it hard to distinguish between her real moods and needs and the ones that she was playing out like a B-list movie star, placing herself centre stage in a kitchen-sink drama.

She was, admittedly, in an awful situation — the constant fights, the physical tussles, the ongoing battle for supremacy with a man who was supposed to be her partner, but only was if you added the word 'sparring' in front.

With them, it was never as simple or horrendous as her being a victim. They drove each other on to increasingly nasty levels of conflict. So sometimes when she was sitting in a tearful heap at the kitchen table, looking around at the smashed plates and overturned chairs, it was genuine. She'd sob and weep and her shoulders would shake with the pain of it all; at the grief and disappointment over what her life had become.

But other times, there'd be a strange sense of glee in her upset. The teenaged me would pat her hand and try and console her, and she'd look up at me, and through the tears I'd see it — I'd see that she was feeling like she'd won. That she was triumphant. It was all very odd and confusing, and definitely taught me not to accept everything she says at face value.

As I trudge my way yet again up the hill to the café, I make a small plan in my mind. I will continue to exchange these texts with my mum; I will continue to try and contact my dad, and I will definitely make a weekend trip back to Bristol to combine seeing my parents and hitting the mega toy stores at the outlet village. Simples.

I don't pause and admire the view down to the bay this time — it's raining too much to see anything other than dirty grey clouds and dirty grey sea. I just plod my way across the garden, which is starting to resemble some kind of marshland nature reserve, and push open the doors to the café.

The warmth wraps around me like a blanket fresh from the radiator, and the aromas of cinnamon and ginger tell me Laura is not only back, she's already experimenting with her Christmas menu. This is a tradition of hers — and a very fine one. We all get to be guinea pigs in the great Christmas bake-off preparation, and I for one am a very willing participant.

Nose twitching, I glance around the room as I shake off my umbrella and stash it in the big holder Cherie has placed near the door. It's made of wrought iron and is in the form of a giant sunflower, which seems cheery even when it's full of soggy brollies.

I see Laura behind the counter, apron on and covered in floury fingerprints, putting together some bacon butties and garnishing an omelette. I see Cherie, standing next to her, waiting to take the orders out to customers. I see the customers — a table full of middle-aged women laughing so hard that I assume someone has just told the world's best joke. They're soaked to the skin, and have obviously been walking the coastal paths.

I see Zoe, leaving the counter holding a mug of coffee and a plate bearing some kind of muffin, heading in my direction as she exits with her takeaway.

'Christmas muffins,' she says, giving me a wink. 'In November! God, I love this place . . . '

I nod in agreement as she bustles past, doing a mad dash over to the bookshop. Her hair is still massive and frizzy from the mad dash over here, and I anticipate it being the size of a Renault Clio by the end of the day.

I see Edie, in her usual perch on a high stool next to the counter, probably playing online Boggle on her iPad. She has an astonishing knowledge of arcane and random words that make her cackle in delight every time she finds them, especially if they sound rude. I thought she might pass out from laughing when she once found 'fellatio' on the grid.

I see Cal, Zoe's boyfriend, watching her as she leaves. His blond hair is damp from the rain, and he's wearing an actual denim cowboy shirt that makes him look like he's about to engage in a spot of rodeo riding. He's sitting at a table for two, chatting to someone with her back to me.

I hang up my coat and make brief eye contact with Laura. She gives me a quick thumbs-up to show that all is well, and then pulls a weird face and nods over towards the tables. She looks a bit like she's swallowed a wasp, and I have no idea what she's trying to tell me. Cherie notices me from the other side of the room, where she's deposited the breakfast orders with the table full of amused ladies, and makes a similar gesture. Her eyes are wide, and she seems to be nodding in Cal's direction.

I nod and smile, and don't question their behaviour too much. I know I don't have Beauty

111

Parlour hair and make-up today, so I'm not too worried. Besides, sometimes the Budbury Cake Club ladies are just plain weird.

There are plenty of empty tables, and I'd usually choose one as far away from the rest of the crowd as usual — that's just been my vibe since I got here. But now, embracing my brave new world, I decide to aim higher, and head for the table next to Cal's. Apart from anything else, he looks like a cowboy — one of life's simpler pleasures.

I nod to him as I walk over, and his eyes crinkle up in amusement. I resist the urge to double-check my hair, but do glance briefly down at my shirt, in case I've missed a couple of buttons or something. Nope. All present and correct.

It's only when I go to pull a chair back at the table beside him that I realise what's going on. When I realise who he's chatting to.

'Better pull that chair over here, love,' he says in his Aussie drawl. 'I've got an old friend of yours here with me . . . '

I stare at him. I stare at her. And finally, I say: 'Mum! What are you doing here?'

14

'What, can't a mother decide to spontaneously visit her only daughter now and then?' she says, sounding half amused and half annoyed. I recognise the tone — it's her Disappointed Joan Collins voice.

She glances up at Cal, sees him watching our interaction, and lets out a ridiculous little laugh. It's the kind of ridiculous little laugh teenaged girls let out when they're busily flicking their hair at a boy they fancy. Mum has short hair, so she can't do that, praise the Lord.

The hair in question, I notice, has been recently touched up, taking her from almost-blonde to definitely blonde. She's wearing more make-up than usual as well, but it doesn't quite detract from the fact that her eyes look tired, and the lines around her mouth more pronounced. She's wearing her favourite jumper, the one with sequinned love hearts on it, which she always calls her 'cheer-me-up-top'.

There's a black coffee in front of her, along with an untouched Christmas muffin that is oozing some kind of spicy syrup filling. She's been 'watching her figure' for as long as I've been alive, my mum — although I have no idea why, as she's still got the build she had as a 20-year-old, and is, like myself, on the petite side. She even joined Slimming World once, where she made herself highly unpopular by claiming to be struggling with her weight in a room full of women who really were.

She's smiling at me, and at Cal, and anyone who didn't know her might think she was perfectly happy and perfectly relaxed. It's probably only me who spots the warning signs of tension: the strain in her face, the gentle tapping of her fingers on the table top, the slightly higher than normal pitch to her voice.

These are all signs I grew up learning to recognise, and signs that immediately put me into placatory mood in an attempt to offset any escalation.

'Of course you can!' I say, blinking my eyes rapidly to shake off my surprise and, if I'm entirely honest, any visible signs of the fact that I'm not 100 per cent thrilled to see her. I'm starting to think that I'm not a very nice person.

'It's lovely to see you,' I semi-lie, 'but why did you come here, and not to mine?'

'I did try yours first, but there was no answer. I thought perhaps you were still in bed so I didn't keep knocking.'

I try not to laugh at that one — as if I'd still be in bed, with Saul in the house! I also feel a bit like she's sneakily trying to make me sound lazy in front of Cal. She probably isn't, I'm just being paranoid. And defensive. And basically acting like a kid. Funny how you slip into your old roles around people you've known the whole of your life.

'Oh, well — no. You must have called while I was taking Saul to nursery. Probably just missed you. Anyway, I'm glad you're here.'

114

Cal looks from one of us to the other, his face set in a pleasant smile, his shirt sleeves rolled up around arms that are thick with muscle from a lifetime of manual labour. It would be easy to underestimate Cal, but he's a lot more perceptive than he looks. He's fitted into this world a lot more easily than I have, even though he grew up on the opposite side of it.

He stands up and stretches. There's a brief moment where I notice pretty much every woman in the room stop what they're doing and watch him, including the table full of middle-aged walkers, Laura from behind the counter, and even, dear God, my own mother.

'Ladies,' he says, placing his battered cowboy hat on his head and tipping it towards us, 'it's been a pleasure, but I have to get to work. Sandy, enjoy your stay, and I do hope we get to see more of you.'

She giggles in response — actually giggles — and reaches out to pat his hand.

'Oh, so do I, Cal, so do I,' she says, with a flutter of mascara-clad eyelashes, waving at him as he leaves.

'Mum,' I say, something of my horror creeping into my voice, 'why did he call you Sandy? And were you . . . flirting with him?'

She shoots me a sideways look and shrugs.

'Well, sweetie, of course I was flirting with him — have you got eyes? I'm fifty-three — not dead. He said he was going to shorten my name to Sandy, because Australians always shorten names, and because I reminded him of a young Olivia Newton-John when she was in

115

Grease . . . anyway, I'm sure he's used to being flirted with. No harm done.'

I nod, and have to concede that she has a point. He is used to it, and frankly seems to enjoy it. He's a man who likes women, and women always seem to know that.

'Fair enough. But if a man called Frank comes in — he's tall and dresses like a farmer, because he is one, and has silver hair — then don't flirt with him, okay?'

'Why not?'

'Because he's Cherie's husband, and she'll squash you like a bug.'

Mum lets out a confident snort, and replies: 'Hah! I'd like to see her try!'

I glance over at Cherie, who is back behind the counter with Laura, helping her get ready for lunch. She's tall, powerful, and a completely dominant presence, both physically and socially. I decide I'd quite like to see her try as well.

Mum and I sit in silence for a moment, looking at each other. As the silence stretches into something more awkward, I can see she's putting on a show here; that her bravado is definitely covering something up. Something she doesn't feel in control of.

She's had her nails done, and decorated with little love-heart gems, and she's wearing dangly earrings also in the shape of love hearts. Combined with the sequinned jumper, that's a whole lot of love hearts going on. She's put a lot of effort into her appearance, but despite it all, she still has the look of a woman brought low. Of someone fighting off the sadness inside.

116

'You'd better eat that muffin,' I say, pushing the plate towards her. Now that I notice it, it looks as though she's lost a bit of weight as well, which she can't really afford to lose. 'They shoot people in here for not eating muffins, you know.'

She uses her knife to slice it in half, giving one side to me. She plays with it a bit, crumbling it up into pieces and moving it around the plate in the syrup that's spilled out, but never actually eats any.

'Sorry, love,' she says, after a few seconds of muffin-bothering. 'I don't have much of an appetite. I stopped at the services on the M5 and had a big cooked breakfast. Wasn't sure if you'd have anything in.'

She's lying about that, and we both know it. She didn't eat breakfast. I'd be surprised if she's been eating much at all. The wave of sympathy I feel is slightly tempered by the fact that she added in that barb about my housekeeping skills, but the sympathy wins out.

'Mum, I'm glad you came. I really am,' I say, holding her hand just to stop her incessant tapping on the table. 'But why are you here? What's going on? The mystery phone calls, the texts, the fact that I've not been able to get hold of you for days? Is everything all right?'

'Well, nobody's died . . . ' she says quietly.

'So I believe. But clearly something else is wrong. You've come all the way here, so you might as well talk to me. I can't help if I don't know what's wrong, can I?'

She bites her lip and stares off in the opposite direction. I see her clock Frank as he walks through the door, and that at least makes her smile.

'That's him, is it? Cherie's hubby? Quite the gent, isn't he? Like a sexy granddad . . . '

'Mum!' I say, slightly louder than I probably should have. I'm getting exasperated now. She's only been here for half an hour and my nerves are already fraying.

She pulls a face at me, and replies: 'All right, all right . . . don't get your knickers in a twist. It's your dad.'

'What about Dad? Is he all right? I thought you said nobody was dying?'

'He's not dying, Katie. He's . . . well, he's very much living. Living with Fiona Whittaker from the next street over, in fact.'

'Fiona Whittaker?' I say, incredulous. 'Fiona Whittaker, the woman who used to drive the ice cream van?'

'Yes, her. She still does drive the ice cream van.'

'Fiona Whittaker . . . the one who looked like she ate all the ice cream in her ice cream van?'

My mum simply nods, and starts opening sugar sachets for no good reason other than to give herself something to do with her hands.

'The very same Fiona Whittaker, yes.'

I am momentarily so stunned by this that I simply can't speak. There is so much wrong with what she's just told me that I can't quite take it in.

No disrespect to Fiona Whittaker, but she's not your stereotypical image of a femme fatale home wrecker. She must be a good twenty stone, and looks a little bit like Jeff Goldblum. I mean, that works for Jeff Goldblum, but it's not so good on a chick. She did, though, always have a jolly smile and an infectious laugh, and seemed to genuinely enjoy her job dispensing ice cream to the children on the estate.

Still, you couldn't get much further away from my mother's physical type than Fiona Whittaker if you actually sat down and designed one for effect. And I'd stood with my dad buying ice cream from her on probably hundreds of occasions, and never picked up on any simmering sexual tension. Then again, I probably wouldn't when I was six.

So him running away with Fiona Whittaker is, by itself, kind of weird. But weirder than who he's run away with is the fact that he's done it at all.

For all of their fighting and all of their mutual contempt, I'd always worked on the assumption that they'd be together forever, my mum and dad. Right up until the point where one of them gave the other a heart attack, or killed each other in a spatula duel gone bad.

I'd genuinely wanted them to split up when I was younger. I yearned for a scenario where I could visit them both in separate houses, and not be caught in the middle of it all; not be used as a pawn or an emotional human shield. Where we could do normal things together without the risk of someone getting shoved into a Christmas tree, or having a bowl of cereal emptied over their head at breakfast.

A world where I could come home from

119

school and not lurk in the garden first, checking that nobody had thrown the other one's clothes out of the window. I once found my dad's Y-fronts hanging off a potted conifer, and never quite recovered.

And yet, they never did split up. They stuck together through what felt like sheer bloody-mindedness, clinging to a marriage that was so long dead it was practically a zombie. They seemed to despise each other, but cling to their stand-off. Maybe, I'd always thought, deep down they love each other — they just do the world's best job of hiding it. And whenever I heard that phrase about there being a thin line between love and hate, I'd think of them — and how they lived their whole lives skipping over that particular line.

Once I'd left home in my teens, it was easier to deal with. Easier to accept them for what they were, and not to spend any more time wishing I could find out I was adopted and that my real parents were out there looking for me. And over time, I stopped being angry — I knew they loved me, and that they did their very best.

Trips home were still sometimes tense, although I'd laid down some pretty strict ground rules once Saul was on the scene. No fighting while he was there — ever. They mainly managed to stick to that, and limit themselves to barbed comments that he didn't understand. So the tension was all on my end, not his — he didn't have a clue; I on the other hand was constantly waiting for the ding-ding of the bell that signified the start of round

9007 in their battle royale.

But one thing I never expected was this. That one of them would finally call time on it all, and leave. That one of them would make a break for freedom and happiness, and presumably, in my dad's case, free 99s with strawberry sauce whenever he fancied.

'So,' my mum prompts, making me realise that I've been sitting in silence doing an impression of one of Becca's goldfish. 'Don't you have anything to say?'

'Um . . . gosh. I don't really know what to say, Mum. I'm completely shocked. What's the situation now, then? When did all of this happen?'

She starts chopping up the muffin with the knife, reducing it to a sugary rubble, scraping the blade on the china and generally looking a little tiny bit psychotic.

'I found out last week, but obviously it'd been going on a while. I knew there was something wrong — or I'd suspected anyway, for a few months. He was all . . . I don't know . . . quiet. *Content.* He started working later shifts, and then going to bed early, and not complaining about anything, and . . . well. He just wasn't himself.'

'You mean he stopped fighting with you?'

She nods sadly, and I see a faint gleam of tears in her eyes. I think, from her body language, that they're real. Only in her screwed-up world would a husband who seemed content, and stopped fighting, signify disaster. And yet it did — and I completely understand why. It must have totally confused her; she'd have felt like the rug of life had been tugged from beneath her feet.

'Have you spoken to him since you found out? Have you sat down and properly talked?'

'Well, he did come around on Monday night. To collect his things. I told him he'd find them in the garden, and that was that. He wasn't even bothered, Katie — just walked back outside and started picking everything up off the lawn!'

I grimace inside, but try to keep my face calm and non-judgemental. That was a typical Mum move — and one that would usually have incited my father into a fit of purple-faced anger. The fact that he didn't even rise to that kind of bait must have been terrible for her — all her expectations dashed. All of mine, too, to be honest.

If he'd stopped caring enough to fight with her, then he'd stopped caring. That would be the simple equation in her brain, and it was one I probably agreed with. I was sad for her, confused for me, and, I suspected, actually pretty impressed by my dad. If he'd done that when I was younger, it might have saved us all a lot of trouble.

'All right, Mum. I'm so sorry. But you're here now, and we can spend some time together, and it'll get better — it really will. I know it might not feel like it now, but it will. You'll stay for a bit, will you?'

'If that's okay, yes. I left my bags in the car. I just couldn't stand it at home any more . . . it was just so quiet all the time. And I kept finding things of his lying around the house, like his shaving stuff in the bathroom and his old copies of *Auto Trader* in the downstairs loo and those tins of Irish stew he likes in the kitchen cupboard . . . and . . . well. I had to get away for a bit, love. The only thing I was grateful for was the weather — so she wasn't driving around in the bloody ice cream van, looking all smug and loved up . . . '

I shudder slightly at the image of a female Jeff Goldblum getting loved up with my dad, and instead start calculating some logistics. Saul can sleep in with me for a few days, and Mum can have his room. She'll have to sleep in a small single bed decorated with *Paw Patrol* stickers, but them's the breaks.

'I get it, Mum. I do. And don't worry. The only way is up.'

'Like Yazz used to say.'

'Exactly. Now, come on — let me introduce you to a few people . . . and remember. No flirting with Frank.'

'I'll try,' she replies, managing a smile. 'But Sandy can't make any promises . . . '

15

After that, my life goes from busy but straightforward to something resembling a complicated American sitcom. Without evil twins or fake deaths — at least so far.

Mum takes root in Saul's room, which he finds hilarious. On the first night, he tucks her in, surrounded by approximately 7,000 cuddly toys, telling her all their names and back-stories in a solemn way that suggests he might test her on them in the morning.

She's tired, and clearly struggling with what has happened in her life, and being put to bed by a toddler beneath a *Paw Patrol* duvet cover must have only added to the sense of the surreal for her. It doesn't get much less surreal, but luckily I have a busy spell with work and college, and she seems happy enough keeping herself amused.

Then, two days after that, The Cat arrives in all his ginger glory. Matt brings him round, fully recovered from his 'small op', but I suspect still harbouring some resentment. He definitely gives Matt an untrusting glare that wasn't there before as he strolls out of the cat carrier, and inspects his new home like the Queen inspecting her guards on parade.

He prowls around the room a while, looking supremely confident and 99 per cent disdainful, while Saul sits on his hands almost bursting with excitement.

I've had some Big Talks with Saul about pet etiquette, and how to handle the cat, and how important it is to let him settle in and get used to things before we smother him with affection. Also, about how pulling tails and tweaking ears isn't a good thing under any circumstances. He's playing along so far, but is literally vibrating with anticipation as the cat carries out his initial patrol.

I half expect him to just take off upstairs, find somewhere quiet and ignore us — but he surprises me by padding over to Saul and curling up on his lap. The look on Saul's face is priceless, and actually makes me cry. There's just something so pure and joyous about seeing a young child react to the presence of a pet — the simplest and most honest of reactions.

Saul looks up at me, as if asking a question, and I nod and tell him it's probably okay to go ahead and touch now, as the cat seems to have made up his mind about us. Or Saul at least.

Tentatively at first, he runs his tiny hands along the cat's back, and when he hears a purr, plunges his fingers into his thick fur. Within minutes, they're best friends, and everyone in the room seems to sigh a communal breath of relief.

One hand on the cat's head, Saul looks up at us with what is officially the world's biggest grin, and announces: 'We're going to call her Tinkerbell!'

I look at Matt. Matt looks at me. We both shrug — what does it really matter? It's not like the cat will ever respond to its name, unless he thinks there's something in it for him. And if

125

Saul has, for some reason, decided the cat is female . . . well, that's not going to do any harm anyway.

The cat looks up at us, snuggled and comfy, and pauses in his leisurely paw-licking to give us a smug cat stare. He's borderline ugly, this fella, with his scar tissue and bald patches and missing ear tip and sheer brute size. If not ugly, then definitely not pretty.

'Tinkerbell,' I say, reaching out to stroke Saul's blond head. 'That's perfect, love.'

After this initial outburst of affection, Tinkerbell becomes slightly more reticent — finding hiding places all over the house, and making his base camp in the dirty washing basket. Saul just thinks it's a splendid game of hide and seek, and even counts to ten (give or take a six) to give the cat time to find a new spot, so that's not a problem.

My mum, after being open and honest that first night, also becomes a bit more reticent — although thankfully she doesn't start hiding in the dirty washing basket.

We have two evenings in, where I cook and she damns with faint praise, and we both shuffle around the small living room trying to be neutral. I'm struggling with her sudden arrival, if I'm honest — I've not spent this much time with an adult human being since I moved to Budbury, and I've definitely become set in my ways.

I'm also confused by what's happening with my parents — and the fact that I'm so bothered confuses me even more. I'm a grown-up. They had a terrible marriage. Why should I be

126

concerned at all that it appears to have come to an end?

I don't really have an answer for that, other than change is hard. Even when it's change that we know, deep down, is a good kind of change, a change that was necessary, it's a tricky fish to land.

So when she's being especially annoying — dusting the TV stand when I only did it the day before; insisting on watching *Gardeners' World* and making saucy comments about the size of Monty Don's pitchfork; rearranging my kitchen cupboards so they 'make a bit more sense' — I remind myself of that.

I remind myself that no matter how confusing this is for me, for her it's a million times worse. Yes, their relationship was beyond dysfunctional — but it was theirs. It was all she'd known for most of her adult life, and suddenly, it was gone. She'd been rejected for a woman she would most definitely not have seen as a love rival, which also had to sting.

She's still not eating much, and still wearing too much make-up, and seems to have developed a taste for skinny jeans — all, I suspect, in an attempt to somehow boost her self-confidence. She's still flirting with everyone from the postman to Scrumpy Joe, which is quite amusing to watch. Scrumpy Joe just looks confused by it, and asks if she likes cider.

Surfer Sam responds like Cal, with a generosity of spirit that brings a smile to her face. Matt simply stares over her shoulder, as though trying to figure out how to escape. Tom,

Willow's boyfriend, engages her in a conversation about Jean Grey from the *X-Men* comics, which is a joy to behold — that'll teach her to say he looks a bit like a much younger Hugh Jackman.

She does, however, leave Frank well alone — she might be in crisis, but she's clearly had the good sense to get the size of Cherie and decide to live another day. Not that Cherie would actually squash her like a bug — not physically. Truth be told, Farmer Frank enjoys a good flirt, and she never seems to mind, but my mum doesn't know that.

By the third night, we're both getting a bit stir-crazy. Tinkerbell is housebound for the first fortnight on the advice of Matt, so he gets used to the idea of this being his home before he's allowed out into the wilds, and he's not especially liking being cooped up with us. I think me and Mum feel exactly the same, as I come down from the stairs after putting Saul to bed.

'So,' she says, stretching out on the sofa that used to be my spot, 'I was thinking we might give Netflix a miss tonight. We've done *Jessica Jones* and watched the best bits of *Friends*, and I did enjoy that one about the president with Kiefer Sutherland in it. But I'm all tellied out, I think.'

I settle down into the armchair and nod in agreement. She's right — we have watched a lot of TV. She hasn't seemed open to much conversation about any issues more weighty than whether Ross and Rachel were really on a break when he slept with the girl from the copy shop, despite my attempts to gently prod her into it.

It's like she's built some kind of wall of unreality around it all, and that's probably easy to do here — where she's away from the house she shared with my dad, away from the risk of bumping into him in the street with Fiona Whittaker, away from the grim everyday-ness of her current circumstances.

I understand that, and in all honesty I've been happy enough to just binge-watch TV with her. We love each other but we've never been especially close, and this enforced proximity is obviously taking its toll on us both.

'Okay,' I say eventually, jolting slightly as Tinkerbell makes a sudden appearance, leaping up onto the back of the chair and splaying himself along it. I can feel his breath on the side of my face, and wonder briefly if he's planning to eat my eyeballs. 'So what do you want to do? Early night?'

I could probably go for an early night, I think. I mean, I usually can — because I will definitely be getting an early morning, and not much rest in between. I love the very bones of my little boy, but he is not an easy bed companion — he tends to sleep horizontally across the mattress, his legs splayed across my tummy, curled up in a comma shape so his face is always millimetres away from mine.

Sometimes it's cute, and I do tend to lie awake staring at his beautiful features, listening to his little sounds, simply adoring this wonderful creature. But other times . . . well, I'm pretty exhausted, let's leave it at that.

Mum looks at me and smirks. It's an annoying

smirk — one that says, 'My God, what kind of a woman are you?'

'Katie, it's just gone half seven. That's no kind of bedtime for a woman in her prime!'

'Right. Yes. You have a point. So . . . what, then?'

'Well, I was thinking I might go out,' she replies, stretching a bit like the cat. My first thought is: *brilliant — if she goes out, I can have the sofa. And the remote controls. And a whole bloody night on my own.*

My second thought is: *hang on a minute . . . aren't I a woman in my prime, like she says? And isn't she the grandma here? And shouldn't she maybe be babysitting so I can go out?*

As soon as I think it, I see that it's a silly thought. A ridiculous thought. I mean, where would I go? What would I do? The café is closed. My friends all have busy lives too. I've not had a night out without Saul since . . . well, ever, actually.

'Is that all right with you?' she asks, arching her eyebrows. 'It's not like you seem to have much of a social life, beyond your cake club and work. Seems a shame for us both to be stuck in. Anyway, you have Tinkerbell for company.'

The cat nuzzles the back of my neck on cue, and I realise that she's kind of right. I am a complete saddo, now I come to think of it. Not even thirty, and already one of those ladies who spends every night with a cat. If I'm lucky, by the time Saul's left home and I reach my own mother's age, I might have fifteen of them and wear a dressing gown twenty-four hours a day and never leave the house at all.

The weird thing is, if Mum wasn't here, I'd actually be quite happy with that prospect — a quiet night in with Tinkerbell, I mean, not my ultimate fate as a reclusive cat lady. But something about the way she says it, something about her expression (I think the best word for it might be 'pitying'), rattles me. Puts my back up. Sends me into a rare mood where I actually think, *no — that's not right.*

I'm used to taking the back seat, and I'm fine with that. I've never enjoyed the spotlight, never been at the heart of a dizzying social whirl. I'm usually happier alone than with other people. All of that is true, but it doesn't mean I want my own mother patronising me because of it.

'Actually, Mum,' I say, firmly, 'I wouldn't mind going out myself. I never get the chance to normally, because of Saul.'

'Oh!' she says, her eyes widening in surprise. 'Why's that? Can't you get babysitters in this part of the world? I'd have thought all your wonderful friends would have been pleased to help!'

There's a definite edge of cattiness to her voice as she says this — and it's a cattiness I've heard many times before. One designed to provoke and push and start a row. She wants me to leap in and defend my friends, and give her the chance to criticise them, and for all of this to end with a big argument where she can slam some doors and storm out.

It usually used to work with my dad — he was just as bad as her, and always up for having his

131

buttons pressed. But I'm not my dad and she's not my wife, and this is not her life. This is mine, and Saul's, and I'm not going down that road, ever.

So instead, I take a deep, calming breath, listen to the sound of Tinkerbell's purring for some extra zen, and reply: 'You're probably right, Mum. They would have, if I'd ever asked. I just haven't for some reason. That's my fault, not theirs. But it's different with you, isn't it? You're Saul's grandma and he loves you, and I'd feel comfortable leaving him with you. But maybe we can do that another time — maybe tonight, you can go out, and perhaps at the weekend I can take a turn. How does that sound?'

She bites her lip, leaving her teeth stained with bright pink lipstick — she wears lipstick all the time these days — and considers what I've just said. My tone seems to have taken the wind out of her sails, which is exactly what I'd hoped for.

'Well, when you put it like that, I see what you mean. It's not my fault you moved away, but I've not done much on the grandma duty front. I do love our little man, and I'd be happy to look after him for you. Anyway, I can go out any time. I was only planning to go to the pub over the road anyway, see if I could make some new friends ... I don't mind staying in if you have something you'd like to do, love.'

Suddenly, of course, I feel guilty. My poor mum, trying to rebuild her life and her self-confidence, was only wanting to make some new friends. And I chose that exact moment to start being selfish about it all. I'm on the verge of opening my mouth to apologise and insist that she goes out instead, when she starts speaking again.

'While you're out, I could give the bathroom a good deep clean. I swear I saw some mould growing around the shower curtain this morning . . .'

Let me make this clear: there is no mould growing around my shower curtain. There is no mould anywhere in my house. My house is very clean, even if it sometimes gets messed up by having a small child around. This is a mould-free zone, thank you very much.

I look across at her and see that she's staring around the living room — the very clean living room — with a critical eye. I follow her gaze and see that yes, there is a pile of toys left out in the corner. That Saul's little art table has a higgledy-piggledy heap of colouring books on top of it. That there may, in fact, be one brightly coloured sock poking out from beneath a sofa cushion. But no mould, anywhere, definitely. I keep a clean house.

I realise, as my nostrils flare in annoyance, that for the good of our relationship, it is suddenly very important that at least one of us gets out of the house tonight.

I stand up, dust myself down and make my mind up.

'Right. That's great then. I'll go out, and you can look for mould, and we'll both be fine.'

'Yes. It's a plan. But where will you go — you know, in case of emergencies? And who will you be with? Everyone here seems coupled up already.'

'Well, I'm not looking for a place on *Love Island*, Mum — just a quiet night out. I'm sure I can find someone to play with, don't you worry.'

Her eyebrows are raised again, and it's starting to really wind me up. I wonder if maybe I could sneak into her room late at night and shave them off without her waking up.

'Okay, sweetie, that's fine. Even if you just go out for a little walk on your own, maybe that'll help calm you down.'

As anyone who has ever had an argument knows, being told you need to 'calm down' is a sure-fire way to strip you of any calm you did, in fact, have left. Again, though, I don't rise to it. I smile sweetly and walk into the kitchen, where I spend a good five minutes crushing up recycling into small cardboard squishes. When you're a single parent, you soon find healthy ways to release your frustration.

After that, I'm left with a problem — I've now won a battle with my mother, and put myself in a situation where I have to actually go out. Minutes ago I was pondering an early night, and now I have to somehow dredge a social life up from absolutely nothing.

I grab my phone, and consider who I can call. Even if it's just to go around to theirs and sit with them for an hour. It's still lashing it down outside, so I can't even resort to plan B and go and hang out at the bus stop with a bottle of cider like a teenager.

I try Laura first — a quick text asking if she's

up for a visit. She replies with the not unsurprising news that she's already in bed, followed by a long line of smiley faces. Then I call Becca, but there's no answer. I'm on the verge of trying Zoe, but then I remember that her and Cal and Martha are away in Oxford for the night, visiting the college Martha's applied to.

Next up is Auburn, who answers on the first ring.

'Madam Zelda's House of Bondage — whom may I say is calling, and what is your safe word?' she says, before erupting into laughter.

'Erm . . . hi, Madam Zelda. It's Katie.'

'I know that. I can see it on my phone. I was just having a bit of fun. How's tricks?'

'Well, I seem to have got myself into a bit of a predicament, and need to find a buddy for the night. Do you fancy a pint?'

'Hmmm,' she says, dragging it out into a thousand syllables, 'ordinarily I'd love to, but I was just out in the garden having a fag, and this passing pterodactyl did an enormous shit in my hair . . . '

I snort out loud at that one, and she continues: 'Seriously, I did actually just wash my hair. Not because of a pterodactyl or anything, obvs. I was planning on having an early night in with Mum. But Van's around. He's doing nothing more interesting than waxing his balls and painting his toenails tonight . . . '

She says the last sentence with such obvious glee that I can tell he's within earshot. I'm tempted to hang up on her, admit defeat, and let

Mum go out while I carry on with a surreptitious mould-check in the bathroom.

I hear a scuffle at the end of the phone, and the sound of Auburn yelping and shouting something about someone being officially the world's biggest bastard. In a way that suggests she really, really means it.

Seconds later, Van comes on the line.

'Hi. Auburn's indisposed at the moment. She was wearing one of those towel turbans on her head, like all you ladies do and men are incapable of making, and someone accidentally set it on fire with a nice lavender-scented candle.'

I'm not sure if he's serious or not. I mean, it sounds like a crazy thing to do — but my only-child mindset understands that in theory, siblings actually do things like that just for fun. The sound of a running tap in the background suggests that possibly Auburn is now dunking her towel in the kitchen sink.

'So,' I say, feeling a little unsettled by it all. 'What colour are you painting your nails?'

Obviously, I avoid referring to his balls. It wouldn't be polite.

'I'm thinking a nice shade of coral . . . but I'll happily sacrifice my mani-pedi if you're finally at a loose end. Assuming I read Auburn's end of the conversation correctly. I'd ask her, but she's busy right now. You know. Putting out the fire and all.'

'Well, it's not that urgent. I was just . . . wondering what people were up to. You don't need to change your plans,' I reply noncommittally. I'm not sure I'm ready for a night out with

136

Van, now or ever. It all feels a bit too delicious. A bit too exciting. A bit too scary.

'In fact I think I might stay in after all,' I add, as much to myself as him.

'Oh. Right. Sorry, I must have got the wrong end of the stick,' he says, sounding disappointed. 'I'll pass you back to Auburn.'

At that moment, my mum bustles into the kitchen, with a whispered 'don't mind me!', and starts poking around in the cupboard under the sink, once she's figured out the child lock. She emerges with a bottle of spray-on Mr Muscle, a wire scrubber and several cloths, waving them in the air triumphantly as she leaves the room.

I watch her skinny-jeaned backside go. If I stay in, there might be blood. I should have told Van yes. I should have agreed to go out with him.

'He is such a wanker,' says Auburn, once she's back on the phone. 'I could have died. I'd have become a cautionary tale on the internet: this young woman died from drying her hair . . . anyway, you okay?'

'Yeah. I'm okay.'

'Really? You sound about as okay as Meghan Markle is ugly.'

'I'm sorry,' I reply, smiling at the way she pulls these crazy images from thin air. 'I'm out of practice at sounding enthusiastic. To be honest my mum's driving me nuts, and I told her I was going out and she agreed to babysit, and now . . .'

'Now you feel like a big fat loser with nobody to play with?'

'Exactly. Don't worry about it. I'll see you at work.'

'Oh no, missus,' she says firmly. 'You have opened the lid to Pandora's Box. Be at the pub in an hour, okay?'

I nod, realise she can't see me, and agree. It's done. I'm going out!

16

It actually feels weird, going out. On my own. At night. Luckily, I'm only actually on my own for about forty-five seconds, which is as long as it takes for me to cross the road from my house and reach the Horse and Rider on the opposite side. It's about three doors down from the Budbury Chemist, which is a slightly longer commute of about a whole minute.

Having set out my stall as a busy woman-about-village for my mother's benefit, I found myself having to go the whole hog. Clean jeans, a fresh top, a touch of grown-up make-up rather than Beauty Parlour style, and even an attempt at doing something with my hair. Admittedly not much — just a slightly off-centre French plait. I always find my arms aching way too much to do them well.

I give myself a spritz of perfume, and pull on my trainers. Okay, so it's not a hike and I could have gone for heels — but it's only my local pub. And it's only Auburn.

It's only Auburn, and it could have been Van, and a tiny part of me regrets my choice. Still, it was the right choice. The sensible choice.

I tell myself this repeatedly as I get ready, tiptoeing around upstairs so I don't wake up Saul. The cat follows me silently, looking at me with what I can only describe as scepticism.

'Don't look at me like that,' I whisper, as he

perches on the toilet seat and watches me put my slap on. 'I'm not ready for anything like that, okay?'

In response, he twists one leg up and elegantly licks his own bottom. Well, that told me.

Now, after bidding farewell to my mum and telling her where I'll be in case of emergencies, I'm out. Standing in the doorway of the pub, wondering if it's not too late to change my mind. The bus stop with a plastic bottle of cider is looking more attractive by the second.

I make my way inside, and am amazed at how different it is at night. I've brought Saul here in the day once or twice, just to fill in time. He likes it well enough, but there's only so long a little boy stays amused by a glass of orange juice and a bag of Quavers.

It tends to be quiet in the day, a few locals, a few walkers, the aroma of pub grub wafting around the place, the tinkling sound of the fruit machine. That sound always makes me smile, and remember holidays to Somerset as a kid, where my nan had pots full of coins to use in what she called the 'one-armed bandits'.

Tonight, though, it's bustling — a veritable cacophony of chatter and laughter and cheers from the corner, where some kind of highly competitive game of darts seems to be going on.

I glance around and nod to the few people I know, giving a wave to the landlord as I walk past the wooden-topped bar. It's a good, old-fashioned boozer, with two main rooms and various tucked-away alcoves and corners, and every chair and stool seems to be occupied.

I search the crowds, looking for Auburn's distinctive hair, and failing to find it. I mill around a bit, checking in the corners and cubbies, wondering if I'm early or if I've gone to the wrong pub. That, though, would be difficult, as there's only one in the village — the other one roughly classed as local is a drive away.

I'm on the verge of giving up and creeping back home in shame when I spot a familiar face over in the back room.

Familiar, but not what I expected. It's not Auburn, for sure. It's Van.

My heart does something skippy and thuddy that under normal circumstances would have me heading straight to A&E, and I stand still, staring at him. He hasn't seen me yet, so I could still make a run for it. I silently curse Auburn and chew my lip, and manage to be both excited and terrified at the same time.

It's Van — not Count Dracula. It's Van, who is my friend, and why can't we have a friendly night out as friends, discussing things that friends do?

Because I fancy the arse off him, that's why. And I think he feels the same about me. And there's alcohol in this pub. And . . . no, this is a terrible idea.

I'm on the verge of turning around and leaving when he spots me, and waves. He's grinning at me, and looks so happy that I can imagine him as a little boy. Damn. I can't just snub him like that. I have to stay, even if it's just for one Diet Coke.

It still takes me a moment to force myself forward, though, climbing over discarded bags and umbrellas and random legs until I reach him.

He's managed to hook a small table by the fireplace, which is one of those that begs to be described as roaring, logs blazing and crackling in a massive stone hearth so big you could roast a suckling pig in it. He already has a pint in front of him, which looks like a member of the real ale family, and probably has one of those borderline rude names like the Bishopric or Old Bessie's Buttock.

Unlike me, he hasn't been able to do much with his hair — it's cut so short — but he is wearing a navy blue T-shirt that stretches over his shoulders and brawny upper arms in such a snug way that I can almost imagine him without it.

This, obviously, is not the kind of thought I want to be having as I walk over to the table, especially as this is not a date. This is just two friends, out for a friendly chat about friend things. As friends. It's not my fault that one of us looks like he does. Probably not his either, but . . . well, he could've worn a baggier top.

I giggle to myself as I think this, as it is a ridiculous thought to have had. This confuses him as it coincides with me arriving at the table.

'What?' he asks, looking down at himself self-consciously. 'Did I accidentally wear my pyjamas or something?'

'No, no . . . just me. Being weird. No pyjamas involved. Do you wear pyjamas? You don't strike me as a pyjama kind of man.'

'You're right. I'm not. I'm usually a buck-naked kind of man. But I don't half feel the cold, living here, after years travelling around much warmer places. Winter in Budbury is not a prospect I'm relishing. Last night I used a sleeping bag and two duvets, and I was still a wuss about it. You look nice, by the way — I like that hair thing. Makes you look like a ballerina. What would you like to drink?'

This is a good question, especially right after his distracting buck-naked comment. It's also skipping right past the other, more glaring question that needs to be asked.

'What are you doing here, Van?' I ask, trying not to sound upset. That would be rude.

'I'm meeting you for a drink . . . ' He frowns, looking as confused as I feel, then continues: 'Didn't you know I was coming?'

'Umm . . . no. I'd arranged to meet Auburn.'

'She said she had a migraine, because I'd set her on fire. She said she couldn't come, but didn't want to let you down at the last minute, and she said she'd told you and it was fine.'

He takes in my bewildered expression, and the way I'm hovering by the chair but not actually sitting on it, and I see a moment of hurt flicker across his face before he wrestles it into something more neutral.

'I take it from your reaction that she didn't?' he says. I nod, and he smiles at me.

'Well, don't worry,' he adds, standing up. 'It's not a big deal. Either stay for a quick one, spend the night with me getting hilariously drunk, or we'll call it a night right now and go home. I

143

don't mind. It's your choice.'

Every single one of those options sounds both acceptable and wrong. There is no right thing to do — so I go for the middle ground.

'I'll stay for a quick one. Or maybe two. That'd be nice.'

'Are you sure?' he asks. 'Because the way you say 'nice' makes it sound a bit more like 'I'd rather be stung by a thousand angry bees.' '

'Sorry. I was just surprised to see you. I'm staying, honestly.'

'All righty then . . . well, as I'm up, what do you want to drink? Arsenic? Invisibility powder? Man repellent?'

'Hmmm . . . just a Bacardi and Coke please,' I reply, grinning. I used to drink that when I was much younger, and it seems as good a time as any to revive the tradition. He raises one eyebrow in what might be surprise, and goes off to fetch it. I quickly grab my phone out of my bag, and see a text has just landed from Auburn. Well, not so much a text as a screen full of devil emoticons and laughing faces. I tap out a reply that informs her in simple language that I am planning to kill her the next day.

'So,' says Van, when he returns with my glass — complete with little umbrella, very fancy — 'how are things going? With your mum? I'm guessing not brilliant if it's actually driven you out.'

'That's a harsh assessment,' I reply, taking my first sip and trying not to sigh out loud. 'But an accurate one.'

'I can imagine. I know how weird it is being

back with your family after years away, believe me.'

For him, of course, it must be even weirder — he's been abroad for so long, and now finds himself not only back in Dorset, but sharing a house with his sisters, and a mother with Alzheimer's. So, yeah, I believe him when he says he understands.

'Well,' I reply, staring into the fire, 'it's a work in progress, I suppose. I mean, it's not easy — she's not easy. But she needs to be here for a while, and that's okay. Half the time I want to hug her, and half the time I want to kill her. But that's kind of normal for families, isn't it?'

'I think so. It's easy to love your family — but not always easy to like them. Have you spoken to your dad yet? And how do you feel, about the whole them-splitting-up thing? Are you sad? I know you're not a kid or anything, but it's still got to hurt.'

I let out a laugh at that one. I can't help myself.

'No, it doesn't hurt. It's confusing, and strange, and part of me doesn't even believe it yet — mainly because I've not spoken to him beyond a couple of texts. He's not good at texting, or apparently using phones at all. Mainly, to be honest, I just wish they'd done it years ago.'

Van looks understandably flummoxed by this, so I explain: 'They've been making each other miserable as long as I've known them. Seriously, I grew up in a war zone, Van. They fought constantly. It was one long line of rows and screaming matches and actual physical fights.'

'What?' he says, looking distraught. 'He hit her?'

'Yes, but it wasn't that simple. She hit him too. She's small but scrappy, my mum. It wasn't one of those mean-dad scenarios — they were both mean. I've seen her literally hanging off his back trying to gouge his eyes during one of their spats. He was more of a shover and a grabber. Basically, neither of them ever came out of it unscathed.'

'And neither did you, from the sound of it. That must have been terrible. My childhood was hardly conventional — you know, born in a hippy commune, Dad died young, moved here and got raised by Lynnie during the Yoga and Incense years. But it was never, ever like that. Mum was all for peace and self-expression — she never even raised her voice. The only violence in our house was between us lot when she wasn't looking.'

'Still the same now, isn't it?' I reply, smiling. 'Did you really set Auburn's towel on fire?'

'Just a little tiny bit. It was all under control, honest. And you're avoiding the subject. Is that why you came here, to get away from them?'

I chew my lip for a moment, and then decide to break the habits of a lifetime and actually talk openly about all of this stuff. *Maybe, I think, it'll help. I've joined the Cake Club. I'm in the pub. Maybe things are changing, and I need to push them along a little instead of being a passive witness to my own life.*

I don't think I'd have had this conversation

with Auburn — we are both highly skilled at talking about nothing of consequence for hours on end — but with Van, it feels more natural. More organic. Maybe that's what scares me.

'Not just them,' I say. 'I needed to get away from Saul's dad as well . . . from everything, to be honest. Me and Jason — well, we were heading down the same path as my parents.'

I see him stiffen slightly as I say this, and his hand clenches into a fist on the table top.

'Don't get all macho on me,' I say, trying to keep my tone light. 'I never let it escalate. It was about me and what I needed as much as him — we were never going to work as a couple. But that's the past, and this isn't one of those situations where some big tough man can come to the rescue and sort my life out, okay? I sorted my own life out, and, I think he's sorted his out too. He lives in Scotland, with the woman who's now his wife, and that suits us all fine.'

'What about Saul? Doesn't he see him?'

'He did, a bit, when he still lived in Bristol. And he stays in touch, sends cards and presents, that kind of thing. He was talking about making a trip down to see him a while ago, but it hasn't materialised . . . I suppose I'm kind of hoping it won't, which is very selfish of me. He's still Saul's dad, at the end of the day, and sometimes I do worry about him growing up without one. I'm not very good at football, you know.'

Van gives me a little grin as he replies: 'I bet you are. And there's more to being a dad than playing football anyway. I grew up with Lynnie as the sole parent, and I turned out . . . well,

147

maybe I'm not the best example, I'm just a professional backpacker and basic New Age slacker. But I did learn how to play football, and Saul will too. He has all of us for that as well — it's not like you're on your own with him.'

He's just vocalised, in a nutshell, the very thing that I struggle with. All of these baby steps — going to the café more, my job, socialising — are taking me somewhere I have mixed feelings about going. Most of me wants to be more rooted, more involved, to give Saul the stability and sense of community that this place offers us both.

But part of me is still anxious and concerned — what if it all goes wrong? What if things break? What if I need to leave? What will that do to Saul, and to me? And more importantly, why am I such a nutter that I always assume the worst? I seem to live my life waiting for the other shoe to drop — in fact, waiting for an enormous great boot to not only drop, but land firmly on my head and squish me into the ground. It's about as much fun as it sounds.

I'm trying to override it, to be brave and sensible and optimistic, but unfortunately, I don't seem able to completely change my world view. It's my default setting. I don't suppose there's any point analysing it — I just have to try and manage it, and not let the fear of things going wrong get in the way of things going right.

Just now, for example, I am sitting in a pub, finishing off a delicious Bacardi and Coke, getting a supportive pep talk from a man who makes my girl-brain tingle. Why can't I simply relax and enjoy it? Maybe I just need to drink the rest of the bottle of Bacardi and go with the flow.

'You're freaking out inside, aren't you?' he asks, grinning. 'You're feeling overdosed with community spirit, and too involved, and wishing you could run away to your nan's house?'

'How do you know about my nan?' I ask, genuinely surprised.

'You told me about her. You told me you used to run away there when you were fed up at home — although you didn't explain why. You told me she was kind and sweet and fed you cake and custard and always smelled of Parma Violets. You tell me a lot of things without even noticing, Katie. I'm like your stealth confidante.'

All I can do to that is make a small hmmph sound, and decide that ever so possibly he's right. When I'm with Van, I do open up more than when I'm with other people — he just seems to have this easy knack of peeling back the layers of self-protection. It's probably why I've avoided being alone in a pub with him for so long.

'Do you want another?' says Van, pointing at my empty glass. I think he's picked up on the fact that this has all got a bit too serious for me, and is giving me time to process it all.

'It's my turn to go,' I reply, preparing to move.

'No. Let me. I have to get rid of my big tough man urges somehow, you know. At least allow me to be a caveman when it comes to your booze requirements.'

He doesn't give me much choice, as he's

already walking away, chatting to people from the village as he goes. I lean back, and feel the warmth of the fire on my face, and the warmth of the alcohol in my system, and I have to say — it does feel pretty good. Like I said, baby steps.

By the time he comes back, I've snapped myself out of whatever morose and overly analytical mood I was heading for, and restart the conversation on a different tack. One that isn't about me. I'm bored of me.

'So,' I say, nodding in thanks for both the drink and the bag of dry roasted peanuts he offers, 'tell me about travelling. Tell me about Tanzania.'

He immediately smiles, but also looks a little wistful. A little sad — like he's happy to be here, but he's also missing his old life.

'Well, that's a big topic. I left home when I was nineteen, and apart from a few visits back for birthdays and such, kept moving until this spring, when I came home again. I'm thirty-three now, so that's a lot of years spent with a backpack on my shoulders. Mainly, I spent my time getting dirty, getting drunk, getting high. They were the early years — when I was hanging around with posh kids called Tristram who were on their gap years. It was a lot of fun, but it does start to wear you down after a while — you start to yearn for more in life, like a clean toilet.

'So then I stayed in Tibet for a bit. That was . . . amazing. It taught me a lot, about myself and others and the whole big world. Made me realise I needed to find a different path, not to go all

Dalai Lama on you or anything. And that's when I started working for charities.'

'In Africa?' I ask, genuinely fascinated. The furthest I've ever travelled is for holidays in the Canary Islands, where you eat and drink yourself to death in an attempt to break even on your all-inclusive deal. And since Saul was born, I've never left the UK — or even the southern half of it. Very lame indeed.

'Thailand initially, then Tanzania. I've been there for the last few years, setting up a school. It's . . . well, it's a beautiful place. But complex, like most beautiful things.'

'Do you miss it?'

He blinks hard, like he's trying to clear his mind, and replies: 'Only every day. I think I left a part of myself there, to be honest. I miss the air, and the space, and the landscapes, and the people. Mainly the people. The kids. The kids were so great . . . it's hard to get used to things the way they are here, you know? Over there, even though life is harder in so many ways, they're also so much happier when things go right. They don't take anything for granted; there's a kind of joyfulness over small triumphs. But I'm okay here, honest. I love my family, even when I'm setting their towels on fire, and my mum . . . well, she needs us, doesn't she?'

'I think your sisters need you too. I can only imagine how hard it is to settle back down to normal life.'

'Ha!' he snorts, laughing. 'Normal is a relative term in our house, between the Alzheimer's and the dogs and the fact that we're all basically

151

crazy anyway . . . but it's all right. I'm enjoying lots of it. This, for instance. I'm enjoying this. It's nice to be out with someone I'm not related to and don't work for.'

I smile at him and nod. This Bacardi is possibly making me a bit more flirtatious than usual. Or maybe it's the dry roasted peanuts acting as a little-known aphrodisiac. Either way, I feel it — I feel the tug of attraction between us; that's always been there, ever since I first met him.

'I can imagine,' I say. 'In fact I think that's the only reason you've been asking me out. You're swimming in a very small dating pool.'

'Outrageous! You do know there are places outside Budbury within swimming distance, don't you? I could have a harem in Applechurch for all you know. Or a cougar in Dorchester. There's even ways to meet people on this wondrous new invention called the internet . . . '

'Have you ever tried that?' I ask. 'I've heard tell there's a whole world of singletons out there.'

'I did sign up to Tinder, yes. But I came off it again straight away when my first match was Auburn. I mean, I know we're in the countryside, but I draw the line at my sister . . . she's really not my type.'

'What is your type then? What was your last girlfriend like?'

'She was called Annika, and she was Swedish. She worked for the same charity as me, and had that whole blonde-one-from-Abba thing going on.'

'Ah. Did she take a chance on you?'

152

'She did,' he replies, grimacing slightly. 'And it's not one that paid off, because I upped sticks and moved back here, didn't I?'

'Oh — was she upset? Are you kind of still together?'

I know this thought shouldn't bother me — we're just two friends, out for a friendly chat about friend things, as friends — but I have to admit that it does anyway. Feelings don't always do what they're told, I've found over the years. I feel low-level anxiety thrum through me at the thought of Van being with someone else, even if she is on the other side of the world.

'No,' he says hastily, shaking his head. 'It's a transient world. People who work in it sometimes make long-lasting connections, but much of the time we're on the move. No, we're definitely not still together, in any sense. Don't worry.'

I'm about to launch into a response about how I'm not worried, I have no reason to be worried, and that I'm worried that he thinks I would be worried — but luckily we're saved all of that by the arrival of Willow and Tom. Who looks worried.

Willow is wearing her pink hair tied up into a scrappy ponytail, and a dress that seems to be made of Miss Haversham's wedding gown, coupled with her usual Dr. Marten boots — extra-long ones that almost come up to her knees. Willow is really, really tall, and really, really slim. Tom is even taller, and must have spent a lot of time since his move to Dorset ducking to avoid banging his head on all the random low-flying beams.

He's wearing a T-shirt that tells the world The Truth Is Out There, and seems stressed. A bit like Matt, Tom isn't one of life's chatters. He's geeky and warm and always a tiny bit awkward, and is currently clinging on to his phone for dear life.

'Mind if we join you?' asks Willow, as Tom troops off to the bar to get us all more booze. We scuttle around making room for their stools, and I end up squashed next to Van in a way that isn't entirely unpleasant.

'What's wrong with Science Boy?' Van asks, nodding off in Tom's direction. 'He looks like he's just found out the Force isn't real.'

'Hush your mouth, big brother,' she replies, reaching out to swat him across the head. 'Of course the Force is real. And he's . . . well, he needed a drink. Rough night at genius camp. He has a house full of mega-brainiac boffins at Briarwood, all trying to build time machines or next-generation handheld microwaves or what-ever — but one of them at least hasn't figured out how to use a toaster. Set one of the kitchens on fire.'

She takes in our shocked expressions, and adds: 'Only a bit. Nothing that couldn't be solved by me and a fire extinguisher. But I think he's worried about it all — some of them are young, some of them are borderline other-worldly, and some of them are partying a bit too hard. So he's playing house dad and not enjoying it.'

Briarwood is a big old Victorian mini-mansion

154

just outside the village, on top of a huge hill. It used to be a children's home — where Tom was raised after his parents died, and where Lynnie used to work, and where he and Willow first met when she was only eight. Tom seems to have made a bundle of cash from inventing some kind of doo-hickey nobody really understands, and bought the old house when it came on the market earlier this year.

He's turned it into a kind of hot-house for budding beautiful minds, people who had brilliant ideas but needed the time and space and investment to bring them to life.

They mainly keep to themselves, but every now and then you'll see a stray wandering around the village or coming into the café — always easy to spot by one or all of the following signs: trendy glasses, awful glasses, bowl-cut hair, long hair, sci-fi reference tops, flannel shirts, odd socks, pens behind their ears, ear buds in the shape of skulls, membership cards to the Stephen Hawking Fan Club, the ability to speak Elvish and/or any of the languages of Middle Earth.

Tom himself fits right in, apart from the fact that he's also very, very good-looking — if mainly unaware of it, or at the very least unconcerned with it. He's also back at the table with a tray of drinks, and yet more snacks.

He sits down, raises his glass in a 'cheers' that we all join in with, and gives us an uncharacteristically outgoing grin.

'I've solved the problem,' he announces happily.

'While you were at the bar?' asks Van.

'Of course while he was at the bar — my man is a born solver of problems!' says Willow, leaning in to give him a quick smacker on the lips. 'Go on then — hit us with it.'

'I'm going to employ someone,' he answers, gazing off at the fire, the cogs of his super-tuned brain almost visible as he fleshes out his plan. 'I'm going to create a new job — I don't have a title for it yet, but for the time being, I'll stick with Star-Lord. Because he or she will be the Guardian of the Briarwood Galaxy.'

Van frowns a little — I guess living in Tanzania has dulled his knowledge of pop culture references beyond Abba songs — but doesn't ask.

'And what will Star-Lord do?' Willow asks. 'Apart from some cool dancing.'

'Star-Lord will live at Briarwood, and basically be in charge of the geek squad. He'll bring order from chaos, and make sure they occasionally sleep, and check the oven isn't left on after late-night pizza, and be the keeper of the keys to the Red Bull cupboard. He'll be part-father, part-boss, part-benign-dictator. I don't suppose you'd be interested, Van?'

Van looks shocked by the very idea, and quickly replies: 'Me? God, no! Thanks for asking, but that would drive me nuts. Little kids I can handle — adult ones, not. I'm happy to carry on doing the maintenance and gardening for you, big man, but I'm not your Star-Lord.'

'Okay,' says Tom, looking temporarily disappointed. 'No worries. I'll find him, even if I have to scour the entire galaxy . . . '

'Or,' I suggest quietly, 'you could go to a recruitment agency?'

'Or that, yes,' Tom says, grinning. 'Anyway. How are you two?'

I finish up my latest Bacardi, and decide that that's enough. I'm starting to get tempted to rest my hand on Van's jean-clad thigh, and that wouldn't be a good idea. Who knows what kind of lovely trouble it could cause?

'I'm a bit drunk,' I reply, and stand up. 'So it's time for me to leave. Saul will be jumping on my head at six a.m., and it won't feel better with a hangover.'

I gather my belongings, and Van insists on walking me home — all the way across the street. We manage that without any incidents at all other than a close encounter with a crisp bag that flies at my head in the breeze, and end up standing awkwardly outside my house.

I feel a bit like a teenager who's been out with a boy for the first time, a feeling that isn't dissipated by the fact that not only is Tinkerbell lying in my windowsill, staring out at us with his all-seeing cat eyes, but noticing a twitch of the curtains as my mother takes a quick peek as well.

'So,' he says, grinning at me, blue eyes somehow managing to pick up on the moonlight and look ever-so-slightly wolfish, 'that was nice. We should do it again some time.'

'Yes,' I reply, fumbling for my keys in my handbag and trying not to gaze up at him in a way that might invite A Goodnight Kiss. He's moved in closer, and he looks so good, and smells even better, and it would be a matter of millimetres for my body to meet his. Holding my keys is the only thing stopping me from reaching out and resting my hand on his chest, just to see what it feels like.

'It was,' I say. 'And we should. And now I've got to go . . . '

I get the key into the door with shaking hands, and slam the door open so hard it bangs the back of the hallway wall.

I dash inside like a woman being pursued by a pack of hyenas, and bang the door shut again.

'You big chicken!' I hear him shout outside, before he starts laughing. I peer at him through the frosted glass at the top of the door, watching his hazy image walk back over the road to the pub.

I take a deep breath and try to calm myself down. I have nothing to be ashamed of — now I just need to convince Tinkerbell that's true.

I lean against the door and breathe hard, and try not to imagine what would happen if I opened the door again. Called him back. Took this to a level that wasn't just friends being friendly.

I'm too much of a big chicken, like he said. Too frightened. Or, being kinder to myself, just not ready. Kissing someone is just no good if you're not ready to lose control, to surrender yourself to it — and I know I'm not.

I stand and listen for a few seconds, making sure there's no noise from above, and tiptoe up the stairs. I go to the loo, and notice the flush on my cheeks that wasn't just caused by the cold, and close myself into my bedroom.

I slump down on the duvet, and wonder if he's back in the pub now. If he's thinking about me. If he even wanted to kiss me at all.

My phone beeps, and I lazily pull it out and look at the screen.

It's a photo, from Van. A picture of the Cowardly Lion from *The Wizard of Oz*.

I smile, and read the message: 'One day, Katie — one day xxx'

I close my eyes and kick off my trainers, and drift off into a sleep full of dreams that make me blush.

17

It's the first Saturday in December, and I am sitting in a Costa Coffee in Bristol, waiting for my dad. This used to be my favourite coffee place, with all the little pastries and biscuits and things, but I think I've been spoiled by the Comfort Food Café now. Or maybe I'm just a bit freaked out by being back here, and knowing I'm about to have an awkward conversation.

I'm stirring my mocha while I wait, feeling slightly nervous about seeing him. Mum has continued to take root at my house, and we have continued to try and find a balance that makes it manageable for both of us. I'm not sure if we're succeeding, but so far, there's been no need to involve the local constabulary or call an ambulance, which is possibly as good as we can expect.

She has, to be fair, started to make herself very useful — the fact that she has a car and a lot of spare time has definitely made my life simpler when it comes to logistics at least. Having someone to give me a lift to college, or drop Saul off at nursery, has been a rare luxury. It's only now I realise how insanely hectic our lives were — a carefully orchestrated performance pulling together times, places, and various bus time-tables.

If the last weeks of November were nothing but rain, then December is so far nothing but pain. The incessant lashing has stopped, but the temperatures are starting to plummet and the wind is wild and unforgiving. Back in Budbury, especially, you feel it whipping up from the bay, slapping your cheeks and making your eyes water as you walk down the street.

Van, who is still doing work for Frank at the farm and also gardening for Tom, is now bundled up in sweaters and shirts and body warmers and gloves, his tanned skin out of place in a small village in England, making him look like some kind of exotic refugee.

We've seen each other a few times, always in the company of others, always as friends — but every now and then I'll catch him looking at me, and he'll smile, and the corners of his blue eyes will crinkle up in amusement, and I'll have to fight off a swoon.

In other news, Tom has a shortlist of potential Star-Lords who he's planning to interview, and Auburn has asked if she can come along. Just for fun and to see if any of them look like Chris Pratt.

Tinkerbell is now allowed out, and has become one of those cats who owns multiple people — I'll be crossing the road from the chemist, and see him draped along Edie's window ledge, or sitting on Becca's doorstep. It seems to fulfil his need to roam, and he always comes home at night to see his best buddy Saul.

Martha has been to her interview at Oxford, and both Zoe and Cal are understandably pipping with pride — now they have to wait and see if she made it through the selection process.

Josh, Scrumpy Joe's son, is hopefully off to East Anglia to study chemistry, which will be quite a change for both him and for Lizzie.

Lizzie herself seems thrilled with two developments in her teenaged life. One is that she's started a 'small business' doing pet portraits. She's always taking snaps, Lizzie, and like most teens seems to feel like life hasn't been lived unless you've shared it on social media. But she does have more of an interest in photography than most, and got a new camera for her birthday. Midegbo, Bella Swan, Rick Grimes and Tinkerbell have all been her test portraits, and now she's promoting herself via Matt's veterinary surgery.

She's also delighted about Laura's news — which has now been made public. I think Cherie had already figured it out, because it takes quite a lot to get one over on Cherie, and she'd already told her sister Becca, but everyone else was shocked. Not, maybe, as shocked as Matt and Laura — when their ultrasound revealed that she's expecting twins.

Apparently this is more common in 'geriatric pregnancies'. She was about as thrilled as you'd imagine at the use of that particular term, and is currently walking around in a state of shock as she tries to get used to the idea of not only one baby, but two.

You'll see her in the café, staring into space as she beats a bowl of buttercream or blends up smoothies, and it's obvious her head is elsewhere. Cherie's made an executive decision that she shouldn't be allowed near knives or the chopping board any time soon, telling her she won't be able to change all those nappies if she lops her fingers off.

So, in the way of life in Budbury, not a lot has happened — but a lot has happened. It's the way things work there, marching to the beat of a gentler rhythm than the rest of the world.

Now I'm here, back in the big city, that feels especially noticeable. There are so many cars and vans and buses and bikes. So many people and voices, and so much noise. Everybody seems to be in a hurry all the time, and have that streetwise always-aware look on their faces as they dash from one crowded shop to another — like they're not being funny, but keeping a close hand on their bags.

I'm probably overthinking it. I usually do. But life in my small, sleepy corner of the world is a lot slower than it is here — and while it was exciting for the first hour of getting swept along by the tide of humanity, blissfully anonymous, I'm now feeling a bit worn down.

I have a heap of bags at my feet at my corner table, mainly for Saul's Christmas stash, and my hands have finally warmed up after being wrapped around my mug for a good five minutes. The place is packed with fellow survivors of the Great Christmas Shopping Disaster of 2018, all of us with the same weary look. Keeping a chair for my dad is getting harder by the minute, and I'm relieved when I finally see him poke his head around the door and scan the room for me.

He comes over when I wave to get his

attention, looking a little bit sheepish but none the worse for the emotional wear of what's happened.

He's only about five ten, my dad — but compared to me and my mum he always seems like a giant. He has dark hair that's thinning on top, and a moustache he's insisted on keeping since the Eighties, and has the tiniest touch of a beer belly. In short, he's a normal-looking middle-aged bloke, wearing a leather jacket that looks like he stole it from *The Sweeney*.

We share a hug when he makes his way through the crowds and randomly discarded shopping bags, and he gets us both another coffee before finally sitting down at the table. I'm guessing, from the look on his face, that he's been feeling a bit nervous as well.

'So,' he says, poking my bags with his toe, 'been shopping for the nipper, have you?'

'Yep. I'm all shopped out. It's like a war zone out there.'

'I know, love — season of goodwill hasn't quite kicked in yet. Still the season of sharp elbows and queue anger. How is he, Saul? And how are you? And how is . . . '

He trails off, staring into his coffee for answers.

'Mum?' I supply helpfully. He nods, and tries to smile.

'She's not so bad, Dad,' I reply. 'Seems to be quite enjoying herself in the village. No idea how long she's staying, but I'm assuming for a bit longer as she asked me to call in at the house and pick up some more stuff for her. I was hoping you could give me a lift there later?'

He nods, looking miserable at the prospect, and stays silent.

I give him a few moments, then have to prod: 'Well, go on then. Tell me your side of the story. Did you really run off with the woman from the ice cream van?'

He stalls for a while longer by helping a woman lift a pushchair over some abandoned coats, then finally sits back down, looks me in the eye, and says: 'Well, it's not quite that simple, Katie.'

'I'm sure it's not — but as I'm the one picking up the pieces with Mum, I think I at least deserve to know, don't you? And anyway — I've been worried about you as well.'

'No need to worry about me, and as for your mum . . . she'll be okay, once she gets her head around it all. And . . . well, no, I haven't run off with the ice cream woman, all right? I am staying at hers, but we're not a couple.'

'What do you mean, you're not a couple? Mum seems to think you're love's old dream . . .'

'Less of the old, cheeky. I told your mum I was moving in with Fiona, and she jumped to that conclusion.'

'Much as Mum's doing my head in a bit at the moment, I can't blame her for that — it seems like a logical conclusion when your husband leaves you to live with another woman!'

He nods, as though conceding that I might have won that point on a technicality.

'Yes, well. It was the wrong conclusion. Fiona — well, Fiona likes ladies, love, you see? And I'm not a lady, am I?'

A trick of unfortunate timing means that as he says this, I have just taken a mouthful of coffee. Coffee that is immediately spat out in one of those full-force snort-laugh-sprays that results in your whole face getting spritzed. After that, I choke for a second or two, while Dad passes me a napkin to dab my chin with.

'She likes ladies?' I repeat.

'Yes. Is that so shocking in this day and age? I thought you young people were all up with that LGBTTQQ stuff . . . '

'Hang on — what's the QQ bit?'

'Queer and questioning. There's also intersex, asexual, allies and pansexual, if you're interested . . . '

'Since when did you become an expert?'

'Since I became housemates with an L,' he replies smugly.

I screw the damp tissue up into a ball and throw it into the saucer.

'Anyway. That's by the by,' I say. 'And of course I'm not shocked that lesbians exist. But I am shocked that you're currently living with one, and maybe even more shocked by the fact that Mum thinks you're loved up with the lesbian in question — and you're letting her think that. Do you have any idea how much make-up she's wearing at the moment? Or how much she's flirting with any man she meets? How much weight she's lost? All to try and make herself feel better because she thinks you've rejected her for Fiona Whittaker!'

He's quiet again by the time I finish, all traces of smugness gone. He reaches out and pats my

166

hand in an attempt to comfort me. I'd been so busy being annoyed by my mum, I hadn't quite realised how worried about her I was.

'I'm sorry, love — no, I had no idea. Though I should have guessed; it's not like I don't know how much of a drama queen she is. I just . . . it seemed easier to let her think that. Fiona's not ashamed of herself for being what she is, and quite right too — but she also doesn't shout it from the rooftops. People can still be old-fashioned, can't they? She's kind of a public figure as well . . . but you're right. Maybe what I mean is it's just easier for me. The truth's a bit more complicated, I suppose.'

I gesture for him to go on, although part of me is convinced that he's about to tell me he's actually gay. That he's been living a lie for the whole of his life, and couldn't do it any longer. And, you know, that would be fine — eventually. Once I got used to it. I'm just hoping he's not one of the T's though — he'd make a terrible woman.

'Okay,' he says, looking at his coffee wistfully. 'Wish I had some brandy in this . . . anyway. I got to know Fiona better over the summer. I've always known her, like you, for the ice cream van. Then one day, when I was getting a Magnum, we started talking about Lee Child books. You know, because it's a gun? And then we talked a bit more, about other books — she's a big fan of James Patterson, like myself. And eventually, she asked me if I fancied joining her book club.'

This conversation is most definitely not going

the way I expected it to. I don't quite know if it's going worse, or going better, but it's definitely heading off in a surprising direction. I find myself thinking, oddly, that the image of my dad sitting in a room discussing Jane Austen is potentially weirder than everything else.

'Right,' I reply, nodding. 'You always did like James Patterson. So, you joined the book club . . . '

'I did. And met some really interesting people, as you can imagine. Broadened my horizons a bit. Then one thing led to another . . . the occasional night at the theatre. A comedy club. Meals out. Even the ballet. All very friendly but nothing more, love, honest. For all my flaws I've never been unfaithful to your mother . . . I think I've become a bit of an A, to be honest.'

There are all kinds of answers to that, but I bite my lip. Being flippant won't help anyone.

'That's why she thought you were having an affair — the nights out, time away from home? She actually said she knew there was something wrong because you stopped fighting with her.'

He looks so sad when I say this that I almost feel sorry for him.

'That's the problem, isn't it?' he says gently. 'For so many years, that's been all we've had. I've done things I'm ashamed of. I've let myself get sucked in, every single time. I don't know, love, I'm no expert on relationships — but I think to make a marriage work, you have to be the very best you can be. And all me and your mum ever did was turn each other into the worst possible versions of ourselves. Spending time away from it, with different people . . . well, it just opened my eyes a bit, I suppose.'

'I can understand that, Dad — I really can. But why now? And why didn't you at least try and talk to her about it?'

'Have you met your mother?' he jokes, absentmindedly ripping open sugar sachets. It reminds me of my mum, that first day in Budbury, trying to find something to do with her hands.

We're both silent for a while, and then he says: 'But you're right. I should have done. I got home from work one day, and we had a huge row. This won't come as any surprise to you, but it was a real humdinger — all over the fact that I said the potatoes were a bit salty. Serves me right, on the one hand — she'd cooked my tea, and I was sitting there moaning about it.

'But then the usual happened, and before I knew it, we're standing up screaming, and she threw the salt mill at my head, and I threw the pepper mill at hers, and . . . God, I was just so tired of it. We'd been there so many times. She'd carry on sniping, and eventually I'd snap and give her a shove, and she'd threaten me with the electric carving knife, and . . . I just couldn't face it any more. It all got worse after you left, Katie.'

I'd like to pretend I'm confused by this, but I know exactly what he means — I was their buffer zone. Without me or Saul around to at least temper them, it must have been a free-for-all.

'Without you there, we only had each other,' he continues. 'And it wasn't enough. So I walked out and went to Fiona's, and she offered me her spare room, and that was that. It's not been easy. Sometimes I miss your mum, love — we've been married a long time, and it wasn't all bad. But I knew that I couldn't go back, not the way things were. I'm sorry — sorry for being such a coward and landing you with her, and sorry for the fact that you must have felt horrible when you were a kid. Trapped in the middle of it all. And I'm glad you got away.'

'Got away from you?'

'Yes, I suppose — although I hope you won't always feel like that. I hope now things are different, eventually you won't feel like you need to escape from us.'

'I can hardly escape from Mum right now,' I reply, pointing my spoon at him accusingly. 'She's living in my house.'

'I know. But again, that won't be forever, will it? It'll get better. And I'm glad you got away from Jason as well. I didn't mind Jason, I really didn't — and you've never told us why you left him. I'm not soft, though, and I can imagine — I think you were following in our footsteps. When your mum said she wanted you to use what was left of the nest egg your nan had left, so you could make your move, I was pleased. I was proud of you for being so strong. I still am, Katie.'

I let out a big breath, and kind of slump back into my seat. I'm exhausted by all of this, I really am.

'Okay, Dad. This is all big stuff. I'm glad you're happier, I really am — but you've got to talk to her, all right? You can't just ignore it. You need to see her and sort things out, and act like a grown-up. Stop letting me deal with it all, because that's what's happening right now, isn't it?'

He nods, and finishes his coffee.

'All right, love. Again, you're right — and I will. Just give me a bit more time, will you? Don't tell her for the time being. Just let me sort my head out for a bit longer, and then I promise, I'll talk to her. Now, after all that . . . shall we nip to the pub for a quick one before I drive you round to the house? Don't know about you, but my nerves are shot.'

18

The next time I go to the café, a few days after seeing my dad, it's turned into a Christmas wonderland.

I'm not a stranger to the café at this time of year, so it's not a total surprise. It's slightly different each Christmas, though, with new decorations added, and old ones revived. The bookshelves are lined with neon green plastic holly wreaths bearing berries in a colour not found in nature; all of the dangling mobiles have been adorned with glittering lametta, and there's a whole display featuring a small electric train whirring through a snowy landscape like *The Polar Express*.

Outside in the garden a giant inflatable Father Christmas is wibbling and wobbling around, almost as tall as the building, tethered to the ground by ropes like a tent. I remember them having a snowman version in previous years, but Midgebo decided it was a chewy toy and managed to puncture claw- and teeth-shaped holes all over it.

It all reminds me that I need to get our house sorted — find a tree, unpack the decorations from the attic, maybe buy some of that fake snow you can spray on windows. Saul would love that. This year, though, we'll have to cat-proof it all.

Today is cold but bright, and I've called in to

fill in some time after pre-school. I've done a shift at the pharmacy, picked up Saul, and walked straight from the bus stop to the café. The alternative was going home, which wasn't that appealing as Mum is on one of her missions.

She's decided to change the curtains in every single room in the house, and I've left her to it. I don't really want my curtains changed, but I don't seem to have much choice. She's also taking the opportunity'to give all the windows 'a proper clean' — as opposed to the improper clean I must have been giving them.

She'd waved at us as we walked past, cheery as heck, still wearing her pink lipstick and a pair of dangly earrings that would look right at home on *RuPaul's Drag Race*. She's super-glammed up to change the curtains, presumably in case Fabio happens to wander down the street and she needs to look her best.

I'd waved back and walked by, noticing Tinkerbell in Edie's window on the way and making a mental note to pick up some soup for her from the café — she's been under the weather with a cold recently.

I've had some cinnamon-dusted coffee and a slice of Green Velvet cake — Laura has decided that it shouldn't be limited to Red alone and is making them in a variety of Christmassy colours. Now I'm sitting at a table, waiting for Cherie to finally say what's on her mind.

She's sitting opposite me, a slight frown on her face. Her hair is in a fat black-and-silver plait dangling over her shoulder, and she looks a bit tired. She's sent Laura home early, and the fact that Laura didn't object tells you how exhausted she must be feeling.

Willow is scurrying around doing some clearing up, assisted by Saul with his very own bin bag, and Frank is fixing the coffee machine, which is temperamental at best. The clanging and hissing provides a melodic backdrop to the conversation I feel is coming.

Cherie is uncharacteristically quiet, and seems to be turning something over in her brain before she speaks. She's looked thoughtful and pensive ever since we sat down together.

'I was thinking,' she says, between spoons of her Green Velvet Cake, 'about your mum. And you. And the twins.'

This is slightly out of left field, as we don't know any twins — so I am assuming she is referring to the as-yet-unborn ones currently exhausting our poor head chef and café manager.

'Okay,' I reply, closing my eyes as I eat my own cake — something about green cake just makes me feel weird, and I don't want my eyes to tell my taste buds not to enjoy it. 'What were you thinking?'

'You've not said much, Katie, as is your way,' she pauses for effect, as though giving me the chance to disagree. I remain true to type, and simply raise my eyebrows in acknowledgement.

'But I get the impression that it's a bit crowded in your house at the moment. Saul says you and him are having sleepovers every night, which I can't imagine is as much fun for you as it sounds for him.'

'You're right there,' I reply, rubbing my side. 'He boots me in the ribs constantly.'

'Ouch. Anyway . . . I also think I need to get a bit of help in here. Laura's doing her best, but she's wiped out — and it's not like it's going to get much easier. So I was thinking about asking your mum if she wanted to come and work with us for a bit. And as part of the deal, if she wanted to, she could also use my flat upstairs?'

I pause with the spoon halfway to my mouth, and hope the disloyal wave of euphoria I feel at that concept doesn't show on my face. She's my mum. I love her. But God, I would so love to get rid of her for a bit . . .

'What would you need her to do? She's okay at cooking, but she's no Laura.'

'Well, we still have Laura to be Laura — she just needs to be a bit less of a Laura. I was thinking she could still do the baking and the creating, but cut down on everything else. I can easily come in and do more, we have Willow, who's a bit more flexible these days, and your mum could give us a hand with the rest. So it'd be taking orders, serving, and preparing the easier stuff — the toasties and paninis and coffees. Plus cleaning up afterwards.'

'She does love cleaning . . . ' I reply, putting my spoon down and giving it some proper thought. To me, it sounds ideal — but my judgement may be clouded by the prospect of her moving out, if I'm brutally honest.

'I'm talking to you about it first because I wanted to check you were okay with the idea,' Cherie continues. 'I know you like to play your

175

cards close to your chest, but this isn't the time to suffer in silence; if you think it's a bad idea, or if you think I'm an interfering old busybody — which I am, by the way — or if you want her to stay with you and Saul, then just tell me. You don't get to be this old and this ugly without learning how to deal with being told no every now and then.'

This, I've learned, is fairly typical of the way Cherie operates. Yes, she is an old busybody. Yes, she does meddle. But she always meddles in a respectful way, if that makes sense.

'Personally I think it's a great idea, Cherie,' I reply after a few more moments of thought. 'It *is* crowded at ours, and it would be nice to get my bed back. But as well as that, I think it might be good for my mum. It might make her feel more involved. Give her a bit of purpose. Make her feel a bit more . . . needed?'

'Well, that's something we all like, isn't it? Whether we realise it or not. Feeling useless is an absolute curse in life. So, tell her to pop in, and I can talk to her about it. Unveil my latest masterplan . . . '

She lets out a fake evil-villainess laugh as she says this. Or at least I think it's fake — if she is an evil villainess, she seems to have very benign motives.

With the masterplan in place, I finish my cake, and ask Cherie if she can carton up some soup for Edie.

'How is she? I must call in and see her,' she says, as she ladles delicious-smelling pea and ham into two takeaway cups and prepares two slices of cake. One for her, one for her fiancé, of course.

'She was on a *Stranger Things* marathon when I saw her yesterday,' I reply, beckoning Saul over to begin the process of re-coating him. 'She was sniffly, chesty, and seemed a lot more tired than usual, but I'll keep an eye on her. Tinkerbell was keeping her company when I walked by this morning; she usually lets him back out about now so he can come home for his tea.'

'In that case, I'll pack him one of these leftover salmon fillets as well . . . ' says Cherie. The pets of Budbury are as pampered as the rest of us.

Once I've managed to get Saul's hands encased in the mittens he has threaded through his coat on a string, we walk back down the hill and into the village. It's still very, very cold, but the sun is shining and that makes it somehow feel better.

We entertain ourselves with one of our favourite games — making animal noises and guessing what they are — and by the time we reach Edie's, I'm letting Saul think he's completely bamboozled me with his silent mouth-gaping impression of a fish.

'Is it a parrot?' I ask, looking confused.

'No! Silly! Parrots go squawk, or say pretty boy! Try again . . . '

He continues his silent cheek-puffing, and I suggest: 'Is it a rhinoceros?'

'No again! Rhinocerosseses . . . rhinose-roos . . . '

'Shall we just say rhinos for short?'

'Rhinos go . . . oh, I don't know what noise

177

they make! But mine was one of Becca's goldfish. I win. Mummy, what noise *does* a rhino make?'

I've trapped myself with that one, because I frankly have no idea, not ever having been up close and personal with one.

'I'm not sure, sweetie. Maybe we'll ask Matt?'

Saul thinks about this, and decides it's a sensible course of action.

'Yes. Matt knows how to talk to all the animals. We'll ask him. Will Matt's new babies be people or puppies?'

'They'll be babies, sweetheart,' I reply, laughing at the look of disappointment on his little face. He continues his chatter as we approach Edie's house, and becomes excited when he spots Tinkerbell through the window.

I, on the other hand, become slightly concerned when I spot Tinkerbell through the window. We have a bit of a routine going, along this street. Tinkerbell eats his breakfast at ours, then we let him out for a wander, and he heads to Edie's or Becca's. They've agreed never to feed him, so he always comes home — and they always kick him out at about three.

It's past that now, and Tinkerbell is still there. He spots us, and is pacing back and forth on the window ledge, tail up, mouth moving in a way that tells me he's making a bit of noise.

'Wouldn't it be funny, Mummy,' says Saul, pressing his face up against the glass and creating a cloud of steam, 'if Tinkerbell could play that game? If she could pretend to be a sheep and baa, or a cow and moo?'

'It would, love, it would . . . maybe she'd know what noise a rhino makes as well . . . Saul, I'm going to drop you off with your nan for a bit, okay, while I give Edie her soup?'

He's perfectly happy with this, thankfully, and I bustle us both further up the road to our house. A house that now has purple and gold curtains in every single window. Yikes.

'What do you think?' Mum shouts, as she hears us come into the hallway. 'Gorgeous, aren't they? Best windows in the street! Move over Laurence Llewelyn-Bowen!'

She looks so proud of herself as she emerges from the living room that I have to agree, even if the new curtains make the house look a bit like the set of an especially gaudy pantomime. Princess Jasmine would love these.

'Beautiful, Mum — thanks so much, you've done a great job. Look, can you keep an eye on Saul for a minute? I just want to check on Edie.'

She can tell from the tone of my voice that I'm worried, so she just nods and hustles Saul away.

'Course I can. Off you go. Saul, do you want to make some cookies with me? I know your mum always buys them from the shop, but they taste so much nicer when you make your own . . . '

I roll my eyes at that one — she has this supreme talent for making digs without even knowing she's doing it — and concentrate on the task at hand.

First, I try the obvious, and call Edie — thanks to her army of nieces, nephews, and the great and great-great versions of both, she's never

179

short of new technology, and actually has a better phone than me. Sadly, there's no reply.

Then I nip out again and try Becca's — she's really close to Edie, and I suspect she has a spare key to the place. Unfortunately there's no answer to my knock on the door there either, so I make my way over to the pharmacy. Auburn's in there, perched on the stool behind the cash desk, looking at her phone and twiddling with her hair.

'Been busy?' I ask, smiling.

'Rushed off my feet. You okay? You look a bit hassled. Nice new curtains, by the way — did your mum buy them at a bankrupt brothel sale?'

'Ha ha, very funny. Look, I'm a bit worried about Edie. I can't see her, and she still has the cat, and she's not answering her phone, and she's not been well, and . . . '

'She's ninety-two?'

'Yes, that. I tried Becca's to get a key but she's not in. What do you think I should do?'

She jumps down from the stool, and replies as she hits buttons on her phone: 'She's probably fine. Knowing Edie, she's out running some committee about allotments or planning her Christmas social life or at one of her niece's houses . . . but I'll get Van over. He has a *very* impressive toolbox, you know.'

She raises her eyebrows at me as she speaks, somehow making a reference to a container for screwdrivers and nails sound filthy. It's a skill.

I listen to her end of the conversation, which is short, to the point, and serious enough to remind me that Auburn is, at the end of the day, a healthcare professional. It's easy to forget when she's puffing away on her ciggies, or making double entendres about me and her brother.

We sit and wait for about fifteen minutes, while Van explains what's going on to Frank and Cal and drives over from Frank's farm. Lynnie's at her day centre, giving the Longville siblings a day to themselves.

We try and make small talk until he gets there, but I'm feeling more nervous by the minute. I don't know why — I have no real evidence that anything is wrong — but for some reason my instincts are all telling me that something is.

'Right,' Van says, once he's parked his truck and jingle-jangled the bell on his way in. 'Let's do a bit of breaking and entering, shall we?'

Frank follows behind him, looking concerned — which is not a look I associate with Frank at all. He's only ten years younger than Edie himself, but apart from the usual aches and pains of getting older, seems stupidly fit. Must be his active lifestyle, although he swears it's down to a pact his mother made in a fairy dell on the night he was born.

Auburn closes up the pharmacy, and we make our way to Edie's in a small pack. We're going to look seriously stupid if she answers the door to us after all this.

We start with a knock, and Frank leans down to shout through the letterbox. Tinkerbell is the only one to respond, running to the hallway and meowing frantically at him through the gap. I call Edie again, just in case, and as we all strain our ears we just about make out the sound of her ring-tone — the *Strictly* theme tune. The phone

181

is in there — which means Edie might be as well.

'Nothing else for it,' says Frank, frowning. 'We need to get in there. She'll forgive us.'

Just to be sure, he shouts through the letterbox again: 'Edie! It's Frank! We're coming in, so make yourself decent!'

Van nudges his way to the front of the small crowd, and inspects the door.

'That's a solid lock on there. Might be easier to go around the back and break a window — and cheaper to fix afterwards.'

We all follow him down the narrow alleyway that intersects the houses after each small terraced block. Edie's is at the end, so he doesn't have to scale everyone else's back wall as well.

He nimbly climbs up onto the top of the wall, pulling himself up with no trouble, and perches on top.

'No point you all following me this way,' he says, eyes crinkled in amusement as we all gaze up at him. 'Much as I'm sure you've all got amazing parkour skills, be easier if you went back to the front door, and I'll come and let you in!'

It seems obvious now he's said it, and I'm glad I'm not the only one who dumbly followed. Frank, Auburn and myself make 'duh' noises and traipse back to the road, feeling a bit stupid. Within seconds we hear the sound of glass being smashed, and soon after Van comes and opens the front door.

Tinkerbell shoots out like a ginger bullet, pausing only to twine himself in and out of my legs for a bit before heading off home. I remember just at that moment that I left all the food from the café in the hallway, and suspect I'll get back to find that he's rooted through the lot of it tracking down the smell of salmon. Such is life.

Frank is first through the door, and I wait until Auburn's in there before I follow. Now we're doing this — going in to find out if she's okay — I'm gripped with fear and reluctance.

My mind's playing tricks on me, associating the sights and smells of Edie's neat little home with my nan's. The embroidered covers on the arms of the chairs; the porcelain figurines; the distinctive smell of mothballs and an old-fashioned perfume that I vaguely remember being called something equally old-fashioned like White Shoulders. It does look and feel familiar — apart from the life-sized cardboard cut-out of Anton du Beke in one corner and the giant flat-screen TV.

Anton and telly aside, it's the home of an old lady — and Edie really is very, very old.

We soon see that she's not in the living room, and Van, who broke a small window panel in the kitchen to let himself through that way, knows she's not in there, so we head upstairs. It's set out like my own house, two bedrooms and a small bathroom, and it's in one of the bedrooms that we find Edie.

She's tucked up in bed, a paperback copy of *The Handmaid's Tale* on the pillow next to her, a glass of water and her little wire-rimmed specs on the cabinet beside the bed. In the corner of the room I see a box full of old black-and-white photos and letters, which I know must be from Briarwood — Tom found them there, all relating to the building's past and its role during the war, and Edie, a former librarian, is archiving them for him.

Edie herself, though, doesn't look like she'll be archiving anything in her current state. She's still, and pale, and looks covered in sweat. Her breathing is coming in fast but laboured chugs, accompanied by a nasty-sounding wheeze.

'Edie!' Frank says, as he dashes over to her side. 'Edie, are you all right?'

I move over to him, kneeling at Edie's side, checking her pulse while he tries to rouse her. It's too fast, and I notice that her fingernails look a bit blue in the sunlight that's dappling through the window. I touch her forehead, and look up at Auburn, who's hovering a little in the doorway. I suppose nurses are more used to this kind of thing — her patients are usually at least capable of getting to a shop.

'She's got a fever. Pulse is up. Don't think she's getting enough oxygen,' I tell her.

'Pneumonia?' she suggests in response. I nod — that's exactly what I think it is. Pneumonia is a lot more common than people think, and isn't usually anything to worry about — but with a woman of Edie's age, no matter how sprightly she seems, there's a lot to worry about.

Auburn bites her lip, and immediately uses her phone to call an ambulance. She also uses all the right terminology to get them here as quickly as possible.

Edie is rambling slightly, her eyes half open,

184

talking but not making any sense. I make out the words 'my fiancé', and 'new dress', and 'legs like Betty Grable', none of which relate to her present circumstances in any way. Edie is lost in her illness, and my eyes sting with very unprofessional tears.

I feel Van's hand on my shoulder, and lean back against his legs for comfort.

'She's a tough one, Edie,' he says gently. 'Don't worry — she'll be okay.'

I nod, and screw my eyelids shut to get rid of the tears, and hope that he's right.

19

The scene in the waiting room at the hospital is, I know from experience, a doctor's worst nightmare. The place is packed with the distraught members of Edie's fan club — friends and relatives, all of them upset, all of them desperate to know how she is.

Her clan of nieces and nephews and their children and grandchildren range in age from teenagers through to her sister's daughter, who is in her seventies, and added into that is me, Van, Cherie, Tom, Frank and Becca, who came as soon as she heard. Becca's a tough cookie, but her eyes are sore and red from crying, and she looks like she wants to punch somebody.

Auburn's gone home to help Willow with Lynnie, who's come home from the day centre in a bit of a state, and that's added to the vaguely apocalyptic sense of doom.

As soon as I see the harassed-looking young doctor walk through into the crowds, I notice the fleeting look of horror that crosses her face at seeing us all in various stages of pacing and worrying and sipping scalding hot coffee from the vending machine.

She looks up, confused, trying to figure out who Edie's next of kin might be amid the mass of humanity. As it turns out, it's her niece, Mary, who strides forward accompanied by Cherie.

The rest of us assemble in a kind of loose circle around them.

'Miss May has been admitted to intensive care,' the doctor explains, doing a great job as she makes eye contact, uses her patient's name and never once needs to look at notes.

'She's currently on strong antibiotics and fluids. We're giving her extra oxygen, and at the moment, that's helping. We think she might have pleurisy as well, which isn't uncommon at her age, but so far she's still breathing on her own.'

This, I know, is very good news — I couldn't imagine Edie getting off a ventilator again if they put her on one. Cherie glances at me, and I realise I probably sighed out loud. She gestures me forward to stand next to her, probably thinking it won't do any harm to get a translator in.

'Will she be all right?' asks Mary, in the no-nonsense voice of a woman who has seen her share of hospitalisations.

The doctor tries to maintain a neutral face, but doesn't quite manage it. Her blonde ponytail is wilting, and a pen has leaked ink in the pocket of her white coat.

'Well, we can't really say at the moment. We're doing everything that we can to help her recover, and to keep her comfortable. But given her age . . . '

It's the second time she's mentioned Edie's age, which is completely understandable as she is in fact ancient. In hospital terms, that's a major factor — but in Budbury terms, it's a complete red herring.

I see Cherie stand up very straight, which must be unnerving for the doc — who maybe scrapes five foot in her flats. She looks fierce, and I suck in a breath — I really hope she's not about to kick off. The doctor is only doing her job, and speaking a truth that medically is extremely relevant. Everyone here might like to imagine that Edie is going to live forever, but science says otherwise.

Cherie squints slightly at the doctor's name tag, and then says: 'Doctor . . . Sullivan? We all know how old Edie is. And none of us are idiots, we know that's a factor. But I'd ask you to remember something, when you're treating her — her age doesn't matter to us. To us, she's just Edie, and we love her. She's treasured, she's precious, and our lives wouldn't be the same without her. We don't expect you to perform miracles, but please — don't write her off.

'That woman has lived through so much, for so long, I really wouldn't give in to the idea that because she's old she won't fight. She will. And I'd like you to help her — when you look at Edie, please don't just see a geriatric patient. See your own mother. See your own grandmother. See Mother Theresa if it helps — but please, see her as someone who deserves every possible chance at surviving. I know you can't promise us she'll make it — but can you at least promise us that?'

The doctor blinks rapidly a few times — she looks tired, as all hospital doctors seem to — and nods.

'Yes. I can. I can promise you that. Now, she's

not really conscious at the moment, and I'd suggest the best thing you can all do is go home, get some rest, and come back tomorrow. If anything changes, I'll make sure we let you know.'

'I'm staying,' pipes up Becca, making her way to the front. 'If that's all right with you, Mary? I'll stay.'

Mary smiles and nods, and pats Becca's hand.

Dr Sullivan looks like she thinks this is a bad idea, but wisely decides not to object.

Becca goes off to one side making phone calls, presumably to explain the situation to Sam and maybe Laura, and everyone else starts to make moving-away noises. It's a strange sight, like the air being sucked out of a room — Edie's family trooping off in twos and threes and fours, all promising to stay in touch and giving Becca smiles and hugs on the way out.

Cherie and Frank stay a few minutes longer before leaving in Cherie's car, and Tom follows not long after.

Eventually only Becca, Van and I are left, in a waiting room that now feels empty and hollow, even though there are still people in it. People dealing with their own dramas and traumas who are, entirely probably, relieved to see the back of the Edie May club.

I glance up at the clock on the wall, and am actually shocked to see that it's almost ten p.m. Everything takes so long in hospitals — or at least it feels like that when you're waiting. When you're on the sharp end, the hours fly by in a frenzy of activity. I definitely prefer the sharp end

— or at least the end that doesn't involve a person who you're very fond of lying in a bed fighting for her life.

Becca comes off the phone and joins us. She looks jittery, and I know she's had too much coffee. She shouldn't be here — but I think Dr Sullivan recognised a losing battle when she saw one.

'Everything okay?' I ask, reaching out to touch her shaking hand. 'Is there anything we can do for you?'

She shakes her head, and bites her lip hard enough to draw blood. I can practically hear the 'pull yourself together, woman' speech she's giving herself.

'No, it's fine. I've spoken to Sam. He'll be okay. Maybe tomorrow you could pop in and make sure he hasn't set the house on fire, or let Little Edie eat Pot Noodles?'

'Of course. And what about you — do you need anything? Clean clothes, a book, some food, anything at all?'

'Nah, I'm good. I don't mind being grubby. And Laura will undoubtedly send Matt over with enough cake to feed the whole hospital before long. You know how she gets.'

I do know. And she's probably right. Laura will have the oven on as we speak, to show her concern in the way that comes naturally to her.

'Was everything the doc said right, Katie? I mean, from a hospital perspective?'

She looks so desperate as she asks this, like she's hoping for me to promise her something I can't in all good faith promise. Like she wants the doctors to be wrong, and for Edie to be twenty-one, and for all to be well in the world.

'From what I heard, they're doing everything they should be doing, Becca. Following all the best protocols. And yes, Edie is old — but they don't know Edie like we know Edie. The odds might be against her, but you see small miracles every day in hospitals, and if anyone can come back from this, it's Edie.'

She nods, and gives me a very quick hug — she's not one of life's huggers; it's like Laura got all of the tactile genes between the two sisters — before backing off again.

'Okay. Well, I'll let you know if they tell me anything,' she says briskly. 'So you two bugger off, all right? I'm just going to grab another coffee . . . '

'Are you sure that's a good idea?' says Van, smiling gently. 'You look kind of wired already.'

Becca snorts out loud in response, and gives a quick laugh.

'Wired? This isn't wired. This isn't even slightly strung out. You know, before I moved here, I don't think I'd had a proper night's sleep for years . . . I was a complete insomniac, one of those people who lie awake looking at the time all night and then finally doze off an hour before dawn? It's Edie who changed that. In a lot of ways, it's Edie who changed everything. Without her, I probably wouldn't have had the guts to stay — and then I wouldn't have had Sam, and Little Edie, and everything . . . '

There's not a lot that we can say to this. She's clearly devastated at even the idea of losing her friend, and for her sake as much as Edie's, I hope those antibiotics are currently coursing through her and kicking some nasty bacterial ass.

'All right, Becca,' says Van quietly. 'We'll be off then — you know where we are if you need anything. And you stay there — I'll go and get you another coffee. Black, right?'

She nods gratefully, and I ask: 'Okay. Do you have baby wipes?'

Baby wipes, as most mums discover, are incredibly useful items.

'Duh!' she replies, grinning. 'Of course I have baby wipes! Plus a packet of organic rice cakes, and an almost-full pack of jumbo crayons in case I get bored . . . the full mama kit and caboodle!'

She taps the side of her bag as she says this, and it makes me laugh. You can probably tell the age of a family's child by the contents of the parent's bag. Mine, for example, does contain a small envelope of wipes, but also two Hot Wheels cars, one of those multi-coloured pencils that comes apart and stacks up again, and a pack containing a strawberry-flavoured Yoyo.

After Van returns with the coffee, we finally leave. It's dark outside, so cold our breath puffs out clouds of steam as we walk across the car park, our way zig-zagged by headlights of new arrivals and the flashing orange of ambulances. I feel a slight crunch beneath my feet, and suspect we're in for the season's first proper frost tonight.

'I got her decaf,' Van says, as he unlocks the truck and we get in.

'Probably a good idea . . . ' I reply, nestling back into the seat and rubbing my hands together as Van puts the hot-air blowers on full. He messes with the radio, and we end up with a show playing Motown classics. 'Tracks of My Tears' and 'Tears of a Clown' and a variety of broken hearts doing a variety of things to a toe-tapping beat.

We drive back to Budbury in relative silence, apart from the music, both processing the day's events. We're tired, and worried, and we both skipped dinner. I know Saul is okay with my mum, because I've spoken to her, but it still feels strange having been away from him for so long. Relinquishing control is a lot harder than I expected.

Van, I know, is also unsettled by the fact that Lynnie has been upset. She's asleep now, Willow's told him, but it had been a rough night. Life, just right now, feels like a lot to handle.

He makes his way through largely empty roads, skimming the coast before driving through the central street that ribbons through Budbury, pulling up in the parking spots on the opposite side to my house.

We both sit for a while, without speaking, waiting for Lionel Richie and Diana Ross to finish singing about their 'Endless Love'. The truck is cosy and warm, and the music is beautiful, and part of me wants to delay reality for a few moments longer. To stay in this cosy bubble for just a little while.

'Tough day,' says Van, once the song draws to a close. He turns the radio off, just in case another impossible-to-leave track starts playing. 'Will you be okay?'

I'm not used to people wondering if I'll be okay, and it takes a second to adjust.

'Yeah,' I reply quietly. 'I'll be okay. I was upset, though. It all reminded me of — '

'Your nan?' he supplies, smiling gently. I look at him in surprise, and reply: 'Yes — my nan. Why are you so clever?'

'I'm not clever,' he answers, reaching out to squeeze my hand comfortingly, 'about anything but you.'

I stare through the windscreen and say: 'You're the only person I told about my nan. And about Jason. And what it was really like growing up. I tell you things I don't tell anyone else. I don't know why that is.'

He twines his fingers into mine and replies: 'You'll figure it out one day, I'm sure. And it's the same for me. I never told anyone else how much I miss being in Tanzania, you know.'

'Oh. Right. What about the fact that you were in a relationship with the blonde one from Abba? Did you tell anyone that?'

'No. That's top secret. The paparazzi will be all over me if that one gets out . . . '

His grin lights up the car, and it's a bit of light relief we both need. A bit of light relief I'm not quite ready to say goodbye to.

'Do you want to come in for a coffee?' I ask, tentatively. 'Or a glass of milk. Or a bottle of whiskey. Might even have a chocolate Yazoo in the fridge if you're lucky. Saul and Mum have gone to bed.'

He stares ahead for a moment, gazing at the dark street and the starlit sky that leads down to the shoreline, then replies: 'Yeah. Thanks. That would be really nice — I'm feeling a bit wired myself, to be honest. If I went home now I'd probably have to sit out in the garden and do some deep breathing while contemplating the meaning of life.'

I have to smile at that — Van might look like a rough, tough kind of guy, but nobody could grow up in Lynnie's house without having mastered some advanced breathing techniques.

'That doesn't sound like fun,' I reply, as we climb out the truck, quietly close the doors — we'll wake up half of Budbury if we slam them — and tiptoe into my house.

Van's never actually been in here before, I realise, as I watch him take it all in. In fact, only Matt has been in here before and even then, he only made it as far as the hallway. I've been so protective of mine and Saul's territory, keeping it safe and cosy and just for us.

That seems to be unravelling these days, and I'm both exhilarated and terrified by it. I've always told myself that if things don't work out, we could just leave — pack our bags and move on. But now I'm not so sure that still applies. We'd be leaving behind an awful lot — friendships and support and free cake and the kind of community that most people dream of. Saul will be starting school in September, and that will be yet another nail in the coffin of my escape plan — perhaps it's time I start letting go of that, and come up with a staying-put plan.

'Nice curtains,' says Van, as we walk through to the living room.

'Auburn's already made the brothel joke,' I say quietly, gesturing for him to sit down on the big, squishy couch that dominates the room. The sofa was my one extravagance when I moved in here. I reckoned if I was going to be spending lots of nights in on my own, I should at least have a place to lounge around.

'I wasn't going to make a brothel joke,' he replies, looking scandalised. 'I was going to make a Sultan's harem joke. And apart from the curtains, your house is really lovely, Katie.'

I'm getting us both a glass of wine while he says this — wine has been appearing in the fridge a lot more often since my mother moved in — and hand it to him as I sit down on the armchair. Just the one — there wasn't enough room for more, and I never anticipated a time when I'd be hosting glamorous soirees.

'Thank you. Although it's just a normal house.'

'Yeah, that's what's nice about it,' he answers, looking around. 'Not an incense stick in sight! No, seriously, it just feels . . . cosy. You can tell a kid lives here, and if I was that kid, it's the kind of home I'd feel safe in. That's all I meant.'

'Thank you again. That's what I aim for. I can barely remember life before Saul came along . . . '

'I can imagine. I can't imagine you without him. Or Budbury without him — he's everyone's favourite little man, and a complete credit to you. You're a great mum.'

I feel my face break out into a smile — what

mother doesn't feel proud of comments like that? I spend way too much time worrying about doing things wrong; it's nice to bathe in a moment of reflected glory.

We're quiet for a few moments, sipping our wine, and I am quite surprised to realise that almost against my will I am relaxing. It feels natural, sitting here, chatting and not chatting, with Van. Just . . . being. I do a quick mental calculation to figure out when I last felt like that, and come to the conclusion that it was sometime round about never.

Me and Jason were never suited, and we plunged head-long into parenthood way too fast. I don't regret Saul for a moment — he was the most blessed of mistakes — but his dad and I shared little other than a sense that we should give it a try, and a tendency to get very drunk and have loud sex. Loud, but not that good, if I'm honest. Apart from Jason, and a few other failed experiments while I was at college, I've never actually slept with anyone who made me feel like we're all led to believe we should feel.

You know, when you grow up watching romantic movies and reading saucy books and thinking that the slightest touch of a man's lips will leave your knees trembling? Nobody really tells you about the reality — that your knees might be trembling, but it's usually because of an excess of WKD in the college bar. That sex can be awkward and embarrassing and many men wouldn't know a clitoris if it walked up and introduced itself.

I find myself shocked at even thinking the

197

word, never mind ever saying it, and cast a quick glance at Van, hoping he can't read my mind. He's sprawled on the sofa, stroking Tinkerbell, who has magically appeared on his lap. For a rough, tough street cat, Tinkerbell likes a bit of TLC.

I have the feeling it would be different with him. The sex thing, that is. I like to think it would, anyway. And as I plan to never actually do it, I am at least preserving the fantasy that this would finally be the man to rock my world in the bedroom.

'I know what you're thinking . . . ' he says, grinning. I blush immediately, and reply: 'I really don't think you do.'

'You're thinking how much nicer it would be if you came and sat next to me. How we both probably need a hug tonight. How we could even have a little snooze once we've finished this wine . . . '

I laugh out loud as he talks. He has his eyebrows raised in an outrageously suggestive way, telling me that he's joking. Probably.

'Right,' I say, putting my wine down and vowing not to drink another glass. 'That would work out well. We'd pass out, and my mum and Saul would find us collapsed in a heap of drool and cat fur in the morning. No, thank you. Drink up, Van — your own bed is calling.'

He grimaces, and I understand why. The cottage he shares with his family has three bedrooms. When he was a kid, he shared one with his brother Angel, and the others were taken by Lynnie and Auburn and Willow.

198

After the older siblings left, and Willow struggled to care for her mum alone, she understandably claimed a bedroom all to herself — and is, again understandably, staying put. Which leaves Van with the options of either sharing a room with Auburn, or sleeping on the couch. It's not ideal for a grown man — a man who is already missing the wide open spaces of the country he left to be here.

Van nods, and is stretching his arms up into the air as he prepares to leave. I can't help but notice his T-shirt untucking from his jeans, because I'm clearly the world's biggest lech.

He's about to stand up and make a move, which Tinkerbell senses. He leaps from Van's lap and disappears off onto the windowsill, where he'll lie above the heat of the radiator like a feline draught excluder.

Before Van gets a chance to stand upright, Saul barrels through the door, slamming it behind him dramatically. He's dressed in his stripy PJs that make him look like a junior pirate, and his blond hair is tufted all over his head. He's unbearably cute, standing in the doorway, rubbing his eyes with tiny little fists as he takes in the scene before him.

He spots Van, and his little face breaks out into an unquestioning smile as he runs straight to him. Van manages to catch him as he stumbles, scooping him up into his arms as though he weighs nothing, and nestles him into his lap. Saul snuggles in, his head on his chest, his small arms thrown around his neck.

'Van! Did you come and visit me?' he says,

199

sounding thrilled at the whole idea.

'Of course,' replies Van, smiling. 'What else would I be doing? I was a bit of a silly, though, and didn't realise how late it was, so I was having a chat to your mum instead.'

Saul nods, accepting this as completely obvious, and yawns.

'It's okay,' he murmurs. 'I'm wide awake now — do you want to play Twister?'

I have to laugh at that one. Saul is basically still half asleep, and Van is exhausted, but I can still imagine both of them at least giving it a try — moving their hands and feet very slowly to the coloured spots and trying not to fall over.

I'm about to pick Saul up and carry him back to bed when my mum follows him into the room. She also pauses in the doorway, and is wearing vivid purple pyjamas that match the curtains in a way that instantly makes me feel a bit nauseous.

Her short hair has been backcombed into a Frankenstein version of a beehive, and her face is covered in multi-coloured make-up. I mean, she usually wears plenty of slap these days, but this is next-level stuff — a kind of space alien Seventies disco look.

'Have you been playing Beauty Parlour with Saul, by any chance?' I ask, biting my lips so I don't start giggling.

She looks momentarily confused, then her hands fly to her face as she realises.

'Yes! Where does he get that stuff?'

'I have no idea . . . but it's taught me the importance of at least glancing in the mirror in the morning before I leave the house. Was everything all right?'

'Yes,' she says, her eyes glued to Van and Saul. They both seem to be snoring — probably getting some rest in before their game of Twister. I can almost see the cogs turning in her brain, and wonder how long it'll take before she has me married off to a man I barely know.

To my surprise, she stays quiet on that subject, and quietly asks: 'How's Edie?'

I check that Saul's not earwigging — he has an amazing ability to hear things he shouldn't — and reply equally quietly: 'She's in the best place. We'll just have to wait and see.'

She nods and yawns, and asks: 'Do you want me to take Saul back up? So you and Van can . . . carry on with whatever it was you were doing?'

I roll my eyes a bit — funny how we all turn back into teenagers again in the company of our mothers — and say: 'We were just having a chat, and he was about to head off home. You get yourself back to bed, I'll sort Saul out.'

She nods reluctantly, her gaze returning to the sleepy pair on the sofa, and replies: 'Okay, love. You can fill me in in the morning.'

I know she'll be reading more into this whole situation, but I'm going to have to disappoint her — because there really isn't anything to fill her in on. Maybe I'll make something up just to keep her happy while we eat our cornflakes tomorrow.

I hear her pad up the stairs, and stand looking at Van and Saul. As soon as I close the door behind my mum, Van opens one eye.

'Is it safe?' he asks, grinning at me over Saul's head.

'It is, you big faker — I can't believe you were pretending to be asleep! Are you scared of my mum?'

'Of course I'm scared of your mum,' he whispers. 'It's the lipstick.'

He gestures down at Saul, who is definitely not faking it, and adds: 'What shall we do with this little fella? Do you want me to carry him back up? To be honest, I'm really comfy — I could probably just pass out for real . . . '

I can hear the fatigue in his voice, and remind myself that he's probably been working since six this morning — farm work starts early. Then he helped us rescue Edie, dealt with the crisis at home on the phone, and was stuck with the rest of us at the hospital before going out of his way to drive me home.

'Stay there,' I say, disappearing off upstairs to the airing cupboard.

I tiptoe, so I don't disturb my mum, but might as well not have bothered. She was clearly waiting to pounce, and emerges from Saul's room with her inquisitive beehived head tilted to one side. I put my finger to my lips to tell her to be quiet, and she nods.

'Just thought you could do with a freshen up . . . ' she whispers, before padding out onto the landing and liberally spritzing me with some Calvin Klein Obsession — her signature perfume for as long as I can remember.

I cough and splutter as it hits my face, and fight very hard not to punch her in hers.

'For goodness' sake, Mum!' I say, trying hard to keep my voice quiet despite my annoyance. 'I'm not heading down there to seduce the man — I'm just getting a blanket! It's not been the sexiest of days, you know?'

She takes a step back, using her hands to waft the perfume around me.

'Well you never know,' she says, giving me a wink from mascara-encrusted eyelashes. 'Never hurts to be prepared . . . '

I ignore her, grab what I need, and walk back downstairs. Saul and Van are out for the count — although both their nostrils twitch in their sleep as I enter the room, bathed in a toxic cloud of Calvin's finest.

I lay a blanket over them both, tucking it in at the sides, pausing to look at them. Saul is completely encased in Van's arms, his tiny body curled into a contented comma, his fingers splayed on his chest. Van has one leg on the sofa, one leg off. I consider hoisting the second one up, but he looks perfectly comfortable. He's loosened the laces of his work boots, and I tug them off as gently as I can, grinning at the fact that he's wearing socks with Homer Simpson's face on them.

He sleeps through my assault on his feet, and I forgive him the fact that they're a bit on the ripe side considering the day he's had. I collapse down into the armchair, and tug a fleece over myself as well. Tinkerbell decides he wants in on the action, and curls into a fluffy ball by Van's feet.

Everyone is settled. Everyone is warm.

Everyone is happy, despite the horrors of the day.

I look at the snoozing threesome on the sofa, and can't quite figure out how I feel about it. I'm exhausted, and I've had a glass of wine, and my brain is a mish-mash of Edie and Saul and Van and my mother. There's a lot going on in there, and I don't have the emotional resources to pick my way through the tangled threads.

I've been worried about how close Saul is to Van. Frankly, I've been worried about how close I am to Van. But right now — here in my cosy home, surrounded by the people most important to me — I simply feel content.

And that, I think, is possibly the most worrying thing of all.

20

I'm woken up the next morning by Saul banging
saucepans at the side of my head. Any parent out
there will understand this: it's perfectly normal. I
startle into consciousness with a rush of
adrenaline, my body preparing me for battle or
buggering off.

Saul is still in his PJs, and is slamming a frying
pan against the milk pan, singing an extremely
annoying song he's learned at pre-school that
seems to be a constant repetition of words
involving 'wake up' and 'shake up'. Luckily this
morning, at least, it doesn't include make up.

'Get up, sleepy-head!' he shouts, clattering his
pans and jumping up and down on bare feet.
'Time for my breakfast!'

I practise opening my eyes one at a time,
eventually building up to the full set. I glance at
my watch and see that it's 630 a.m. Oh joy.

The sofa is empty, the blankets neatly folded
up and left in a squishy square on the corner.
Tinkerbell is mewing by my side, having clearly
been woken, and shaken, and now looking
forward to some food. I can hear footsteps
upstairs, and the sound of the toilet flushing.

I stand up, stretch myself out, and force myself
out of my stupor for long enough to give Saul a
morning cuddle.

'Where's Van?' I ask, yawning.

'He's gone up for a wee-wee,' says Saul,

putting his hand over his mouth and giggling. Bodily functions — is there anything more amusing to a 3-year-old boy?

'Okay. Right. Well, what do you want for breakfast?' I say, hoping he says cereal. I don't feel up to anything more complicated. Even that might be a challenge.

Saul ponders this important question, looking serious for a second, then bangs his pans together as though creating a drum roll.

'Pancakes!' he announces gleefully. 'With blueberries! And squirty cream! Just like Laura makes them!'

I frown at this. I'm not sure I have blueberries. Or eggs. In fact I think I only have the squirty cream.

'How about something even better than that . . . ?' I say, as I walk through into the kitchen. He looks as though he's going to argue, but his face lights up when I get the cream canister out of the fridge and wave it in his face. I squirt a cream beard on his chin, and he dissolves into a fit of laughter as he tries to manoeuvre his tongue low enough to lick it off.

Tinkerbell jumps up onto the table to try and help him, and I shoo him away. I know as soon as my back is turned Saul will let him, but it's my parental duty to at least try and stop the human-feline bacteria exchange.

I pop some bread into the toaster, and sip a glass of water, leaning back against the sink. I'm already thinking about Edie — if I'm honest, wondering if she's even made it through the night. It's by no means guaranteed that she has, and I can't imagine how Budbury will look without her. I feel tears sting the back of my eyes, and shake it off — no use worrying about that until I know for sure.

The toast pops up, slightly burned as usual, and I put it on one of Saul's dinosaur-patterned plastic plates. He watches closely, fascinated by what I'm planning, as I cut it into triangles. I then take the cream, and squirt it all over the slices, so thick it wobbles.

'Squirty cream on toast! Mummy! That's brilliant! I can't wait to tell Auntie Babs about this . . .'

I give him a mock curtsy, and hand him the plate. I smile, but inside I'm grimacing. Auntie Babs is one of the ladies who runs his pre-school, and she's a bit of a dragon. A retired head teacher who will probably report me to social services for serving my child such a nutritionally reprehensible breakfast.

I'm wondering how I can avoid seeing her for the next few days when Van walks into the room. He's clearly had a quick shower, and his closely cropped hair is still damp and shining. He's wearing yesterday's T-shirt, his plaid flannel jacket thrown over one shoulder. He looks like a lumberjack, and way too big for my small kitchen.

'Squirty cream on toast?' he says, peering at Saul's plate as he trundles off towards the sofa to watch TV.

'Yep. I thought it was about time I gave someone else a shot at winning the Mother of the Year Award.'

'Can I have some?' he asks, grinning at me and looking for all the world like an overgrown kid himself. 'Such delights were only dreamt of when I was growing up . . . Lynnie was way ahead of the curve on the whole holistic diet thing. It was a multi-grain and lentil kind of house.'

I nod, and do the honours on the next slice. He crunches into it, his face blissfully happy, a huge cream moustache left above his lips.

He suddenly leans in and kisses me on the cheek before I have time to dodge him, holding me by my shoulders so I can't escape.

'Right — I'll be off!' he says, darting out of the kitchen in case I retaliate. 'Just wanted to leave you with a little reminder of the first night we spent together . . . '

I hear him say goodbye to Saul, and the sound of the front door closing behind him, closely followed by the clunking of his truck doors and its engine revving up.

I'm still standing there, wiping squirty cream off my face, when my mother walks into the room. She has a full face on — a fresh one, not the one Saul did in his Beauty Parlour, which was possibly slightly less garish. She's still in her pyjamas, and the pink lipstick set against the purple fabric is not something easily beheld on an empty stomach. Or probably any stomach. I pop some more bread in the toaster for us both and hope I don't get a migraine.

She raises her perfectly plucked eyebrows at me, takes in my face — by now bright red as well as creamy — and says: 'I thought we had company?'

'He's gone to work,' I reply, pouring us both some orange juice and sitting down at the little dining table. I clean up my cheeks with a wad of kitchen roll and hope she doesn't ask what happened.

'These countryside types don't half start early . . . ' she says, sitting herself down. She stares at the toast — devoid of cream — and pushes it around her plate a bit before taking a tiny, mouse-like nibble. I am reminded again that despite the newly found obsession with make-up, my mum is still in a painful place.

'Any news? About Edie?' she asks, for which I give her credit. I know what she really wants to ask about is Van, but she reins herself in and makes an effort to be polite first.

'Not so far,' I reply, having checked my phone and not seen anything. No news, I tell myself, is definitely good news in this particular case.

'So . . . what's going on with you and Van then? He's quite rugged. Reminds me of a young Clint Eastwood when he was in those Spaghetti Westerns, but, you know, bigger. And without the poncho.'

It's taken her over a minute to get there, which is longer than I expected.

'Nothing's going on, Mum,' I reply patiently. 'He's just a friend, that's all.'

'He's great with Saul, isn't he?'

'Yes, he is.'

'And he seems to really like you . . . '

'Well, yes. I like him too.'

She ponders the whole thing for a few more moments, still barely touching her toast, before saying: 'Mind you, they say Alzheimer's runs in the family, don't they? Might be for the best to keep him at arm's length.'

I'm initially left speechless by this. Not only has she thought as far along the line as me and Van having a future together, possibly even procreating — she's decided it's potentially a bad idea because of the tragic circumstances Lynnie and her children have found themselves in.

I shake my head and take a deep breath. She really is quite a piece of work, my mother.

'All kinds of things run in families,' I reply. 'And that's irrelevant. I'm not looking for a man, Mum. I don't need one.'

She nods and chews on her lip, and looks thoughtful. I wonder what kind of fresh hell I'm about to be subjected to, before she says: 'Not need, no. Maybe not. But perhaps you might . . . want one, at some point?'

I say a silent prayer that she's not about to start talking about my libido, at least partly because I have no defence on that front — much as I try and play it cool, Van definitely sets off a few earthquakes whenever I'm near. Even if he's just kissed me with squirty cream.

'Maybe I will,' I answer. 'And I promise you'll be the first to know. But at the moment, I've got my hands full with work and college and mainly Saul. I want things to just . . . settle down for us.'

She lets out an unladylike snort and replies: 'Settle down? Crikey, Katie, if your life gets any more settled you'll be comatose! I know you've got Saul to think about, but you're still a young woman. You need to think about living a little. Think about your future. You don't want to end up like me, a dried-up old crone, useful to no one, thrown into the gutter like yesterday's chip wrapper . . . '

She delivers this speech with such fervent pathos that I'd feel sorry for her if it wasn't also a bit funny.

'Mum, you're not dried up, or a crone! You're in the prime of your life. And Dad . . . well, maybe it's more complicated than it seems. I'm sure it's not just that he threw you in the gutter.'

Of course, I have the advantage of knowing more about it than she does. I've promised my dad I won't say anything just yet — but his time is running out. I decide to text him later to express exactly that. It's not fair on Mum, and it's definitely not fair on me, being caught between them. Again.

'Well, that's what it feels like! All those years together, and now this . . . dumped for the ice cream lady! It's . . . well, it's crap, to use a vulgar word. Just crap. And I'm lonely, if I'm honest. And sad. And . . . I don't want you to end up the same way. I want you to find someone, Katie — someone nice, who'll treat you and Saul well, and build a good life with you.'

She doesn't add 'someone like Van', but I wonder if she's thinking it — or if she's discarded him as a potential suitor and provider of further grandchildren due to his suspect gene pool.

'I understand that, Mum,' I say, reaching out to cover her hand with mine. She's so thin her bones feel like a sparrow's beneath her skin.

'And I know you want the best for me . . . but I'm not convinced that getting married and spending the rest of your life with someone is the answer. I mean, I can't deny that I find Van . . . not disgusting. And it might start out well. But how long would it last? How long before we started to annoy each other, or get bored, or start being cruel and snippy? How long before all the excitement magically disappears, and we start fighting about whose turn it is to put the bins out? How long before Saul gets stuck in the middle of it, and ends up losing Van all together? What if it ended up getting so messy, we had to leave Budbury, just as we've started to fit in? It's a small place, you know — we wouldn't be able to avoid each other, it'd be terrible! And then we'd have to start all over again . . . '

Once I start, I find I can't stop. The words pour out, vocalising the exact thing that worries me about the whole situation. Mum squeezes my hand and stares at the table top. I see a tear sneak its way from one of her eyes, and feel terrible.

Before I can apologise, she speaks: 'Well, I'm really sad you feel like that, love. It's not always like that, you know? You and Jason weren't right for each other . . . but that doesn't mean it always has to end badly. Look at your friends here in the village, and how happy they seem to be with each other.'

'I know, and I'm happy for them,' I say. 'Every single one of them. But I'm still not sure that's part of my future.'

She draws in a deep breath, and looks up at me from her spidery lashes.

'I know you're not, Katie. And I know you probably didn't have the best role models, did you? Me and your dad were hardly examples of marital bliss when you were growing up. We did our best, but I'm not stupid — I know our best wasn't good enough.'

We're both silent for a moment, and it strikes me as strange that the only time either of my parents have acknowledged my less-than-idyllic childhood is now, when their marriage is in tatters. It's taken a complete breakdown in their relationship for them to see it as it really was, rather than the way they probably had to tell themselves it was in order to survive.

I always thought I'd relish this moment — feel some sense of victory or vindication. But now it's happened, I just feel sad. The way she's talking isn't the way you want to hear your mother talking — she's broken, defeated, lost. The fact that all of this is unfolding to the background sounds of Saul chortling away at a mega-loud TV show about a family called the Thundermans, who are all secretly superheroes, makes it even more weird.

Meanwhile, back in the real world — literally feet away in the kitchen — none of us are superheroes. None of us are villains. We're all . . . just doing our best, like Mum said.

'I had an interesting conversation with Cherie . . . erm, yesterday, I suppose. God, it feels like a longer time ago than that. But it was yesterday.'

'Oh? What about?' asks Mum, apparently

welcoming the opportunity to change the subject, swiftly wiping her purple pyjama arm across her leaky eyes.

'About you, actually,' I say, raising my eyebrows at her. She perks up immediately, sitting straighter and suddenly looking much more lively. She might be an ego-maniac — but she's my ego-maniac.

'Me? Why? What was she saying? Was it about my lipstick? She was admiring it the other day and I did offer to give her a few make-up tips . . . I don't mean to be rude, but I think she needs them.'

I grimace inside but manage to keep my face neutral. The thought of Cherie in a full face of slap simply does not compute. She's a woman who would never dream of hiding a wrinkle or dying her hair — she's happy with who she is and doesn't give a damn if the rest of the world disagrees.

'No,' I reply slowly, 'but that was very kind of you. She was actually saying that she could use some help at the moment. That they're struggling for staff, what with Laura being in a delicate condition and all that. She was actually wondering if you'd like to work there . . . and even live there?'

I add the last part cautiously, not wanting for a minute for my mum to feel like I'm trying to get rid of her. I am, of course — but it's a secret, much like the Thundermans' super-powers. She's in far too fragile a state to be able to cope with another perceived rejection, so if she quails even slightly, I want her to know that she's still welcome here.

'She has a flat,' I explain, 'in the attic of the café. It's really nice, she used to live in it before she married Frank. So if you wanted to, you could use it for a while. But only if you wanted to. You're a huge help here, and I'd miss you, obviously, so don't feel any pressure. I love having you here, and you're welcome to stay as long as you like.'

I'm treading carefully, not to mention outright lying, all to spare her feelings. I really needn't have bothered.

'Oh God, yes! I'd love to!' she shrieks, jumping to her feet as though she plans on running right upstairs and packing her suitcase this exact moment. She realises that might have sounded a little overeager, and sits down again.

'I mean . . . only if it's all right with you, Katie? I'll stay if you want me to, you know I will. Family comes first.'

I'm laughing inside as we look at each other across the tiny kitchen table. Laughing at the games we all play in an attempt to be decent — the lies we tell in an attempt not to be hurtful.

It's completely obvious to me now that my mother has been struggling with our enforced proximity as much as I have — she couldn't have been keener on moving out if I'd offered up Cal and Sam stark naked and covered in icing sugar to help her with her luggage. She's been hiding it as much as I have — and now we're both sitting here pretending that we want to do whatever the other one wants. If we're not careful she'll let me talk her into staying, and we'll both lose.

'That's okay, Mum,' I reply, without a trace of laughter in my voice — we both need to keep up the pretence of enjoying each other's company a little while longer so we can escape with our mother-daughter dignity intact.

'I think it'd be really good for you,' I add, watching as she actually starts eating her toast. 'And Cherie needs the help. Maybe you're not as dried up and useless as you thought, eh?'

'Maybe not!' she says, her eyes sparkling.

It's the happiest I've seen her in years.

21

A couple of hours later, Mum sets off to take Saul to pre-school, still full of verve after my news about her new life and new temporary home, and I make the long commute across the road to the pharmacy. There's a light sheen of frost on the windowsills, and the air is bitingly cold again. Tinkerbell didn't follow me out onto the street but stayed glued to the radiator, and I can't say that I blame him.

The shop door is open, but nobody seems to be at home. I walk through, and predictably I find Auburn out back, having a cigarette. Less predictably, she's jogging on the spot as she smokes, the cigarette waving around between puffs in her fingerless-gloved hands.

'Why are you doing that?' I ask immediately.

'Smoking? Because I have an addictive personality, an oral fixation and no will power. Have you met me?'

'Yes, and I get all of that. But why are you jogging on the spot?'

'Oh!' she says, her ponytail bouncing. 'It's my new fitness plan. You're supposed to do, like, 10,000 steps a day or something stupid, aren't you? And even with walking to and from here from the cottage, I don't do anything like that. So I thought I'd maximise my time by doing a quick thousand or so every time I'm on a ciggie break. Cool, right?'

It is, of course, one of the most counter-intuitive things I've ever heard — but possibly it's better than having the smoke without the jogging. I nod, still feeling bemused at the psychedelic wonderland that is Auburn's mind.

'I'm going to patent it,' she says, sounding slightly out of breath now. 'I'll call it the Fag Break Fitness Plan. I'll start a blog, and I'll probably get a book deal, maybe even an exercise DVD . . . '

'Excellent idea,' I reply. 'Not long now until you're on one of those health promotion posters we have on display in the shop. You and your Marlboro Gold.'

She grins, and smokes, and then starts to jog more slowly.

'It's important to always cool down after vigorous exercise . . . ' she announces, eventually reducing her speed until she looks like a man on the moon in gravity boots, taking super-slow steps.

I'm about to leave her to it when she speaks again: 'Talking of which — did you get any vigorous exercise last night, Katie?'

I frown and shake my head. I have no idea what she's talking about until she adds: 'Because I couldn't help noticing that my big brother didn't make it home at all . . . '

'You have a dirty mind,' I reply, turning my back on her to go and make some tea. I'm blushing, and don't want her to see my weakness.

'Maybe,' she says, following me back in, puffing and wheezing slightly, 'but my lungs are

218

clear as mountain air! Did he stay over, though? At yours?'

'He did,' I answer, busying myself with less troublesome things like a kettle and tea bags. 'But in case you were wondering — '

'I was.'

'He slept on the sofa. Nothing happened, and even if it did, I wouldn't tell you.'

'Spoilsport,' she says, sounding like a sulky child. She leans back against the sink, and I notice that she looks tired too. There are dark circles beneath her eyes, and the nails showing through her fingerless gloves are chewed so far down the skin looks raw.

'Everything all right at home, with your mum?' I ask, putting the pieces together.

'They've been better,' she replies, shrugging and looking sad. 'We've made an appointment to go and see her consultant. She was really wound up yesterday, one of those 'I don't know who you are, why are you holding me captive?' scenarios.

'When Willow suggested she read her book — the one that reminds her who she is and who we are and where she is — she threw it at her head so hard the spine cut her eyelid. After that, Mum went and barricaded herself in her room with the bookcase and a Buddha bust. She's done this before, and we know it's possible to move it all eventually — but if you do it while she's still upset, it just makes her even more scared and agitated.

'So Willow let her cool down, and Tom came over, and they waited until it was quiet and managed to get in. In the meantime Lynnie had conked out, and went to sleep for about twenty hours — except it didn't look restful, you know? More like she was in a coma, which she'd wake up from every hour or so to have a good shout and thrash around in bed like she was fighting someone.'

I hand Auburn her tea — plenty of sugar — and say: 'That's awful, for all of you. I'm so sorry. What do the team at the day centre think?'

'They think maybe it's a sign she's going to decline. Or maybe it's a sign she has some other illness she can't tell us about. Or maybe it's a sign that her meds need upping. Or maybe it's a sign her meds are having side effects. Or maybe a sign she's in pain, but we don't know where. Basically it's a sign that nobody has a fucking clue.'

It's not uncommon for Auburn to swear — she's that kind of girl — but it's usually in fun, or for comedic effect. This time it's a reflection of her frustration and anxiety.

'I'm so sorry, Auburn. You've done the right thing making the appointment. She's really fit, your mum, physically — but there might be something else going on. She might have another urinary tract infection, like she did earlier in the year. They can test her easily for that. Or she might have a bump or a strain or any number of things. Is she up to date with her routine scans and checks?'

'Hmmm . . . I don't know. I'll check,' replies Auburn, already fingering her cigarette packet in a way that implies she might soon be going for another jog.

'You might ask if she can have her bowels looked at as well. It's a common problem, and anything going wrong down there can make even the most healthy of people get wound up and cranky. Have you noticed any changes in her toilet habits?'

Auburn sighs, and I can't say that I blame her.

'No, but I've not been paying close attention. I will now . . . that'll be fun.'

'Well, it's worth asking the doctor about. Anything like that could be what's causing the problem.'

'Or,' she says, staring at me while she chews her lip viciously, 'it could be that she's entering the end stages. I should know this — in fact I probably do but I've deliberately forgotten it — but what is life expectancy with Alzheimer's?'

I do know the answer to this, but it's not one she's going to like.

'It varies massively,' I say, cautiously. 'All kinds of factors come into play — her physical health and wellbeing, the level of support she has at home, her treatment plan. All of which I'd say are excellent.'

'Yes, but . . . ?'

'For someone diagnosed like your mum was, in her early sixties, it averages between seven and ten years. But it can be much longer.'

Auburn nods abruptly, her nostrils flared and her lips pinched tightly together. I can only imagine what she's going through, how complex and devastating all of this is for them, and say a little prayer of thanks for the fact that my mother, no matter how annoying, is still my

221

mother. Hopefully she'll be annoying me for a long time to come.

I'm wondering if Auburn's going to ask me more questions, and decide that all I can do is answer them honestly, when both our phones make beeping noises to tell us a message has landed. We exchange a glance, knowing it's likely to be about Edie, and both reach to check.

Sure enough, there's a text on mine from Becca — obviously sent in a round robin to everyone waiting to hear the morning's news. I hold my breath slightly as I start reading it, telling myself that if it was bad — if there was no more Edie — then Becca wouldn't be telling us by text. She just wouldn't.

Luckily, I'm right on that — and the news is good.

'Ahoy sailors!' it says, bizarrely. 'Better news on the Good Ship Edie. She's awake and talking and drinking her tot of rum. Waiting to see the Captain on her rounds. Jolly Roger that, over and out, Able Seawoman Becca.'

I smile — because it really is good news — and then frown. Because it's also confusing.

'Why did she go all nautical-but-nice on us?' asks Auburn, also frowning.

'I have no idea!'

'And do you reckon they really give you rum for breakfast in hospital?'

'Not in my experience, or it'd be a lot more popular. But it's good news anyway — really good. Becca's probably just knackered. Have you seen Sam this morning? I said I'd check in on them for her.'

'Yep, I saw him when I was opening up — he was taking little Edie into work for the day. Said it's never too young for your first ammonite.'

Sam works as a ranger, and gives guided walks along the Jurassic Coast, pointing out the fossils that get washed up on the shore or are embedded in the cliffs. Looks like Little Edie's getting her first lesson in fossil hunting.

'Anyway . . . didn't get a chance to say it yesterday,' says Auburn, putting her phone down on the counter. 'But well done. You were a bit of a hero.'

'What do you mean? What did I do?' I ask, genuinely bewildered.

'You saved Edie's life. Didn't want to actually say that out loud until we knew how she was doing — but you did, Katie.'

'Don't be daft,' I scoff, embarrassed. 'All I did was notice the cat in her windowsill and call for help. It hardly makes me Natasha Romanoff, does it?'

'Well, I'm sure you'd make a great Black Widow, but heroes come in different forms, don't they? You could just as easily have not noticed the cat. Or not wondered why the cat was still there. Or decided it didn't matter. Or told yourself you were imagining things, and ignored your instincts and gone home. You're a nurse — you know how bad she was. You know it was touch and go. If we hadn't found her when we did, she might not have made it through the night. So don't argue — you saved her life.'

I don't agree, but I also don't argue. There's no point with Auburn. I just smile, and walk back through into the shop with my tea.

I settle in on the scary lipstick sofa for a minute, and text my dad, telling him he needs to get his arse into gear and sort stuff out with Mum. She's happy right now, because of the obviously exciting idea of moving out of my house, but it's still not fair.

I don't expect any kind of reaction from him, because he's usually so bad with his mobile, but I actually get a reply straight away. A reply that makes me want to scream, but I don't suppose you can have everything in life.

He's going away for a bit, he says. On a mindfulness retreat in Tenerife. With Fiona and some of her friends. But, he assures me, he'll be down before Christmas to talk to Mum.

I sit still for a moment, drinking my tea, and trying to be more mindful myself. Maybe it's a good thing, I decide. I have my blood pressure to consider.

Maybe it's for the best, I think. Maybe he'll come back with some answers. And long term, who knows? He was definitely a changed man when I saw him — and that can't be a bad thing. Mum's a changed woman as well, but that's different, and a lot less positive — hers is change she's had forced on her rather than chosen. No wonder she's a mess.

I shake my head, and leaf through the sex aids catalogue almost without realising what I'm doing. As soon as I get to a brightly coloured page full of pastel-shaded vibrators, I throw it away, wondering if I now need hand sanitiser.

It's all so strange, this family stuff. Here, in

Budbury, I've made friends better than I've ever known. I've become part of an extended family that I chose for myself, rather than the one I was born with. But family is still family — still part of my history and my genetic make-up and my future. I wonder about Saul, and what he'll make of it all when he's older. Right now, he accepts that his dad lives in Scotland and he lives here and that's all fine.

But Saul is only very small, and knows no different. This is the only way he's ever known it to be. Maybe that will change once he's old enough to ask questions. When he's at school, and has his own friends, who all might have perfect little Mum-and-Dad set-ups. He's bound to be curious — to want to know why his dad isn't around; why we split up, why he's not in his life more. It's only natural, and I know that day will come — and I'm surely dreading it.

I idly mess around on my phone, feeling low-level stressed about pretty much everything. About Edie, about my parents, about Lynnie, about Van, about Saul. I find myself on Facebook, which I rarely use as I never have any pictures of nice meals to post.

I flick through my newsfeed, laughing at the fact that Lizzy's page is now full of photos of Tinkerbell and the dogs, and press like on them all. I see that Laura's shared a picture of her Green Velvet Cake and like too.

I see that my mum has updated her profile pic — the first time she's posted since she set up her account four years ago. It's a selfie with trout pout, taken against the backdrop of my purple curtains, and looks frightening. Still, I like that as well, as Facebook hasn't as yet introduced a button for 'that scares the shit out of me'.

Barely thinking about what I'm doing, I type in Jason's name and search. I scroll through the results, and find that there are an improbably large number of people with the same name as him online. Eventually, after investigating a few, I find him.

Feeling guilty and sneaky and really hoping he can't tell I've been looking, I open his page. I'm met with a photo of him and his wife, Jo, at their wedding. It looks nice, one of those candid shots with confetti fluttering across their laughing faces. She's about my age, Jo, but couldn't look more different — she's brunette, almost as tall as him, with one of those Amazonian figures that makes her look like Wonder Woman.

I know she's a teacher, and that they've been together for the last two years, getting married this summer.

I roll the page down, looking at their various joint posts, at the numerous pictures — Jason and Jo on honeymoon; Jason and Jo at a barbecue; Jason and Jo on a mini-break to Paris; Jason and Jo eating spaghetti.

They look happy. They look good together. I feel strange about it — not out of any sense of jealousy, but out of a weird sensation that I'm intruding on a life that has nothing at all to do with me. Except it does — because for better or worse, this is Saul's dad.

Jason and I communicate mainly by email, which is easier because we both get to think carefully about what we're saying. He always remembers Saul's birthday, and Christmas, and even sends Easter eggs and boxes full of creepy chocolate treats at Halloween.

He's mentioned coming to see him a few times, but it's never happened. I don't know whether that's down to distance, or something deeper — whether Jason doesn't push for it to happen because he doesn't want to see me. I don't suppose my lukewarm response has helped — I've never said no, but I've never shown any enthusiasm either.

That, a tiny little voice whispers into my ear, probably isn't fair. Maybe if I'd been more open, more encouraging, he'd have made the effort. The way Jason and I ended was horrible — but I don't for one minute see him as a threat to me, or to Saul. Not a physical one, anyway.

With the hindsight of a couple of years away from him, and with my parents as examples, I can see quite clearly how easy it was for us to descend into the arguments and bitterness. It wasn't by any means inevitable that it should end the way it did — not all men who fight with their wives slap them. But I also don't think it was typical of Jason, or indicative of the way he is now. I genuinely believe it was a one-off — one he was as horrified by as I was. Although maybe that's what all women think, who knows?

I do know, though, that in some ways it gave me an excuse to finally end a relationship we both knew wasn't working. And then I ran away, and I've kept him at arm's length ever since. He's probably still ashamed, and hasn't pushed as hard as he could have to stay in Saul's life — and perhaps I need to have a think about it all. I don't like thinking about it, obviously — things go much more smoothly when I don't think at all.

But with everything that's been happening — my parents, Edie, even Van — the time has come. I don't want the complications. I don't want the mess. I don't want my orderly little life to be disrupted by all this tangled emotional stuff. But this isn't about what I want; it's about Saul's future.

On the spur of the moment, I hit the button that sends a friend request. I immediately feel a little tremor of panic run through me as I do it, and jump up to do something else. Anything else. I don't know why it feels weird — it's not like we never communicate. We do. But somehow a 'friend request', and this little foray into his personal life, feels too intimate — like I'm inviting him to be more to me than he currently is.

I need to find work to distract myself, and decide to rearrange our display of Rimmel make-up — the lipsticks are all in the wrong places, so it's pretty urgent. I'm still stubbing plastic tubes into plastic holes when Auburn trots through from the back room. She's taken her coat off but is still wearing her fingerless gloves after goodness knows how many cigarettes while she pulled herself together.

'I feel great!' she says breezily, completely transformed from the maudlin state she was in a few minutes ago. 'I think I might run the

London marathon next year!'

'Will you smoke while you do it?' I ask, wondering if anybody has ever done that — and whether they'd get on TV cameras if they did.

'Only a few — you know those little places they have set up on the course, where they give you bottles of water and whistle pops?'

'I've never seen them handing out whistle pops, but I know what you mean.'

'Well, maybe I'd just stay there for a minute, and have a quick puff. I don't think I'd actually smoke while I was running — it wouldn't be ladylike . . . anyway, there's time to plan for all of that later. I've got some prescriptions getting sent in from the surgery in Applechurch — let me know when they land, will you? And by the way — there's a big dinner at the café tonight. By royal decree of Cherie — says she wants everyone to get together to have a feast to celebrate Edie being on the mend.'

The nurse part of me is worried by that — because while the Good Ship Edie might be doing better today, it's by no means guaranteed that it's plain sailing from this point on. She's fighting pneumonia, she's 92, and she's in hospital — where there will be other people, with other infections, potentially sharing their germs with her. She's still very, very poorly.

It seems churlish to mention this right now, though, so I keep my thoughts to myself. Dinner at the café will be lovely. Saul will be the centre of attention; there'll be dogs for him to play with, and the food will be a heck of a lot better than the chicken kievs I have in the freezer. Plus my mum can talk to Cherie about her glamorous new life as a member of Team Comfort Food.

Van will probably be there too. Which is fine, I tell myself — that will also be lovely, and I won't be drinking. It's all under control.

'Okay. Great,' I reply, finishing with the lipsticks and moving over to the dispensing area to turn the computer on. We get prescriptions sent electronically from local GPs, and get them ready either for patients to collect, or for us to sometimes deliver. Auburn does most of that part due to my childlike inability to drive a car.

I'm checking through our files, keeping myself busy, when I hear an alert from my phone. I get it out of my pocket, and check to see what it is.

It's a notification from Facebook. Jason has accepted my friend request, and Facebook wonders if I'd like to send him a message or wave to him.

What I'd actually like to do is rewind the last hour, and not contact him at all. But I somehow suspect that's beyond Facebook's power.

22

I'm grateful to be in work for the rest of the morning, and equally grateful to have to go to college in the afternoon. I've passed three of the four modules I'm studying already, and only have one more to go. Having Mum around has, at least, taken off a lot of the pressure around childcare.

Before, it was a workable but ad hoc arrangement with my various friends — and with Laura now very much in the family way, and Lynnie taking a downward swing, I'm glad I don't have to impose.

I'm also glad I've had something to occupy my mind, as Jason and I have been exchanging messages all day. There's something about the whole messaging thing that makes it feel more personal than an email — like we're talking to each other in real time.

He's now seen the few photos I have of Saul on my account, and seems interested in all of them — and in our life here. I suppose that's kind of what I wanted, but it also feels vaguely unsettling. Like I've opened a can of worms that's now going to crawl all over me; that I'll still be shaking off my skin even when they're gone.

It also seems that Jason was on the verge of contacting me anyway — partly to ask what Saul might want for Christmas, and partly to share some news.

His wife, Jo, is pregnant. Again, this weirds me out — not because I still have feelings for Jason, but because it means that Saul will be getting a little brother or sister in about six months' time. Logically, I knew that my life would always be connected to Jason's through our son — but this news makes it all the more real. More complicated. A whole lot more difficult to ever run away from. I feel strangely trapped by it all, and can't quite understand why.

The absolute last thing I feel like doing is going to the café for a big group dinner. I love my pals, I really do, and I've taken big strides in getting more involved with village life. But I now realise that when I feel conflicted, or worried, my instinct is still to hide away from the world and sort it out myself. To shut all the potential stress factors down and retreat to my bunker.

It's a pattern I'm now familiar with, but only really identified when I briefly attended a support group for single mums. We had a group counselling session where we were all asked to mark important turning points in our 'journeys'.

I left the support group after two weeks — to be honest, I'm not very communal, and I also felt like a bit of a fraud. I definitely hadn't suffered enough in comparison to some of the other women there, and was worried I might start making things up just to fit in.

But I do always remember that session. I remember sitting in a circle on a hard plastic chair, Saul in the crèche off to one side, probably trying to eat Duplo, my eyes closed and hands wrapped around a plastic cup of hot coffee. I think that was half the attraction, the hot coffee.

I sat there, eyes closed, and I saw that pattern. Saw it, and took it home with me to examine later. That night, when my precious baby boy/demon spawn was finally asleep, I sat sprawled across the sofa, watching repeats of *Through The Keyhole* and remembering things I'd thought dead and buried. Reliving moments so painful I'd hidden them deep under seventeen layers of denial.

I'm feeling the same now, and the sensation of being under attack reminds me of when I was a kid, and things were getting heated downstairs in the Land of the Lunatics. The way I'd lock my bedroom door and listen to music, or walk the streets for hours on end just to escape from the insanity and the noise and the anger.

I kind of want to do that now — or at least to not have to be in company I'm not fit to be in. I know how this will go: I feel pressurised, so I'll retreat. It'll be like the time earlier in the year when Edie was having her ninety-second birthday at Briarwood. I'd been to all the dancing lessons, I'd helped plan the event, but when it came down to it, I couldn't face it — there were too many people, and too much attention.

I'd wussed out and stayed at home with Saul instead.

On the bus ride home today, I'd briefly toyed with the idea of coming up with some excuse to wuss out again, but the text messages from pretty much everyone I know reminding me to be there by 7.30 were making it patently clear that that wasn't an option.

So, my brain a simmering pot of stress stew, I find myself walking to the café on my own, through village streets that feel deserted — probably because everyone is at the café.

Mum has headed over early with Saul, keen to talk to Cherie about her job and the flat, and I'd had time to get ready on my own. It should have felt like a luxury — but it actually felt like torture. My make-up was applied half-heartedly, and I wasn't even sure what my hair was supposed to be doing.

In an empty house, I had too much time to think, too much time to worry, too much time to wonder about how my life would look if Saul wasn't in it. If, for example, he was spending time away in Scotland — with his dad and his new baby brother or sister.

The whole thing feels like a case of 'be careful what you wish for' to me. Hours ago, a lifetime ago, this morning in the pharmacy, I'd been thinking that it would be a good idea for Saul to get to know his dad better. To not grow up feeling unwanted or rejected in any way. To not only rely on me for love and nurturing and approval.

Now it looks as though that might be happening, I'm frankly terrified. I know that doesn't say anything good about me, but it's how I feel. I can't change the situation — it is what it is — all I can do is try to adapt. To stay calm, and get through it. If life crises have taught me anything, it's that with time, things won't always feel as bad as they do in the heat of the moment.

I tell myself this over and over again as I walk, far too slowly, towards the café. It's dark, and chillingly cold, and snow has been forecast overnight. I'm wrapped up warm but, without a balaclava, still have icy cheeks that feel as though Jack Frost has rubbed his bony fingers all over my skin.

By the time I get to the café, lit up with its fairy lights, I've decided that I'll only stay for an hour. I can fake it for an hour — then I'll come up with some reason, like Saul being tired or Tinkerbell needing a foot massage, so I can make my excuses and leave.

I trudge my way reluctantly up the path and into the garden, where the giant inflatable Father Christmas is wobbling around, half in shadow from the illumination spilling from the steamed-up café windows.

I take a deep breath, tell myself I can hide in a corner and leave as soon as possible, and push open the door.

I'm immediately struck by two things. One is the heat — the place is warm and crowded and suddenly makes all my coats and scarves and gloves feel unnecessary. The other is the noise.

As soon as I step through the door, the whole place erupts into a chorus of 'For She's a Jolly Good Fellow', loud and discordant and threaded through with the one or two voices that are actually hitting the right notes.

I freeze, rooted to the spot, and actually look behind me — checking to see who it is they're singing to.

As there's nobody else there, and there's also a

huge banner strung up along the serving counter that says 'Well done Katie!', I come to the inescapable conclusion that they're actually singing to me.

I don't know how I must look to the assembled masses standing in front of me, but I'm guessing that it might involve the words 'deer' and 'headlights'.

Saul dashes forward and hugs my legs. He's getting bigger now, taking after his dad in height rather than me, and I kneel down to hug him back. And, you know, to hide the look of sheer horror on my face.

These people, these wonderful people, have thrown me a party to congratulate me for doing something that wasn't even a big deal. And in return, all I feel is a driving need to run screaming back down the hill, through the village, and into my own little house. Except my own little house doesn't even feel that safe any more — it has weird curtains, and my mum's stuff all over it, and people have started to visit me. I've had Matt in the doorway and Van on the sofa and in my shower, and it all feels too big — too invasive.

I school my face into something that hopefully doesn't reflect this — because I know I'm being crazy — and stand up straight.

Everyone is there — apart from Edie, of course. Everyone is looking at me, and grinning, and cheering. There's a trestle table set up and groaning with food and drink, and the whole place is draped with little fairy lights in the shape of Christmas presents.

If I was here in the background, celebrating somebody else's heroism, I'd be thinking how pretty and lovely it all is. Instead, I'm still wondering how quickly I can escape.

Becca steps forward and envelops me in a huge hug.

'Thank you,' she whispers into my ear. 'The doctors are all amazed at her. They keep bringing students in to meet her — I think they're considering writing some kind of paper on the Edie May miracle! Nobody thought she was going to survive, but she is. I know she is. But she wouldn't have done if it wasn't for you.'

'And Tinkerbell,' I add, overwhelmed.

'Yeah. Tinkerbell too. Cherie has a whole plate of salmon for him as well.'

I nod, and smile a stupid smile, and keep the stupid smile on my face as everyone troops over to thank me and hug me and pat me on the back. Laura's there, looking tired but happy; Zoe and Cal; Sam and Little Edie; Willow and Tom and Auburn and Van and Lynnie.

Lynnie's looking confused but not distressed, which is a blessing, and Van gives me an extra tight squeeze when he reaches me.

'You can do it,' he murmurs into my ear. 'Just keep on smiling!'

That does at least make me laugh — he's obviously seen right through my less-than-brave face. I just hope all the others haven't.

Finally, after a large round of thanks from Edie's family, Cherie is by my side. She's wearing a kaftan — an actual kaftan — decorated with tiny pom-poms, like something she picked up from a little boutique in an Aztec village.

'We made you these,' she says, 'me and Saul. Just for you.'

First, she shows me a big cardboard love heart, decorated in pink glitter, with the words 'Our hero!' written on them in neon-coloured marker pen. The heart is attached to some stripey blue and white fabric used as a necklace. I think it might possibly have been a tea-towel in a previous life. She drapes it around my neck like a medal, and flips my hair out at the back.

Next she produces a kind of cape, obviously made from an old tablecloth, also decorated in glitter. It shimmers under the fairy lights as she wafts it around, shining specks of glitter flying off and into a sparkling cloud around our heads.

There's a makeshift clasp at the corners made out of glued-on press-studs, and she fastens it around my neck.

'There,' she says, smiling at her handiwork, 'your very own superhero cape. Give us a twirl!'

I blink rapidly and do as she says — it's the path of least resistance, and I'm hoping that once I've endured this last suffocating act of kindness, I can fade into the background.

Everyone cheers and claps as I twirl, and then, thankfully, attention starts to move away from me. Cherie calls out for music, and I see Matt, who always seems to end up manning sound systems at parties, switch it on. I think it's his way of hiding — the anonymity of being the guy in charge of the buttons.

Bizarrely, the first song on is Beyoncé's 'Single

Ladies', and everyone immediately starts busting out some dance moves and laughing. I feel the beat, and wish I could join in — I love dancing, and I'm good at it, but right now I just can't. I wish I was the kind of person who could just twirl their superhero cape and throw herself into the party, but I'm not. I'm too much of a coward.

I see that Saul is doing that thing that kids like doing, where he's got his feet on Cal's feet, and Cal is dancing him around the room. I see Laura sit down with a sigh of relief, and Matt bring over a glass of water and a paper plate laden with food. I see the teenagers, dancing in their own little circle, mock-twerking and pulling faces as they look at the old people gyrating. I see Willow and Tom cutting it up, and Auburn to one side, sitting with Lynnie. I see my mum, and she catches my eye across the room, giving me a huge grin and making a 'thumbs up' sign.

Everyone is happy. Everyone is relieved. Everyone is grateful that Edie has lived to fight another day.

I, on the other hand, am shrivelling up inside, and hating myself for it. I slink away to the ladies, smiling and chatting to people as I move through the room, feeling more and more brittle with every conversation.

I finally make it, leaning back against the door once I've locked it, breathing a sigh of relief. I just need a moment, I tell myself. A moment to regroup. To calm down. To shake off the feeling that I'm some kind of imposter — that I shouldn't be here, amongst all these people, on

239

the receiving end of their love and support and thanks. That if they really knew me, they wouldn't like me at all.

Even as these thoughts flitter through my mind, I realise how silly they sound. Why shouldn't they like me? What have I ever done that's so bad? I shoplifted a mascara once, when I was fourteen. Technically, that's about the worst of my sins.

But this runs deeper than that, I know. It started young, feeling like I was a spare part in my parents' drama. It developed into my teenaged years, where I always felt I had to keep people at arm's length, that I needed distance from people who might hurt me.

Now, I'm here, with a child and with friends and with a life. And yet I still feel like I don't quite belong. Like I can't quite connect with them in a genuine way. I'm still playing a part — and it's not the one of a superhero.

I splash my face with cold water, and swish my hair around to get rid of some of the glitter, and stare at myself in the mirror.

'Don't freak out — just don't,' I tell myself out loud. It's been a big couple of days. Edie being ill. Everything that's going on with Dad. Van sneaking further and further into our lives. And, with ultimate bad timing, facing up to the fact that I need to sort myself out when it comes to Jason.

It feels like things are changing — and I don't want them to. I've only just steadied myself with the basics of this community, my place in the world. And now I feel like I'm being fast-tracked on to an advanced level I'm not quite prepared for. Like if I'd gone into work as a nurse and someone expected me to perform brain surgery.

I'm taking some deep breaths — the kind Lynnie has taught me to do when I'm feeling stressed — and turn the taps off.

I'm preparing to leave when there's a knock on the door. I assume I've been a toilet hog for too long, and someone — probably Laura — is desperate for a pee.

'Coming!' I shout, aiming to sound perky and bright and happy. In other words, the exact opposite of what I actually feel.

I open the door, fake smile plastered onto my face along with the stray glitter, and see Van standing outside, leaning against the wall. He looks at me and grins.

'Nice look,' he says, pointing at the glitter. 'I'm here to rescue you.'

'What do you mean, rescue me? What makes you think I need rescuing from anything?' I reply, my voice rising about seven million octaves by the end of the sentence.

'The look on your face when you walked through the door. The fake smile you're currently using. The fact that your voice sounds like Minnie Mouse on helium. And the fact that I know you, Katie, and know that this isn't your idea of a good time. Come on — let's sneak through the kitchens and out the back door. Saul's fine, and if we're quick nobody will notice we're gone. I promise I'll have you back by midnight so you don't turn into a pumpkin.'

I look beyond him, to the packed café, where

The Mavericks are helping everyone just dance the night away. Saul is now on Cal's shoulders, tangling up some of the dangling lametta in his fingers, and my mum is doing her usual Eighties party dance with Frank. The idea of plunging back into it all makes my stomach clench into knots.

I look back at Van, who has somehow figured all of this out, and nod.

'Okay,' I say quietly. 'I'll let you rescue me.'

23

We make our way through the kitchens, for some reason tiptoeing as we do — I don't know why, it's not like anyone would be able to hear our footsteps over the music.

Van pauses at a cupboard near the back, where Cherie keeps a stock of plaid fleece blankets for customers to use when they're sitting outside in winter, and grabs a couple before we leave.

We head off down the path, and I find myself smiling at the thought of anyone noticing us — two dark figures, doing a runner like a pair of fugitives. My superhero cape is fluttering behind me in the breeze, and I kind of wish I was also wearing tights and red pants just to make it even more ridiculous.

Once we're down by the bay, I feel a physical sense of relief wash over me. It's as though gaining even this amount of distance from the party has allowed my adrenaline levels to calm down to something approaching normal.

We walk out onto the beach, which is completely deserted. I can still hear the beat of the music from the café, and when I look up I can see its bright lights and the dancing figures inside, but it's all small enough to feel less intimidating.

Van was right, I think, sucking in some cold night air — *I did need rescuing. And maybe, once the shock and surprise of the ambush party has worn off, I'll be able to simply go back in and enjoy myself, like a normal human being.*

I just walk, grateful for the chilly air against my overheated skin, while Van amuses himself in the way of overgrown boys everywhere — by throwing sticks and stones into the sea. As we get further along the coast, the sound of the music fades, and all I can hear is the gentle hiss and fizz of waves lapping up onto the sand, and the occasional splash when he lobs one of his beachcomber finds into the water.

Eventually, after about ten minutes or so, I decide to stop. I can't just keep walking until I hit Devon — I've left my son in the café, apart from anything else. I sit down on one of the big, water-smoothed boulders that line the bay by the cliffs, and Van joins me.

He places one of the fleece blankets over our knees, and one over our shoulders.

'We could have had one each,' I say, smiling.

'I know. But that would have foiled my masterplan to get you to snuggle up to me. Anyway, it's not too disgusting, is it?'

I feel my thigh crushed up against his, and his arm around my shoulder, and realise that I feel small and warm and safe.

'Not completely, no,' I admit, staring out at the sea and the shimmering stripes of the moonlight, rippling across the undulating waves.

'So, what's up, then? Apart from the party, that is. I can tell there's something else going on. Is it your mum?'

I shake my head, and wonder how he can possibly see so much in me. It's like he has some kind of spyglass set up in my brain.

'No, she's fine. In fact she's more than fine — Cherie's offered to let her stay in the flat for a while, so she'll be moving out.'

'I hope she takes her curtains with her.'

'Me too. But that's all good . . . it's other stuff.'

'Oh,' he says, seriously. 'Other stuff. Well, that can be a bastard. Would you like to be more specific, or should I start guessing?'

I laugh, and gently poke him in the ribs. After that my hand somehow finds its way to his thigh, where it decides to stay. He covers my fingers with his, and links them into mine.

'I was in touch with Saul's dad today,' I explain. I clearly need to talk to somebody about this, and Van is the person who knows more about it than any of my new friends. That I've been here for two years and not shared any personal information with anyone else probably tells me all I need to know about my privacy issues.

'Okay. Is that uncommon?' he asks.

'Hard to say. We've always stayed in touch, but it's been by email — maybe three times a year. All very civil. Very distant. Very grown up — like we were both trying to make up for the lack of civility we were displaying by the time we split up. This time, though, we were messaging each other on Facebook, which I know makes me sound like a teenaged girl — '

'Teenaged girls wouldn't use Facebook,' he says, grinning. 'They think it's for old people. They think it's something from the past, like thimbles, and soap dishes, and flip-phones.'

'Thank you, Mr Down-With-The-Kids. Anyway, being an old person, I do use Facebook. Occasionally a soap dish, but never a thimble. So, we were chatting. Jason and me. And he wants to see Saul, and his wife is pregnant, and Saul is going to have a baby brother or sister, and — '

'It all feels like a bit too much right now?'

'Exactly! He's even talking about meeting up when he's back in Bristol for Christmas. And I know it's not a bad thing — I know he's Saul's dad, and I don't want to be the kind of mother that keeps them apart, and ends up giving Saul all kinds of daddy issues. But even though I know that, I still feel worried.'

'Do you trust him?' he asks, frowning. 'After . . . what happened with you two?'

I know what he's alluding to, and I reply: 'Yes. I think so. He wasn't ever that keen on being a dad, to be honest. He was too young, and we were incredibly ill-matched. But when he was with Saul, he was never anything but kind.

'After we split up, before I moved here and he moved to Glasgow, we saw each other — and there weren't ever any problems. No rows. No raised voices. Nothing . . . else. Just two people who had gone quite a long way down the path of destroying their self respect. I don't think it's a coincidence that we both ended up relocating — it's like we both needed a fresh start. That was right for us both, then — but now I suppose I also need to think about what's right for Saul.'

He nods and ponders this silently, his fingers

tracing swirling patterns on the palm of my hand.

'And I suppose,' he says eventually, 'that this has all assumed monstrous proportions in your mind? In your imagination, it's gone from something small, like meeting up for a coffee, to something huge? Like Saul going there for holidays, and his dad deciding he wants to keep him, and your whole life falling to pieces?'

I let out a short, sharp laugh. He's battered the nail on the head.

'Of course. I am female. That seems to be one of our specialist subjects, doesn't it — blowing things out of proportion?'

'I couldn't possibly comment. I live with three women and I'm not falling into that trap, thank you very much. What I would say is that perhaps you need to break it down; take it one step at a time. Deal with each development as it comes, rather than try and control it all and freak yourself out with the what-might-be scenarios. That's one thing I've learned through Lynnie being in the state she is.

'Maybe you could try to concentrate on the what is happening, rather than the what-could-happen — and at the moment, the thing that's actually happening could be really positive. He's not talking about abducting Saul and running away to Marrakesh — he's talking about meeting up in your home town. And if his wife is having a baby, maybe you'd like to meet her as well? If — and I mean 'if' — Saul ends up spending any time with them, it would be good to meet her. It could put your mind at rest.'

I think about what he's said, and know that he's right. So right there's no way I can argue with it — except, I do.

'That's all true,' I say sadly. 'But somehow it's not helping. I know what I should do — but at the moment, I don't seem able. It's like it's all set off some kind of chain reaction inside me, and I'm on the verge of exploding. And yes — I need to meet his wife. And I want Saul to like her, and her to like Saul. Eventually, if it goes that far. But if I'm being honest, even that freaks me out . . . because what if she's so fantastic, Saul prefers her to me?'

There, I think. *I've said it.* It makes me feel like poo, but at least I've made myself acknowledge it — the deep, dark fear that's stubbornly lurking inside me.

I don't know quite how I expected Van to react to that admission, but I have to say, it wasn't with laughter.

Laughter is what I get, though — big, full, whole-hearted laughter. The arm around my shoulder squeezes me in tight, and he rests his chin on top of my head, his body shaking with amusement. I'm taken aback by this, and also considering punching him in a place no man likes to be punched.

'Oh, Katie, I'm sorry,' he says, once he's regained control of himself, 'but that is so stupid the only sensible response is to laugh! I can actually understand why you feel like that — it's always been you and Saul against the world and this feels threatening. But to even think for a minute that the little man would prefer someone else to his mum? A mum who loves him and laughs with him and makes him feel like the centre of the whole world? Well, that's a step too far.

'I know you don't have a lot of confidence, and I know life has taught you not to believe in yourself as much as other people do. As much as I do. But you have to listen to me when I say this: you are a great mother. Saul adores you. Nothing will ever break that bond — Saul's world getting bigger just means he'll have more people to love him, not less love to give. Is there any way you can try and believe that?'

I nod, and tell myself he's right. That I'm being foolish. I'm not sure I'm convinced, but I need to take my anxiety down a notch or ten before some vital part of my brain snaps in two.

'I'll do my best,' I say. 'And thank you. For the cheer-leading.'

'It's one of my specialist subjects,' he replies. 'I'll dress up for you next time, if you like.'

'With pompoms and everything?'

'If that's what floats your boat. Look, if you want me to, I'll come with you. When you go to Bristol. If you need the moral support or, you know, a lift.'

'I'm not sure that would help,' I answer honestly. 'It's only going to make an already awkward situation even worse, me bringing my . . . friend along. And I'm not convinced you won't go all macho on me.'

'I promise I wouldn't. I might look like a caveman, but I don't always act like one. Anyway. No pressure — just keep it in mind.

You're not alone in this. Not if you don't want to be. Now, do you think you might be ready to go back to the café? They might have noticed they're missing their guest of honour by now.'

I make a sound that is a suitable expression of my lack of enthusiasm for being the guest of honour — the noise a whoopee cushion makes when you sit on it — and he laughs again.

'I get it,' he says, 'I really do. This place can be so claustrophobic sometimes. Everybody is always in your face — in the nicest possible way. I struggle with it too. At least it's by the sea. Sometimes, when I'm feeling a bit hemmed in, or the cottage feels like a battery chicken cage, I come and sit out here and tell myself it's all okay — I'm perched at the edge of the world.'

'It must feel so small,' I reply, gazing around us. 'The village. Compared to what you're used to.'

'Well the village itself feels like a major metropolis to be honest — there's a fish and chip shop for starters. Running water. Usable roads. All the big city attractions. But yeah — the landscape is very different. The culture? Not so much. People get in your face in Africa too, once you're part of the community. But you're only ever minutes away from the most beautiful wide open spaces; the best sunsets and sunrises, the animals . . . it's a special place. Maybe I'll take you there one day.'

I stand up and stretch out my limbs. Now we've been still for a while, the cold is catching up with me, and even my eyelashes feel frosty.

'Maybe you will,' I reply, smiling at him.

'Wouldn't that be something?'

'It would,' he answers, standing up to join me. 'We'll do it, I promise. When Saul's all grown up, and I'm not sleeping on a sofa, and life is simpler. If life ever does actually get simpler. But for now . . . I'll settle for this . . . '

He's standing so close to me I can feel the warmth of his body, and the touch of his breath. He places his hands on my shoulder, and leans forward to kiss me.

It's tentative at first, as though he's giving me the chance to slap him away. I probably should, I know.

But when I don't, his arms close around me, pulling me closer, his hands sliding up to tangle into my hair, the intensity of the kiss building.

I can't deny that I've fantasised about this moment. I've imagined the touch of his lips on mine; the feel of his fingers on my skin. Of my hands, splayed across the width of his chest. I've thought about it many times — and I can honestly say that everything I'd hoped it would be is nothing at all compared to the reality.

From the minute we make contact, I'm swept away. Every thought, every anxiety, every worry — swept away. Every doubt, every question, every self-recrimination — swept away. Every pain from the past, or fear for the future — swept away. All that's left is the present: me, and Van, and the sound of the waves and the bright stars in the dark sky around us.

I don't know how long we stand there, tangled up in each other, tangled up in the moment. It could have been a minute. It could have been a lifetime.

All I know is that when we finally pull apart, our bodies still touching, our eyes locked, every part of me is tingling and alive.

'Wow,' says Van, giving me a crooked smile, his fingers still stroking my hair, his breathing coming fast and hard. 'You really do have superpowers.'

24

Laura takes forever to get out of the car, me and Saul waiting by her side as she constantly finds reasons not to leave it. She checks for her glasses in the glove box (where she just put them); she carefully places the CD we've been listening to back in its sleeve, and she puts the handbrake on and off repeatedly. Once she's out, she uses a bottle of water to clean an already clean windshield.

Eventually, when that's done, she locks the doors approximately sixteen times, checking each one individually, before slowly walking with us out of the car park. When we reach the entrance to the building, she pauses, and eyes it slowly and warily — as though it's a rabid dog about to bite her.

'Are you okay?' I ask, laying a gentle hand on her arm. Frankly, she looks like she might be about to pass out. Her skin is drawn and pale, and her pretty face is furrowed into a deep frown.

'Yes. I'll be fine. I just . . . don't like hospitals,' she replies, shaking her curls and very clearly trying to snap out of her fugue state.

'Not many people do,' I say, keeping a tight grip on Saul's hand. He's jogging up and down, pipping to get inside and visit Edie.

'I'll be okay. I just need a minute. It's because of David, you see . . . he died after a head injury,

253

and we had to turn the machines off, and it was all very, very grim. So sometimes, in a hospital, I have a bit of a funny turn. If I do, don't worry — it's not related to me being pregnant or anything.'

I nod my head, and keep my hand on her arm. Between her and Saul, I'm fully occupied now.

'I understand,' I say quietly, 'take your time. If you want to stay in the car, that's not a problem — I'll tell Edie you weren't feeling well.'

I'm not a stranger to hospitals, and they hold no fear for me — luckily they're places I see as work, not vivid reminders of hellish personal trauma. But I've been around them long enough to appreciate the fact that for most people, they don't signify a long shift and beans on toast in the canteen — they signify something much more upsetting. Especially in a case like Laura's.

Saul picks up on some tense adult thing going on around him, and gazes up at Laura's face. He inserts himself between the two of us, and takes one of our hands in each of his.

'It's okay,' he says to Laura. 'I'll look after you.'

She stares down at him, her distress causing a bit of a time lag between him speaking and her processing the words, then breaks out into a big smile.

She ruffles his hair, and beams at him as she replies: 'Thank you, sweetie. I feel much better now. Shall we go and see Edie?'

She puts one brave foot in front of the other, and together we make our way inside. Through the familiar corridors, through the familiar smells, through the familiar worried faces and harassed-looking medical staff. She blanches slightly when we pass a room with a bleeping monitor, but shakes it off and carries on.

Eventually, we reach Edie's ward. It's evening visiting, and busy, crowded with family and friends all searching for extra chairs and looking for a spare surface to lay down their chocolates and flowers and cards. I can hear that weird low-level buzz from the strip lighting humming behind the bustle and chatter, and resist the urge to start looking at charts.

We find Edie in a corner spot by the windows, propped up on pillows, her silver head bowed over her iPad. I pause for a moment myself, and say a little prayer of thanks to whoever might be listening. I don't think anybody quite realises how miraculous this is — for a woman of her age to recover from pneumonia. If I'd been pushed at the time, having seen the state of her lying in her bed at home, I'd have bet against it.

Saul breaks free as soon as he spots her, dashing straight over to her bed, and clambering right up to sit next to her. He throws his small arms around her shoulders, and gives her a kiss.

I follow on quickly, worried that she might still have an IV in, or be in some discomfort that an agile three-and-a-half-year-old chunky monkey might exacerbate.

I needn't have been concerned. Edie is hugging him back, and is blessedly free of a drip. There's still a cannula in the back of one hand, and the skin around it is purple and bruised, but other than that she looks good. Frail, as is to be expected, but good.

I gently pull Saul down from the bed, and lean forward to give Edie a kiss on the cheek. Her wrinkled skin feels like parchment, but her grip is firm as she takes hold of my hand.

'Thank you,' she whispers. 'For finding me. I'll be home in no time, and it's all down to you.'

I smile and tell her it was nothing, and settle myself in the chair next to the bed, Saul on my lap. Laura hovers at the end of the bed, apparently not quite ready to commit to actually being seated.

'How are you, my dear?' asks Edie, peering at her over her tiny specs. 'How's the precious cargo?'

Laura's hand instinctively goes to her tummy, and she manages a smile.

'All doing brilliantly, thanks, Edie. You look great. I'm so sorry I haven't been in before, but . . . '

She trails off, and Edie waves her papery hands, dismissing the comment.

'Don't be foolish,' she replies firmly. 'I wasn't fit company for the first few days anyway. Afraid I put poor Becca through the mill, acting as though it was still wartime, all kinds of nonsense! It's wonderful to see you all . . . especially you, Saul. There's a new episode online, you know.'

Saul perks up at this, stops fidgeting, and stares at her intently.

'Can we watch it? Can we? Please?'

Edie nods, and fiddles with the screen of her iPad while Laura and I exchange confused looks. Within seconds, she's found what she was apparently looking for, and hands it to Saul. I peer over his shoulder to try and see what it is that they're both so excited about.

It's something on YouTube — something that comes with some terribly cheesy music, some vivid coloured graphics, and lots of animated cartoon make-up and hair products who have tiny hands and feet and faces. They all do a little dance around one of those lightbulb framed mirrors you see in film versions of a star's dressing room, and then the lipstick speaks: 'Kick off your heels, kittens! Sit back, and prepare to be pampered . . . it's time for your session at the Beauty Parlour!'

Saul is completely enraptured as a lady with a pink beehive, wearing a Fifties style pencil skirt and a pink polka-dot blouse, starts to explain that in this episode, we'll be able to discover 'everything you ever wanted to know about the bouffant and the bob'. I can't say that I ever wanted to know very much about either, but Saul is fascinated by the flashed up pictures of Jackie Kennedy and Grace Kelly and other Fifties stars, along with the voiceover that promises that within the next fifteen minutes, you'll learn all the secrets to recreating your own Hollywood look.

It does, of course, explain a lot — including my frequent makeovers. It also, thankfully, looks like it's going to keep Saul thoroughly entertained. I'm guessing he's been a regular viewer with Edie, all those times he's been sitting with her in the café.

'Mummy,' he says, without even taking his

eyes from the screen, 'these are really nice looks. Maybe I can do one before Van comes to have tea with us . . . '

Laura's eyes widen, and she makes a 'oooh' noise as she grins at me. Edie follows up with a speculative 'Oh my!' I try not to take the bait, but can't help a very small smile.

It's been four days since Van and I kissed on the beach. Four very busy days — the usual stuff, like work and college and Saul, but also sorting Mum out in her new temporary abode, helping Sam with Little Edie while Becca's been doing shifts at the hospital, and spending a few hours with Lynnie when all three of the siblings were otherwise occupied.

Busy is good. Busy distracts me from worrying about things, like our impending trip to Bristol to meet Jason and Jo. It distracts me from the fact that my dad is AWOL, getting all mindful in the Canary Islands. It distracts me from the fact that my mum is now at the café, which makes it no longer a place of refuge. It distracts me from the fact that Christmas is almost here, and I don't feel quite ready for it.

It also distracts me from my main distraction — which is reliving that one kiss, over and over again. That wouldn't be a problem if not for the fact that even thinking about it makes me go all wobbly and weird, like I suddenly start seeing the world through a soft focus lens. I try and keep a lid on it as I go about my daily business, but I usually find my mind drifting in his direction as I lie in bed at night. Which, you know, leads to some interesting dreams.

If you'd asked me how I'd feel before it happened, I'd have expected the kiss to have made things more complicated. To be concerned about it, and what it might mean, and how it might affect our future.

In reality, something quite strange has happened — all I actually feel about it is happy. And excited. And curious as to how it would feel to do it again. To kiss him, and touch him, and lose myself in him. Basically, I think I've probably turned into a sex maniac, and that's somehow managed to override the worries about what could go wrong. And all it took was one kiss. Who'd have thought it? Not me.

'It's nothing to raise your eyebrows at, ladies,' I say, hoping none of my newfound lustiness shows in my face. 'Just a friend, coming round for some dinner.'

'He's bringing us a Christmas tree,' pipes up Saul, eyes still glued to the screen, a slight lisp on the 'r' of his words that makes him sound super-cute.

He's sounding less babyish every day now, apart from the brilliant way he gets words mixed up — the radiators are the 'radios', yellow is sometimes still 'lellow', hedgehogs are 'spikely', a combo of spiky and prickly. The rolled 'r' only comes when he's distracted or sleepy, like now. I can't believe he'll be going to school next year, my not-so-tiny baby boy.

'Oh! How lovely!' gushes Laura in response to Saul's comment, finally bringing herself to perch on the end of Edie's bed. 'Matt brought me a tree the first Christmas we were together . . . it

259

was so macho I almost melted into a puddle! Lizzie said I was betraying the spirit of Emmeline Pankhurst by being such a pushover!'

'We're not together,' I reply hastily, hoping that Saul isn't listening any more.

Edie and Laura share knowing looks, and Edie adds: 'You just tell yourself whatever makes you happy, dear. But I'm betting the Budbury magic has worked its charm again. Give it time — you might be in the same state as Laura in a few years!'

Saul, obviously, *is* listening. He looks at me, and then looks at Laura, frowning in confusion.

'You mean she might have curly hair?' he asks innocently.

'That's exactly what I mean, young man,' replies Edie seriously. 'Now, ladies . . . fill me in on all the gossip! I don't want to lose touch with the real world, like some of the old dears in here . . . '

As Edie herself is 92, I'm slightly flummoxed by what her idea of an 'old dear' is, but Laura and I oblige. We stay for another half hour, telling her all about the party, and updating her on Tinkerbell's bird-hunting missions, telling her about my mum being added to the café staff, and describing the new range of Christmas-themed puddings that Laura's put on the menu.

Edie sounds excited about that, and declares that 'my fiancé' will love it too. I know she's asked Becca to keep an eye on her fiancé while she's been gone, and Becca, bless her, has actually gone and stood in Edie's empty house. She said it was quite spooky, and she was half

260

expecting the ghost of the long-gone Bert to wander in from the kitchen.

By the time we leave, Saul is yawning, and so is Edie. He gives her another full-body hug, and we make our way out of the hospital.

'Phew,' says Laura, once we're safely back in her car and Saul's installed in his car seat. 'I actually feel like I can breathe again. She looks great, doesn't she? I'm glad we came — but I'm relieved to be out of there. I'm dreading the whole birth thing, you know? I was trying to persuade them to let me have the babies at home, but apparently that's a no-go, because it's twins and because I'm so . . . *geriatric!*'

She hisses the last word with about as much enthusiasm as any woman would, as she starts the car engine and navigates us out of the car park.

'Well, obviously you're not geriatric in the real world, Laura. It's just one of those terms medical people sometimes use without thinking it through. And twins can be more complicated, so I have to agree that maybe you'd be better off in hospital . . . anyway. Maybe it'll change the way you feel about them.'

'What?' she scoffs. 'Hours of agony followed by an emergency C-section? I can't imagine that's going to be a barrel of laughs!'

'No. Probably not — but there's no guarantee it'll happen like that. It'll probably all go smoothly. And after it, however it happens, you'll be a new mum. You'll have two beautiful, healthy babies, and Matt will be a dad, and Lizzie and Nate will have little brothers or sisters, and it'll be the start of a wonderful new adventure. I bet that's worth a trip to hospital, isn't it?'

She keeps her eyes on the road, but I see a slow smile creep over her face as she thinks about it.

'You know what, Katie? That's completely true. It will be worth it. And maybe I'll replace my last hideous hospital experience with something so much nicer . . . new life, rather than losing someone I love.'

'Exactly. It's so exciting.'

'Exciting, and a tiny bit terrifying . . . it always is, starting something new. Especially when you have kids to factor in. I can imagine that's how you must be feeling, about . . . Van!'

She whispers the last word, presumably for Saul's benefit — but she needn't have bothered; he's completely conked out behind us, head lolling on one side, chubby fists splayed at his sides. Like someone's taken out the batteries.

'We're just friends,' I insist, though I suspect the twitch in the side of my mouth might give me away.

'You'd make a terrible poker player,' she says, laughing. 'But if you don't want to talk about it, that's fine. Do you? Want to talk about it?'

She sounds so young and so curious and so hopeful that I'm almost tempted to crack. It would be a relief in some ways, to get it out in the open — to gossip about it like a pair of teenagers, discussing the cute boy in the year above who always winks at us outside the PE hall.

'No,' I say, firmly — because I'm not a

262

teenager any more, and I don't even know what's happening with Van myself — never mind enough to discuss with anyone else.

She makes a disappointed 'hmmph' sound, and we make the rest of the journey without touching on the subject again — for which I am truly grateful.

By the time we reach the village, the roads are quiet, the night's frost already adding a diamante sheen to the pavements. I see fairy lights glittering in Becca's window, and the outline of a tree in Cal and Zoe's house, and have to admit that it's beginning to feel a lot like Christmas.

Even more so when we spot Van, standing at the back of his truck, wrapped up in a body-warmer and a dark beanie hat, his gloved hands waving at us as we approach. Laura pulls up in her Picasso, but doesn't get out — can't say that I blame her.

She waves at Van, gives a beep of the horn, and then drives off in the direction of the Rockery. I wonder briefly how they're going to sort their living arrangements when the twins arrive — at the moment Laura and her kids are in a three-bedroomed cottage called Hyacinth; Matt is in the biggest of the buildings, Black Rose. Maybe they'll merge. Maybe they'll keep it like it is. Maybe it's none of my business.

I gather a sleepy Saul in my arms and cross the road, standing in front of Van and eyeing the contents of the back of the truck.

Saul briefly wakes up, grins at Van, and passes out again. He's slobbering on my neck. One of those lovely motherhood moments.

263

'Your truck is taking up half the pavement,' I say, smiling to show I'm joking. 'That's very inconvenient for people with pushchairs, you know.'

'I can only apologise,' he replies, reaching out to swirl his fingers gently across Saul's tufty hair. 'But as the street is completely deserted I think we'll get away with it. I'll move it after I've unloaded; I didn't fancy carrying this beast any further than I need to. Not that I'm not strong enough or anything, before you go doubting my manliness.'

I raise my eyebrows — that's one thing I definitely don't doubt — and stagger to the front door. This boy of mine is getting very heavy now. I manage to get the key into the door and kick it open, a complex manoeuvre that mothers soon get used to — juggling a child in one arm, doing something completely different with the other. I can make tea, load laundry, and put pizza in the oven, all with one hand.

Tinkerbell rushes to greet us in a flurry of ginger fluff, then suddenly seems to remember he's a cat, and starts to play it cool instead. He winds around my ankles a few times, then heads off into the street to investigate his kingdom.

I carry Saul into the living room and lay him in the corner of the sofa. I hand him a cushion, and he hugs it to him, like I knew he would.

He's awake, but still half asleep, if you know what I mean. On any other night I'd take him straight up to bed, but I know the chances of him sleeping through Van being here, and the Christmas tree arriving, are non-existent.

Besides, I wouldn't want to deprive him of the chance to start the decorations. He's far more aware of Christmas this year, and is at the age where he totally believes in all the magic — I know that won't last forever, so I need to treasure it.

As ever, my brain does a complex analysis of when Saul last had a wee, and if he might need to go to the toilet — he's at the stage where he's definitely out of nappies, but still occasionally has an accident if he leaves it too late to ask, or is so engrossed in doing something exciting that he forgets. This can include, but is not limited to, watching cartoons, playing with his Crocodile Dentist game, eating Mr Freeze ice pops, applying my make-up, or reading *The Gruffalo*.

I remind myself he went just before we left the hospital, so all is good. I get him a beaker of watery juice from the kitchen, and he sits sucking on it, curled up in a ball with his cushion, still recovering from the trials and tribulations of being three.

I sit myself down on the armchair, and prepare to be entertained. I hear the clank of the truck gate being lowered, and some huffing and puffing as Van hoists the tree down. The huffing and puffing develops into a full-on swear as he attempts to get it up the front step and into the house. There's a sudden pause, as he realises what he's done, then he shouts: 'Sorry for the language!'

'Do you need any help?' I shout back, kicking off my trainers and tucking my legs up beneath myself on the chair. I'm guessing he'll say no.

'Nope, I'm fine . . . ' he yells. 'Or at least I will be, once I get this . . . *flipping* thing through the door!'

Eventually, he makes it, and emerges into the living room with the tree trunk over his shoulder, and the green pine-needle laden branches drooping all around him. His face peers out, like he's in a jungle filming a wildlife video, and he grins in victory.

'Where do you want it?' he asks, trying to hide the fact that he's slightly out of breath.

'In the corner . . . or maybe by the window . . . oh, I really can't make my mind up. Can we try it in a few places and see which looks best?'

He stares at me from behind the foliage, eyes narrowed, until I crack: 'Just kidding. Over in the corner. Thank you.'

He nods, and carries the tree to the spot I point at. He's already attached a kind of wooden disc at the bottom for it to stand up on, and he fluffs the branches out once it's stable.

'What do you think?' he asks, standing back, wiping sweat from his forehead.

'It's not as big as I thought it would be . . . ' I say, actually delighted at that — I'd expected him to bring the biggest he could find, which would have been a mistake, as our house is only small.

'I bet you say that to all the boys,' he replies, laughing. 'Have you no respect for the fragile male ego?'

'Well, perhaps I should rephrase that. What I meant was, it's not too big, and not too small, and not too bushy, and not too sparse. It's

266

perfect. It's the kind of tree Goldilocks would have chosen — exactly right. Thank you. It's really kind of you.'

He nods, once, and looks pleased, before noticing Saul curled up on the sofa, back asleep. I gently take the juice beaker from his hands and put it down on the table. He murmurs but doesn't open his eyes.

'What shall we do about the little man?' he asks quietly. 'Let him be, or wake him up with a party popper?'

'Let him be for twenty minutes. We'll wake him up to do the decorating in a bit. He'll be cranky if he needs a nap, and it'll give me time to start dinner, and you to . . . I don't know. Whatever it is that fragile male egos need to do.'

'In my case, move my truck so I don't inconvenience any passing pushchairs. But before I do that, just nip into the hallway for a minute, I've got something for you.'

I tear my gaze away from admiring the tree, and tiptoe out of the living room door behind him. I'm still pondering how much tinsel we're going to need when he takes hold of my waist, pushes me back against the wall, and kisses me. I use one foot to kick the door closed in case Saul wakes up, then wrap my arms around his neck and kiss him back.

It's another absolute powerhouse of a kiss, and definitely proves the first one on the beach wasn't a fluke. I let my hands explore the bulk of his shoulders, the firm outline of his arms, drifting down to his side and slipping my fingers beneath his T-shirt. He's pressed up hard against

267

me, and the touch of his skin beneath my hands is completely intoxicating.

His lips move to the side of my neck, kissing their way down to my collarbone, and I groan as I feel his hands pull my hips even closer to his. I'm on the verge of losing what little self-control I have by this point, and am wondering how it would feel to wrap my legs around his waist and get even closer.

When Van puts his hands on the wall either side of my face and pushes away a few inches, my first thought is, *please bring back the nice thing.* The second is, *pretty please bring back the nice thing.* But my third, to be fair, is, *my son is sleeping in the next room and could walk through at any minute.*

Van takes in my disappointed expression, the flush I can feel creeping over my cheeks, and smiles. He leans his forehead forward so it touches mine, and says: 'I didn't want to stop either. I promise. Don't look so crestfallen. But . . . '

'Yeah. I know. But. I'm pretty sure we could tell Saul we were playing a game, but he'd just tell everyone else all about it next time we're in the café. This is tricky, isn't it? Not that I really know what this is.'

He nuzzles my neck for a few seconds before replying: 'Me neither. But I like it. I like you. And I don't want to rush it — it took me months to even persuade you to come to the pub. I know it's complicated. I know you'll want to take things slowly, and that's fine with me.'

I drape my arms around his waist, and close

the small gap he's opened up between our bodies. I can feel that he's still very, very interested in the physical aspects of this, and it makes me grin. It's been a long time since I had that kind of effect on a man, and I can't deny it feels good. Especially as I feel exactly the same.

I duck from beneath his arms and sit on the stairs, patting them to invite him to join me. He tugs his rumpled T-shirt into shape and sits by my side, one arm thrown across my shoulders.

'Thing is,' I say, laying my hand on his thigh and telling it to behave itself, 'that at least part of this is very simple. The sex part. As in, I want to have sex. With you.'

He jolts very slightly, and I realise I've shocked him. To be honest, I've shocked myself as well.

'Look,' I say quietly — this is not the kind of conversation I want Saul overhearing — 'I know there are all sorts of complications. Both of us are at this weird stage of our lives where everything seems to revolve around other people. For me, it's Saul mainly, but also my parents right now. For you, obviously, Lynnie's needs come first.'

'Go on,' he says, nudging me. 'I'm intrigued.'

'Well, despite all of that, I still can't stop thinking about you. Specifically, about kissing you. And touching you. And being . . . with you.'

I glance up at his face, and see that he's grimacing slightly — which isn't the reaction I'd anticipated.

'Sorry,' he says, when he notices me looking. 'It's just that I'm a bloke. A bloke who's just kissed a hot woman. And now you're saying things like this, and it's making me . . . uncomfortable again, if you get my drift.'

I do indeed get his drift. I can pretty much see his drift as well, which is both amusing and gratifying.

'So,' he continues. 'You're saying you want this to . . . progress?'

'Yes. I do. But even as I say it, I'm a bit worried about it. Because it might get messy. It might get complicated. We might screw everything up, and neither of us has time for drama. I have to be totally honest with you, Van — I'm not looking for a big heavy relationship. I don't have the time or the energy or the courage. That's why it took me so long to go to the pub with you — maybe I always had a sneaky suspicion that we'd end up like this.'

'With me in agony on your bottom step?'

'Not precisely, no . . . sorry about that. But I knew I found you attractive, and I was worried about where it might lead.'

'And now you're not? Worried?'

I sigh and bite my lip, struggling to find the right words to express how I feel — mainly because I don't even know.

'I am about some aspects of it. But I'm also . . . ready. More than ready. For the physical side of it, anyway. I know it's complicated. Everything is — and I'm sick to death of complicated. But the way I feel when you kiss me? That's the only time things feel simple.'

'So,' he replies, a smile in his voice, 'the obvious solution is that I should just kiss you twenty-four hours a day?'

'That's a nice idea,' I say. Because it is. 'But I don't think it's practical. Might cause a few issues at work.'

He nods, and I see him turning all of this over in his mind. I'm hoping he has some answers for me, but I'm not sure any of this makes sense to me any more.

'I'm just trying to decide,' he eventually says, 'whether I feel insulted at being used as your sex toy, worried about breaking your heart, or excited about the prospect of seeing you naked. I've got to say, option number three keeps intruding on the other two — but the other two do matter.

'As I've said, I like you. I'm not getting down on one knee and proposing or anything, but I like you enough to think this might be more than sex. More than just physical. I enjoy your company, and feel relaxed when I'm with you, and see you as a friend. A friend I fancy. I'm not quite sure how all of that fits in with your version of things?'

'Me neither,' I reply, shaking my head and laughing. 'And I must warn you, I usually overthink things — so it's entirely possible that I'm saying one thing now, and then I'll feel differently later. It's a rollercoaster. You're so lucky to have me in your life to confuse you.'

He tugs me up against him, and kisses the top of my head.

'I am lucky,' he says. 'And horny. And yeah, now very confused. I was all set for a slow burn here, just to feel things out and see how we worked through it. Now you've gone and messed

271

up the masterplan.'

'My specialist subject,' I say, leaning my head against his chest. 'Anyway — I don't suppose it's something we need to decide right now. As my son is asleep in the next room, this is about as sexy as it's going to get tonight. And I don't know when that will change — I share my house with a curious toddler who already thinks you're God's gift to the planet and follows you everywhere, and you share a cottage with your elderly mother and your sisters. We're not exactly rocking it on the *sexy night in* front, are we?'

'I suppose not — not yet at least. Though I had a chat with Tom about that the other day. He found me on the floor in a sleeping bag. Auburn was being a nightmare — she was all hyper because she's helping Tom out with these interviews to find his Star Lord. I couldn't face another night in a single bed in a room with her, and my legs are wrecked from being crammed on a too-short sofa, so I ended up on the floor. As you say, not sexy. So Tom offered to lend me his camper van.'

'His camper van? Doesn't he live at Briarwood? Aren't there enough rooms there for him?'

'He does have rooms at Briarwood, and a flat in London and, knowing Tom, a bolt-hole on the moon as well — but he also has this really nice, retro VW van he used when he first moved here. It's parked up in the woods near Briarwood.'

'Oh. So would you move there?' I ask, frowning. It's very possible the excitement of the last few minutes has blown a brain circuit.

'No. It's on wheels, see? It's mobile. He'll drive it to the cottage and we can park it up on the drive, so I'm still around, but everyone gets a bit more privacy.'

'I'm not convinced that's much better. I'd feel a bit . . . weird, right outside your cottage. What if your mum heard us?'

'How loud are you planning on getting?'

'I don't know . . . you tell me!'

We grin at each other, and it feels good. Natural. Easy. I haven't flirted for many years, and I'm enjoying it.

'Well, we'll have to wait and see,' he replies. 'But again, I refer you to the fact that it's on wheels. The world's our lobster.'

I nod, and roll that around in my mind. Okay, so it's hardly a mini-break to Paris — but the idea of spending a night with Van in a camper, somewhere secluded and quiet and beautiful, isn't exactly repellent. And with my mum here at the moment, I could probably even make it happen, if she agreed to have Saul for a sleepover.

Crikey. I'm starting to think this might even happen. And I'm even starting to think I might go for it.

I hear muffled movement from the other room, the sound of small feet padding around, and then the ever-so-gentle screech of 'MUMMY!!! Come and look at our tree! It's giant-gantic!'

It might happen, for sure. *But not*, I think, standing to my feet and walking back into the living room, *tonight*.

25

I'm not especially keen on reptiles, but at least it's warm in here. Outside, it's bitterly cold, and snow is forecast for later today.

I've dragged out the snakes and geckos and giant tortoises for as long as I can, and Saul's attention is waning. He wants to see something more exciting, like the gorillas or the lions or the little hippos. Or his dad — one of the lesser known exhibits at Bristol Zoo.

Frankly, I'm nervous, and would probably rather walk into the lion enclosure than stroll across to the café, where we're due to meet Jason and Jo. I've played it as casually as possible with Saul, trying to strike the balance between this being a real treat, and it not being too big a deal. He knows his dad lives in Scotland, which he talks about as though it's an incredibly exotic place, and he knows his dad loves him and always sends him presents and cards.

He's spoken to him on the phone as well, on his last birthday, but he hasn't actually seen him since a time he was too small to even remember.

Saul actually seems very cool about it all, accepting it without too many questions and with an open-hearted sense of anticipation that reassures me I'm doing the right thing. The right thing for him, anyway.

Because while Saul might be okay with today's

meeting, I'm basically pooing my pants. It's all very, very strange.

We came to Bristol last night, and stayed in my parents' house. That in itself was weird and a bit melancholy. Mum is down in Budbury, and Dad is due home from Tenerife very soon, and the home I grew up in felt oddly quiet and empty without them.

Saul enjoyed it, laughing at the photos of me on the wall in frames: me with pigtails and missing front teeth; me in my ballet outfit after a dance performance; me on the beach on a family holiday to Cornwall. No child ever easily imagines their own parents as young, do they? Even when we're adults, and technically know they were, once, tiny little humans — it still seems unlikely.

Saul thinks the photos are hilarious. I on the other hand feel sad when I look at them. Sad because I'm always on my own — no brothers and sisters, no playmates, not even any happy, smiling family group shots.

For me, they're a reminder of lonely times. A reminder of the chaos around me that the lens never quite caught. The night of that dance recital, Mum locked Dad out of the house because he'd turned up with the smell of beer on his breath.

After the triumph of the show itself — I must have been about eight, I suppose — I recall the rest of the night being fraught with drama, Dad banging on the door and Mum screaming at him from the bedroom window. That might have been the night one of the neighbours actually called the police, I don't know — they all fade into one big row with the passing of time.

And the family holiday in Cornwall was one of the worst weeks of my life — all three of us crammed into a two-bedroomed caravan on a park near Bude. They'd drink too much in the leisure club where we'd watch the entertainment staff sing hits of the Seventies, and a giant bear mascot prowled around scaring the kids. After the drink, there'd be the fighting — and the walls of a caravan are even thinner than the walls of a house.

I'm not sure it was a good idea, going back there. But again, Saul seemed happy with the arrangement, and that's what matters. He got to sleep in my old bedroom, and I showed him pictures of my nan and told him all about her, and I took him to the little play park nearby where I'd gone as a child myself.

And now we're here. In the zoo. Approximately five minutes away from meeting my ex and his new wife and soon-to-be mother of Saul's baby brother or sister. I tell myself it's a good thing. That it's important for Saul to feel good about his relationship with them. That maybe having a sibling will make his childhood a lot less lonely than mine, because it seems unlikely I'll ever be providing him with one.

I can't even find it in myself to commit to a relationship, never mind have a baby. I do wonder sometimes if something inside me is simply broken, and I'll never be able to fix it. Having Van in my life should feel wonderful — and when I'm with him, it usually does.

But when I'm away from him, like now, it all feels different. It feels frightening and anxiety-inducing and probably not worth the risk. I turn into a big fat coward, basically. Poor Van. He deserves better. Like the blonde one from Abba, or at the very least a woman who doesn't blow hot and cold like a faulty car heater.

I glance at my watch, and tell Saul it's time to go.

'Will my daddy be there now?' he asks, scurrying along so fast he's taking two steps to every one of mine as we leave the reptile house and emerge into an arctic blast of wind that makes my eyes water.

I quickly bend down to fasten up Saul's coat and tug his bobble hat back down over his ears, and nod.

'He will,' I reply, trying to put some much-needed enthusiasm into my voice. 'Isn't that exciting?'

'It is,' he replies, gripping my hand with his mittened fingers. 'He's come all the way from a different country. Do they have lions in Scotland? And will Daddy be able to make a lion noise? And will the lady called Jo speak in a different language because she's from Scotland?'

I answer all his rapid-fire questions as well as I can — only in zoos, definitely, and no — as we make the short walk to the café. We pause in the entrance, and I take off his hat and unbutton his coat again. It's an exciting life, looking after a small person. A rollercoaster of indoor-outdoor clothing logistics.

I scan the room, filled with shivering refugees

from the icy weather, looking for them. Maybe, just a tiny bit, hoping they haven't turned up.

Of course, they have — I spot Jason easily, even after all this time. He's very tall, even sitting down. The woman with him is almost the same height, and it occurs to me that their child is going to inherit some mighty genetics.

Jason waves hesitantly, and I suspect he's just as nervous as I am. Maybe he was secretly hoping we wouldn't turn up as well.

'Is that him? Is that my daddy?' Saul asks, when I wave back. I nod and smile, and feel a creaking sensation inside me, like a rotten floorboard being stepped on.

We walk over to their table, and as we approach, Jason never takes his eyes off Saul. Saul, who is keen to run towards them, and possibly the muffins they have on a plate. I let go of his hand, and he dashes the last few feet, the mittens on strings streaking behind him.

He stops right in front of Jason, who crouches down to be on the same level as him, and smiles at him. He plays it just right — not grabbing hold of him and freaking him out, not showing his own tension, just talking to him in a soft voice, saying how lovely it is to see him and asking what animals he wants to see and wondering if he prefers chocolate or blueberry muffins.

He hasn't changed that much, in the last few years. He looks a little leaner, maybe, and his hair is a bit longer. Jo, sitting beside him, glances up at me and smiles, giving me her own little wave. I linger a few steps away, not really sure of how to behave. There aren't really any rule books for this kind of situation, and I'm sure we're all scared of getting it wrong.

Luckily, we have a talkative toddler with us — possibly the world's best ice-breaker.

'I like blueberry,' Saul says, perching himself on the seat next to Jason and chattering away as though all of this is completely normal. 'Laura makes blueberry cake for me at the café.'

'Does she? I bet it's yummy,' replies Jason, looking on as Saul tears off his coat and grabs hold of a muffin. He's going to perform his usual trick of reducing one cake to a billion small pieces, I know — but I don't suppose it matters.

'It is. The yummiest. You should come and taste it.'

'Maybe I will,' says Jason, glancing at me over Saul's head. I finally make the move to sit down, and he nods at me. 'Saul, this lady here is Jo.'

'Hi, Saul!' she says brightly. I know she's a primary school teacher, and it shows in her voice — the kind of voice that kids automatically respond to; that you can imagine leading an assembly or singing the times tables. 'It's really nice to meet you. Blueberry's my favourite too.'

Saul squints at her slightly, while he chews his first mouthful. His fingers are working on the rest.

'You sound funny,' he eventually says. 'Mummy said you wouldn't speak different.'

'I said she wouldn't speak a different language, Saul,' I add, explaining. 'Not that she wouldn't sound different. People who come from different parts of the world have different accents. Like

Laura is from Manchester and she sounds different to your nan, who's from Bristol.'

He chews this over as thoroughly as his muffin and decides it makes sense.

'Did you have to come on an aeroplane?' he asks, perking up again. He's obsessed with going on an aeroplane at the moment, and decided after watching a film called *Monsters vs Aliens* that he wants to be an astronaut when he grows up, so he can make friends with little green men.

'Not this time, no,' replies Jo, automatically sweeping some of the crumbs from the table in a way that suggests she's done it many times before. 'We came in the car, but it took us two days.'

'Did you sleep in the car?' Saul asks, frowning.

'No, we stayed overnight in a hotel on the way. A nice one with a swimming pool that had pancakes for breakfast.'

'I like pancakes,' he concedes. 'Laura makes those too. Mummy does as well, but Laura's are nicer.'

I raise my eyebrows and let out a small laugh. I can't argue that point, and it's good that he's honest, after all.

Saul stops destroying his muffin, and looks at the map of the zoo that they have spread out on part of the table. Jason uses his finger to point out where we are, and where the reptile house is, and where some of the other animals are.

'Do you know a lot of animal noises, Daddy?' he asks earnestly. It's the first time he's addressed him like that, and I see a quick and sudden sheen of tears in Jason's eyes. I bite my lip, because I feel a bit like crying too. I know my reasons for agreeing to this were sound, but I'm simply not a big enough human being to not feel threatened by it. I need to toughen up.

'Yes. It's one of my best things,' answers Jason seriously. 'What do you want to hear?'

The two of them spend the next few minutes challenging each other to recognise various roars, squeaks and howls. I go to get myself a coffee to give them a bit of space, and to give myself a breather. I kind of wish there was a brandy in it.

By the time I come back, Saul is on his feet, doing that mad little bouncing-on-the-spot thing he does when he's excited about something.

'Mummy, can I go and see the gorillas with Daddy? We both want to see if they answer us when we make our gorilla noises! Please please please!'

Jason's eyes meet mine across the table, and I'm so nervous I slosh my coffee into the saucer. The gorillas are literally only minutes away. He's not asking for custody, he's asking for ten minutes. It's normal, it's natural, and it's nothing to get choked up about. I gulp in air, and manage to nod.

'Of course you can,' I say, aiming for relaxed. 'Just make sure you put your coat and hat back on. Say hello to the gorillas for me.'

Jason mouths the words 'thank you' at me, and the two disappear off in a flurry of scarves and excitement. I see Saul slip his hand into Jason's, and feel a mix of relief and desperation. He'll be back before I know it, but he still takes a tiny

281

piece of me with him.

'He's gorgeous,' says Jo, as I sit down opposite her. Her accent doesn't sound Glaswegian to my admittedly untrained ear. It's soft, and lilting and gentle.

'He is, isn't he?' I reply, smiling as best as I can.

'He'll be starting school next year, will he?'

'Yes. The local primary. He can already read some words and write his name, as long as you have a liberal stance on which way round the letter 'S' should face.'

'Well he'll be off to a flying start then. I teach P1, which is like reception in England, and I can tell he won't have any problems at all — I bet he'll be more than ready.'

I grimace as I sip scalding hot coffee, and reply: 'I hope so. I'm not sure how ready I am, though.'

'That's always the way,' she replies, using a napkin to clear up the coffee I've now spilled. 'The kids come through the gate full of excitement, and the mums are weeping in the playground.'

I nod, unable to think of a single thing to say. It's like my brain has gone completely blank, and my tongue has superglued itself to the roof of my mouth.

'This must be weird for you,' she says eventually.

'Um . . . yes. But I think it's probably weird for everybody, apart from Saul, apparently.'

'That'll be down to you, raising a happy and confident little person. Look . . . it doesn't have to be weird. I can only imagine how you must be feeling, us turning up, a baby on the way, suddenly part of Saul's life. All I can say is that we're genuine — both of us — about wanting to get to know Saul better. You're his mum, and obviously a good one — but one day before too long, he'll have a brother, and it would be great for them to know each other.'

I stare at her, my eyes flickering to her stomach against my will. She's wearing a thick jumper, so I can't tell if she's showing or not yet. I remember those days — the combination of excitement and terror. Or maybe, in her case, there is no terror — she's older than I was, and obviously happy in her marriage, and she teaches kids for a living. Maybe she doesn't just look like Wonder Woman. Maybe she is Wonder Woman.

'Yes, it would,' is all I can manage. 'It's a boy?'

Her hand goes to her tummy, and she grins.

'At least that's what they think, yes. So thank you — for this. For seeing us. It means the world to Jason, and to me. He told me, you know . . . what happened between you. All of it.'

For some reason, I cringe as she says this. I don't know why. I have nothing to be ashamed of, and it's only natural that he has. Proof that they have a much better functioning relationship than Jason and I ever did. But I still feel somehow exposed — like this woman knowing so much about one of the darkest times in my life makes me somehow vulnerable.

'Oh. Okay,' I murmur, still apparently in shut-down mode.

'And you should know, it changed him. He

probably won't tell you all of this, because he's a man. But it changed him. He's not touched a drop of alcohol since that day, and he went to counselling. Still does, every now and then. He hated what he'd done, and that's probably why he left Bristol. But . . . well, I'm sure you know that.'

I nod, and avoid her eyes. She has vivid blue eyes that I suspect can see right into my soul.

'I know. We . . . brought out the worst in each other. It's why I moved as well. But you two . . . you seem to bring out the best in each other.'

She beams at me, and passes me another napkin. I'm really not managing very well with this whole advance level coffee-drinking business at all.

'We do, I hope. I just wanted you to know that I understand. And that we won't be putting any pressure on you, or on Saul — we just want to know him. To be part of his life in any way that works for all of us.'

I know she means well. I know she means every word she says. I even know she's right.

But that still doesn't take away the fear. The fear that bit by bit, I'm falling to pieces. That all the control I've worked so hard for is crumbling. That everything is about to change, and I don't want it to. That I want to take Saul, and possibly Tinkerbell, and run as far away as we all can.

That, I realise, is ridiculous. It's an outdated impulse, a knee-jerk response to a perceived threat. Something I need to manage or analyse or possibly just ignore until it goes away.

I nod firmly, and force myself to look up from

the napkin-strewn table and meet her eyes.

'Okay,' I say simply. One word. A lifetime of meaning.

26

I get three calls from Van during the journey home, and I ignore all of them. Then he texts me, asking if I want a lift from the train station in Applechurch. Then I turn my phone off, and slam it into my bag. I can't face anyone right now — I need some space to process all of this.

The rest of our visit with Jason and Jo passed well enough. Nobody cried, even me. Saul was happy to see them, but happy to say goodbye as well. Jason bought him a giant stuffed toy gorilla from the gift shop, and it takes up its own seat on the train. Saul drifts in and out of sleep all the way home, tired out from all the excitement and walking. He cuddles up on my lap on the bus for the last part of the journey, and is perfectly content to collapse in a heap on the sofa when we finally get home.

He's watching *The Jungle Book*, the old cartoon version. The gorilla next to him, Tinkerbell curled in a ball by the toy's side. The three musketeers.

Once he's settled, I wander into the kitchen and make myself a cup of tea. It takes a lot longer than it should, due to my impaired mental state. First I put the kettle on to boil without any water in it. Then I put the water in, but forget to switch it on. Then I put both coffee granules and a tea bag in the same mug. Then I add a lovely dollop of mayonnaise to the tea instead of milk.

I'm really not feeling like myself.

It's not that late — just after 8 p.m. — but it's pitch black outside. The snow is coming down in gentle flurries, and I'm grateful for the warmth and cosiness of our little house. The Christmas tree lights are switched on, a blaze of yellow sparkles, and the sound of the movie fills the house. I'm here. Saul's here. We're safe. The bear necessities of life.

I lean back against the kitchen counter, and sip the tea I've finally managed to make. I look through to the other room, at Saul with his juice, and the gorilla and the cat, and realise how exhausted I am. Not just by the journey, but by everything.

My parents. Jason and Jo. Van. The trip down memory lane in Bristol. The complications of everybody else's lives — Lynnie, and Edie, and Laura. Love them as I do, they all add extra layers of mess to my life — a life that used to be much tidier.

It used to be me and Saul. Saul and me. It was straight-forward and simple and all very, very manageable. Yes, sometimes I was lonely — but, to use a comparison that would probably fit if I could drive, I was like the only car on a secluded country lane, going at my own pace, never worrying that someone might crash into me if I braked too suddenly.

Now I feel like I'm driving on a crowded multi-lane motorway at rush hour. Everybody seems to want to be part of my life. Everyone seems to want something from me.

Even as I think that, I know it sounds awful.

I've gained far more than I've lost, and usually I like the hustle and bustle of my life here. But right now, when I'm physically and mentally wiped out, it all feels like too much. Too many people. Too many complications. Too many demands. I just need to shut it all down for a while. Get Saul settled in bed, and follow right behind him. Get some sleep. Clear my mind. I'm sure everything will feel different in the morning.

I finish my tea and rinse the cup out in the sink, deciding that there's no time like the present. So what if I go to bed at 8 p.m.? There's no one around to judge.

I walk through into the living room, and scratch Tinkerbell behind the ears, making him purr. I scratch the gorilla behind the ears as well, but luckily he doesn't.

'Ready for bed, kiddo?' I say, looking down at Saul. He's staring at the TV screen as Bagheera and Baloo discuss Mowgli's future, but his eyes are glassy and tired. He's basically already asleep, he just doesn't know it yet.

I can sense an argument coming on, and steel myself for it by putting my hands on my hips — the no-nonsense-mummy stance. He stares at me and rubs his eyes with screwed-up fists, opening his mouth to say no. He doesn't throw many tantrums, but I can feel this one in the air — mainly because he's exhausted.

We're interrupted from escalating our minor disagreement by a knock at the door. I stand there, hands still on my hips, and really want to swear out loud. Saul stares at me, then back at the TV.

'You'd better answer the door, Mummy,' he says, grabbing hold of his gorilla and hugging it tight. I have been dismissed, it seems.

The knock comes again, and I roll my eyes in a very mature fashion. Just when I'd really like the whole world to piss right off, it decides to come and visit.

I stomp to the door, trying to get a hold of my bad mood, and swing it open.

Van is outside, leaning against the wall, peering at me as I finally materialise. He's wearing what looks like nineteen layers of clothing and his beanie, dusted with snow. His breath is gusting into clouds on the cold night air, and he looks freezing. I feel the usual little skitterry-skit when I see him, but even that is overruled by the fact that I don't want to talk to him. Not that it's personal — I don't want to talk to anyone.

'Hey,' he says, jamming his hands into the pockets of his body-warmer. 'You okay? How did today go? I tried calling but I couldn't get through . . . '

'It was fine,' I say, knowing I should invite him in but not really having the energy to follow through. 'There was something wrong with my phone.'

He takes in my positioning, the arms I realise I have crossed defensively across my chest, and the fact that I'm not budging, even though I'm letting the cold in. His eye twitches slightly, and his mouth twists into an almost-but-not-quite-amused grin.

'You're lying, aren't you? You never usually lie.'

I sigh, and admit: 'Yeah. I am. There's nothing wrong with my phone. Auburn said I needed to start telling fibs so I could be socially acceptable . . .'

'Ha!' he scoffs, looking at me intensely, as though he's trying to figure out what's wrong. 'Auburn is in no position to tell anybody how to be more socially acceptable. And you don't need to lie to me, Katie.'

'Don't I, though?' I ask, letting out a big breath from all the tension. 'I wouldn't have done, not so long ago. But now I'm worried about hurting your feelings, or saying the wrong thing. So here I am. Lying.'

'Well, stop lying. Tell me the truth.'

'The truth? Okay. Basically, Van, I'm exhausted. It's been a big day. It's been a big month. All I want to do is curl up in a ball in bed on my own and hope tomorrow's different. I can't deal with . . . people right now. Any of them.'

He doesn't reply for a while, and I see him trying to control what may very well be the first flash of anger I've ever seen from him. What can I say? I've still got the magic.

He backs off a few steps, and holds his hands up in the air in a gesture of surrender.

'No problem,' he says, his voice controlled. 'I understand. I'm sorry to have crowded you. And don't worry about hurting my feelings, Katie — I'm a big boy. I can handle it. You get some rest, and I'll see you soon.'

He doesn't give me the chance to reply, just turns on his heel and jogs over the road to his parked truck.

I feel terrible, as soon as he walks away, and know I should shout him back. Apologise. Explain. Invite him in. I try to, I really do — but all that comes out of my mouth is a whisper, his name murmured so quietly that even I can't hear it. I go back inside and close the door behind me, leaning back against it and shaking my head.

I listen to the sound of his engine starting up, and hear a slight squeal of tyres as he pulls away a lot faster than he usually does. Shit. I've been a complete cow to someone who really didn't deserve it.

I go back to the kitchen and get my phone out of my bag. I decide I'll bite the bullet and text him right away. Say I'm sorry and offer to meet him for a drink tomorrow after work. I really do need a night on my own — but there are far nicer ways of saying it. It's not like he wouldn't have understood — I just snapped at him without giving him the chance to.

All the fight's gone out of Saul now, and he's lying limp and splayed across the sofa, one hand caressing the gorilla's furry head as he tries to stay awake. I watch him, my precious little boy, as I wait for my phone to switch back on.

When it does, I see that I have three new text messages. I'm ashamed of the way I behaved with Van, and don't want to read anything that's going to make me feel even worse.

I'm about to start tapping away on the keys when there's another knock at the door. I sigh and put the phone down. Maybe he's come back, I think. Maybe he's so annoyed with me, he's come to give me a piece of his mind. Maybe we'll end up screaming at each other on the doorstep — fast forwarding right past the honeymoon stage and into more familiar relationship territory. For me, at least.

Wearily, I trudge back through the living room and into the hallway. I take a deep breath, and open the door.

Waiting outside, complete with an uncharacteristic suntan and wearing a weird shirt with a mandarin collar, is my dad.

'Hi, love,' he says, sounding pretty exhausted himself. 'I've been doing some thinking, and I've decided you're right. I need to sort this out. Is your mother in?'

27

'No, she's not . . . come in, Dad. But be quiet, Saul's just gone to sleep and I'm going to try and put him down for the night.'

I feel exhausted in every way possible. If I have a tether, I think I've just reached the end of it. I tiptoe into the living room, and manage to hoist Saul up into my arms without really waking him.

It always amazes me how kids can sleep through things — when we were potty training, I used to be able to do the same late at night; I'd hold him on the loo on his special make-the-seat-smaller device, and he'd do his business, all the while his head lolling and his eyes closed.

I do the same tonight, before carrying him through to my bed. Looks like I've got a guest for the evening, and Saul is back to sleepovers.

I tuck him under the covers, and pause for a minute, stroking back his hair and giving his smooth forehead a kiss. He looks so peaceful when he's asleep, and I feel a wave of love wash over me. This, I remind myself, is what life is all about — the purity of the way this little person makes me feel. All the rest of the complications can bugger off.

I call into the bathroom to splash cold water on my face in an attempt to wake myself up, and go back downstairs with as much of a smile as I can muster.

I find Dad in the kitchen, making tea, looking weirdly exotic with his trendy shirt and his tan.

'Want a cuppa, love?' he asks, holding up a mug and waving it at me. I nod, and get the milk out of the fridge for him.

'What's with the new look, Dad?' I ask, watching as he stirs the tea bag. He likes his tea strong, my dad, and always spends a good minute pressing the tea bag against the side of the cup with a spoon until every last drop of flavour's been squeezed out.

'Oh . . . you mean the shirt? It was a gift from Miguel, who was leading our course. We all got them, in different colours. To match our auras.'

He at least has the good grace to look a bit embarrassed by that last sentence, which makes me laugh. They're at this weird stage in their lives, my parents — both of them changing; like they're starting to emerge from cocoons as different people.

'What's your aura like, then?' I ask, taking the tea he offers and gesturing for him to follow me through to the living room.

He glances down at the shirt and replies: 'Apparently, it's turquoise.'

I gaze at the sofa with something approaching adoration, put my tea on the table, and immediately collapse down onto its lovely squishy softness. I'm next to the gorilla, and remind myself to take it upstairs when I finally get to bed — maybe Saul can practise Beauty Parlour on it in the morning. Tinkerbell has disappeared off somewhere, which he tends to do when he meets new people — he's probably watching us from a corner, doing a feline risk assessment.

Dad sits in the armchair, and we're both silent for a moment. I'm too tired to start a conversation, and he doesn't look too perky himself.

'I did text you, honest. I dropped my stuff at home and drove straight down,' he says eventually. 'Were you there? While I was gone?'

'Yeah, I stayed there last night,' I reply, wondering how he knew.

'Right. Makes sense. Saul left me a picture on the fridge door — looked like a penguin, but could have been a panda. Maybe in space, there were stars all around it.'

'That sounds about right — he's currently obsessed with both animals and becoming an astronaut. We were . . . there because we met Jason. And his wife, Jo. She's having a baby.'

Dad leans forward in the chair, and looks me over, as though checking for damage.

'How was that? Was it all right?' he asks. He sounds genuinely concerned, and for a moment I let myself bask in it. No matter what problems I had growing up, he's still my dad — and every now and then, it's nice to still feel like a little girl.

'It was fine. Nice for Saul. Jason seems good. He's given up booze, sees a therapist — right up your street, Dad. Jo's lovely too. Everyone was on their very best behaviour. I'm just . . . well, I'm secretly glad they live so far away. Probably makes me a terrible person, doesn't it?'

'Course not, love. It's completely natural.

You've done a great job with Saul on your own — better than me and your mum did together. I know you'll always do what's right for him.'

I nod, and hope he's right. I'm feeling a bit off kilter tonight, and don't trust myself quite as much as I should. I was mean to Van, and that's still bothering me.

'So, where's your mother, then?' he asks, looking around the room, a bit like he expects her to leap out of a cupboard dressed as a pantomime villain.

'She's moved out. Got herself a new job and a new place.'

His eyebrows shoot up into his forehead, and he seems temporarily thrown by the whole idea.

'What did you expect, Dad?' I ask, half amused by his reaction, half annoyed on Mum's behalf. 'Did you think she'd be here waiting for you, like a good little woman, all apologetic and submissive?'

'God, no,' he says quickly, shaking his head. 'I'd never expect that of your mother! But the way you were talking about her last time, it seemed like she wasn't doing so well.'

'People change, don't they?' I say, pointing a finger at him. 'When you least expect it. They run off with the ice cream woman, and start wearing turquoise shirts, and going on mindfulness retreats.'

'Fair point,' he concedes, grinning. 'And . . . well, I'm happy for her, then. I think we both needed to realise there was a life out there for us that didn't involve battle stations at the breakfast table. I just got there a bit earlier, that's all.

What's she doing, then?'

'She's working at the café — you know, the one I told you about? She's living there as well. One of the staff is pregnant and they needed an extra pair of hands. There's a flat she's using. She's . . . happy about it. She feels useful again. So, lovely as it is to see you, Dad, I have to ask — why are you here? Are you going to mess it all up?'

'No, love, I'm not. I just thought I owed it to her to talk about everything. Explain about Fiona. Whatever our faults, we loved each other once. We built a life together. We've been married for a long time, even though if we're honest most of it fell into the 'worse' category, not the 'better'. And we had you — we did at least one thing right.'

He sounds so genuine when he says that, so emotional, that it makes me realise that I'm his Saul. I might be all grown up, with a child of my own, but to him, I'm the equivalent of that magical little boy I was gazing at in his sleep.

I stand up, yawning, and walk over to him to give him a hug. He looks like he needs a hug.

'All right, Dad. Look, I'm knackered. I need to go to bed. Saul's in with me, so you can take his room. We'll sort it all out in the morning, okay?'

'Okay, Katie,' he says, holding on to the hug for as long as he can. 'And I promise, I won't mess anything up.'

Those, I think, as I trudge up the stairs yet again, *sound suspiciously like famous last words.*

28

I leave Dad in bed the next morning, despite the fact that Saul is desperate to see him. In particular, he wants to jump on his head making gorilla noises.

I channel his enthusiasm away from that concept, by telling him he can take his toy gorilla — now named Marmaduke for some unfathomable reason — into pre-school, along with the map of the zoo we brought home as a keepsake.

'And,' he says excitedly as we make our way on the bus, 'I can tell them about my daddy too!'

Great, I think, gritting my teeth. I will now officially be the Jeremy Kyle mother of Applechurch pre-school. Just another day in paradise.

I promise Saul that his granddad will still be there when he gets home, and try not to think about the alternative — that he goes to the café unannounced, Mum skewers him with one of Laura's posh chopping knives, and disposes of the evidence by feeding his body into the smoothie blender.

They're grown-ups, I tell myself. I can't control them or their lives, and I shouldn't even want to. I have enough problems of my own.

I called Van early this morning, because I know he's always up at the crack of dawn, but he didn't answer. It feels weird, being potentially at odds with Van. It throws everything off balance, and I hate it. I hate the fact that I'm worried about him, I hate the fact that I might not even see him for days to sort this out, and I hate the fact that he's not answering his phone.

The fact that I did exactly the same to him the day before does very little to make me feel better about the situation.

I try and put it out of my mind and concentrate on what I can do — go to work, after getting Saul safely dropped off at nursery. It's his last few days in before they break up for the Christmas holidays, and both the staff and the kids seem to be going giddy with excitement about it. Possibly for different reasons. I don't have any more classes at college until the New Year either, which also feels like something of a Christmas miracle.

As I push open the door of the pharmacy, setting off the tinkling bell, Auburn leaps up from the giant red lipstick chair and rushes towards me. She seems to have been lying in wait, which is slightly terrifying. Her red hair is loose and flowing behind her as she makes her dash, and she looks a bit like some kind of super villain in her white coat — one of those beautiful but mad scientists who's trying to create a mega-virus to wipe out the human race because she was bullied at school.

Before I even have the chance to take my coat off, she throws her arms around me and physically lifts me up off the floor, spinning me around like a child. Did I mention how tall the Longville sisters are? And how short I am?

I splutter and protest and struggle to breathe,

and she eventually puts me down again, where I wobble slightly on unsteady feet and feel confused.

'What the hell, Auburn? What was that all about?' I ask, backing away from her slightly in case she tries to do it again. You never know with Auburn. She can be strange and unpredictable, it's all part of her offbeat charm.

'I just wanted to say thank you!'

'What for? And since when did spinning someone until they're dizzy constitute an accepted way of showing gratitude? I would have preferred flowers, or cake, or a diamond necklace!'

'Well, I'll get you all of those as well,' she replies, grinning at me. 'Or being realistic, maybe a cubic zirconia necklace off the shopping channel . . . '

'Okay. I'll look forward to it. But what have I done that's made you all thankful? If it's for sorting out that new delivery of Gaviscon, then don't worry, it's all part of my job . . . '

She frowns and perches her head on one side, like some kind of exotic parrot.

'I thought you'd heard?' she says mysteriously. 'Didn't Van come over last night?'

'He did,' I reply, biting my lip in shame at the memory. 'But I was tired, and he left, and we didn't really get a chance to talk properly.'

Her lips form into a small 'oh' at that, and I can tell she's picked up on the fact that there's something wrong from my tone. I'd never make it as a Russian spy.

'Right. Well. I'm sure you'll sort it out,' she

says eventually. 'But I wanted to thank you because of Mum. You know we were taking her for her health checks because she's been so off recently?'

'I do. Wasn't that a few days ago?'

'It was, and because of your suggestion, I basically insisted they check her bowels as well. It was all pretty hideous — you've not met hideous until you try explaining a camera up the bum to an Alzheimer's patient. Anyway, they found something, and they took a biopsy, and the results came in yesterday. Bowel cancer.'

I stare at her, blinking rapidly as I try and digest this news.

'What . . . why is that good news? Why are you thanking me? How is she? What happens next?' I splutter.

'Well, it's good news because we've caught it really early. It's only stage one, and the docs are sure they can sort it out. She'll need surgery, which will be another barrel load of laughs obviously, but hopefully that'll be all. They'll know more after some CT scans, but fingers crossed it's a small op — '

'A local resection?' I ask.

'Yes. Forgot how clever you are. Hopefully one of those, yes. And if the margins are clear and the lymph node tests come back okay, she won't need any chemo or radiotherapy. So that's why I'm thanking you — because of you saying we should get it checked, we've found it now. While it's just a teeny-tiny bastard tumour, rather than a ginormous flesh-eating bastard tumour.'

This isn't a funny subject, but I have to laugh

301

at her language. I wonder if she used terms like that when she was sitting her pharmacist's exams.

'You're welcome — although I really did nothing. I don't like this new trend for treating me like I'm a hero just for doing normal things. Promise me you won't throw me a party and make me a cardboard medal?'

'I make no promises,' she replies, punching me in the arm. 'But probably not — it's going to be a bit busy anyway. We'll know more soon, once the other scans are done. Sorry to ambush you — I genuinely thought Van had told you. I heard him come home last night, but he just disappeared off into his new man cave straight away.'

'His new man cave?'

'Yeah. His new man cave on wheels.'

'Oh! Tom's camper van? It's arrived?'

She nods enthusiastically, and replies: 'It has, and it's a thing of beauty. I wish I'd thought of it to be honest. I'm hoping he'll let me have a turn. I might just move in when he's out at work one day, and cover all available surface space with bras and knickers and tampon boxes so he can't face the thought of stepping foot inside ever again . . .'

She's gazing off into the middle distance, and I recognise the signs that she's gone off into some kind of mindscape known only to herself. Auburn World. She's tapping one toe, and chewing a fingernail, and tugging at her hair — never still, always hyper.

It does, at least, give me the chance to scuttle

302

off to the back of the shop, and put the kettle on. I fill it, up with water without even thinking about it, then realise that I don't actually want a cup of tea. All I seem to have done for days is drink hot beverages.

I'm doing it because I'm on auto-pilot. I'm looking for something to do with my hands while my mind is busy elsewhere. My mind is busy making me feel awful.

I put the still-empty mug down, and notice that Auburn has tacked up some tinsel along the stock shelves, along with some mistletoe. I better watch myself.

I wash up the mug — which is still clean — and realise that no matter how busy I try and keep myself, I'm going to carry on feeling awful.

Van was standing there, on my doorstep last night, knowing that his mother has cancer. He'd been calling me all afternoon, knowing that his mother has cancer. He got sent packing by a selfish cow he was foolish enough to think of as a friend (that would be me), knowing that his mother has cancer.

Van's mother has cancer. As well as Alzheimer's. And I didn't even give him the chance to tell me — I assumed he was there to find out about my day, and didn't even engage with the concept of his day. I shrivel up inside a bit more each time I remember our non-conversation. The tone of my voice. My body language. The fact that I kept him on the step. That I gave him the impression he was a burden, that he was crowding me.

Even if he had only come there to check up on

me, it would have been unforgivable. What a nasty way to behave. But under the circumstances I've just been made aware of, it's even worse. He probably needed someone to talk to who wasn't a member of his family. He probably needed some space, away from the cottage. He probably wanted someone with a medical background to talk to. He probably just wanted a hug, and for me to tell him it was all going to be all right.

Instead, I rejected him — because I was tired. Because I was stressed. Because I'm probably fundamentally evil.

No, not evil, I tell myself — but I definitely have issues. Van was getting too close, on a day when being around Jason and Jo had rattled my cage already. I shut him out, and it wasn't right, and it's especially not right now I know about Lynnie.

'Are you going to wash that mug again?' asks Auburn, jolting me out of my self-hatred meltdown. 'You've already done it three times . . . '

I stare at the sink; at the mug, still in my hands, submerged in soapy water. I pull the plug out, and grab a towel to dry myself with.

'You okay?' she says, leaning in the doorway, watching me while she sucks on a whistle pop.

'Hmmm . . . I don't know. Would you be all right without me for a bit?'

She glances back in to the shop. Mrs Newton from the local butcher's shop is browsing hand cream.

'Not sure. The rush might kill me . . . of

304

course I can. Where are you off to?'

That, I realise as I get my coat from the hook, is actually a very good question. Where am I off to? There are any number of places.

'I don't have a clue, but maybe you can help me. Where's Van working today?'

She screws up her face, trying to remember, then replies: 'Briarwood. I remember because we had a conversation about it yesterday. I was there for some Star Lord interviews in the morning, before we had our appointment. And he said he was there today, fixing a whatsit with a whoojit. Or possibly something more technical than that. Why?'

'I was a complete bitch to him when he called around last night, and I want to apologise.'

She pulls a face, and says: 'You? A bitch? It seems unlikely.'

'It was likely. So . . . I need to get to Briarwood. That'll take ages to walk, won't it?'

'Yes. Can you teleport?' she asks.

'Not as far as I know.'

'Maybe if you think about it really, really hard?'

'It's okay . . . I'll walk.'

I remember how cold it is outside, and the fact that Briarwood's nickname with the locals is the House on the Hill. And I remember exactly how steep that hill is. Arrrgh.

'You can use my bike if you like?' she suggests, shrugging her shoulders in a 'this is a crazy idea but it might just work' way. 'I cycled in today. New fitness regime and all. It's out back. Not sure I'll do it again; too hard to hold a fag and control a bike at the same time.'

I am not the world's greatest cyclist, even when I'm not holding a fag. In fact, I'm pretty awful, unless I'm going in a straight line. Still, it seems like a plan — and it's the only one I've got.

I nod, and tell her I'll be back as soon as I can.

Just as I'm about to leave, she shouts: 'You could just call him, you know?'

I shake my head, give her a wave, and go back out into a freezing cold winter's day, to cycle up a steep hill. It doesn't sound like fun, but it has to be done. I was a bitch to his face, so I need to say I'm sorry to his face as well.

29

I gracefully arrive at Briarwood by skidding to a halt on the circular gravel driveway that leads up to the house.

Unfortunately, I skid to a bit too much of a halt, a bit too quickly, braking so hard the whole bike wobbles and judders and inevitably throws me so much off balance that I end up on the ground, a tangle of legs and feet and swear words.

This bike is pure evil. It absolutely hates me. I decided this on the way here, which was a journey fraught with peril. Seriously, it was like something out of *The Hobbit* — scary trees at the side of the road, tangled roots jutting out into my path, overflowing brooks, crows flying inches past my face, evil wizards. Well, okay, not evil wizards as such — but van drivers who overtook me with inches to spare. The Saurons of the Highway.

By the time I actually make it to the House on the Hill, I'm not only out of puff — that is one supremely steep hill — I'm a jibbering wreck. Every nerve I possess is frayed, which might explain my not-exactly-proficient braking technique.

I lie on the ground for a moment, looking up at a vivid blue sky and catching my breath. I'm not injured precisely — maybe some chunks of gravel in the palms of my hands, maybe a

307

bruised coccyx. Most definitely a wounded sense of dignity.

I kick my way out of the bike, and climb to my feet. By this time, I seem to have an audience, which is a new kind of wonderful.

Several of Tom's budding geniuses have emerged from the house to see what's going on, which leads me to believe that I made a lot more noise than I thought I did. It was probably the swearing that attracted them.

They stand in small groups, staring at me like I'm a member of an alien species, in various stages of surprise and fascination. None of them have put on outdoor clothes, and most of them are dressed in variations of T-shirt and jeans. Some of them are even barefoot, or wearing flip-flops. They all look cold, as they stand shivering around the fountain that's in front of the big old Gothic building, but it doesn't seem to occur to them to go back inside.

They all look curious about who I am and why I've been rolling around on the floor, but none of them asks who I might be or what I'm there for.

Suddenly, I understand why Tom is looking for a Star Lord. These are not practical people we're dealing with. Clever, but also stupid, if you know what I mean.

I dust myself down, brushing gravel off my legs, and then put the bike upright again. It's basically way too big for me, as well as being evil and hating me. I'm wheeling it away to the bike stands at the side of the house when the spell seems to break, and the geniuses finally realise that I am actually a real human being, not something conjured up by brains way too mashed on caffeine drinks and science all-nighters.

'Are you okay?' a henna-haired girl asks as I walk by. She's one of the barefoot ones, I notice.

'I'm fine, thanks,' I reply. 'But you really should get back inside before your toes get frostbite.'

She stares at her own feet as though surprised to see them there, and nods.

'Yeah. Good call. See ya!'

She turns to go back inside, where presumably she can continue her world-changing research without the need for socks or shoes. All the others follow her, as though they have one hive mind, trailing back in through the big wooden front door.

I notice as I walk past the fountain that the cherub-style figure in the middle of it has been decorated for Christmas, and is wearing a Santa hat on its head and has tinsel draped around its chubby midriff. Frankly, it looks terrifying.

I lodge the bike in the rack, and grimace as I stand up straight. My back has been in a weird position for the whole cycle ride, and the fall didn't help anything. This, I decide, was not one of my more brilliant ideas. I glance around, and have no clue where Van might be, which makes it an even less brilliant idea.

He does maintenance and gardening for Tom here, which means he could be anywhere. He could be in the house, fixing a leaky tap, or he could be miles away, in the deepest, darkest jungle of the Briarwood grounds. It's a bit of a dilemma.

I walk away from the bike, and into the hallway of the house. I never saw it when it was a children's home, where Tom spent part of his childhood, and I never saw it when he bought it earlier in the year, when it was neglected and abandoned.

Now, though, it's clean and bright and filled with light: The impressive staircase and original wood panelling are polished and shining, and I can hear the sounds of music coming from deep within the building. I follow the sound towards what used to be the ballroom, where Edie had her birthday party last time around. The one I chickened out of.

It's a grand room, with high ceilings and intricate plasterwork and dado rails and a huge, ornate fireplace. The bay windows are massive, the frames restored, the curtains thick red velvet drapes. If you screw your eyes up and only concentrate on those parts, you can totally imagine this place hosting dances during Victorian times and beyond.

If you don't screw your eyes up, though, it's harder — because then you get to see lots of young people with weird hair and flannel shirts and beards and bare feet, working in small teams at their work stations. The work stations contain various things I don't recognise, like machine parts and computer casings and tools that look like torture devices, and various things I do, like soldering irons and laptops and spirit levels.

I have no idea what they're doing, and decide it's probably better not to ask. I glance around the room, eardrums throbbing from the bass beat of the music, and hone in on the henna girl from earlier — the one who actually spoke.

She's staring at her laptop screen, chewing the end of a pencil, her face frowning in concentration. I walk over, and wave my hand in front of her eyes to get her attention. I have some nasty scrapes on my palm from my plummet from the bike, I notice, and probably should get them cleaned up. Soon.

'Hi!' I say, once she's torn her gaze from the screen.

'Hi?' she says, staring at me like she's never seen me before in her life.

'We just met, outside . . . I fell off my bike?'

'Oh yeah!' she says, grinning and pointing at me. 'That was funny! Are you all right, though?'

She adds the last part in quickly, as though she feels guilty for laughing at my misfortune, and continues to look slightly confused by the whole exchange.

'Yes, I'm fine. I was just wondering if you could help me — I'm looking for Van? You might know him, he comes and does work in the house and gardens?'

She nods and smiles, and taps out a message on her screen: 'Anyone know the location of Van the Man?' She presses a button, and it must ping around the whole room on some kind of internal system, because I notice everyone else looking at their screens as well.

Within a few seconds, she gets a reply from someone called LostInSpace666, who says: 'Van the Man was heading to the second floor living area. He had his Toolbox of Justice.'

311

Henna girl points at the words to make sure I've read them, and I nod in thanks.

'Cheers,' I reply, pausing before I leave. 'Erm . . . wouldn't it have been quicker to just ask out loud?'

'Nah,' she says, raising her voice slightly. 'Then we'd have had to turn the music down.'

Okay. Well. I am clearly about 108 years old and living on a different planet to these guys. I leave the former ball-room, wondering what Ye Olde Dancers of Yore would have made of its current inhabitants, and head back to the staircase.

I make my way up, admiring the way Tom's managed to bring the place back to life, combining the character of the old with the functionality of the new. On the second floor, I find a row of individual rooms, and at the end of the corridor, a big communal living room and kitchen.

I find Van — or at least part of him — in the kitchen. He's lying on his back on the floor, with his head and chest beneath the sink. I can hear the clanging of tools, and assume that he's fixing something — loudly.

His legs are bent, his body twisted with the effort, and he's wearing cargo pants and thick work-boots that look like they have steel caps in the toes. Plus, I can't help but notice, one of those tool belts that automatically makes a man look macho and sexy. At least to me.

I'm quite keen on not surprising him so he jumps and bangs his head, so I cough a little, clearing my throat in the time-honoured manner of warning someone you're in the room. Naturally enough, it makes him jump, and he bangs his head.

He scoots himself out from the space under the sink, and emerges rubbing his scalp with one hand, holding a wrench with the other. He stays there for a moment, like he's doing a weird stomach crunch, staring at me, before getting to his feet.

'Sorry!' I say immediately. 'I didn't want you to bang your head . . . '

'No worries. My head's tough enough to take a few knocks. Just trying to get a plastic Yoda figure out of the drainage pipe. Apparently it's quite valuable.'

'Really?' I ask, surprised. 'How did Yoda end up down the drain?'

'Have you met any of the residents?'

'I have . . . and yes, well. Fair enough. Look, Van, I just wanted to say that — '

'Are you all right? What did you do to your hands?' he interrupts, taking hold of my wrists and examining the gravel-scraped skin.

'Oh, nothing . . . well, I kind of fell off Auburn's bike. In front of all the geniuses. That was fun.'

He shakes his head, wearing one of those expressions that people get when they decide not to even ask. He leads me off to the next door along, which turns out to be a bathroom, and waits while I give my hands a scrub.

He produces a first aid kit from a cupboard by the fire extinguisher — clearly essential items at Briarwood these days — and leads me back through into the kitchen.

'Sit down,' he says, firmly, 'and don't argue. I know you're a nurse, but you have grit in both hands, and nobody is good enough to do that on their own.'

His tone is stern, and I don't know exactly what he's annoyed at — me for last night, me for today, the unfairness of his mum's situation, of life in general. Whichever it is, I'm sure me disagreeing with him isn't going to help.

I sit on one of the chairs, and he drags one next to me. He reaches out and takes hold of one of my hands, spreading it out on the table so my palms are facing upwards. He picks up the tweezers he's just cleaned with a sterile wipe, and very, very gently begins to pluck out the biggest lumps of gravel.

I force myself to relax, because I know that will make this all so much easier, and look on as he works. At the broad hunch of his shoulders as he leans in; at the still-tanned face with its tiny white laughter lines; at the big hands that hold mine so delicately.

Watching him now, under the strip lighting, I can see the strain on his face. His usual smile has faded; his eyes look tired and dull, and he seems half asleep still, concentrating hard on what he's doing.

I reach out with the hand he's not treating, and gently run it over his hair. It's short and soft and lovely, and I let my fingers briefly caress his cheek before I say: 'I'm really sorry about last night, Van. I was a complete dick, to use a technical term. I took all my frustrations out on

314

you, and didn't even give you the chance to tell me the news about Lynnie. I was selfish, and rude, and I hope you can forgive me.'

He tenses slightly — at the touch or at the words, I don't know — and pauses in his work to look up at me. He raises his eyebrows, staring at me as though he's trying to weigh something up.

'Are you just saying this because you feel bad about my mum?' he asks. 'Because I didn't expect you to be psychic and somehow know.'

'No! Well, of course I feel bad about your mum — but even if that wasn't part of it, I'd still be apologising. I wanted to apologise as soon as you'd gone. I felt awful, and was going to text you right away . . . '

'Why didn't you, then?'

'Well, my dad turned up on the doorstep, fresh from becoming Mr Mindfulness 2018 — so I couldn't. As soon as I found out where you were this morning, I quite literally got on my bike and came to find you. And I am honestly a really shitty cyclist.'

This, at least, does make him laugh, and I feel some of the tension fizz out of the room.

'I can see that,' he says, taking hold of my hand again. 'Now try and keep still and be quiet until I've done this, all right?'

I nod, and do as he asks. He's good at it — I'm guessing all those travels abroad and working in a school have taught him a few first aid lessons the hard way. He's gentle and steady, and somehow, even though 'picking gravel out of your bloody hand' isn't on anyone's list of Top

10 romantic occasions, the physical contact with him still makes me feel alive.

'Okay . . . ' he says eventually, turning both my hands up to inspect them. 'I think we're all done. You've been a good patient. I'll give you a lollipop and a sticker on the way out.'

'Thank you. And I'm sorry,' I say, 'please believe me.'

He nods, and leans back in his chair and yawns and stretches at the same time.

'Katie,' he says, evenly, 'it's okay. I get it. I know you're sorry. Anyway, you're perfectly entitled to keep the riff-raff standing on the doorstep whenever you want to. Don't worry about it, apology accepted. Was your day all right then? With the ex?'

'It was fine. Just left me with a bad case of crazy bitch-itis afterwards. How are you, more importantly?'

He shrugs and gazes off into the distance, as though he'll find some answers there.

'I don't know. All right, I suppose. Can't quite reach Auburn's giddy heights of enthusiasm, and Willow's pretty bummed too, but . . . well, I keep getting told how lucky we are it was caught early. All I keep thinking is that 'lucky' isn't a word easily used in association with Lynnie these days. Still, we shall overcome and all that — no use moping about it or complaining.'

The words sound a bit rehearsed — as though this is what he's been telling himself. That he shouldn't mope, shouldn't moan, shouldn't make a fuss.

'You have every right to mope, and to

complain,' I say firmly. 'And if you don't want to bring your sisters or your mum down, you can mope and complain to me. I'll be your mope mopper-upper.'

Just a day or so ago, he'd have found that amusing. He'd have made a suggestive comment, and we'd have flirted a bit, but also known it was true — that we could confide in each other.

Today, he just nods and smiles — perfectly pleasant, perfectly civil, perfectly contained in his own headspace.

Despite him telling me that all is forgiven, things still feel slightly strained. I'm probably overreacting, and making everything about me when it's actually about him and his mum, but I get the sense that he's keeping his distance. That he still seems a bit wary of me.

That makes me feel even worse than I did before I came here. I've always seen this budding thing with Van from my own perspective — I've measured it in terms of what *I* have to lose, what I'm risking, what could go wrong for me and Saul.

Now I'm starting to realise that Van has opened himself up to risk as well, and that maybe right now he's decided to err on the side of caution.

He has no idea how much I want to fix that. How much I want him to trust me, to see me as an ally in life at a time when he needs one. To be honest, I didn't have any idea how much I wanted that until just this minute.

'So, Auburn tells me you have your camper van all set up,' I say, trying to lighten the mood.

'She seems very jealous.'

'Yep, she is,' he replies, grinning. 'But it's mine, all mine . . . '

I pause, and wonder if he'll invite me round. If we'll go ahead with our scheme, and sneak off for the night together. If everything we planned will actually happen. He stays silent, and I don't know quite how to interpret it.

'I can't wait to come and see it,' I say, mustering all my courage.

He doesn't quite meet my eyes, and is tapping the table top with his fingertips.

'Or not,' I add quietly. 'No pressure. Whatever you need, Van.'

I realise that I need to get out of there pretty quickly, or I might start crying. That I'm starting to feel overwhelmed by emotions I don't quite understand, and don't want to drag him down with me. He's got enough on his plate without me turning into a wailing woman at his workplace.

I stand up, and start bleating on about needing to get back to work, and then to pick Saul up from pre-school, and how first I have to do battle with evil road wizards and low-flying crows.

He gets up from his seat, and puts the palm of his hand gently over my mouth to stop me from bleating any further. Thank God for small mercies.

I look up at him, and nod. He lets his hand drop, and twines his fingers into mine.

'It's all a bloody mess, isn't it? Our timing?' he asks, leaning into me as my head rests against his chest. He smells of oil and manliness and Fairy Liquid.

'I guess so,' I reply, nodding against his T-shirt. 'And I'm really sorry about last night. And about Lynnie. And I would like to come and see your camper van.'

He nods, and wraps his arms around me. When he speaks, I can feel his lips moving against my hair.

'I think I'm probably breaking some kind of man code here, Katie, but I'm not sure the whole no-strings sex thing is a good idea right now. I'm not sure either of us is capable of it . . . not physically, I mean. I am capable of that, honest. But last night, I was upset — no, please don't apologise again! It's not necessary. I know you're sorry, and it wasn't that big a deal — but it did make me realise that I'm maybe already in a bit deeper than I thought I was. And that's okay — but I know you're not. Not yet, at least. I think maybe we need to figure it out a bit more before we get even deeper.'

I slip my arms around his waist, and listen to his heart thudding quietly away through the soft fabric of his T-shirt.

I want to tell him I'm in as deep as he is — or at least that I'd like to be. I want to tell him we should wade out together, and see just how deep we get. I want to tell him all kinds of things — but none of them would be fair, because he's right.

We need to figure things out a bit more. We need to make sure we'll float, and not drag each other down.

'Now come on,' he says, pulling away from me. 'Let's get Auburn's bike in the back of the truck, and you back to the village. I'm not sure you'd survive the return route.'

30

We just about manage horrendous small talk on the blessedly brief journey back to the village. It feels so odd, all of this — so different to the way I usually feel when I'm with Van. He hasn't said it, not out loud, but I recognise when somebody has put their defences up. I should do — I'm a world expert at hiding behind my own.

He pulls up outside the pharmacy, and I turn to him before he gets out to retrieve the bike.

'Are we all right, Van?' I ask, quietly. 'Are we still . . . friends?'

He stares out of the windscreen for a moment, then turns to face me with a smile.

'Of course we are, Katie. That won't change, I promise. If you need me, let me know — I'll be there.'

'And what about you? What about if you need me? You know it applies in reverse, don't you?'

He nods, and swipes his hands over his hair, as though brushing off dust.

'I do. I promise, I do. I'm not trying to be an arsehole here — I'm just tired. Didn't get much sleep, and my brain feels like some kind of black hole, sucking all logical thought out of my head. Look, don't worry about it. It's all good. Come on, I need to get back to Briarwood before Yoda makes it to the great sewer in the sky . . . '

He gets out of the truck, and I watch as he lugs the evil bike out of the bed. He hands it over to me, and I stand holding it steady as he gives me a quick kiss on the cheek, climbs back into the driver's seat, and toots his horn as he starts the engine.

I watch the truck pull away onto the road, knowing he'll do a U-turn at the car park by the café and come back up again. Part of me wants to stay there, rooted to the spot, so I can wave at him again as he drives past for the second time.

Luckily I realise this would be an insane and counter-productive thing to do. He's exhausted, and needs a bit of space, and it's probably a sensible choice to ditch the crazy lady and her complications and lose himself in some mindless plumbing tasks. It might just keep his head from exploding.

I wheel the bike down the entryway and through the gate into the back yard at the pharmacy. I half expect to see Auburn there, smoking, but she's inside. Only the big pink shell she uses as an ashtray remains.

I lean the bike against the wall, and resist the urge to kick it. I'd probably get my ankle trapped — that bike is definitely the boss of me.

I make my way inside, shedding my coat and scarf, and wonder if I should make some tea. Because, you know, I haven't had enough of that recently.

I glance through to the shop floor and see that there is, by Budbury standards, a rush going on. Two people are sitting on the lipstick sofa, presumably waiting for the prescriptions I can see Auburn working on, and there's a man standing at the till holding a packet of corn plasters and a roll of wrapping paper. I hope the two aren't connected, or someone's in for a big disappointment on Christmas morning.

I dash right through and serve him, then go and help Auburn with the prescriptions. I hand them out to the waiting ladies, checking their addresses first, while she carries on getting together some asthma medication that needs delivering later in the day.

We're busy for a solid hour, with customers and preparing scripts and taking a delivery that needs to go straight into the fridge, and by the time the coast is finally clear, it's nearing the end of my shift. I have to go and collect Saul, and then go home to see my dad, and then possibly referee a meeting between him and my mum. Even without the bedrock of anxiety about Van, it wouldn't be a vintage day.

'Cor blimey,' says Auburn, her eyes wide and slightly manic. 'That was intense! I think we should get more Christmas stuff in . . . we're almost out of the scented candles and snowman mugs, did you notice?'

'I did. I'll order some. Plus maybe some more gift wrap and tags. Might as well make hay while the sun shines.'

She nods, and glances out of the window.

'Or while the snow falls . . . ' she says, as I follow her gaze. It is snowing, she's right — but not heavily, just a gentle dusting that probably won't settle. At least I hope not, or the buses might not be running.

She leans back against the counter, and I see her reach for a whistle pop, then think better of it and shove her hand into her pocket instead. Must be that health kick she's on. She'll probably have a fag instead, replacing sugar with nicotine — her whole life seems to be one big juggle between potentially harmful substances.

'So, did you find him?' she asks, staring at me, as though daring me to try and avoid the subject. 'And are you coming to the big bash at the café on Christmas Day?'

There are two questions there, but delivered in one rush of words. This is often the way with Auburn — her mind moves so fast that her lips can barely keep up.

'I did find him,' I reply, chewing my lip and wondering how much to tell her. I decide on 'not very much', as she is, after all, his sister.

'Everything okay?'

'Yeah. Fine. All sorted. Thanks for the loan of the bike. And as for the café . . . when was this decided?'

'I got a text from Cherie a bit ago. You might have done as well, have you checked your phone?'

I haven't, not since I did my last 'making-sure-Saul-is-okay' surveillance for missed calls from his pre-school. I look now, and see a couple of messages. One from my dad, saying he's okay to go and pick up Saul if I let him know the address of the nursery, and one from Cherie.

First I answer my dad, telling him I'll be home in five and will drive there with him. It takes a lot of pressure off, knowing our journey will be so much quicker. I really must learn to drive; I'm sick of relying on favours to get through the basics of my day. And if I learn to drive, I'll never have to cycle again.

Cherie's text is simple and to the point: 'Your presence is requested at the Comfort Food Café for a Christmas feast, in thanks and celebration for all we have. Fancy dress optional, from noon onwards. Bring nothing but your Christmas spirit xxx'

I slide my phone back into my pocket, and try not to feel stressed. It's an invitation to a party — one that will undoubtedly be splendid, which Saul will love, and which will surely do away with the need for me to overcook a turkey and peel parsnips.

But as I chat to Auburn, and gather my coat and belongings, I can't quite shake off the feeling that maybe a party at the café might be a step too far for me right now. That maybe I'd prefer to be at home, on my own with Saul, the same way I have the last couple of years.

That maybe I'd even prefer to be somewhere else entirely, like on a last-minute flight to the Caribbean. Or, being realistic, somewhere cheap and cheerful in Spain.

I had a brief spell, I realise, where everything was settled. A brief spell where I happily sat with the café ladies and gossiped; where I started to relish my place in their lives, and feel safe and secure in the home I'd built for Saul and me in this community. A brief spell where I even began to open up to the idea that Van could be something more to me than the friend I flirt with.

Now, it feels like that brief spell is over. Like

325

things have changed up again, just when I least wanted them to.

There's been drama, and hospitals, and illness, and exes coming back on the scene. There's been the reappearance of my parents, inserting themselves into my life with their usual carelessness. There's been Van, basically rejecting me when I feel like I offered myself to him. Not that simple, I know — but that's how it feels right now.

No matter how much I understand what he's saying, and even partly agree with it, the rejection still feels raw. It still stings. I'd almost forgotten how bad it does sting, as I've not been rejected for so long — keeping my emotions under bubble wrap has its advantages.

Now, I feel like the walls are closing in, and I might get crushed. I might suffocate. I'm trapped in a web of other people, and suddenly need to get out. It's irrational, I know, and I'm going to try and ride out the storm. Take things one step at a time, and not overreact. Not go into shut-down mode at the first sign of trouble — or, to be fair, approximately the first ten signs of trouble.

It's a party. At the café. It will be splendid.

Auburn is looking at me with some concern, as I faff around getting ready to leave.

'You might want to take a few deep breaths,' she says, placing a hand on my arm. 'You've gone super-pale, and you look like you're about to fall over. Do you want a whistle pop? Is your blood sugar messed up? Is anything messed up?'

Pretty much everything feels in some way or

another a bit messed up right now — but Auburn has enough to deal with without adding my pathetic personal crises to the list.

'Nope, I'm fine, honest — just having a moment. It's probably a delayed reaction to the shock of riding your bike! Anyway, I'm off — let me know if you get any more news about Lynnie, all right?'

'Aye aye, captain,' she says, saluting me as I leave.

31

I've tried calling my mum to warn her we're coming, but there was no answer. I texted as well, but got no reply. I should have done it last night really, or at the very least earlier this morning, but . . . well, I had other things on my mind. Way too many other things.

So now, as Dad pulls up in the little car park by the bay, I have no idea how this is going to work out. Saul is incredibly excited, clutching his gorilla by its arm with one hand, holding his granddad with the other.

'That's our beach, Granddad!' he says, pointing down at the shoreline. 'And our sea!'

'It's lovely, Saul,' my dad replies enthusiastically. He's been here before, to the beach at least, but it was when we first moved, and Saul doesn't remember it.

'And that's the path to our café,' he adds, pointing upwards. 'And our snowflakes.'

Dad takes in the hill, and the café perched on top of it, and the snowflakes, and smiles.

'That looks even lovelier. Do you think they'll have cake?'

'They have ALL the cake! Every cake in the world! Come on, come on . . . they'll be waiting for me!'

My dad and I share a look over Saul's bobble hat as he dashes off, scrambling up the path like a baby goat. If you can't be an egomaniac when you're three, when can you?

We follow on a bit more slowly, Dad grimacing at the sharp slap of sea air on his tanned face. It's still beautiful here, but climate-wise, it's not quite the Canary Islands.

'So, how is this going to play out, do you think?' I ask, as we trudge upwards. We're both taking our time. Probably both a bit nervous. 'And are you sure we should even be doing it? Why don't we just arrange to meet her somewhere else, later? This is all a bit . . . public.'

'I know, love,' he says, grinning at me. 'That's why I chose it. She won't stab me in public, will she?'

'I don't know, Dad. Maybe she will. And if she does, it'll be your own fault. I don't feel comfortable with this at all.'

'I can understand that, Katie, and you don't have to come with me, you know? Feel free to give it a miss. Leave it to the grown-ups to sort out.'

I make an involuntary snorting noise at that. *The grown-ups.* Ha. He might have changed, but it'll take more than a few weeks to convince me that he's not the same dad I've always known — the dad with a temper, who's quick to anger, who can be loud and hurtful and just as up for a fight as my mum.

He glances at me, and I know he heard me. That he knows what I'm thinking. That he wisely chooses not to engage with a debate about his newfound maturity as we finally emerge through the wrought-iron Comfort Food Café sign and into the garden.

The garden is, understandably on a day like this, deserted. The dog creche field is empty, and only the inflatable Santa greets us, his tiny arms wobbling in the wind like a festive T-Rex, his flowing red hat dusted with snow.

Saul has already run ahead and gone inside, and I can see him through the windows, giving Laura a big hug. We follow him in, and I immediately cast my eyes around, searching for my mum. I have my phone in my hand, in case I need to call 999, and have already planned to take Saul for a rapid walk down to the beach if things look as though they're going to turn nasty.

I don't want to see them fighting — and I'm determined that he won't.

Laura straightens up, tucking her curls behind her ears as she smiles at us both. There's a question in her gaze, and I say: 'Laura, this is my dad. Colin. Is Mum around?'

She blinks rapidly, and chews her lip as she nods, and looks basically as nervous as I feel. I haven't seen Mum for a few days, not since she moved in here — I've been busy, and felt like we both needed some space to decompress from our enforced house-sharing. I didn't even tell her about meeting Jason, because I knew she'd have some strong opinion or another on it, and I needed to stick with my own.

I can tell from the expression Laura's currently wearing, though, that Mum has clearly filled them all in on her domestic situation, and probably painted Dad as some kind of evil philandering monster who broke her heart.

'Nice to meet you, Colin,' she manages,

staring at him as though searching for the devil horns. 'And yes, Sandy's around — she's was just out back getting some fresh milk from the fridge . . . she should be through in a minute. Come on, Saul, let's go and get you and Marmaduke a snack, shall we?'

She leads him away by his hand, and I mouth a quick 'thank you' to her.

Dad hasn't really noticed Laura's cool reaction. I don't suppose he even realises it was cool, as he doesn't know how warm Laura usually is.

Mainly, though, he's too busy doing what most people do when they come into the café for the first time, and looking around at the decor. It's especially glorious with its Christmas clothes on, and he seems completely bemused by it.

As Laura disappears off with Saul in tow, he looks at me and says: 'Nice place. Great atmosphere. And since when did your mother become Sandy?'

'Gosh, Dad, let me think — probably about the same time you were sitting in Fiona's front room discussing your feelings with a bunch of strangers? Change isn't a one-way street, you know.'

As my mother wanders out from behind the counter, I realise that I have never spoken truer words. My mother has changed — into some kind of chameleon, who adapts her colours to her surroundings. Living here, in Cherie's rock chick lair, has clearly had an effect.

The garish make-up has gone; her hair is free of its usual sheen of lacquer, and she's wearing a tie-dyed T-shirt she's obviously filched from Cherie's wardrobe. It's way too big, and she's cinched it in at the waist with a belt made of seashells. Matching shell earrings drape down from her lobes, and she's completed the ensemble with open-toed Birkenstocks she'd never previously have been seen dead in. In summary, she looks exactly like the kind of woman who would go on a mindfulness retreat in the Canary Islands.

She stops dead still when she spots us, and I look on in horror as she lets go of the plastic milk bottle she's carrying. It seems to happen in slow motion — her look of shock; her fingers loosening; the bottle upending and falling to the floor, milk cascading in a river of white all over her feet.

Nobody reacts for what feels like forever, but is probably only a few seconds. Frank, who was sitting at his usual table in the corner reading a newspaper, jumps to his feet and grabs the bottle from the ground, stopping any more milk spilling out. Cherie, who was making cappuccinos at the machine, grabs the towel that lives next to it and spreads it over the liquid, stamping on it to mop the worst of it up.

Laura joins in, unspooling what looks like a whole tube of kitchen roll around the edges, and swiping it over the rest of the milk.

My mum seems to suddenly notice that she's in the middle of a hive of activity, and jumps, holding her hands to her face and bursting into tears.

Cherie abandons her cleaning duties, and puts

her arms around her, squeezing her in tight. I have no idea what she's saying, but I'd be surprised if it doesn't include the words 'crying', 'spilt milk', and 'no use'.

Whatever it is, it seems to do the trick, and Mum emerges from their huddle blinking and pale but looking more together.

I take a few steps towards her, but am deterred from getting any closer by a combination of the still squishy floor, and the look on her face. It's a look that says she feels betrayed, and it makes me feel terrible. Like I've let her down.

I glance back at my dad, and he's equally horrified, although at what I'm not sure. In fact, only Saul seems to be all right, and is using Marmaduke's feet to soak up some stray milk splatter. Gorilla in the washer tonight, then.

'Hi, Mum,' I say, hearing the waver in my own voice. 'I'm sorry we surprised you. I did call, and text, and . . . '

'It's not her fault, Sandra,' says my dad, stepping forward. 'Don't blame Katie. I insisted on coming. I'm sorry I did . . . I didn't want to upset you . . . '

Mum stares at him, and I'm actually relieved to see some anger flash across her face. Anger is good. Anger I'm used to. Pale and weak and betrayed? Not so much.

'Well, how did you expect me to react, Colin?' she snaps, pointing one shaking finger at him. 'I've not seen you for an age, and then you turn up out of the blue like this? Were you expecting a red carpet?'

Cherie, Frank and Laura are watching this

333

exchange with curious expressions, sensing the momentous shifts in mood, the emotions that are swirling across the surface of the words. Laura meets my eyes, and gives me a small, sympathetic smile.

'Saul — do you want to come and help me make sponge cake?' she says, holding out her hand to him.

'Can I crack the eggs?' he asks in delight.

'Course you can . . . ' she replies, pulling a face at me over her shoulder. Laura knows as well as I do that letting a 3-year-old crack eggs is going to end in one almighty mess of yolk. Still, it gets him away, and keeps him amused, and distracts him from whatever might happen next.

It also, I realise immediately, takes away my excuse to make a sharp exit as well. There are a couple of tables' worth of customers in the café, all of whom are pretending not to be fascinated by the unfolding drama, and Cherie starts towards them, undoubtedly to offer them free top-ups on their drinks. Frank looks at me, raising his eyebrows in a question, and I nod.

'You know where I am if you need me,' he says quietly, heading off to his table and his hastily abandoned tea.

Eventually, the mood settles, and it's just the three of us. Standing there surrounded by damp towels and wads of kitchen roll and stray rivulets of spilled milk.

'Can we just sit down, and talk?' my dad says, holding his hands out in a gesture of surrender. 'I need to explain some things to you. And apologise.'

Mum is holding on to her glare, but I can tell it's waning. It's probably his timely use of the word 'apologise' that does the trick. That or she's planning on pushing him off the cliff.

She nods abruptly, and stomps off to the furthest table away from everyone else. Normally, new visitors to the café get swamped with cake and creamy beverages and a hearty welcome. Not today — everyone's far too sensible to get involved in this powder keg.

And, as my dad gestures to me to follow him, I decide that includes me as well.

'No, Dad,' I say firmly. 'You got yourself into this mess. You need to get yourself out of it. I'm going to do like you suggested, and leave it to the grown-ups to sort out.'

The look on his face as I stay still, arms folded across my chest in determination, is an absolute picture. I almost feel sorry for him.

I glance around, and notice the way everyone is very deliberately not looking at us. Very deliberately trying not to make an already embarrassing situation any worse.

I don't actually feel embarrassed, although I know I should. I feel annoyed, and exasperated, and trapped. Trapped in a situation I don't like, surrounded by drama I don't enjoy, in a cauldron of emotion that feels all too familiar.

I need to draw a line between their lives and mine, but I'm not entirely sure how to do that, as they seem to have followed me here. Part of me would like to scoop up Saul, and leave immediately. I could change the locks, or move house, or use my savings to buy us false identities and begin a new life in rural Canada. A fresh start, away from my mum and dad and Jason and Jo and even Van. Away from all the complications.

As my savings would probably only stretch to starting a new life in Wales, and I have no clue how to get us false identities, I stay put.

Besides, running right now wouldn't be fair on several different levels. Especially not to Saul, who I can hear chuckling away as he bangs eggs against the side of Laura's mixing bowl.

I turn my back on my parents — I don't want to be staring at them, analysing their body language, listening for the raised voices and changes in posture I recognise as familiar warning signs. I don't want to be a teenager again, sitting at the kitchen table, trying to gauge if it was safe to stay or if I needed to bunker down in my room with my head-phones on.

Instead, I walk over to Frank's table. He looks up from his reading, and gives me a welcoming nod. He peels off a section of his paper — travel and leisure, very nice — and hands it to me. Then he chops the cherry scone Cherie's delivered to him in half, and pushes it towards me.

He straightens the crease out of the sports pages, and gives me a wink over the paper, blue eyes twinkling.

'Just leave 'em to it, love,' he says, before going back to his reading.

That, I think as I start an article about eco-friendly northern lights tours, sounds like great advice.

32

A very strange thing happens with my parents after that initial showdown at the Comfort Food Café.

They actually talk. And talk. And talk some more. It strikes me as an odd and serendipitous thing that via different routes, and for very different reasons, they've both ended up at a place in their lives where they seem open to change.

Dad stays at mine, and Mum stays at the café, but they meet often and apparently without bloodshed.

I'm wary about crossing the line I've drawn for myself and getting further involved, but today, as Dad helps me to wrap Christmas presents, I finally feel able to ask.

'So,' I say, biting off Sellotape while holding together edges of paper around Saul's new gardening set, 'what's going on, then, with you and Mum?'

He smiles at me, and carries on encasing a set of plastic zoo animals in paper decorated with bright red Santa heads.

'I thought you didn't want to know,' he replies. 'I thought you were leaving it to the grown-ups to sort out.'

'I am. And it looks like you have been. And now I'm . . . surprised?'

He nods, and finishes his wrapping, adding it

to the ever-growing pile on the floor between us. Saul is over at the cottage with Willow and Lynnie, at Willow's request. They've had their scan results, which were as positive as they could be, and she's due to go in for her op in the New Year. Now they've pinpointed what the problem is and got her on pain meds, her mood has improved, and she asked if 'that little boy who looks like Angel' could come around and help them bake mince pies.

We're making the most of it to get ready for the Big Day, filling up the two red Santa Sacks that Saul will find under the tree in a few mornings' time.

'That's a shame, isn't it?' he says, sounding genuinely sad. 'That we've surprised you by acting like civilised human beings?'

'Well, yes . . . but better late than never, I suppose?' I reply, patting him on the hand. 'Do you think you'll . . . you know . . . get back together?'

He ponders this, leaning back against the chair, staring at the purple curtains.

'I don't know, love. Long way to go. We need to be apart for a bit, I think, see what happens. See if any of this is just skin deep. What do you think anyway? Should we get back together?'

I have to confess that my first instinct is to scream 'No!' in his face. But that instinct comes from the cowardly part of me that struggles to trust them and their newfound behaviour. The part of me that thinks the same as I did when I was a teenager and old enough to understand what was going on: *you two should never even*

338

be in the same room as each other, never mind married — please get a divorce, for all our sakes!

I manage not to say it out loud, but my lack of an immediate response doesn't go unnoticed.

'You don't think we should,' he says, resigned. 'And I don't suppose I blame you. You've seen too much, heard too much. Can't expect to undo years' worth of damage with a few days, can we?'

He's right, but I feel mean about it. Like I'm somehow dismissing them and their futures, either together or apart.

'Well, whatever happens, I'm glad something did,' I reply, moving on to wrapping a set of picture books about astronauts. 'And don't listen to me — I'm just a worry wart.'

I expect him to laugh, or tell me I'm not, or make a joke. Instead, he looks serious, and says: 'Yes, you are. And that's what upsets me most about all of this. About the way we've affected you. Your mum says you were close to Willow's brother, Van. She thought maybe you'd even get together. But you've not mentioned him since I've been here, and I hope that's not because you think all relationships are doomed to take the same turn as mine and your mother's did.'

I bite off some Sellotape with way too much enthusiasm, and hammer it over the astronaut books. I don't want to talk to my dad about Van. I don't want to talk to anyone about Van. I don't even really want to think about Van. It still confuses me, and hurts me, and stings like a patch of skin when you've burned it on a hot pan.

I've seen him, a few times. At the cottage,

when I've called around to see Lynnie. In the pharmacy, when he's dropped Auburn off and called in for a cuppa. At the café, obviously, where everyone sees everyone.

We've chatted, and laughed, and shared news. He's been around, being useful as always. He fixed Edie's window, in advance of her coming home in the New Year. He fitted me a cat-flap in the back door, with Saul's invaluable help, so Tinkerbell can come and go as he pleases. Obviously, with usual cat-like contrariness, he's not been out since.

We've talked about his mum and what happens next. We've talked about my mum and what happens next. We've talked about Christmas, and the weather, and Saul, and about the new Star Lord Tom's taken on for Briarwood.

We've met. We've talked. But we've never gone back to the way we were. I don't just mean the kissing and cuddling and the excitement of anticipating what might happen next. I mean the casual intimacy I suppose I'd only just started to accept, only just started to appreciate, before we lost it.

We're both making a big effort to appear normal — but we're not. I know we're not, and it's painful.

'Earth to Katie . . . Earth calling Katie!' my dad says, prodding me back into the here and now. I look up at him, and smile.

'Sorry! Got lost in space . . . I think we're done here, don't you? I can't face another single gift-wrapping challenge.'

He smiles back, and replies: 'Sore subject?'

'No,' I say, getting to my feet in a way that I hope looks decisive. 'Just nothing to discuss.'

Nothing to discuss, I tell myself again. Nothing to cry about. Nothing to mourn. Nothing to regret. Just life, going on as normal.

I'm not at all unhappy. I'm not at all lonely. I'm not at all missing him.

I'm not at all telling the truth, even to myself.

33

By Christmas Eve, Saul's excitement levels have reached a fever pitch. He engages me in numerous conversations about the logistics of Santa's action-packed schedule, and I need all my wits about me to at least try and answer them. It's not long, though, before I am forced to revert to replies that involve frequent use of the words 'because he's magic'.

We've got a programme on the iPad that shows us Santa's route that night, tracking his whereabouts in 'real time', and that's got him even more hyper. He tells me he thinks maybe Father Christmas is an astronaut, and spends a good few minutes wondering how Rudolph gets his antlers into a space helmet, and is generally obsessing in the way that all little people do at this time of year.

I've taken him on a massive walk along the beach, where we used big sticks to write our names in the snow-covered sand. I've taken him to see Edie, who is out of hospital and recuperating at her niece's farmhouse. I've taken him to the café, where he was delighted to find both Tom's dog, Rick Grimes, and Willow's border terrier, Bella Swan, in residence.

I've taken him to the pharmacy, where Auburn had him helping to wrap her gifts. When I say helping, I do of course mean hindering, but in such an adorable fashion that all is forgiven.

I've taken him on an adventure through the village, snapping photos on my phone of everybody's Christmas decorations so we can print them out and make a collage.

I've taken him to Matt's surgery, where Lizzie has Midegbo dressed up in a Santa hat and a tinsel collar for a festive photoshoot.

I've taken him, basically, everywhere I can possibly think of — and he's still on some kind of insane Christmas high. It's way worse than sugar.

I'm now insisting he sits still for at least two minutes, while he eats a bowl of grapes and crackers and drinks some juice and watches *Elf* in the living room.

By the time he's accepted this, and is happily giggling away with Buddy and his friends, I am in a state of near catatonia in the kitchen. I make myself a coffee and slump down into the chair, resting my head on the table top and wondering what time it's going to be feasible to get him to bed.

Personally, I'm ready for sleep right now — but it's actually only just after six. I need to get him to decompress, and feed and water him, before even considering calling an end to the day.

I glance through at him, and see him curled up in a ball, wearing his T-shirt that has a picture of a Christmas-hat-wearing T-Rex on it. Tinker-bell's next to him, and he looks so cosy and happy.

It makes me smile, despite my fatigue levels. Isn't this what I wanted for him? This kind of

Christmas — crammed with magic and friendship and excitement and ginger cat hair? He lives in a little world that is full of laughter and fun and anticipation, and I created that world for him. I kept away the nasties, and I cocooned him in comfort, and I made his life jolly and safe. I did good.

Now, though, I just have to navigate my way through the tricky next level — maintaining it. That, over the last few days, has been getting even trickier.

First, there's the stuff I can talk myself out of. The stuff I know is bound up with my own issues, and which I work hard to overrule. Stuff like wanting to dodge tomorrow's big Christmas bash at the café, because I feel a bit overwhelmed by it. Stuff like me booking driving lessons for the new year, purely so I can always have a quick escape route if I need it. Stuff like me feeling as though someone is punching me in the chest every time they mention Van.

I never had anything with Van, not really. Not in reality — nothing actually happened. But things don't have to be real to hurt, do they? And maybe the thing I now realise I did have with Van was hope. Hope that I could change, hope that I could reach out to someone, and take a different path.

Having that hope taken away — in fact, being such a coward that I've agreed to let it go, been complicit in it all — is dragging me down. I've toyed with the idea of calling him, arranging to meet. Telling him how I feel. Telling him I've done like he asked, and figured stuff out — that

I'm ready to plunge right in and see what happens.

I don't, though. Because I'm not. I'm stuck somewhere in between — suffering without him, not convinced I should be with him. And seeing Van, if I'm honest with myself, is a big part of what's stressing me out about tomorrow. Christmas. At the Café.

That, and my mum and dad. After a frankly befuddling period of calm, the cracks are starting to show again with my parents. I don't think they ever went away — they just both managed to paper over them for a while. A kind of honeymoon period.

They've been going for walks, nights out in the pub, talking. She's cooked him dinner in Cherie's flat, and he was smiling when he came back to mine afterwards. I even saw them holding hands once, as they strolled down from the café to the bay. I didn't know quite what to make of it, so chose to pretend it hadn't happened.

Most children would probably be delighted at the prospect of their estranged parents getting back together. But then again, most children probably hadn't put 'Mum and Dad getting a divorce' on the top of their secret Christmas wish list ever since they'd been old enough to know what a divorce was.

Today, though, when Saul and I arrived at the café, things seemed different. As we walked through the door, I saw Mum leaning back in her chair, arms crushed across her chest, nostrils flared and eyes narrowed. Dad was banging the salt and pepper pots together so hard I could hear them clanging, and he was staring out of the window, deliberately avoiding making eye contact with her.

The moment Saul ran towards them, they both seemed to snap out of it, making an effort to shake away whatever was causing the tension. I know them too well, though; I know the signs too well — I can sense the simmering resentment, the slow build-up of anger. I know where that usually leads, and it's nowhere good.

I suspect it's because my dad has told her he's heading back to Bristol on Christmas Day. He's agreed to pop in to the do at the café, but then go for a late lunch with Fiona and her girlfriend. He probably assumed that once he'd explained the situation to Mum — that there was no romance, and that he definitely hadn't dumped her for Jeff Goldblum — that she'd be chilled about it.

What can I say? He's clearly developed a blind spot about how evolved Mum's newfound sense of self actually is. I knew she wouldn't be happy about it, but I guess he didn't.

At least they do put whatever it is they're fighting about on hold while we're there — and hopefully they'll continue to do that tonight, when they're both due to come here for dinner. It'll be the first time I'm alone with them since their not-quite-reunion, and frankly I'm not looking forward to it. There are far too many ways for this to go sideways.

My parents aren't the only ones stressing me out right now. Jo sent me a friend request on

Facebook, and I kind of had to accept it. So we're now just one big, happy cyber family. I could have lived with that — but the message she sent this morning wasn't so easy to dismiss. Partly it was just to wish us a happy Christmas, and ask if it would be okay to chat to Saul once he'd opened his presents. Which, you know, it will be — that's not unreasonable.

Less joyful was the second suggestion — that Saul maybe spends a weekend with them at some point in the New Year. Perhaps somewhere in between our homes, she thinks — somewhere in the middle. I can either drop Saul off, or I can come too, if I want to.

Neither option is appealing. The idea of spending a weekend with my ex, his pregnant wife, and Saul isn't enticing. But the whole concept of leaving him with them is even less so. It's a bit of a conundrum, and it's messing with my head. In the end, I just send a non-committal reply saying we'll talk about it after Christmas. Maybe, I think, they'll have decided to emigrate to Australia by then.

For Saul's sake, I keep smiling. I keep on keeping on. It's Christmas. He's three. There should be no downside to this.

I drag myself to my feet, and open the fridge door. Laura called round with a scan photo yesterday — the generic blobs of black and white that still make you go 'aaah' even though they look like a Rorschach test — and as is her way, didn't come empty handed. She also brought a chicken casserole, which has been waiting to get heated up ever since.

Today, I decide, knowing that my parents will be here soon, is that chicken casserole's chance to shine.

I stick it in the oven, and spend the next hour finishing my wrapping. Saul is starting to crash, slowly but surely, fighting against it but losing the battle. He's rubbing his eyes, and hugging his now-washed gorilla, and generally displaying the signs of a toddler who needs to go to sleep but really, really doesn't want to.

I parcel up a few bits and bobs for my parents, glad that Cherie and the rest have instigated a no-gift rule. Money isn't exactly free flowing, and neither is time — not having to search for the perfect present for the café bunch has simplified everything.

I do, however, have a gift for Van. I had to get it handmade, so I'd ordered it weeks ago. I give it a shake, then set it on the kitchen table. It's a snow globe — of Tanzania. The snowflakes that I assume would never actually fall there in the real world are sparkly and glittering, landing on the backs of tiny zebra and lions.

It seemed quirky and fun at the time I ordered it — but now it makes me feel sad. I pick it up, and put it in a gift bag. I don't want to look at it, and I don't want to think about Van, and I don't want to feel sad.

I put the presents and all the gift-wrapping paraphernalia away and walk through to the living room. The casserole is smelling divine, and Saul is barely awake, and Tinkerbell has given up his latest fight with the Christmas tree. All is relatively calm.

I slump down into the armchair, and watch Saul for a few minutes. He looks so sleepy and content, and I try and focus on that — at how excited he's going to be in the morning.

I'm just about managing to escalate my mood from 'somewhere in the region of doldrums' to 'passable' when I hear the front door opening, and the sound of my parents arriving. There's a couple of minutes where they are obviously taking off coats and boots and dusting snow from their heads before they join us in the lounge.

I can tell, immediately, that things are going badly. I am like a fine-tuned receptor for their vibes, and the one they're giving off now puts me straight onto high alert.

Dad nods at me, and stomps straight off into the kitchen. He starts slamming cupboard doors and is somehow managing to even transform making tea into an act of aggression.

Mum says hello, and glances at Saul. He sleepily waves at her, and she stands with hands on hips, looking down at him. I can feel her tension, but she does at least dredge up a smile for his sake.

'I like your gorilla,' she says, reaching down to pat the furry toy clutched under Saul's arm.

'My dad got him for me,' replies Saul quietly, not even taking his eyes away from the TV screen. He's almost zonked.

'Yes,' she replies, turning to look at me. 'I heard about that. From your granddad.'

Her hands are lodged on her hips, and her eyes are narrowed, and she's looking at me as

349

though I'm a small mouse and she's a hungry boa constrictor. Anyone else might think she's mad at me, for not filling her in on the Jason situation.

I, however, know her too well. I know she'll be annoyed and possibly hurt that I didn't confide in her. But this is more than that — this is the kind of mood that somehow makes the air around her crackle with the anticipation of a great big screaming row. I'm just the nearest target — I suspect the one she really wants to aim it towards is in the kitchen, abusing my kettle.

In the meantime, it seems, I'll do. I'm really not up for that, and I glance at my watch, seeing that it's now getting on towards half seven. Time, I decide, for the little man to go to bed.

He starts to argue when I scoop him up to take him upstairs, but it's half-hearted. He winds his arms around my neck, and I feel his tiny fingers twine into my hair, the way they do when he's really tired.

I feel his warm breath on my neck, and think again how big he's getting as I trudge up the stairs. I can still carry him at the moment, but he's not a baby any more. It's all so fleeting — it feels simultaneously like yesterday and like several lifetimes ago that he was so tiny I could hold him in one arm.

He's so wiped out he lets me undress him without any protest, raising his arms in the air for me to take his jumper off, holding onto my hair as I fasten up the buttons on his tartan pyjamas. He looks very Christmassy, decked out in his black and red.

I muss up his hair and give him a kiss, and draw the covers of his bed up to his chin.

He stifles a yawn, and holds my hand.

'Mummy,' he says, dozily, 'when will Santa be here? Can we check?'

'Course we can, sweetie,' I say, getting my phone out and finding the page with the Santa-finding device. I lie down next to him, snuggling in while we both gaze at the screen.

We see that Father Christmas isn't too far away now — heading in our direction.

'He'll be here soon,' murmurs Saul, sighing with contentment.

'He will, my love,' I reply, stroking his hair from his forehead. I decide I'll stay here for a few minutes, with this precious boy, making the most of every moment of innocence he has to spare. Before I know it he'll be drinking cider in the park and choosing his Christmas swag from the Argos catalogue instead of doing this.

I lay my head next to his on the pillow, and watch as he tries to keep his eyes open and fails. His lids close, and his breathing steadies, and his face goes slack in that way that tells me he's in the Land of Nod.

And then I hear the first raised voice from downstairs that tells me my parents are in the Land of Arguments. I bite my lip and close my own eyes, and fight the tension that starts to sweep through me.

Maybe, if I just stay here and stay quiet and stay still, it'll all go away. I know, from too many years of experience, that it won't — but it's Christmas. I can but hope.

PART 3 – GO?

34

I've had enough. My head is pounding, and my eyes are sore, and every inch of my body from my scalp to my toes feels like it's clenched up in protest.

All I can hear is the screaming, rising in shrieks and peaks above the sound of festive music, a playlist of carols I have on my phone to try and drown it all out. The mix is horrendous: the sublime choruses of 'Hark the Herald Angels Sing' alternating with yells of abuse.

Saul is sleeping, but restlessly, in that way that children will — I can see his eyes moving around under his lids, and his little fists are clenched, and every now and then his legs jerk, like a dreaming dog. It's the night before Christmas — maybe he's thinking about Santa, flying over the rooftops in his sleigh. I hope so, anyway. I hope he's not about to wake up, and hear all the rowing, and the banging, and voices. I worked hard to protect him from this, but it's chased me down, rooted me out.

I'm in my own little house, but I don't feel safe here any more. I'm in my own little house, and there are too many voices. Too much conflict. I'm in my own little house, and I'm hiding up the stairs, cowering beneath the bed sheets, paralysed by it all.

I'm in my own little house, and I have to get out. I have to get away. I have to run.

The problem is, I have nowhere to go — and no way of getting there. I'm barricaded into this room, with Saul, by my own emotions — just as securely as if I'd moved the wardrobe in front of the door.

It's been going on for almost two hours now. I only make out the occasional word from down the stairs, and none of those words are kind. None of them are mindful, or progressive, or belong in the mouths of people who have changed.

I want to just go down and tell them to shut the eff up. I want to kick them out. I want to scream at them myself, and tell them how much I despise this, how angry I am that they've brought their drama into my home on this night of all nights.

I want to do all of this, but somehow, I just can't. Maybe I'm a coward. Maybe I'm exhausted. Maybe I have no resources left.

Maybe hiding away and drowning it out with music is just too engrained in my behavioural DNA for me to do anything different.

I glance at Saul, and see that he's fine. I know he's fine. He sleeps deeply, and neither the racket from below nor the sound of the carols has roused him. He's fine — it's me who isn't.

I tiptoe out of his room, and into my own. I sit on my bed, and stare at the window. I get a rucksack from the cupboard, and I start to fill it. I place a few items of clothing inside, mine and Saul's. I put the framed photo of my nan I keep by my bed inside. I put the bag down on the floor, and kick it, several times, careful to aim at the clothes and not the photo.

There's a lull downstairs, and part of me wonders if it might be safe to come out. To creep down and take a peek into the living room. But I know better than that — I've been here too many times. I know it's only temporary, while they both catch their breath.

The door creaks and opens, and Tinkerbell leaps up onto my bed. He curls his face into the giant ginger fluffball that is his tail, and looks at me. I swear to God he looks sad, but I'm probably projecting.

I get up, open the wardrobe door. The two big red sacks are in there — Saul's presents. I want to take them out and carry them downstairs, and somehow get hold of Saul and run for the hills. I want this so badly it's like a craving.

I've done it before, and I'm starting to think that maybe I should do it again. I have a cat and friends and a job here. But now, I also have psychopathic parents and a man who somehow has become my ex without ever being my boyfriend. I have complications and ties and responsibilities.

I'm not sure I want any of it any more. It all feels sour, and joyless, and I decide I'm a fool for ever thinking it could be any different. For thinking I could escape the fate of the now-resumed screaming match below me.

I hear the familiar sound of my mum's high-pitched screech, the one I always think of as her war cry, and wait, head cocked to one side, for what I know will follow soon after — the sound of something breaking.

Sure enough, seconds later, I hear a crash and a thud. No shattering, so my plates and glasses are probably safe. It might be a book, or even the wooden fruit bowl, and I picture all the apples and tangerines scattering over the carpet.

I want to run, but I'm not sure I can. The logistics are challenging. It's Christmas Eve, it's snowing, and I have nowhere to go. I have the keys to the pharmacy, and I could set up camp there. I have the phone number for a taxi firm in Dorchester, who might charge me double-time but would at least get me out of here. I could go to Bristol as the first stop, to my parents' house. I could leave them to it, and decide what fresh start to make tomorrow.

I could wrap Saul up warm, and load those Santa sacks into some stranger's boot, and disappear. It's not like my parents would notice my leaving — I've learned this much by now. Everything else, including their own daughter and grandchild, is invisible to them when they're this deep into it.

Tinkberbell would be fine, I tell myself. I could text Matt, and ask him to get him. Auburn could find someone else to do what I do at work — it's not like it's rocket science. People might be surprised. Laura might cry. But eventually, nobody would really care — they'd all get used to my absence. They have each other, and their own busy lives, and after a while, it'd be like I'd never even lived here.

And maybe, I think, feeling a self-indulgent tear slip down my cheek, Van would even be relieved. He's trying to be a friend. He's trying to be steady. But wouldn't it, just possibly, be better for both of us if we made a fresh start? Whatever we might have had, we've messed it up. It might be my fault. It might be his. It might just be a great big enormous dollop of bad timing. But it's gone now — it was barely even there.

Better to go now, before it all gets worse.

I haul the present bags out of the wardrobe, and stare at them. Imagine how all of this would affect Saul. If there is any way I could sugar-coat this one — pretend it was a game, an adventure, an exciting piece of Christmas fun.

I slump back down on the bed, and feel like screaming in frustration. No. Of course there isn't. Waking him up on Christmas Eve, loading him into a cab on a freezing cold night? Taking him away from everything he loves, everything he's used to?

That wouldn't be fair. It wouldn't be okay, not even a tiny bit. There's another burst of vicious yelling from downstairs, and a bellow from my dad, and yes, right on cue, the sound of something actually smashing. Maybe my plates and glasses aren't so safe any more.

When I was a kid, I used to find ways to pass the time while I was exiled upstairs. Listening to music, texting my friends, reading magazines, even doing homework. A lot of the time, I even managed to sleep — with my headphones in, to drown out the cacophony from the floor below.

Now, I can't risk the headphones. I can't risk not hearing Saul. I'm trapped up here, with nothing to do.

I pick up the rucksack again, and for some reason hold it to me, like it's a baby I'm cuddling. I wander to the window, and look outside. The snow is falling more heavily now, piling up on rooftops and pavements and the swinging pharmacy sign. Under other circumstances, it might even look pretty. Christmassy, in that way that English Christmases are always portrayed in American films.

I notice the usual lights on in the usual homes; see the silhouettes of movement in bright windows. If I strain my ears, and turn off the phone carols for a minute, I can almost hear — or maybe just imagine — the sounds of laughter and companionship coming from the pub. It'll be busy in there, the log fire blazing and hissing, every table full, bar staff wearing their traditional elf and snowman hats.

I notice a car parked by the pharmacy, and realise that it's Auburn's. I frown, and squint so I can see better, and realise that a light has just gone off in the pharmacy. Weird. I hadn't even noticed the light was on until it all went dark again.

I watch, in my dimly lit bedroom, wondering who's there. It's a lot better than wondering how long the screaming downstairs will go on for. It could be almost over. It could go on all night. They're certainly showing no signs of letting up so far — I suppose they have months' worth of steam to blow off, after all.

The pharmacy door opens and closes, and I watch as a figure emerges. Tall, broad, dressed in dark clothes. It's Van, although I have no idea

360

what he's doing. I look on as he locks up, and turns to walk back to the car. He pauses, beneath the yellow light of a lamppost, frozen in a circle of shining shadow.

The snow is flurrying around him, and he's holding a box of some kind. His beanie hat is pulled down over his ears, and he's wearing his body-warmer.

He stands still, and looks across towards my house. I feel momentarily guilty, standing here spying on him, and wonder what he's thinking. Whether he knows where I am, or even cares. Whether he'd miss me if I left. How long it would take him to even notice.

I realise that I'm crying as I stand there, staring down at him, and wish so hard that I could be the kind of person who could reach out. Tell him how much I appreciate him. Tell him how much he's come to mean to me, and how much I need a friend right now.

But I'm not that kind of person. I'm not strong enough to be that weak.

I wipe the silent tears from my eyes, and at that moment, he looks upwards. He sees me. He waves, once, hesitantly.

I wave back, and close the curtains, and collapse onto my bed, too sad to even care about my parents any more.

35

I'm tangled in my sheets, eyes red and stinging and barely open, as my phone rings. I ignore it, but it's enough to wake me up — or at least drag me even more into consciousness.

I've not exactly been asleep. Not properly. I've just drifted in and out of a restless and traumatised state, and now I feel disjointed and bewildered. I blink my eyes open and shut a few times, and look at my watch. It should be four in the morning, but I see it's only just after eleven.

I can still hear my mum and dad hard at it — they obviously have a lot to sort out. I sit up, and slap myself in the face. I need to wake up properly, go and check on Saul.

Before I can mobilise — my body really doesn't want to cooperate — my phone rings again. I snatch it up from the pillow, where it had been playing carols to me, and look at the display. Van.

I want to ignore it again — I feel too compromised to add my feelings about Van into the mix tonight — but something tells me he'll just keep calling. And anyway, it could be something urgent.

I answer it, and say nervously: 'Hi? Is everything all right? Is your mum okay?'

'Everything's fine. She's at home with Willow and Auburn and the dog.'

'Oh. So, where are you then?'

'Look out your window,' he says, sounding amused.

I stand up, and walk my wobbling legs over to the window. I tug the curtain aside and see him there, in the street, holding his phone in one hand, waving at me with the other.

He's standing beside what I assume is Tom's camper van, and the camper van is decorated as brightly and colourfully as the Father Christmas sleigh that the Rotary Club used to ride around our estate every December.

The VW is draped in strings of fairy lights, in pink and yellow and blue, twinkling on and off in a frenetic spasm up and down the body of the van. Their brilliant blinks are swallowed up in the snow, shining through the flakes and making them multi-coloured.

Against the odds, it makes me smile — the first smile I've managed for some time now.

'I've come to rescue you,' he says simply, looking up at me from the street. It's weird, watching his lips move in real time out there, and hearing his voice in my ear. 'I was outside earlier, and I heard your parents. To be honest I think people in Applechurch heard your parents. I . . . well, you'd told me about it, what they were like, but I don't think anything could have prepared me for those kinds of sound levels. Jesus. Is Saul managing to sleep through it?'

'He is, thank God,' I reply, still groggy and still confused by what he's doing here.

'Well, get your stuff together. Get his presents. Get him. And come to me. We're going to run away together, just for the night. I'm going to hang up now, so you can't say no. If you don't come out, I'll just stay here, and sleep in the van all night.'

He promptly does exactly what he said he would, and hangs up. I stare at the phone. I stare at him. I stare at the decked-out camper van taking up most of the road.

Then, I do exactly as he says. I do it quickly, because I know that if I pause — if I let myself think about it — I'll talk my way out of it. I'll persuade myself that this is a terrible idea. I'll come up with a million and one reasons why this is wrong.

First, I make two journeys up and down the stairs with the Santa sacks and my bag. Then I put on my trainers and a coat and a hat, ready to go out into what I know will be a freezing cold night.

I make my way into Saul's room, and wake him up. Kind of. He's still asleep, really, clinging on to me as I plunge his head into the neck of a chunky sweater and encase his feet in thick socks. He clings onto my neck as we creep downstairs, whispering into my ear as we go past the living room door.

I pause for a moment, and hear my mum's high-pitched voice telling my dad he's 'a useless lying piece of shit', and him replying gruffly that he wouldn't need to lie, if she wasn't an evil bitch with no soul.

If ever I needed any further prodding, that was it.

Tinkerbell has padded down the stairs after me, and is sitting on the bottom step, his green

364

eyes glittering as he watches us sneak away. I hold the door open for a few seconds, as if inviting him to join us, but he starts licking his front paws instead. I take it that he's decided to stay where the radiators are, and I leave him to it. He's a cat. He'll be fine.

Van's waiting outside for us, rubbing his hands together in the cold. His face breaks out into a huge smile when he sees us, and I gesture to the bags in the hallway.

I carry Saul up into the van, and he follows, hefting all three bags at once, like a super-human Santa.

Inside, the van is even more Christmassy. There's a small fake tree set up on the fold-down table, decorated with tartan bows and glittering angels, and all the windows have tinsel tacked up around them.

There's a double bed, which again I assume can possibly be folded up, and I gently lay Saul down on top of it. The heaters have obviously been working overtime, and it's warm and cosy in here — warm and cosy and quiet.

Saul stirs as I tuck him in, looking up at me with big blue eyes.

'Is he here?' he murmurs, grabbing hold of my hand. 'Is Santa here?'

'Not yet, sweetie,' I reply, smoothing down his hair and soothing him. 'But we saw on the Santa tracker that he's very near . . . and . . . Van came round, to see if we'd like to go and find him. How does that sound?'

'Nice. Wake me up when we find him . . . '

Van's in the driver's seat, and all the doors are

closed. He glances back at me, tugs off his beanie hat, and grins.

'Ready to go Santa hunting?' he asks.

I nod, and grin back. This is crazy. This is insane. This is probably completely wrong.

'I really, really am,' I say.

36

Van drives us to Briarwood. The snow is still coming down, and he knows the path into the clearing where Tom had the camper parked up for months.

It's tucked away in a wooded glade, the boughs of the trees heavy with snow, the moonlight filtering through them to dapple on the ground. It's dark and quiet, the only sounds the occasional hoot of an owl, cry of a fox, or snow slithering from the branches. I peer out of the window, curious, and it all looks unbelievably magical — like he's actually brought us to some kind of fairy glen.

Any worries I had about Saul being upset at not waking up at home disappear — this is so much better. This actually looks like somewhere a Santa hunter might do a stake-out.

Saul himself is out for the count, curled up beneath the blankets, looking so much more peaceful than he did back at the house, where the noise of background arguments must have been filtering through into his dreams.

Van clambers through to the back, and perches on the edge of the bed next to me. There's a dim light on in the cabin, enough for me to see his smile, and to give one in return. He reaches out, and gently strokes my face. I lean in, and kiss the skin of his palm.

I feel so much better now. Whether that's

because I've escaped my parents, or because I'm with him, I don't know. And I'm not planning on spoiling the moment by trying to figure it all out. Some things are beyond my control.

'He looks happy enough,' Van says, glancing at Saul.

'He does. Thank you. For coming to get us. I would never have asked that of you.'

He grins and raises his eyebrows.

'I know that!' he replies, taking hold of my hand and keeping it. 'You'd probably rather chop off your own limbs than ask for help. But when I saw you . . . standing there, in the window, clutching that rucksack . . . well, you looked like you needed to get away. In fact I thought you might be gone by the time I got back — you were holding onto it for dear life; it reminded me of those go-bags that spies have in movies? You know, the ones that contain wads of different currencies and a gun and a fake passport?'

I nod, because I know exactly what he means. I've often yearned for one of those.

'Sadly, mine only contained some clean socks. But . . . yes. I needed to go — I just didn't know how. I didn't know how I could leave, and not wreck Christmas for Saul, and not spend the night on the lipstick couch in the pharmacy. Mum and Dad . . . well, they were really going for it.'

He shakes his head, looking befuddled by it all.

'I noticed,' he says, squeezing my hand. 'I've never heard human voices that loud, or that nasty. I'm so sorry you grew up with that. Have you ever considered . . . I don't know . . . telling them to fuck off?'

I laugh out loud at the uncharacteristic swearing, holding my hand to my mouth to dull the sound in case we wake Saul up.

'I have considered it. And I think, tomorrow, I actually need to do it. Tonight, I just didn't have the strength. There's been too much else going on, and I turned into the world's biggest wuss.'

'Why?' he asks. 'What else has been going on?'

I look at him, with his bright eyes and chestnut hair and his kind smile. I look at him, and realise how much better I feel when I'm with him than when we're apart. I realise that leaving here would mean leaving him — and that might break me. This isn't about Saul, or my parents, or Jason and Jo, or my own supremely screwed-up attitude to life. This is about a simple choice: I need to take a risk and try to be happy, or I don't.

'Mainly,' I reply, quietly, 'you. And me. And it being all screwed up. I don't know how it all went wrong so quickly . . . before we'd even given it a chance to go right. I've been an idiot, and I'm sorry. You told me we needed to figure things out. You told me you I needed to figure things out. That you were already in deeper than you thought.'

'I did tell you those things, yes,' he replies, gazing through the window into the moonlit clearing, as though preparing himself to hear bad news.

'Okay. You were right to. And I have. I won't lie — I wanted to run. I wanted to grab my sub-standard go-bag, and leave. Some of that was because of my parents, and the new situation with Saul's dad. Some of that was just me being a coward, and feeling like I was getting too tangled up in other people's lives. In this place.

'But mainly, I think, it was because of you. You called me out, Van — you made me think about us, and what we were to each other, even if I didn't want to. You pushed me away, and that made me realise how much I wanted you. How much I needed you. I'm not proud of it, but it's the way I'm built — contrary, I suppose.'

He turns his gaze back to my face, and his eyes meet mine. His hand is still holding mine, but his expression is unreadable. I feel my breath hitch in my throat, and wonder if I've blown it. If I've left it all too late. If he's decided I'm more trouble than I'm worth. If he's got back together with the blonde one from Abba.

'So,' he replies eventually. 'Refusing to sleep with you made you realise what . . . that you wanted to sleep with me?'

'I already knew I wanted to do that, Van,' I answer, nudging him. 'I thought I'd made that clear enough. But now . . . well, I also know that this is more than that. This isn't just physical, is it?'

He laughs, and wraps me in his arms, and kisses the top of my head.

'Duh. Of course it isn't. That's what I was trying to say. Took you long enough to cotton on, though, didn't it?'

I smile, and slide my hands around his waist,

and stay exactly where I am for a few moments. Because — well, why wouldn't I?

'I know. What can I say? I'm a slow learner. Thank you for tolerating me.'

'S'okay,' he replies, holding me tighter. 'Nobody's perfect. So. Where does this leave us, then? Not that I'm expecting a life plan and a marriage proposal, Katie — I just want to know that I'm not going to wake up one day and find a note saying you're relocating to Vatican City or anything.'

'I'd never do that,' I say. 'Maybe Cardiff. But . . . well, I suppose it leaves us here. Me, and you, and Saul. In a camper van in the woods. Spending Christmas together. That's step one.'

'I'll settle for that,' he says, reluctantly pulling away from me. 'And on that note, we'd better get our Christmas act together. There's a little man here who's going to wake up expecting all manner of merriment. I dressed the van up for him, and you've got the presents — do you think he'll be okay with it? Will it be magical enough for him?'

I look around, at the little Christmas tree and the tinsel and the beautiful snow-bound woods outside. I look at Van, and recognise how special he is — that even now, after our big grown-up discussion, he's still thinking about Saul. He is, to put it simply, pretty much the best person I think I've ever met.

'It'll be magical enough,' I reply, leaning forward to kiss him. 'For all of us.'

37

We wake up at the same time as Saul. This is unsurprising, as Saul is bouncing around on the bed, accidentally kicking us in the face and screeching with excitement.

We spent the night lying either side of him, our hands meeting in the middle, a cosy trio of humanity curled up together like a litter of puppies.

Now, what feels like approximately one hour later, we're up again. Saul is screaming, 'He's been, he's been!', and scampering to the end of the bed to reach the two bulging sacks of presents. He pauses at the end, and turns around to look at us in confusion.

'Where are we?' he says, apparently noticing that he's not in Kansas any more for the first time. 'And why are you here, Van?'

Van yawns, and stretches, and drags himself out from beneath the covers.

'We're in the woods. We saw on the Santa tracker that he was coming here first. And I'm here because I didn't want to miss seeing you open all your presents. Is that okay?'

I realise I'm holding my breath at this point, watching Saul for any signs of distress, hoping he's not going to have a meltdown. I needn't have worried. He nods and jumps off the bed, and plunges right into the sacks. Little people are so much more sensible than big people.

We spend the next hour or so in a flurry of discarded wrapping paper, as Saul undoes all that time and effort I put into the gifts with ruthless efficiency. It takes a while, because he wants to play with everything as he opens it, and we let him. He's operating on around 700 per cent more energy than we are, so we're not in a position to argue.

Once that's done, Van makes us all some toast, and we eat it outside, in the snow. I'd brought Saul's wellies from the hallway, and he blows off even more steam by running around, making footprints and snowballs and shaking low-lying branches and laughing as the snow comes flying off.

Eventually, once he's calm enough to sit still for more than two seconds, he comes back inside and curls up on the bed with one of his astronaut books.

I make the most of the lull in the proceedings to give Van his Tanzania snow globe. He loves it, which is nice. I'm not expecting anything from him, but he produces a white envelope containing a card.

'Got this for you a little while ago,' he says sheepishly, handing it to me. I open the sealed envelope, expecting to find some kind of Christmas confection inside, but am confused to come up with a colourful card featuring a picture of Herbie, the VW Beetle from the movies. I open it up, and inside there's a piece of paper that's clearly been printed off from a computer at home. I scan the page, and start to laugh.

'Driving lessons?' I say, grinning. 'Are you trying to get rid of me?'

He smiles — one of those slow, lazy smiles that makes me feel warm inside. The kind of smile that promises so much more than I ever thought I'd deserve.

'No,' he replies, 'the opposite. I thought if you learned to drive, you wouldn't feel as trapped. And then you'd be more likely to stay.'

'Ah. I see. Reverse psychology . . . very clever. Thank you. I wanted to do this anyway, so it's perfect. Though now I feel bad, because this cost a lot more than a snow globe.'

'Not that much more,' he says, laughing. 'I'm not rich. If you don't crack it in ten lessons, you're on your own. Anyway . . . I'm glad you're pleased.'

I am pleased. Pleased with all of this. With being here, in this place, with these people. At the way my originally horrific Christmas has shaped up. With the idea of what the future might hold for us. All of the problems still exist — my parents are still psychopaths. Jason and Jo still want to be in Saul's life. Lynnie is still ill. But while those problems might still exist, they exist somewhere else. They don't live here, with us, in this place and this moment.

I want to kiss him, so badly. I want to throw my arms around him, and tell him how much he means to me. But there's a young boy lying on the bed, flat on his tummy, legs waving in the air, planning his first trip into space.

I settle for taking Van's hands in mine and kissing his fingers.

Saul gazes over his shoulder at us, and his eyes go wide.

'Are Van's fingers cold?' he asks, when he sees what I'm doing. I always kiss Saul's little hands to warm them up, so it must seem logical to him.

'Yes, love. That's exactly it,' I reply lightly. 'All that snow.'

'Okay. We have to go soon,' he says. 'To the café. They'll be waiting for me.'

He goes back to his book, and I think he's probably right. They will be waiting for him. For me. And that is absolutely fine.

38

The café is postcard pretty in the snow, the path up the side of the hill glistening in the weak sunlight that's filtering down through the clouds.

The sea is grey and white, rolling in to snow-dusted sand, the bay quiet apart from a few dog-walkers and desperate parents trying to wear out their kids.

We arrive together, leaving the camper van in the small car park, making the walk up to the Comfort Food Café sign in a row of three. Saul is between us, his small hands in ours, swinging and jumping and laughing. For him, this is just another lovely day with his mummy and his Van. For me, it feels different — like the start of something. Something wonderful.

Van has one of the Santa sacks hoisted over his shoulder, so Saul can show off his gifts, and I am carrying a box of whistle pops.

That's what he was at the pharmacy for the night before — Willow and Lynnie had made mince pies and snowman cupcakes to take to the party, and Auburn didn't want to go empty-handed. Not being as much of a domestic goddess, she'd sent Van to collect the lollies instead.

Once she'd heard about his plans to come and rescue me from my dysfunctional Christmas Eve fun, she'd put them in the camper van for Saul, after helping Van quickly decorate it before he left. We didn't get around to any whistle pop shenanigans the night before, so the box is still unopened.

We pause outside the café doors, Saul clinging on to our hands and trying to drag us through, and Van's eyes meet mine.

'Are you ready?' he asks, his tone serious.

I know what he's asking. Am I ready to walk through these doors, and become part of all of this? Am I ready to let the world see us together? Am I ready to see my parents again? Am I ready for whatever the heck it is that might happen next?

I nod, and smile, and say: 'Yes. For anything.'

He smiles back, and we go inside. Saul immediately disentangles himself from us, and makes a beeline for Laura. He barrels into her arms and snuggles up on her lap, and I see him starting to tell her all about his magical Christmas in the woods. I can tell exactly when it is that he mentions Van being there when he woke up, because Laura looks up at me, her eyebrows lost beneath her curls, her eyes wide, and a big 'oh!' forming on her mouth.

I nod and make a thumbs-up sign, and she reciprocates. Looks like we just went public — because if Laura knows something, she's constitutionally incapable of keeping it quiet.

Everyone is there already. The teenagers are in a corner on their own, playing what looks suspiciously like rock, paper, scissors. Matt is talking to Frank, a can of Guinness in his hand. Cherie is bustling around serving up ginger snaps, Willow behind her with a jug of what looks like orange juice but is undoubtedly Buck's Fizz.

Tom is with Lynnie and Auburn, Rick Grimes curled up at their feet with the love of his life, Bella Swan. Midgebo is here, following Cherie and Willow, hoping for a tragic tray accident that might see all of the ginger snaps fall at his paws.

Zoe and Cal are dancing to The Pogues singing 'Fairytale of New York', yelling all the words in each other's faces as they jig. Scrumpy Joe is arranging bottles of his cider on a trestle table, a length of green tinsel tied around his head like a bandana.

Over in the corner, by the bookshelves, I see Edie, set up like a queen on a throne of cushions, a tartan blanket over her lap and a glass of sherry in her hand. Becca is with her, and I feel my heart soar at the sight. Edie is back, and she looks frail but all right, and for the first time I am convinced that she's going to be okay. She spots me across the crowd, and raises her glass in my direction. I wave back at her, and continue to scan the room.

Eventually, I spot them — sitting together at a table for two near the window. Nobody is near them, even in this packed room. It's as though they're emitting some kind of forcefield of bad energy that's keeping people away. Mum is leaning forward, fingertips drumming on the table, lips moving rapidly. I can't tell what she's saying, but I'm guessing it's not 'happy Christmas and peace to all men'.

Dad is on the opposite side of the table, leaning back, arms crossed over his chest, as though he's trying to be physically as far removed from her as he can. I can see the effort he's making not to respond, but I'm not convinced it'll last. He's like a ticking time bomb waiting to go boom.

I stride towards them, determined to sort this out once and for all. I've had enough of tolerating this bullshit, and now is as good a time as any to make that clear.

I drag a chair over to their table and plonk myself down. They both stare at me, as though I'm an alien visiting from another planet. Eventually, Dad speaks: 'Katie! Where were you? We got your text saying you were fine, but we didn't have a clue where you'd disappeared off to . . .'

'No, we didn't,' adds Mum, pulling a face at me. 'That was very selfish of you — taking Saul off when we'd been looking forward to Christmas with him!'

I shake my head and let out a sigh, and hold up my hands to shut her up. She's in that kind of mood, I can tell, where I could tell her she had beautiful eyes and she'd somehow manage to turn it into an argument because she felt I'd insulted her ears.

'No, Mum — just stop,' I say, before she can regroup. 'Both of you, just stop. At exactly what time was it that you even noticed we'd gone?'

There's a silence from both of them. Mum suddenly finds the view from the window fascinating, and Dad starts to rearrange the salt and pepper pots. Yep. Thought so.

'I'll take it from your silence that it was either

very late last night, or this morning. I'll also assume that you carried on your slanging match without even hearing us leave.'

'That's not fair!' pipes up Mum angrily. 'It wasn't a slanging match . . . we have a lot to sort out . . . it was — '

'She's right,' interrupts Dad, reaching out and placing his hand over hers. 'It was a slanging match, love. And we didn't sort anything out, did we?'

Mum looks as though she wants to disagree, and I decide that I'm not going to let her.

'Look, Mum, Dad — I really don't care what you want to call it, okay? All I care about is that it doesn't happen again, anywhere near me, or Saul. If you want to have a slanging match, or punch each other in the face, or kill each other with a million paper cuts, that's your business. It's not mine, and I'm not going to let you make it mine.'

They're both silent for a while, and then Mum replies: 'But Katie, don't you want us to sort it out? Don't you want us to get back together?'

I look at her — at the sad eyes, and the new flower-power vibe, and the face that only seems to come alive when she's angry — and wonder what the answer to that is. Do I want them to get back together? In all honesty, no. I think they've been making each other miserable for way too long, and they should probably go their separate ways and find whatever pleasure and fulfilment they can in life while they're both still young enough and healthy enough to do it.

I don't say that, though — because that's not

my place. Marriage counselling is not part of the job description of 'daughter', or at least it shouldn't be.

'I don't know, Mum. I can't say what you should do, or how you should do it. I can't live your lives for you. All I can say is this: keep it away from me, and Saul. I will not — ever again — put up with your drama. If it means not seeing you, then so be it. I hope it doesn't, because I love you both very much — but I've had enough. From now on, I'm concentrating on my own life. I'd suggest you do the same with yours.'

Dad nods, and looks sad but resigned. Mum bites her lip, and I can see her fighting the urge to answer back. She can't agree with me, but at least she's not arguing — which I suppose is a step in the right direction.

Before she can take a step in the wrong direction, I stand up.

'Right. I've said my piece. Now I'm going to spend some time with my friends, and my son, and enjoy my day. Happy Christmas.'

I walk away from their table, and into the crowd of people. I walk through the laughter and the chatter and the exuberance of a room full of my friends. I give Cherie an unrequested hug as I pass, which leaves her speechless. I tell Edie how fantastic she looks. I find the box of whistle pops, and I give them all to Auburn. I see Laura, reading an astronaut book to Saul on her lap, and give them both a peck on the cheek.

I walk all the way to Van, who is drinking a bottle of Joe's cider and chatting to Frank.

I take the cider bottle out of his hand, and I kiss him — properly. He looks down at me afterwards, both confused and delighted.

'What was that for?' he asks, laughing. 'Not that I'm complaining.'

'That was a thank you,' I reply, 'for the best Christmas ever.'

I'm aware that I've caused quite a stir, and hear Cherie whooping and cheering in the background, and Edie cackling, and Auburn blowing relentlessly on her whistle pop. Then, in a voice I'm biologically programmed to recognise over any other noise, I hear Saul.

'Mummy,' he says, sounding happy. 'Are Van's lips cold?'

'Yes, love,' I reply, as Van slips his arm around my shoulders and pulls me closer. 'That's exactly it.'